About th

Scott Hunter was born in Romford, Essex in 1956. He was educated at Douai School in Woolhampton, Berkshire. His writing career began after he won first prize in the Sunday Express short story competition in 1996. He currently combines writing with a parallel career as a semi-professional drummer. He lives in Berkshire with his wife, Kathy.

IN THE KEY OF DEATH

Scott Hunter

A Myrtle Villa Book

Originally published in Great Britain by Myrtle Villa Publishing

All rights reserved
Copyright © Scott Hunter, Anno Domini 2024

This book is sold subject to the condition that it shall not, by way of trade or otherwise, be lent, resold, hired out, or otherwise circulated without the publisher's prior consent in any form of binding or cover other than that in which it is published and without a similar condition including this condition being imposed on the subsequent publisher

The moral right of Scott Hunter to be identified as author of this work has been asserted in accordance with Section 77 of the Copyright, Designs and Patents Act 1988

In this work of fiction, the characters, places and events are either the product of the author's imagination or they are used entirely fictitiously

Acknowledgements

Thanks to Stuart Bache (Books Covered) for the cover design, to my man on the inside (he knows who he is), and to my insightful and excellent editor, Louise Maskill

This one's for Archie

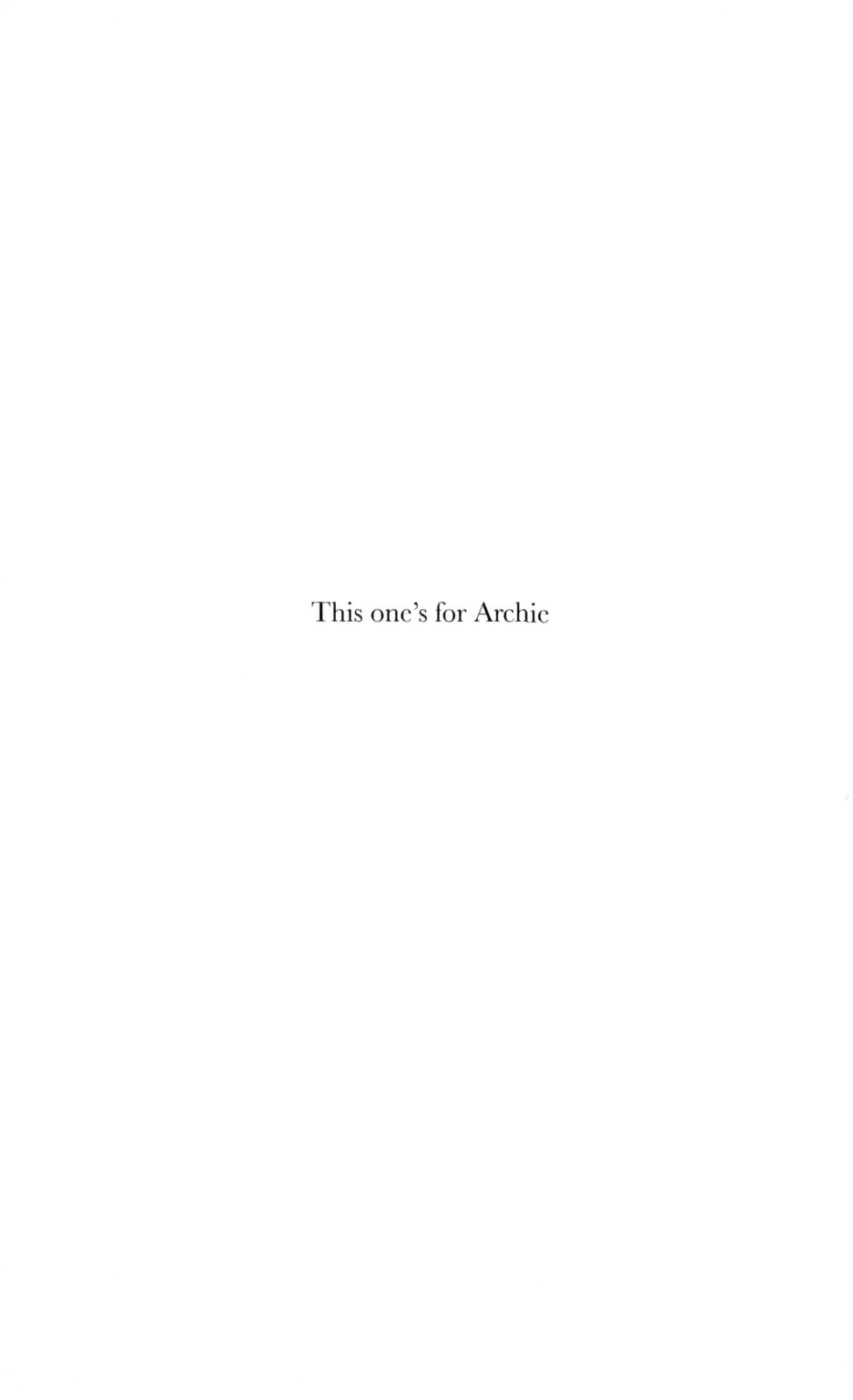

'Things are not always what they seem; the first appearance deceives many; the intelligence of a few perceives what has been carefully hidden'
—**Phaedrus**

Author's Note

This is the tenth book in the *DCI Brendan Moran* series. There are elements of the plot which follow on from *Closer to the Dead* so, as usual, it's probably best to read that first if you want to understand the background to some of the issues Moran's team have to face in the following pages. I hope you enjoy it!

SH
April 2024

Prologue

My vision blurs as I stretch my fingers to cover the octave. It's happened before at moments like this – moments when I know I'm going to fail. I strain to extend my hand to the required position, but I can't quite make it; my pinky is just not long enough. Maybe in a year or so, when I'm fourteen, it will have grown enough for me to play the piece correctly. But a year or so is too far ahead. I must play the piece correctly *now*, or I know what will happen.

I look at the music manuscript, open on the piano's music stand in front of me. A bust of Beethoven glowers at me from its strategic position on the closed piano lid. Is it meant to inspire? It's always terrified me, right from the first time I came here; the expression is stern, almost accusatory. How is it supposed to help? It's an ugly thing, and music is supposed to be a thing of beauty. How can such an ugly man have composed such sublime music?

The notes on the stave swim in and out of focus, the tiny interconnected black dots mocking me. The groupings of semi and demisemiquavers are beyond my limited ability to execute. The tendons in my hands ache with the effort and I feel beads of sweat on my brow.

I notice that the white keys are yellowed with age. I've probably noticed that before, but my mind is doing what it always tries to do – take me away from the situation, free me from my obligation to sit for the required hour and play faultlessly to my tutor's satisfaction.

'No!'

I flinch in anticipation an instant before the steel ruler comes down on my wrist. As always I'm tempted to snatch my hand away, but experience has taught me that worse will follow if I do.

'From the same bar. Again.'

And so it goes on.

My hands shaking, I repeat the phrase. Somehow I manage to convey the required mood, find the correct notes.

'Better. And again.'

My collar is damp. I want to moisten my lips but there is no saliva. I stumble over the second phrase, my finger straying onto an F sharp instead of a G. My muscles tense; I close my eyes as I hear the swish of air that precedes the ruler's descent.

'No! Again.'

I repeat the phrase but my concentration is broken now and I'm incapable of following the music. Fear has the upper hand.

The next ten minutes are hell.

Finally, the mantel clock strikes the hour. I rejoice through the pain. It's over, until the next time.

'We'll leave it there. I'll see you tomorrow. I hope to see a considerable improvement – or you know what will happen.'

I know. Oh yes, I know. I stand up and hear myself thanking my tormentor, as though I've enjoyed the experience. I know that if I fail to show the appropriate degree of politeness, it will be fed back to my parents. And that would be bad. Very bad.

Beethoven glares sightlessly as I pick up my manuscript and slip it into my leather satchel. The walk to the front door seems to take a lifetime. I want to run but I must show no emotion, not give away how I'm feeling. No weakness; it is not approved of. My wrist tingles, the skin raw and sore as I reach for the door knob that leads me to freedom – for a time, at least.

Until I get home, where once again I'll be consigned to the salon, to the grand piano that awaits me like a gibbet.

As I stand at the bus stop I blink the tears away. The futility of it all hits me hard, as it always does in these fleeting moments of respite.

I'm an imposter.

I'm not what was wanted.

I'm an inadequate replacement, that's all.

I make a firm resolution; I'm a child now, but one day, some time in the future, when circumstances are different, someone is going to pay.

Chapter One

DCI Brendan Moran rinsed his hands and examined his reflection.

The mirror never lies, someone had once said. He remembered his late mother's insistence that she would only ever use what she considered to be a "true" mirror to apply her make-up. There had been one such mirror on the dressing table in the guest bedroom, which the family had always referred to as "Gran's room" because of his grandmother's biannual billeting in the large, Georgian-bedded chamber. Moran remembered peering into the dusky glass and thinking that, rather than showing a true image of his face, it seemed instead to soften the contours, darken his pale complexion so that his reflection was presented in a more flattering light. Rather than being a true mirror, he recalled, he'd secretly rechristened the dressing table glass "the Hollywood illusion".

But this particular washroom mirror was true, he was pretty certain of that. The harsh strip lighting showed the lines and crevices of his face in stark detail: the dark circles beneath his eyes, the loose skin sagging beneath the chin, the greying at the temples. The image was confirmation enough, as if he needed it.

It was time. Time to bow out.

He sighed as sounds of merriment swept in through the opening lavatory door. The music was too loud, pounding over the racket of simultaneous conversation as colleagues shared information they'd probably regret divulging in the morning, the clink of glasses, the gales of laughter at some old joke retold.

'Guv! Wondered where you were skulking. They're all waiting for you.'

'Thanks, Bola. I just needed a moment – you know, to compose myself.'

'Never seen you *un*composed, guv. Well…' Bola paused with a half-smile. 'Not often, anyways.'

'Better than *de*composed, I guess.' Moran smiled ruefully at his reflection. 'Not far off that either, by the looks of me.'

Bola guffawed. 'You've got *years* ahead of you, guv. Look at DS Phelps – he's having the best time as a retiree by all accounts.'

'Robert? Yes, well,' Moran dried his hands, 'he has his books.'

'Everyone has something they want to do, guv.'

'Do they?' Moran inspected his hands, flicked away the last beads of moisture. Bola had hit upon one of Moran's most troubling considerations. What *was* he going to do with his retirement? He had no hobbies, apart from maybe walking, or the odd pub lunch. He wasn't particularly interested in following sport on TV, nor was he drawn to joining the local bowls club as another colleague had suggested.

'Hold up, guv. I'll come in with you. Give you some moral

support.'

Moran paused at the exit of the gents. 'I suppose I'll have to make a speech?'

'*De rigueur*, I'm afraid guv.'

'Hell. What shall I say?' He'd scribbled a few paragraphs five times over, consigned each draft to the wastepaper basket.

Bola grinned. 'Doesn't matter, guv. You're here, that's enough – and your lady too, so that's great.'

'Guess I'll just have to wing it, then, eh?'

'Why change the habit of a lifetime?' Bola's grin widened.

Moran raised a warning finger. 'DC Odunsi, there was a time when I'd have—'

A head poked around the door. 'Brendan? What *are* you doing in there?'

'Alice! This is a gents' toilet.' Moran blocked the doorway. 'I mean, really!'

'I know what it is, but you've been in here for ages. I was beginning to wonder if I'd been stood up.'

'It's all right, Mrs Roper,' Bola said. 'My fault. I was just giving DCI Moran some friendly advice.'

'Oh yes? Well I'm sure Brendan will put your wise words into practice, DC Odunsi – *if* he deigns to join the party.'

'Yes, I was just…' Moran sighed. 'Look, this isn't easy for me. It's not every day a man retires.'

'Indeed not.' Alice peered over her glasses. 'And that's why there's such a good turnout. So come on. Time to face the music.'

Moran gave a mock groan and rolled his eyes.

Bola guffawed. 'Right behind you, boss. Knock 'em dead!'

Alice held out her hand. Moran was again struck by her

elegance. She was wearing a stylish blue midi-dress with matching clutch bag and her hair pinned so that it framed her face, enhancing her high cheekbones. She looked stunning. Moran still couldn't quite believe they were together, even after all these months. He took her proffered hand. 'Right. Let's do this.'

Alice led him along the main corridor of Atlantic House towards the source of the merriment. Moran's disquiet intensified as he realised that the hubbub had abruptly cut off in favour of an expectant silence, so that their footsteps, padding across the thin carpet, were clearly audible.

They turned the corner and pushed open the door to be greeted by an explosion of party poppers and a deafening cheer. Moran grinned sheepishly, raised his hand in wry acknowledgment. Bodies pressed in on all sides. An overlapping chorus of "Welcome to the party, guv", "Great you could make it, boss", "What'll you have, guv?" competed with the thudding bass and drum music as it resumed at twice the previous volume so that Moran felt himself instinctively backing away towards the door. However, Alice took his elbow and guided him firmly to the drinks table, where DI Charlie Pepper was clearly having trouble making herself heard above the din, DC Bernice Swinhoe cupping her ear and leaning in close to Charlie's moving lips.

Moran made an effort to relax his shoulders. Alice was a canny woman, guiding him towards two team members with whom she knew he'd be comfortable. As they squeezed through the press various colleagues patted him on the back, offered their hands, grinned their greetings. He felt like a celebrity and it was a distinctly uncomfortable sensation. How did film stars cope?

The room itself had been lavishly decorated with balloons and bunting, and now he saw that an enlarged photograph of a much younger version of himself, seated at his desk at the old station, had been propped up on an easel by the drinks table.

*Saints preserve us… I wonder where **that** fella got to…*

'Brendan!' DCS Higginson intercepted them, glass in hand, a wide smile lighting up his face. 'Thought you'd got cold feet.'

'Sir.' Moran forced a smile. 'Well, Alice wouldn't have let me get away with that, I'm afraid.'

'Quite right, too.' Higginson nodded approvingly. 'Nice to see you again, Mrs Roper.'

'Alice, please.'

'Very well. Alice it is.'

'Hi guv.' Charlie greeted Moran with a peck on the cheek as Bernice refilled her glass. 'Informal is OK now, right?'

'Of course.' This time Moran's smile was genuine.

'Still feels odd, though.'

'You'll get used to it.' Moran winked. 'And you can try *Brendan* too, if you like.'

Charlie mock-grimaced. 'A step too far, guv, sorry.'

Moran made a face. 'Why do they have to have the music so ridiculously loud?'

'You know what they say, guv?'

'What do they say?'

'If it's too loud, you're—'

'Too old? Right. Great, I admit it. Can't you have a word with Collingworth? Whose idea was it to put him in charge of the disco?'

Charlie laughed. 'He's a DJ in his spare time. An expert, he told us.'

'Well, he would.' Moran glanced over at Alice, who was a few feet away deep in conversation with Higginson. 'D'you think she's all right?' he yelled in Charlie's ear.

'I think she can hold her own, guv.'

Moran cupped his ear and Charlie repeated her statement. 'Ah. Yes, I do believe she can.' Of course she could; Moran could see that Higginson was enthralled. A swell of pride rippled through him. How had fate brought Alice to him? It was a marvel, and even now he still found it hard to believe his good fortune.

There was a pause in the music. Moran took the opportunity to speak at normal volume. 'How's young DS Luscombe? All well between the two of you?'

Charlie flushed. 'All good, guv.'

'It's been a while now, hasn't it?' Moran probed gently.

Charlie's embarrassment was headed off at the pass by Collingworth's introduction to another song, although Moran wouldn't have described the noise in such favourable terms. What had happened to music? Was it just that he was old? This song seemed to consist of relentless drums and thumping bass with someone talking at great speed over the top. What had become of melody? Verse and chorus?

He became aware that Charlie was grinning broadly. 'I know what you're thinking, guv,' she shouted. 'Why didn't we opt for a quiet drink somewhere far from the madding crowd?'

Moran nodded helplessly. Was it too early to escape? Alice was still talking animatedly to Higginson, but at that precise moment Higginson caught his eye, patted Alice on the arm by way of disengagement and headed for the microphone next to

Collingworth's machinery.

Moran's heart sank.

Here we go…

Higginson tapped the microphone, curled his hand around it and spoke a tentative "hello", signalling to Collingworth to cut the music. Collingworth obliged, only for the microphone to issue an ear-splitting squeal, prompting a collective covering of ears and general grimaces from the gathering.

'Take your hand away from it, sir,' Bola called.

The normally unflappable Higginson let go of the microphone as if it were red hot. The feedback tailed off.

'Ah, thank you DC Odunsi. Yes, that's better.' Higginson tapped the microphone again and cleared his throat. Conversation faltered as he surveyed the room, and only when the DCS was happy that he had their full attention did he begin.

And he began with a beckoning gesture that made Moran groan internally.

'Come on over, Brendan.'

To a scattered chorus of applause and catcalls, Moran made his way across the room and joined Higginson by the microphone. The DCS patted him on the shoulder, but to Moran's relief he declined to rest his arm there. Moran respected Higginson but they'd never been great buddies. He braced himself for what was to come.

'Well, here we are,' Higginson beamed. 'We've arrived at a day I never thought we'd reach. DCI Brendan Moran has been with us for as long as I can remember. Indeed, he preceded me by – how long was it, Brendan? Three years? Four?'

Moran confirmed that his arrival at Thames Valley had been, in fact, six full years before DI Higginson had joined them and made his efficient way to DCS in record time. Higginson carried on with an obviously prepared speech, and as Moran looked out on the sea of faces he felt an unexpected lump in his throat.

Until, that was, his gaze fell upon John Herbinson, the Major Crimes Investigations Manager. The straight-talking Canadian had ruffled more feathers than Moran cared to remember – including his own on more than one occasion. Herbinson was nonchalantly propped against the far wall, soft drink in hand, regarding the proceedings with studied indifference. Moran's eye traversed to Herbinson's left, to the shambling shape of the newcomer, DCI Frank Dawson, his successor, with his mop of unruly, Boris-Johnson-like hair, and noted the quiet exchange between the two men. Dawson hadn't wasted any time getting alongside Herbinson, then – and by the look of it they were already as thick as thieves.

Ah well, good luck to them. What did it matter? Personalities sometimes clashed, sometimes complemented. Moran silently wished them both well as Higginson's carefully rehearsed – and no doubt thoroughly polished – speech went on, interspersed by bursts of appreciative laughter as he recalled a few of Moran's amusingly eccentric habits. Moran joined in with as much good nature as he could muster.

Higginson finally drew to a close with an invitation. 'Would you like to say a few words, Brendan?'

Moran took a breath, smiled genially. 'Of course.'

The evening was drawing to a close. The hardline crew were

the only ones left. Bola, Collingworth still spinning his disks, although at a quieter volume now, Charlie and Alice deep in conversation in a corner of the room, George and Tess, heads together like two teenagers on a first date, and the officer Moran was currently chatting to – DCI Dawson. Dawson was recounting a tale from his old posting in Birmingham, but Moran was only half-listening. The guy had obviously had one too many, and the story had deteriorated into a rambling, fragmented discourse that Moran had given up trying to follow. In desperation he interrupted. 'Can I get you one for the road, Frank?'

Dawson stopped mid-flow and thrust an empty glass into Moran's hand. 'Capital idea. Large Scotch'll do the trick.'

'Sure?' Moran frowned.

'As eggs is eggs.' Dawson swayed and maintained his balance only by making a grab for the wall.

At the bar table Moran found a half-empty bottle of Jamiesons and poured a tiny measure, reasoning that Dawson was too far gone to notice the difference between a double and a single. George and Tess were similarly refreshing their glasses, but only, Moran noted approvingly, from a bottle of elderflower Shloer. George was doing great, and Tess was nothing short of a miracle after what she'd been through; Moran felt protective, fatherly almost, towards all the members of his team, but particularly these two. He wondered how they were going to relate to Dawson and his reputation for cold stand-offishness when sober, effusive over-familiarity when inebriated.

'Good speech, guv.' Tess grinned. 'Reckon you out-Higginsoned Higginson there.'

'Ha. That'll be the day.'

'Making friends, boss?' George nodded towards Dawson who was now leaning his entire weight against the wall and gazing with unfocused eyes at the flotsam and jetsam of the party as it wound down. At that moment Collingworth took the microphone and interrupted their conversation with a final announcement, delivered in the style of a sleazy Radio One presenter.

'Ladeees and gents, please take your partners for the Last Waltz.'

'Seriously? Tess grimaced as the intro to the Humperdinck classic swelled across the room.

'Finally, a decent tune.' Moran grinned. 'Englebert was all the rage back in the day. They don't write stuff like this any more.'

'Aye – and that's a blessing, right enough,' George muttered.

'Oh come *on*, Mr Grumpy.' Tess giggled and propelled George, still protesting, into the centre of the room.

Moran chuckled as Tess whirled George around in a frenetic waltz that would have caused even Englebert himself to raise an eyebrow, but his smile quickly faded as he spotted Collingworth approaching.

'All right there, guv? Enjoying the music?'

'Not really.'

'Ah well, I'm not surprised.' Collingworth grinned as he sloshed red wine into a half-pint mug. 'Val Doonican more your thing, eh?'

Moran shook his head. 'Hardly.'

'Drinking for two?' Collingworth nodded at the drinks Moran was holding in each hand.

'One for me, one for your new guv'nor,' Moran replied patiently.

'Yeah?' Collingworth made an exaggerated gesture implying inebriation. 'He's had enough, if you ask me – if the wall wasn't holding him up, he'd be on the floor.' Collingworth winked, took a swig of claret and sashayed back to his music station.

Moran watched the dancers for a while before reluctantly making his way back to Dawson.

'Ah, cheers Brendan. Listen, I want to wish you all the best, you know?' Dawson took the proffered drink and downed it in one. 'Different styles you and me, but I'll get the results, don't you worry.'

Moran winked as Alice made 'time to go' signals towards him from her cosy corner. 'I'm not worried,' he replied. And he wasn't – not about results, at least. He was more concerned about how the team would respond to their new boss.

'Time to ring in the changes.' Dawson nodded. 'Me and the Mrs – we always wanted to move this way anyhow. And here we are.' He spread his arms by way of illustration.

'Your wife wasn't able to make it tonight?'

'She doesn't like these kind of dos. Very private person, Sheila.'

'I see. Well, her prerogative. I'm not so keen on them myself.'

'Got to attend, though, right?' Dawson regarded his empty glass. 'One of those events you can't wriggle out of. Like your own funeral.' He guffawed.

'Maybe time you headed back to Mrs Dawson,' Moran suggested gently. 'Looks like we're all done here.'

'All done. That's about right.'

'Listen, I can give you a lift.' Surely Dawson wouldn't attempt to drive?

'No need, old fella. Got my pushbike in the car park.'

'Really? Even so…'

Dawson stuck out his hand. 'All the best to you, Brendan. You won't miss it, I'll wager. Enjoy the garden, golf…' he waved a hand vaguely, 'whatever it is you're into.'

Moran gave up, shook his hand. 'Sure. And all the best to you, too. They're a good team. Be kind to them.'

'Absolutely. Kind is my middle name,' he slurred.

Alice arrived at Moran's side, and together they watched Dawson walk unsteadily towards the lift.

'Is he OK?' Alice whispered in his ear.

'Not really. But he's got his bike, not his car, so …' Moran shrugged. 'He won't accept a lift.'

'He's a grown-up. He'll be all right. Are you fit?' She held out her hand.

'As I'll ever be.'

'Then let me escort you away from all this, Mr Moran.'

Collingworth raised a hand in farewell from behind his decks, while Charlie waved and Bola executed a mock salute. The waltz over, George and Tess held hands in the middle of the room, and watched them leave.

Chapter Two

'That's it, then.' Moran's hands were clamped on the steering wheel, the engine idling. 'Will I pop over tomorrow?'

'Yes, do.' Alice retrieved her handbag from the floor. 'Peter wants to help with a little gardening project of mine. You can supervise – in case you miss exercising authority,' she added mischievously.

'Dawson doesn't reckon I'll miss anything.'

'What does he know? He's a buffoon, Brendan. He can't fill your shoes, not by a country mile.'

'Well, that's kind of you to say so, but…'

'Now, I don't want any of this feeling sorry for yourself business,' Alice said firmly, opening the door and stepping gracefully onto the pavement. 'It doesn't suit you. You've made the decision. It's the right one, and now you're going to live it out.'

'Live *with* it, more like.'

Alice shook her head in exasperation. 'What am I going to do with you?'

'I can think of a few things.' Moran grinned.

'At this time of night? You can forget it, mister.'

'Tomorrow, then.'

'Tomorrow.'

As Moran drove away, his anxieties surrounding his retirement shifted in favour of another potential change in his life. He was thinking more and more about moving in with Alice. How many more times would they part company at the end of a day, each to their separate homes? Neither of them had broached the subject, it was true, but there was an implicit tension in their relationship that needed to be resolved. They were both thinking the same thing, he was certain, but neither had yet articulated the suggestion to the other.

It was complicated, of course. There was Peter, Alice's autistic brother, to consider, not to mention the shocking history of Alice's sister, an ex police officer who had suffered traumatic amnesia and found herself living in a different city, with no memory of her past life. Moran's team had traced her and all was now well – or as well as it could ever be, he supposed. Emma and Alice had been reunited, but Emma had elected to remain in Carlisle with her partner. They visited once or twice a year, but Peter still found it hard to understand why Emma had been taken away from them, and why he only got to see her infrequently.

In short, there was a lot of baggage, and that was without even considering his own not-insignificant collection. Moran sighed. The day was too long in the tooth for serious reflection; he was weary, but relieved that the ordeal of the farewell do was over.

He found his way through the sparse town centre traffic onto the Oxford Road and ten minutes later arrived in Pangbourne, passing the still burned-out service station on his left. There'd been no new development on the site since the explosion, a puzzling oversight. For one thing, it meant the inconvenience of having to drive beyond Theale to the Bath Road for petrol, or else backtrack to the Reading end of the Oxford Road. The block of flats next door, a residential care home, which had been damaged by the same explosion, had been quickly restored and, presumably, new residents moved in, but the service station remained a shell.

Moran turned into his road, parked the car and sat quietly for a few minutes, reflecting. What would he do? How would he fill his days? Perhaps, in a few months, he'd be living with Alice, gardening, helping to look after Peter, shopping, visiting friends…

Well, that wasn't such a bad picture, was it? As Bola had reminded him, his ex-sergeant, Robert Phelps, seemed to manage well enough in retirement. The last time Moran had visited Phelps had been a picture of contentment, happy with his Shakespeare and, of all things, his three-dimensional decoupage. Even now Moran found it hard to reconcile the brawny yet incisive copper he had worked alongside for so many years with the sight of burly Sergeant Phelps' meaty fingers delicately positioning paper on paper to create a sailing boat, or a country cottage, or complex floral arrangement for his wife's birthday.

The house was dark as he entered. Hall bulb gone again. He missed the pattering of canine feet since Archie had passed away. His faithful spaniel had enjoyed a long and happy life, and saying goodbye had been tough. Should he get another dog? Or maybe wait to see how things worked out with Alice? He couldn't be sure how Peter would react to a dog.

Questions, questions. Why couldn't life be simple? Heaven knew his career had had its share of complications, and it looked as though retirement wasn't necessarily going to change much in that department.

Moran went through to the kitchen and fixed himself a nightcap. He'd been deliberately abstemious at the party, a necessary precaution since he'd offered to drive, which had the added benefit of ensuring that he wouldn't make too much of a fool of himself at the microphone. As it turned out, judging by the warm applause he'd received his parting words had been well received. He'd adopted an optimistic tone when speaking about his successor, Dawson, purely for the benefit of the team. Privately Moran had reservations, which Dawson's casual attitude this evening had done little to dispel. But maybe his fears would turn out to be unfounded. His team were a capable lot and he was proud of their achievements, proud to have served as their guide through so many trials and challenges. Dawson just had to recognise their skills and guide them when necessary.

Later, in the wee, small hours, he lay on his back. Sleep was eluding him; he wondered about tomorrow, and the day after that, all the tomorrows to come, how he would spend his time. There were no answers.

Eventually he drifted off, but his dreams were filled with images of parties, loud music, insistent drum beats hammering into his skull like nails. DCI Dawson was at the record deck, leering at him as he increased the volume until Moran was forced back against the far wall, hands over his ears. Oddly, no one else seemed to be affected; the dance floor was a mass of writhing bodies. Even DCS Higginson was dancing, dressed bizarrely in the style of a punk rocker from 1977.

Moran closed his eyes, but the racket continued unabated. Eventually, he lay on the floor and covered himself with straw – where the straw had come from he couldn't quite pinpoint, but it might have had something to do with the fact that the partygoers had all transformed into animals, and the room into a stable.

He awoke to the insistent ringing of the telephone. Cursing, he swung his legs out of bed and limped through to the hall. Snatching the landline handset from the receiver, he croaked a brief greeting.

'Brendan. So sorry to call you this early.'

Higginson.

'Early? What time is it?' Moran rubbed his eyes with his free hand.

'Just after six. I apologise – the morning after, and so on.'

'I wasn't drinking, it's OK.'

'Ah, good. Well, I'll get straight to it. We have a problem.'

'I gathered that much.'

There was a short pause, then Higginson said, 'It's DCI Dawson.'

'Dawson? What about him?'

Higginson sighed. 'He's in ICU at the Royal Berks. Came off his bike last night and hit his head – they've put him into an induced coma. It's not looking great, I'm afraid. A lot of internal swelling, apparently. They may operate to see if they can alleviate the pressure – if they think he can cope with the procedure, that is.'

'What happened? Hit and run?'

'No one knows. No witnesses; an earlybird dog walker found him an hour ago. Bike's a write-off.'

'Sounds like a hit and run to me.'

'Maybe, but that's not all, I'm sorry to say.'

Moran frowned and his head shot a spasm of pain across his forehead. 'Meaning?'

Another sigh. 'Look, Brendan, I'm very sorry about this, but I'm forced to prevail upon your good nature.'

Moran didn't like the sound of that. 'Well, I'll visit the guy, obviously, when he stabilises.' Moran suddenly remembered his last conversation with Dawson. He'd brought him another drink – a small one, yes, but still … could that have contributed to the accident?

'Of course. I'd expect nothing less, Brendan, but there's something else.'

'Go on.' Now Moran was wide awake.

'We have a body. It's pretty, grim, I should warn you.'

That explained it. 'O … kay. But I still don't see…' The penny dropped. 'Oh no, you're kidding. You want *me* to…'

'It's a big favour I'm asking, Brendan, I know that. But – I'll be frank with you, I've no one else to turn to. No one of your seniority is available.'

'Really? DI Pepper is more than capable of—'

'Yes, I know, but I have other plans for DI Pepper, and they are about to be realised. I can't change what has already been put in place.'

'I see.'

'So you'll help us out?'

'In what capacity? As a freelancer? I'm not sure that HR will take kindly to—'

'Don't worry about HR – I'll sort them out. We'll get you reinstated on an ad hoc basis. This is a bad one, Brendan. If we encounter any red tape I'll slice it open.'

Moran was thinking of Alice. What would she say? What would she think? After a moment he sighed.

'All right. Tell me more.'

'I can't, not right at this moment – I have to prepare a press statement, lickety split. Ten-minute briefing is at nine.'

Moran sighed. 'OK. I'll be there.'

'Oh, one other thing.'

'Yes?'

'I'm appointing DS Collingworth as your deputy on this one.'

'*Collingworth*? As DSIO?' Moran could think of a thousand objections. 'I'm not sure that's—'

'It's a done deal, Brendan. The promotion board were very impressed with him, and he's been hanging around waiting for a posting for long enough. He needs something to get his teeth into.'

'Sir, as SIO, don't you think it's my call to—'

'That's all, Brendan. I'll catch up with you later.'

And with that, Higginson was gone. Moran replaced the receiver and, shaking his head, went through to the kitchen to brew a reviving cup of coffee.

Chapter Three

The brief had been just that. An elderly woman had returned home from visiting a friend to find her younger sister dead. It was murder, no question – and a brutal one, at that. Collingworth had outlined the salient points and then cut the questions short, prioritising preparation of the incident room and the allocation of initial tasks. As the team dispersed Moran went over to the acting sergeant with the intention of offering his full support, but also because he wanted to survey the crime scene while it was still fresh – preferably before the pathologist departed.

'Morning, Chris.'

'Guv.'

'Comfortable holding the fort while I take a look at our body?'

'Sure.'

Moran paused. Even without the monosyllabics, Collingworth's body language was speaking volumes about his reaction to Moran's unscheduled reappearance. 'Look, you probably weren't expecting to see me again – well, not in this context anyway. But we'll have a less bumpy ride if we work together, agreed?'

'Of course.'

Moran was unconvinced. Perhaps a change of subject. 'Any news of Dawson?'

Collingworth shook his head. 'Not heard. But he's out of it as far as this is concerned.'

Moran nodded. 'Yes, I just wondered if—'

'You'll have to excuse me. Higginson wants a word.'

Moran watched him go, the rolling shoulders and swagger a touch more emphatic than usual. The acting sergeant had doubtless been looking forward to taking the lead on the next case to come along, while showing the new DCI the ropes. Dawson was an experienced officer, but it always took time to bed in to a new posting. Of course, that wasn't going to happen now.

No point dwelling on it, Brendan. Back to the job in hand…

Collingworth had already obtained Coroner sign-off, which meant that the body could be moved to the mortuary for a forensic post-mortem on Moran's say so. So far they had a name, an address, an occupation, probable cause of death, no apparent motive, and little else.

He found George in the incident room. 'Fancy an onsite, George?'

'Aye. Could do with some fresh air after the hot variety.'

Moran smiled. 'I thought your new sergeant was commendably concise.'

As they headed for the car park, Moran decided to sound the Scot out; his opinion would likely be shared by the rest of the team. 'You all right reporting to Collingworth, George?'

'I'll be honest, guv, it's not the best news I've had this year.

But it seems to me we don't have much choice.'

'It seems not. But rest assured, I'll keep an eye on things. Don't worry.'

'Good to know, boss.' George cracked a smile. 'Nice to have you back after so long.'

'Ha ha.' Moran pulled a face. 'There's no one more surprised than me, that I can tell you.'

But there would be – once he'd told Alice. That wasn't a conversation Moran was looking forward to.

After a short drive, they pulled up outside the house, a nondescript terraced property in a quiet suburb of Reading. Parking was an issue here, as in many of the terraced roads in and around the town. Traffic was effectively one way with cars lining each side of the road – a necessity, with no available garages for residents. Not that traffic could move along the road at that moment in any case, though, since a squad car was parked four square in the middle and a second was blocking the end, effectively shutting it off. Between the two vehicles the forensics van squatted, a tell-tale harbinger of doom.

A small crowd had gathered on the other side of the blue and white police tape. Arms folded, faces pale in the morning grey, they chatted amongst themselves, aired theories as to what might have happened to their neighbour. George parked behind the squad car and Moran took a mental deep breath.

'Right,' he said, 'let's get this done.'

'It's not a pretty sight, guv, by all accounts.' George walked alongside Moran as he approached the duty constable. The PC nodded a greeting. 'Morning, sir. Forensics are still at it.'

'Pathologist still in situ?'

'I believe so.'

'Good.'

Moran approached the front door with care, using the anti-contamination stepping plates laid down by the forensics team. As they reached the threshold, a suited figure appeared in the hallway.

'Ah, Brendan. *Quel surprise.*'

Sandy Taylor sounded anything but surprised. 'And hello to you, Sandy.' Moran rifled through his pockets and found a pair of plastic gloves.

Taylor put his case down and pulled his mask over his chin. 'Had a funny feeling I might see you today.'

'Prophecy at this hour?'

Taylor laughed. 'Not at all. I just wondered who else they might call out for something like this, and yours was the only name that came to mind.'

'You heard about DCI Dawson?'

'Yes. One of the PCs told me. Bad luck for him, eh?'

Moran let it go. He couldn't shake off a nagging feeling of guilt over that last shot he'd poured.

'Anyway, this won't do much to cheer you up, I'm afraid.' Taylor shook his head. 'I've not seen anything like it for a long, long time.'

'Care to walk me through?'

'All right. Come this way – oh, hello George,' he added as George joined them in the hallway. 'All well with you?'

'Could always be worse, doc.' George's reply was typically downbeat. 'No complaints so far, but it's only nine forty-five.'

'Indeed so.'

Taylor led them into the main living room where the

dominant piece of furniture was a baby grand piano. The room was plainly furnished and had an unmistakeable air of the old-fashioned about it. 'The sister?' Moran wanted to know. 'Where is she?'

'On her way to the RBH, guv,' George piped up. 'PC Rugg just told me they left in an ambulance fifteen minutes ago. Terrible state, apparently.'

'And who can blame her?' Moran murmured as he scanned the scene.

A woman was slumped at the piano, her head resting on the keyboard. Her arms, however, were spread on top of the piano casing, held in place by two nails, one driven into each palm.

'Excuse me a moment – thank you.' Moran stepped around a kneeling forensics officer to position himself behind the victim. He blew his cheeks out. 'I see what you mean, Sandy.'

'Grim, eh?'

'Cause of death?'

'Not necessarily the nails themselves – nowhere near the vitals. In my humble, she died of a massive heart attack.'

'Before, during or after the nails?'

'I'd like to say before, but I'm afraid the blood tells another story.'

'Lord. Poor woman. What's her age, George?'

'Sixty-six, guv.'

Moran studied the corpse. 'What an end to a life. Time of death, Sandy?'

'I'd say sometime between five and eleven last night.'

'The sister came back this morning, guv,' George chimed in. 'Been staying over with a friend. Found her like this.'

'Right. What a homecoming. Two spinsters living together?'

'Yep. In their own world of music, by the look of things. The sister plays the oboe.'

'Hmmm. A bygone age. The house certainly feels like it.' Moran stroked his chin. 'Right. Pop over to the RBH, George, would you? Have a word with the sister when the opportunity presents.'

'Will do. Do we have her name?'

'Reyka, I believe,' Taylor replied. 'Surname is Szarka.'

'Polish?'

'Hungarian.'

George frowned. 'Er – not my forté, guv.'

'They've lived here for many years, George,' Taylor reassured him. 'If she can understand a Scotsman's accent, the King's English will be fine.'

'Aye, maybe, but it's not an English king I'll be thinking of.' George shot them a wink on his way out.

Moran smiled. 'Our George isn't a fan of the English monarchy.'

Taylor made a face. 'I don't suppose many Scotsmen are.'

They stood in silence while the background sounds of forensic activity went on around them.

Moran was thinking about Charnford Abbey, the fate of Gregory Neads, his acting sergeant at the time. The scene before him had reawakened long-buried memories. He took a breath. 'The victim's name, Sandy?'

'Ah… Marika, I believe.'

Moran leaned in close, examined the wounds on Marika Szarka's hands. The nails were galvanised steel, wide-headed, length indeterminate – at least for the time being pending extraction. Just two had been used, driven through the centre of each palm. Interesting, Moran reflected. It would have been easier just to hammer the shaft through the back of the hand, surely, save twisting the arm?

'You a DIY man, Sandy?'

Taylor had retreated to the middle of the room, was fiddling with his case. He looked up. 'The odd repair job, you know. I might stretch to creosoting the shed every so often. That's about it. Too busy most of the time.'

'These look like roofing nails to me. The wide head.'

'I bow to your greater knowledge.' Taylor grinned. The smile died on his lips. 'Bloody painful for the poor woman, whatever they are.'

'Hammer found anywhere?' Moran glanced around.

Taylor shrugged. 'Not my department. Best ask the CSM.'

'Of course – where do I find him?'

Taylor shut his case and cocked his head towards the ceiling. 'Upstairs, last I saw. And it's a she.' He gave Moran a half wink. 'Attractive, too.'

Moran raised an eyebrow. 'Thanks for the tip, Sandy, but I'm spoken for.'

'Well, you know. Always nice to see a pretty face – especially in circumstances like these. Good show about your other half, though – I had heard a rumour or two.'

'I'll bet.'

'Anyway, the CSM's name is Pauline Harris.' Taylor picked up his case and made as if to leave. 'Experienced, so you'll be all right – so long as you toe the line, of course.'

'Don't I always?'

Taylor's response was a knowing grin.

'Keep me posted, Sandy.'

'Sure. I'll arrange for the body to be removed, if you've no objection?'

'No, that's fine.'

Moran made his way into the tiny hall and carefully negotiated the narrow staircase. The house was a typical Victorian terraced property which, judging by its decor, hadn't been changed a great deal since it was built. Despite its brevity, Collingworth's briefing looked to be accurate: two elderly spinsters living together in genteel harmony, a perfectly preserved time capsule, presumably keeping themselves pretty much to themselves and, apart from private pupils coming and going, very little in the way of a social life to intrude on their cosy domesticity. Necessary trips to the local shops, of course, perhaps the odd excursion to the local theatre, but not much else. Quiet, contented, respectable lives.

All of which made the current situation even more incomprehensible. What kind of person would stoop so low as to commit such an atrocity? No wonder the sister was traumatised. How would she ever recover?

He reached the landing. To his right was a small bathroom, and just ahead a door presumably led to a bedroom – the spare, he thought. The main bedroom would be at the front of the house, overlooking the street. Moran followed the scraping noises and buzz of masked conversation, nudging the spare bedroom door open with his knee.

'Hello?'

A white-suited figure, down on their haunches attending to some detail, glanced up. 'Can I help you?'

'I'm looking for Pauline Harris. DCI Moran, SIO.'

'You've found her.' Harris pulled her mask down, extended a

gloved hand. 'Nice to meet you. Bit late to the party, aren't you?'

'I wasn't expecting an invitation,' Moran said. 'I retired yesterday.'

'Oh.' Harris frowned. 'Then what—'

'My successor was involved in an accident last night. I'm here as a favour.' But a favour to whom? To himself, or Higginson? He'd work that one out later.

'I see. Well, nothing concrete to report so far, I'm afraid. No prints, aside from those of the two sisters. No murder weapon – we're assuming that the nails were hammered with a conventional hammer, but it could have been any heavy object.'

'Indeed. Signs of forced entry?'

'Not that we can see.'

'She knew her killer.'

'Don't they always?'

'Not always, but often.'

Harris fixed him with an appraising look. 'I'll let you know if we find anything significant. The photographs and video will be available on request by noon.'

'Thank you. I'm particularly interested in the nails.'

'I'm sure. We'll see what analysis reveals.'

'Thanks.'

Harris nodded and returned her attention to her interrupted task.

That's it, then Brendan. Dismissed.

He stepped along the narrow landing to the main bedroom. Forensics had finished in this one, as evidenced by the light dusting of fingerprint powder on the windowsills and surfaces.

The bed, a single divan, was neatly made up with a floral-patterned counterpane. On the bedside table lay a leather-bound Bible and a music manuscript book. Moran picked it up and flicked through the pages of handwritten notation. As a non-reader it didn't mean much to him, but it was clear that great care that had been taken, each note and symbol painstakingly transcribed using traditional black ink. Neat and fastidious.

He went downstairs; Sandy Taylor had departed, but the detail to remove the body had just shown up. One of Harris' team emerged from the lounge with a claw hammer in one hand and an evidence bag in the other. Moran caught a glimpse of the bloodied nails inside and looked away. The forensics officer nodded to the new arrivals. 'All yours, chaps.'

Moran waited at the foot of the stairs as the body was carried out. He bowed his head; no one deserved such a fate. He took a breath and went into the lounge.

The air was musty. It reminded him of visits he'd made to his grandparents, long ago. The rooms had smelt odd to him then – a mixture of camphor and polish, the dusty fragrance of old books and fading, charmless curtains. This room had the same smell. He studied the objects on the mantelpiece: two cheap porcelain figures, a shepherdess and a vagabond, bookending a carriage clock and a bronze horse on a marble base.

By the armchair was a circular occasional table. On its polished surface rested a small black book, a fountain pen and a pair of half-moon spectacles. He picked up the book. A diary. He turned to today's date. There were two entries:

4pm – James Cordell – R
4.45pm – Mary Jennings – R

R for Reyka, presumably. He flicked to the previous day.

10.15am – Roger Barnes – R
3.30pm – Fiona Manning – M

So, two lessons booked for yesterday. Had they taken place? Perhaps Fiona Manning had noticed something out of place. Whatever, they'd need to speak to all the students.

And tomorrow:

9.00am – Gillian Steadman – M
10.00am – Francis Penman – R

One for Marika. They'd both need cancelling. Moran flicked to the end of the book where he found a list of names and addresses, all painstakingly recorded in the same elegant handwriting. He dropped the diary into an evidence bag, slipped it into his coat pocket and was about to leave when he remembered Sandy Taylor's comment about toeing the line and retraced his steps to the upper floor, where he found Pauline Harris on the landing.

Moran waved the diary. 'I'll need to refer to this – we'll talk to their students.'

'OK.' Harris brandished her clipboard. 'Let me log it first.'

Moran headed it over and waited as Harris affixed a sticker to the evidence bag. She returned it with a flourish. 'All yours. I hope it helps.'

Was that a sparkle he detected in Harris' eyes?

Don't be daft, Brendan ...

He coughed. 'Thanks. You'll let me know if anything turns up that might prove useful?'

'We've already covered that, DCI Moran. Now, if you'll excuse me.'

Second dismissal, Brendan. Time to go.

It had started raining, fat drops falling from a leaden sky. Moran turned up his collar, nodded to the duty officers and only then remembered that he'd arrived in George's car.

Oh well, a short walk wouldn't do him any harm, even in the rain. Thinking time was always useful.

Nice looking girl, Pauline Harris. Mid-forties, maybe?

Wait. You're spoken for, Brendan, remember?

Should he call Alice now? His footsteps slapped on the wet pavement.

No, not yet. Later.

Chapter Four

'OK, thanks.' Collingworth looked anything but grateful. He examined the evidence bag a second time with pursed lips.

'Problem, Chris?' Moran was wet through. The heavens had opened half way back to Atlantic House and he wasn't in the mood for ingratitude.

'No, not at all.' Collingworth pasted a smile onto his face. 'We'll get on to this pronto.'

Moran ran a hand though his soaking hair. 'Let's get one thing straight, shall we? I'm not here to step on your toes. You're more than competent to run with the nuts and bolts of the investigation, but I like to see things for myself. I'm a visual person, that's how my mind works. And as the SIO, the buck stops with me.'

'Sure, I understand, guv.' Collingworth nodded. 'They need a figurehead. Dawson is out of the frame, so here you are.'

Moran elected to ignore Collingworth's less than complimentary assessment of his recall to duty. Instead he said, 'Just keep me informed, Acting DS Collingworth. In the meantime, I'll keep the hounds at bay. And believe me, they'll be scenting blood before long.'

'You're referring to the press, I take it?'

Moran lowered his voice. 'I am, but it won't just be the press. You'll be surprised at what pops out of the woodwork to point the finger if a quick result isn't forthcoming.' He paused to let the point sink in. 'And even if we do get a fast result, don't expect gratitude. The hounds will sniff out any deficiencies in the investigation and gobble up those responsible. That'll be you. And, more significantly, me.'

Collingworth chewed his lip. 'Thanks for the pep talk, guv. Wait – should I still call you that? I mean, seeing as how you're not officially a ranking officer as of yesterday?'

Moran jutted his chin. 'Whatever I am in terms of official HR-speak, Acting DS Collingworth, I'm still your senior, and you can call me whatever you like. Just keep me in the loop, and manage your team. That's all I ask. There's a dead woman on the pathology table right now who deserves justice, albeit posthumously. That's all that concerns me. So, in order to bring about said justice we'll have a full briefing at two o'clock, at which I will outline the investigative strategy and thereby ensure that we're all on the same page. Once that's complete and we have the key team managers in place, it's over to you to manage the daily tasks: house-to-house enquiries, tracking down the students, potential witnesses and whatever else you deem necessary to bring this sad situation to a conclusion. I'll be available as and when you require guidance or advice, which I hope to God you'll follow. You can arrange regular team briefings at times suitable to team activity.'

Moran turned on his heels, angry at himself more than with Collingworth. He needed to dry off, and he needed a quiet place to think. That would be his office.

Moran rested his elbows on the desk he had cleared just hours before. The walls were naked, the blinds drawn. He could hear the murmur of conversation filtering through the glass from the open-plan outside, the occasional purr of an incoming telephone call, the clatter of a printer, but in this space there was nothing apart from a desk and two chairs. Even his desktop PC, the machine he'd refused to exchange for a laptop, had been removed.

The office was featureless, an empty space, but his mind was buzzing like a crowded room.

Come on, Brendan, focus...

Two sisters. Unmarried – 'spinster', he suspected, was not a politically correct word to bandy about these days. Mature ladies then, immersed in a world of their own, archaic and musical. Did they socialise much? Doubtful. It sounded as though the world mostly came to them rather than vice versa, in that pupils would visit for piano and oboe lessons. Reyka had been out at a friend's, though, so maybe she'd been the social animal?

Relatives? Checks would be mandatory. Contractors, for sure – had there been any recent remedial work done on the house? Carpentry in particular.

Moran rubbed his eyes. The image of the nails driven through Marika Szarka's hands would haunt him for a long time to come. His iPhone beeped an alert. A text message. He knew who it was from, but he still winced when he read it.

Good morning, Mr Leisurely! Can I expect to see you later today? A x

Explaining the current situation via text was probably a bad idea. He should drive over to Alice, sit her down, go over the facts gently. The conversation, he knew, would follow a predictable trajectory: look, it'll only be for as long as it takes for the culprit to be caught, that's all. How long will that be? Well, it's not that easy to say. Well, surely someone else can handle the job? Well, not really, not at this short notice, and the early hours and days following a crime are the most vital, and the DCS insisted, and no one could have predicted Dawson's accident, and so on and so on.

It would close with Alice's disappointed expression, the same mixture of personal affront and resentment he'd seen on previous occasions when he'd referred to current and future work commitments.

Moran's fingers hovered over the iPhone's keyboard. A sharp rap on the door made him jump.

'Enter.'

George poked his head into the office. 'You free, guv?'

'As a bird.'

George grabbed the visitor's chair and sat down. He was bristling with nervous energy.

'Out with it, George.' Moran knew George well; sometimes the diminutive Scot would get so wound up that he couldn't articulate what was bothering him. Instead he would turn puce, chew the edge of his hand and mutter some Celtic invective under his breath before finally launching into his primary area of complaint. Moran encouraged him gently.
'Did you find the sister?'

'Aye, I did, but she's a mess, guv. I was given five minutes by some tosser of an A&E nurse, but the woman's incoherent. All I got out of her was the name of her friend – the one she was staying with. And that was hard enough, I can tell you.'

'Well, that's a start. He can corroborate Reyka's whereabouts at least, confirm times and so on.'

'It's a she, actually, guv.' He consulted his notebook. While the younger DCs all used smartphones or iPads to make notes, George was stubbornly old school. Moran approved. 'A Fedelma Goosens.' George tapped the notebook with a scrupulously sharpened pencil. 'Of 12 Christchurch Road. Lives alone. Widowed.'

'Fedelma? Now there's a good old Irish name.'

The office door opened and Collingworth appeared. 'DCI Moran, sorry to interrupt. Can I borrow George?'

George, his back to the door, shot Moran an evil expression.

'I think we're finished for now, Chris,' Moran replied. 'Be my guest.' To George he said, 'Thanks, George. We'll catch up later.' He followed this with a look that he hoped conveyed supportive empathy, or something close to it.

George scowled and followed Collingworth, closing the door behind him with a firm click.

Moran sighed. Keeping the peace was always going to be a challenge with Collingworth as his deputy.

Thanks a million, DCS Higginson…

Chapter Five

DC Bernice Swinhoe was trying hard to concentrate on the task in hand, but that was easier said than done, distracted as she was by the imperative to maintain a good distance between herself and Collingworth. In his new role as acting sergeant, he was swanning about like a cat that had got the cream *and* the sardines to boot, and he had taken every opportunity over the past two hours to invade her personal space with some new instruction or demand. If he carried on like this she'd have to resort to bluntness, which was not at all in her nature.

Sitting at the opposite workstation, DC Bola Odunsi was watching her with concern.

'You OK, B?'

'For now, yes thanks.'

Bola sniffed. 'I get it. He's a pain.'

'Nothing new there.'

'Except now he's a grade-higher-pain.'

Bernice pushed her mouse away and stretched in her chair. 'We're all going to suffer that.'

'Uh huh – but the guv'll keep him in check.'

'He won't be around all the time.' Bernice folded her arms.

Bola shrugged. 'There's always HR.'

Bernice sighed. 'I don't want to come across like a little girl who can't look out for herself.'

'Sure.' Bola rubbed his chin. 'I get that.'

'Do you?'

Bola maintained eye contact, and Bernice read the unspoken question. 'I'm all right, Bola.'

'You sure?'

'Yes!'

A pause. 'How was your weekend? You were away?'

'Yep.'

'Another trip to my favourite guy's stately home?'

'Not this again.'

Bola had been acting like her elder brother ever since the moment she'd confided that she'd visited Alastair Catton at his *Simplicity* commune. Not commune, she reminded herself; *living space* is what Alastair liked to call it. For some reason Bola had taken against Alastair, who was the sweetest, most interesting guy she'd ever met. Were they an item yet? That was Bola's unspoken question – as though it were only a matter of time.

She liked Alastair. He was attentive, kind, he hadn't forced himself on her. On the contrary – when she'd tentatively asked if she might stay for a few days he had welcomed her discreetly, kept his distance, made sure she'd had time alone to unwind, and only approached her the once to ask her to dinner, during which he had behaved like the perfect gentleman he clearly was. No pressure, just fascinating conversation, good food and wine, and a beautiful location to wake up to. Bernice had been captivated by the experience. She wanted to go again soon and as it happened she had a perfect excuse; she'd left her smartphone behind. It had her life on it and the week had been correspondingly difficult as she had struggled to manage without it.

'I'm just looking out for you, that's all.' Bola drummed his fingers on his desk.

'I'm a grown up, Bola. I can handle myself.'

'Oh I know, I know.'

'There's a *but* lining up.'

Bola cleared his throat. 'I just got a feeling, that's all. There's something not right at Catton's Utopia.'

'Simplicity.'

'Whatever.'

Bernice sighed. 'I'll be careful, Bola, OK? Promise. But nothing's going to happen.'

'If you say so. Anyway, you've got my number if you need it. When you do go?'

'What makes you think I'm going there anytime soon?'

'The look in your eye, B. Dead giveaway.'

Bernice glowered. 'As it happens I do have to go back pretty urgently – I left my phone there.'

'Oh yeah? Get him to send it on. We're on the Szarka case for the foreseeable, right? And I can't see Captain Dickhead authorising any absences until we have this thing under control.'

'Alastair doesn't trust the postal services. It'll only take a few hours. I really need it.'

'Your funeral.'

'Come on, partner. You can cover for me for a few hours, can't you?'

Bola groaned. 'Really?' He sighed. 'As it's you, I suppose.

But don't say I didn't warn you.'

'Thanks, Bola.' She grinned. Bola was one of the good guys. She'd got lucky working with him. 'No warning necessary, though,' she added with a frown. 'Alastair's OK, really.'

Bola gave a weary shake of his head. 'I just got a vibe, that's all. And what about that creepy young guy hovering around, like he's a manservant or something?'

'Johnny?' Bernice laughed. 'He's all right. He's a musician. Alastair lets him stay in the main house rent-free so he can compose. Alastair's like a benefactor – so generous. And Johnny is really talented. I think he could make a big splash in the neo-classical market, given the right opportunity.'

'Yeah? Weird set-up if you ask me.'

'Let's change the record, Bola. Bored of this one.'

'Retro, eh?'

'Ha ha. I do own a turntable and a vinyl collection, I'll have you know. Anyway, look, I have to get on with this – our Vice Captain will be looking for timescales anytime now.'

'The music students?'

'Yep.' Bernice pursed her lips. 'Fifteen of them, mostly pre-teens. They all live locally, except for one adult who travels from London.'

'Wow. Dedication.'

'It's worth travelling for a good music teacher.'

Bola winced. 'I don't get it. An old woman, never harmed a soul. Why?'

Bernice waved the Szarka's diary. 'That's what we're going to find out – you and me, George and Tess. *Not* Mr Knobhead – even though he'll try to steal the credit.'

'Happy to step out with you, if you'll have me?'

Bernice grinned. 'You know I will. As long as said knobhead sanctions the partnership.'

'Speaking of whom—' Bola glanced at his watch. 'It's almost two. Shall we?'

'Everybody clear?' Moran surveyed the room. There were nods, and a confirmatory chorus of *yes, guvs*.

'Good. House-to-house updates to Acting Detective Sergeant Collingworth, forensics results as they come in to myself in the first instance, please.'

More nods.

'Off you go then.'

Moran watched them disperse. Collingworth and George were having another crack at the sister, now discharged from the Royal Berkshire Hospital and staying with the same friend she'd been visiting the previous day. Hopefully by now she'd be in a calmer frame of mind. Was Collingworth the right personality for the interview? Probably not, but there wasn't a great deal Moran could do about that. He consoled himself with the thought that George's interview manner was, if not ideal, then certainly less abrasive than Collingworth's. He could always pop over himself this evening, or tomorrow, perhaps, if they found that Reyka Szarka's composure was still wobbly this afternoon.

Tess and the new detective constable, DC Schlesinger, were taking care of local enquiries. Neighbours were usually a good source of information, and it seemed likely that the Szarkas' eccentricities would have been observed and commented on by the other residents. Moran tried to imagine the sisters' antiquated lifestyles: no mobile phones, no computer – and therefore no social media presence – no television or radio, not even a modern kitchen. The scullery looked like something from a museum – a basic sink with a rudimentary work surface, an ancient gas cooker and a pantry for cold storage. The decor hadn't been altered since the house was built.

All in all, there was much less than usual to go on. The nearest CCTV was half a mile away and the Szarkas didn't own a car. But – Moran stroked his chin – someone had come to visit, and that meant an arrival and a departure. Which would leave some trace, however small, on the premises, or on the body.

And that was his next port of call: the post-mortem at half past four. The wall clock told him he just about had time for a late lunch and a much-needed infusion of caffeine.

Moran took a last look at the whiteboard, in the centre of which was a black-and-white portrait photograph of Marika Szarka taken maybe twenty or thirty years ago. Not a conventionally pretty woman, but handsome enough in her own way. He wondered about her back story, her past, whether there had been suitors or a wider family. Perhaps the house search – or Reyka – might satisfy his curiosity. In the meantime, he didn't know what he didn't know – never a comfortable feeling.

His mobile vibrated in his pocket and he headed back to his office for some privacy. Sustenance would have to wait; he knew he owed it to Alice to explain his absence. He read the short text message.

Have I been sent to Coventry?

Moran sat at his desk and attempted to compose a conversational opener. None hit the right tone and after a few minutes he gave up, found her number and stabbed the call icon. She answered immediately.

'Brendan. I was getting worried.'

'Sorry – I meant to call earlier. All is well.'

'Good. Well, I'm glad to hear it. Are you … coming over, or —?'

He took a breath. Here we go. 'There's been a … development.'

'Oh? What kind of development?'

'A work development.'

A pause. 'But you're retired. I don't under—'

'Last night. DCI Dawson – the guy hanging on your every word, remember?'

'Your successor, yes, of course. What's happened?'

Moran explained.

'God. That's terrible.'

There was another, longer, pause as Alice digested the information. Then,

'But why do they need you? I mean, surely there's someone who can step in and fill the gap until the poor man recovers, or…' she tailed off, uncomprehending.

'There's been a serious crime. A homicide.'

Another brief pause, ominous this time. 'Oh. I see.'

A note of resignation had crept into Alice's tone. Moran grimaced. She went on, 'Peter was looking forward to seeing you.'

A wave of irritation washed up Moran's spine. Emotional blackmail was not something he expected from Alice.

'Look, I know this is inconvenient. But a murder – well, it has to take priority.'

'So it would seem.'

'Don't be angry, Alice. I didn't ask for this.'

'No? I'll bet you bit Higginson's hand off.'

'That's not fair.' He bristled. 'I didn't arrange Dawson's accident.'

'Maybe you contributed to it, though.'

'And what's that supposed to mean?'

'The man was drunk, and I saw you hand him another glass of Scotch.'

The observation rendered him momentarily speechless. 'It was scarcely a mouthful – I made damn sure of that. The guy was already three sheets to the wind by then, anyway.' Moran clamped his mouth shut as he felt himself slide towards incoherence. Despite his efforts a final protest slipped out through gritted teeth. 'That's bloody unfair, Alice and you know it.'

'I have to go. Peter's calling me.'

The line went dead, and Moran slammed the phone on his desk.

Two sharp raps on the door and DCS Higginson entered without waiting for a response, uniform buttons gleaming, knife-edged trouser creases, hair neatly parted. His eyes, however, were dark and brooding.

'Bad news, Brendan, I'm afraid. Dawson didn't make it.'

Moran nodded. Of course. It was always going to end like that. Worst case scenario, as per usual. A cold shiver ran through him.

Higginson was still talking. 'I'll speak to the widow; you've plenty to be getting on with. Can't tell you how much I appreciate your stepping in on this one, Brendan.'

Moran's response was automatic, delivered without conscious thought. All he could see in his mind's eye was that last drink, a finger of Scotch. A finger too many.

Chapter Six

Bola consulted the list. 'OK, numero uno – Fiona Manning. Last student booked. The only other adult on their books, apart from the London commuter. Three thirty.'

Bernice swung the car into Poole Road. 'And time of death, according to pathology, was between five and seven-ish, possibly later.'

'So Ms Manning could be the last person to see Marika Szarka alive.'

Bernice found a parking space and adroitly eased the car into the gap. 'If she attended.'

'Indeed.'

It was an unprepossessing house – a red-bricked, late Victorian semi-detached. Very middle class, sited in a prosperous area, catchment for the best state schools. Unlikely, in Bola's opinion, to be the type of household where family members regularly nailed old ladies to pianos.

'I know what you're thinking,' Bernice said as she rang the bell.

'Enlighten me, do.'

'You're thinking no way, not from a middle class setup like

this.'

Bola grinned. 'Psychic too, huh?'

The front door swung open. A man in his early forties stood on the threshold, rounded John Lennon glasses, open-necked shirt, jeans. His hair was short and gel-tufted at the hairline, a nod to modern fashion, although in Bola's judgement he was five to seven years too old to carry it off. His eyes narrowed and Bola knew what the guy was thinking: Jehovah's Witnesses, or some new sales scam.

He produced his warrant card before the guy opened his mouth to tell them to get lost. He examined the card minutely before asking the obvious question.

'Detectives? What's going on?'

'Is a Ms Manning in?'

'Fi? Yes, why?'

'Perhaps it would be better if we came in for a chat?' Bernice suggested.

'That sounds ominous. All right. If you must.'

They followed him along the hall into the living room, a tastefully furnished space with wall-mounted TV, an expensive looking sofa and two matching armchairs, a stylish coffee table and, taking up most of the bay window space, a lovingly polished upright piano.

'Is that a Steinway?' Bernice asked aloud, almost to herself.

'Yes, it is,' a female voice replied.

Bola and Bernice turned as a slim woman in a long skirt and white blouse entered the room and positioned herself slightly to one side but behind the man, as though using him as a shield.

'My mother owned one very similar.' Bernice smiled in a

friendly fashion. The woman looked as though she might take fright at the slightest provocation. 'I still play it a little, although I'm not very good.'

'Not another damn pianist,' the man muttered.

'Don't mind Clive,' the woman said quickly. 'He's not a music fan.'

'You're Fiona Manning?' Bola pressed on.

'Yes.'

'And you are...?' Bernice smiled sweetly at Clive.

'Clive Brooks.'

'We're together,' Fiona Manning clarified. 'Not married, I mean. Just together.'

'That's fine, Ms Manning,' Bernice said. 'We're not here to judge your domestic arrangements.'

Manning gave a demure nod.

'Can we get to the point?' Brooks said. 'I have things to be getting on with.'

'Sure,' Bola indicated the sofa. 'May we sit down?'

'Why not?' Brooks sat down, but Fiona Manning hesitated and Bola caught an imperceptible nod of acquiescence from Brooks. Only then did Manning join him, arranging her hands neatly on her lap.

'We believe you attended a piano lesson yesterday afternoon?' Bernice began.

'Yes, that's right. Why do you ask?' Manning's confirmation and question quavered a little. Nervous. Maybe her disposition, or maybe something else. Bola watched her carefully while Brooks drummed his fingers on the armrest.

'I'm afraid I have some rather bad news,' Bernice said gently. 'Marika Szarka was found dead early this morning.'

'Marika? But … I don't understand. She was fine, she was…'

'I'm sorry. It's a shock, I'm sure.'

'What happened? I mean, *how* did it happen?'

Bola was keeping an eye on Brooks. No reaction, just irritation. He gave it to them straight. 'We're treating the incident as murder.'

Brooks' eyebrow twitched. Manning blanched, the blood fleeing from her already pale face.

'Did Ms Szarka seem her usual self yesterday, Ms Manning?' Bernice asked.

'Yes … yes, absolutely. I mean, she was *fine*. But who would harm someone like Marika? It makes no sense.' Manning's eyes were wide with shock. The reaction looked genuine to Bola.

'How long have you known Ms Szarka?' Bernice asked. 'Have you been attending lessons a long time?'

'Around a year, maybe a bit longer. You see, I used to play, but I stopped because … well…' Here she glanced sideways at Brooks.

'Bloody waste of time,' Brooks said. 'What good does tinkling on a piano do? Plenty of other things to occupy our minds.'

Manning went on quickly, as though trying to play down Brooks' hostility towards her musical endeavours. 'Clive's not a fan, as you can see.' She laughed nervously. 'But he's happy to let me play a little nowadays, aren't you Clive?'

Brooks' grunted response could have meant anything.

'So, you arrived at half past three?' Bola let the awkward exchange pass.

'Yes. Maybe a few minutes later. It was a rush.'

'And you drove?'

'Yes. I always drive. I don't like buses, or—'

'Anything that might bring you into contact with germs,' Brooks finished for her.

'That's right. I like to be careful, after Covid, you know?'

'Of course. Very wise.' Bernice encouraged Manning with a brief nod. 'Were you alone in the house with Ms Szarka?'

'Yes. Her sister was away.'

'Do you know Reyka well?'

Manning shook her head. 'Not really. She answers the door occasionally, but I've never really had a conversation with her. She's usually teaching in the dining room. Oboe, not piano,' she added.

'And there was nothing about Marika Szarka's demeanour that suggested stress, or unusual agitation of any kind?'

'No. Not at all.'

Bola turned his attention to Brooks. 'And what about you, sir?'

'What about me?' Brooks parroted. 'Why has any of this got anything to do with me?'

'We're just trying to build up a picture of the circumstances, Mr Brooks,' Bernice explained patiently. 'We're not implying anything.'

'I've met the woman once or twice, when I've dropped Fi off on occasion. That's it.'

'And what were you doing yesterday afternoon, sir?' Bola asked. 'Between three and seven.'

'Shopping. I was at B&Q, if you must know.'

Bola stroked his chin thoughtfully. 'I see. For four hours?'

'No.' Brooks' tone veered sharply from testiness and made a beeline towards outright hostility. 'For an hour or so, then straight back here. And if that question isn't an implication I don't know what is. Are we done here?'

'Almost, sir. We appreciate your time.'

'Right, Ms Manning,' Bernice broke in smoothly. 'We may need to speak to you again, but in the meantime, if you recall anything you feel might be relevant, no matter how trivial it may seem, please get in touch.'

'Have you any idea who might have … who…' Manning's fingers worried themselves on her lap.

'Not yet.' Bola stood up and shot Brooks a beaming smile. 'But we will. Very soon. Criminals always leave a trace, no matter how hard they try to cover up.'

Brooks gave Bola a filthy look and Manning made as if to rise, but Bernice held up her hand. 'We'll see ourselves out. Thank you again.'

Bola waited until he reached the lounge door to deliver his parting comment. 'Oh, I almost forgot. We'll need to check your landline and mobile call history, social media and so on. All standard procedure. We'll keep it confidential, of course.'

Bola left the room with a smile without waiting for Brooks' reaction.

As they crossed the street Bernice gave him a look. 'I can't see you and Brooks forming a close friendship any time soon.'

'He's all wrong, that guy,' Bola said as Bernice clicked her key fob. 'He's hiding something.'

'I can't help but agree. Did you see the way she looked at him?'

'Abusive relationship?' Bola hastily fastened his seatbelt as

Bernice pulled out of the parking space, accelerating towards the T junction at the end of the road. 'Jumping Jehosephat, B, take it easy, will you?'

'Sorry. Bad habit.' She spun the wheel and deftly slipped in among the queuing traffic on the main road. 'Overbearing, for sure, but maybe not abusive. I didn't see a mark on her. She's timid, deferential. Gentle. *She's* no killer, Bola.'

'Maybe,' Bola growled. 'But I ain't so sure about him.'

Chapter Seven

'Can't you leave the poor woman alone? She's had a frightful time of it. Can you imagine how she feels? No, I don't suppose you can. I've a mind to complain to your superior.'

'That'll be me, Miss Goosens,' Collingworth elbowed George aside and flourished his warrant card. 'As this is a murder inquiry I'm afraid we can't afford any delay. I appreciate that Ms Szarka is upset—'

'Upset? She's lost her sister, her lifelong companion. Marika was her all-in-all.'

'We do understand, Miss Goosens. This won't take long, but I must insist.'

'I prefer *Ms* these days, if you *don't* mind.' Goosens exhaled and rolled up the sleeves of her cardigan with terse, quick movements of her fingers. For a moment George imagined that she might try to physically resist their entering the property, but instead she stood to one side and gestured for them to proceed. 'No more than ten minutes. Maximum.'

George followed Collingworth inside. The house was a new build, the old row of three-story semis having been demolished half a decade before.

A show home. George could smell fresh flowers, although that was probably the numerous bowls of *pot pourri* placed strategically on top of each gleaming surface. The carpet felt like thick cotton wool under his feet. He felt as though he were soiling the house just by being inside it.

'Shoes.' Goosens blocked their path into the living room.

George removed his slip-ons and watched Collingworth do likewise without a murmur. He was beginning to feel like a schoolboy on a visit to the headmistress' study.

'Now you may enter.'

Reyka Szarka was seated in a plush cherry-coloured armchair holding a lace handkerchief to her nose. When she saw George she allowed her head to fall back on the antimacassar with a small groan of resignation.

'You have nine minutes precisely.' Goosens stood by the door, arms folded.

'How are you feeling, Ms Szarka?' George began.

Collingworth opted for a rather more direct approach. 'We'd like to know precisely when you got home this morning, and your first thoughts on finding your sister's body.'

Reyka Szarka stared hard at Collingworth as though she were trying to make him disappear.

Goosens gave a huff of indignation. 'Might I suggest a little sensitivity?'

Collingworth pressed on as though he hadn't heard; George felt like a spectator helplessly watching two fast-moving vehicles on a collision course. However, to his surprise Reyka gathered herself and began to speak in a low, clear, voice with just the hint of an accent. If George hadn't been aware of her origins he would have assumed her to be English, possibly from somewhere in the West Country or maybe the Welsh Borders.

'I returned home just after midnight,' she began. 'I opened the front door as usual and immediately knew that something was amiss. I—'

'By taxi?' Collingworth interrupted.

'Yes, the local minicab company. I always use them. AB cars.'

Collingworth made a note. 'OK. You say you knew something was amiss. How's that?'

'Because my sister always retires at ten o'clock, but I noticed that the light in the lounge was still on. Marika always makes sure the lights are off when she takes herself to bed.'

Here she glanced at Goosens, still standing guard by the door. Her friend returned a sad, sympathetic smile, and Reyka dabbed the handkerchief to her eye. 'Always … always *made* sure, I mean.'

'I know this is hard, Ms Szarka,' George encouraged her. 'Just five minutes, that's all. If you can think of anything that might help.'

'*Four* minutes,' Goosens corrected, glancing at the carriage clock on the mantelpiece.

'Rather late to come home, isn't it?' Collingworth's interrogation went on. 'After midnight?'

'I wasn't intending to be so late,' Reyka replied evenly, 'but our evening was so enjoyable that we completely lost track of time, didn't we, dear?'

'We did,' Goosens agreed. Now she came and stood behind Reyka's armchair, laid a protective hand on her shoulder.

'And what were you doing that was so absorbing?'

Collingworth demanded.

'Why, playing music, of course.' Reyka fluttered her handkerchief. 'I play the oboe, and Fedelma plays the piano.'

'I don't see a piano.' Collingworth cast about for some nook or cranny capable of disguising something as large as a piano.

'In the music room – behind the louvre doors,' Goosens said wearily. 'We meet once a week to play together. It's our little routine.'

Collingworth came straight back at her. 'Why wasn't your sister included, Ms Szarka?'

'Marika didn't care to leave the house. She's become very nervous over the last few years – she'd become, I mean. She was happy for me to visit Fedelma, though. She knew it was important to me.'

George was impressed by Reyka's composure. Though obviously distraught, she'd been able to control her emotions and remain calm in the face of Collingworth's provocative line of questioning.

'I have to ask you this,' George said. 'And I'll have to be direct, I'm afraid.' He took a breath. 'Was Marika dead when you found her?'

A wordless nod, pursed lips.

'And you called the police straight away?' George went on quickly.

A shake of the head. 'No. I stayed with her for an hour or so. I wanted to remove the … you know … but I had no … no *tools*. I didn't want to hurt her anymore.' Reyka's composure crumbled and she buried her head in her handkerchief, sobbing.

Goosens rapped the back of the armchair. 'Right. Time's

up.'

'I'm not finished.' Collingworth locked eyes with Reyka's minder. 'We're not done until I say so.'

Reyka spoke up. 'Really, Fedelma, it's all right. Let me think.' She placed her hand over Goosens'. 'Don't you want to help?'

'Of course. But I have things to do.' Goosens pulled her hand away and strode across the lounge. 'I'll thank you to be as quick as possible.' This to Collingworth as she left the room.

Collingworth declined to reply, keeping his attention on Reyka. 'Any issues with pupils? Disagreements?'

'No. None that I can think of.'

'And have you had any remedial work done on the property over the last eighteen months?' George asked. 'No matter how small.'

Reyka frowned. 'We had the gutters cleaned a while ago, but that was all outside work – a very nice gentleman, as I recall. And a little gardening last year sometime, I think – the same gentleman. We pay our bills promptly. There's no reason to imagine that anyone might bear any kind of grudge, if that's what you're thinking.'

'Does anyone else visit regularly – for any reason?' Collingworth sat on the sofa arm and tapped his foot on the deep carpet pile.

Reyka clasped her hands and closed her eyes. Once again George was struck by the way she had gathered herself, found a new self-possession. Collingworth's tapping accelerated as Reyka remained silent. George held his peace.

Let her think…

Just as Collingworth took a breath to butt in, Reyka opened

her eyes. 'Well,' she said. 'There's Matthew.'

'And Matthew is?' Collingworth clicked his fingers.

'The piano tuner.'

'Tell me about him.'

'Matthew? He's rather … eccentric, I suppose. An odd bod. I don't think he's married. He's pleasant enough, apart from his horrid habit.'

'What habit would that be, Ms Szarka?' George asked. In the near distance Goosens could be heard clattering dishes in a not-so-silent protest.

Reyka wrinkled her nose. 'Snuff. He uses snuff. Takes a pinch and sneezes into a revolting brown handkerchief. And he clears his throat with an equally ghastly noise. I have to leave the house when he comes.'

'I see. And do you have his contact details?'

'In our telephone book. At home.'

'Surname?' Collingworth stood up and stretched.

'Potter. Matthew Potter.'

'Thank you. Do you have any relatives?'

A hesitation. 'Not now. Our mother passed away a few months ago.'

'OK, great.' Collingworth made a note. 'Thanks. George? Anything to add?'

George shook his head, embarrassed by Collingworth's insensitivity. He just wanted to leave the bereaved woman in peace. She needed quiet, rest, and time. A lot of time. 'I'm sorry to hear about your mother, Ms Szarka.'

A slight inclination of the head. 'Thank you.'

A further thought did occur to him, though. 'Will you be staying here … for the foreseeable future?'

'As long as Fedelma will have me, yes. I can't go back. Not yet. Maybe not ever.'

'I understand. We'll be in touch.'

Collingworth was already at the door. 'Come on, George.'

Goosens appeared at the far end of the hall and wordlessly watched them leave, arms folded, expressionless, like an over-protective chaperone warding off unwanted suitors.

Chapter Eight

Moran wrinkled his nose at the all-too-familiar smell of the autopsy room. Even the thick glass of the viewing window couldn't keep the smell out; the scent of death had a knack of seeping through the cracks. Sandy was hard at work and already had Marika Szarka's chest open; he acknowledged Moran's arrival with a nod and a cheery flourish of some razor-sharp tool he was holding in his gloved hand.

'Anything yet, Sandy?'

The loudspeaker came to life with a pop. 'As I suspected,' Sandy's voice said, 'cause of death was coronary failure. Probably attributable to her predicament.' Sandy gave a slow shake of his head. 'Not unexpected for a woman of her age in such a position.'

'Yep. Can't argue with that.'

'No other signs of trauma to the body. Lungs are in good nick for her age, as is the liver.' He probed with the instrument while Moran studied the wall. 'And the kidneys. She'd have lived to a ripe old age, I'd say, had she been allowed to.'

'Makes sense. Non-smoker. Teetotaller. A vice-free existence – if you discount the obsessive composition of arias and chamber music. Over a hundred scores between them in the music desk, according to Forensics.'

'Prolific, indeed.' Moran could make out Sandy's grin beneath his mask. 'Ah, this is interesting.'

'What?' Moran leaned forward until his nose made contact with the glass.

Sandy was standing at the end of the dais by the head block, looking down at Marika's scalp – still intact, but as Moran knew from previous experience, it would not remain so for long. Marika's brain would be subject to the closest scrutiny, which necessitated the removal of the top of the skull. Moran intended to be long gone by then; for some reason it was always that stage of an autopsy that unsettled him the most. He had no idea why; perhaps it was the consideration that the brain was the most mysterious organ in the body. Neurosurgeons understood enough to be able to identify which areas of the brain took care of the various necessary bodily functions – speech, movement, feeling and so on – but essentially they hadn't the faintest idea how this spongy, unappealing-looking mass was able to generate that most perplexing phenomenon, consciousness itself.

Sandy didn't answer straight away. He was examining the hair, carefully pulling something from the grey-black scalp. 'Hm. Here's something you might be interested in.'

Moran squinted. 'What is it?'

'A piece of glass, or … wait, no, ceramic, I think. Pottery?'

'Pottery? Not a piece of ceiling plaster? Place hasn't seen a decorator for decades.'

Sandy was holding the object up to the light. 'Nope. Definitely not. I'd say it's a fragment of an ornament, or maybe a table lamp or similar.' He consigned the fragment to a glass dish.

Interesting. Broken ceramic implied a struggle of some kind, or at least some deliberate act of destruction. 'Right, we'll need to get that to the lab asap.'

'Will do.'

'How about her hands?'

'Yes, I'm coming to those.'

Moran watched as Sandy lifted Marika's right wrist, almost gingerly, and examined her hand. 'Small entry wound on the palmar side.' He turned the hand over. 'Exit wound on the dorsal. Severe trauma to the flexor pollicis brevis muscle.' Sandy repeated the procedure on Marika's left arm and reported the same conclusion.

'That would have hurt.'

'Undoubtedly. But as I said before, it was the heart failure that killed her.'

'Murder either way you look at it,' Moran muttered.

'Want to scoot this to forensics yourself?' Sandy reached for the ceramic fragment and held it up. 'I can get it bagged for you.'

'Would you? That'd be helpful, thanks.'

A few minutes later Moran departed with the item in question safely sealed in a plastic bag in his pocket. He felt a familiar tingle of excitement. It might be nothing, but his instinct told him otherwise.

In the car park he drew a lungful of fresh air and fished out his mobile. He tapped in a number and the call was answered after one ring.

'Pauline Harris.'

'Moran here. Just wondering if your team found any pottery fragments or similar in the lounge?'

'We're still collating, Chief Inspector.'

'Any objection if I pop in?'

'No. Just don't expect my undivided attention. Once we're finished, we're finished, and you can have all the information you need.'

'I just need to know if, in your opinion, there were enough fragments found to represent a recent breakage. I have a sample to cross-check.'

'Autopsy found said fragment on the body, I take it?'

'You take correctly.'

'I'll see you shortly then, Chief Inspector.'

The line went dead in the middle of Moran's thank you, reminding him of her predecessor, the now retired Mrs E. Maybe spending too much time with the dead made one forget how to be cordial to the living.

He walked thoughtfully back to his car. Before starting the engine he scrolled down his contacts list. Roper, Alice. He exhaled, allowed his head to fall back on the headrest. Face-to-face is always better. Who had said that? Some wise man. But when? It was coming up to half past five and he really wanted to check out Pauline Harris' findings before doing anything else, but truth be told, Alice's tone earlier had shocked him. He'd never known her to be so cold. She'd stoically put up with his workload for months, and mostly with good humour. But this … she'd taken his unexpected reinstatement as a betrayal, there was no doubt about it. How could he make amends?

If he went to the house now, he'd only be able to repeat what he'd told her earlier. And there was the added complication of Peter – not that Peter himself was a complication; Moran had established a good relationship with Alice's autistic brother, but his presence would inevitably inhibit any attempt on Moran's part to re-establish the emotional status quo. Things could get heated, and Peter responded badly to raised voices. It wouldn't be fair.

Moran banged his head against the headrest. Just when things were settling down, just when he felt that he might actually be able to make a go of this relationship...

His mobile rang. 'Moran.'

'Inspector Moran?'

'Chief Inspector, yes.'

'Oh, good. Listen, a Sergeant Collinghurst gave me your number. He thought I should tell you what I told him earlier. Well, to be completely honest, he didn't really give me the chance to tell him much at all. I mean, I know you lot are always busy with crimes and murders and all things like that, but you know, when I saw what was happening across the way this morning I thought I'd better fill you in on the—'

Moran broke into the rapid-fire monologue. 'Who am I speaking to?'

'Oh, sorry, yeah. My name's Levi Cambridge. I live across the road from the old dears. Well, old *dear*, if my understanding of today's events is correct.'

'Mr Cambridge. It's not entirely appropriate that we converse on the phone. If you have any information relating to today's events, I suggest you come into the station and one of my officers will interview you.'

'But Sergeant Collinghurst said—'

'It's Colling*worth*, and I don't care what he said. Call Atlantic House please, and ask for DC Martin or DC Schlesinger. They'll arrange a time for you to come in and be interviewed.'

'How's that? Sledge what?'

Moran patiently spelled the names.

'OK. Got it. So, you don't want to know about the burglary then?'

'Burglary?'

'That's what I'm saying. The old biddies were burgled two weeks ago. Scared stiff they were. One of 'em comes over to my place and bangs on the door. Almost midnight it was.'

'Mr Cambridge, this is potentially of interest to us, but please do what I asked and contact my officers.'

'All right, sure. I just thought you'd want to know – you know, in case it's relevant. I mean, the guy could have snuck back and done the poor old thing in, right? I mean, two old uns on their own, nothing to defend themselves. Sitting targets, right? No way a burglar's gonna pass up that kind of chance once he's sussed out they're easy meat.' The verbal machine-gunning stopped abruptly. 'And all things like that,' Cambridge added.

'Thank you, Mr Cambridge. Now, if you'll excuse me.'

'Pleasure chatting, Inspector. I'll call them officers straight away.'

'Yes, do that.'

'Bye bye, then.'

Moran signed off. He wondered if he should warn Tess in advance, but quickly decided against it; better for her to discover Cambridge's quirks for herself. She could ask the new chappie, Schlesinger, to talk to him. Schlesinger seemed a competent enough officer, but his skills were as yet untested. Cambridge would be on Tess's neighbour list, but now she'd got herself an early-doors interview, so to speak. He hoped Cambridge wouldn't prove to be a waste of their time.

Quarter to six. Time to go. Moran gunned the engine and set off for the forensics laboratory.

Chapter Nine

'Tess?'

Tess Martin turned her head as she waited for the lift to see George bearing down on her. 'Hey.' He popped her a bright smile. 'Off home?'

'I thought I'd sift through tomorrow's list. Finish my paperwork. Get my head in order.'

'Don't fancy a quick bite somewhere?'

Tess flashed a sympathetic smile. 'I do, but … you know. We've got a case on, right?'

George's chagrined expression made her reach out and touch his arm. They hadn't spent much time together of late, and that had been down to her. The truth was that George's concern for her wellbeing – as endearing as it might be – was beginning to stifle her. And then there were the headaches. At first she'd put them down to the strain of returning to work after such a long period of illness and recuperation, but as time went on they'd become increasingly severe. Was it some kind of reaction following the trauma of finding her parents unwittingly exposed to a serial killer? Connie Chan's surprise visit had caused her more sleepless nights than she cared to remember, but her mum and dad had shrugged the whole thing off; the naivety of old age had come to their rescue. They seemed unaffected in themselves, but the thought of what *might* have happened had taken up residence in her subconscious and would not be evicted.

Or was there was something more sinister going on between her ears? The drugs she'd been given during the incident with Ilhir Erjon had so far defied chemical analysis. Last she'd heard, the lab was still trying to figure out exactly what kind of cocktail had been responsible for her near catatonic condition. In a way she'd rather not know the whole truth; maybe that was why she hadn't bothered to get an update, despite George's constant prompting. What if it turned out to be bad news? What if she turned out to be like Robert de Niro in *Awakenings*? Up and running for a time, only to sink back eventually into a zombie-like state, unaware of what was going on, unable to communicate with the outside world…

She shuddered. True, at the time of the incident she had reached some kind of cathartic point of breakdown, and had compliantly succumbed to Erjon's seductive encouragement to end it all, to draw a line under the constant struggle to keep herself afloat on the waters of depression that had expanded to oceanic proportions since she'd joined the team. But that was then, this was now. She wanted to live. She wanted to be normal again.

So why was she feeling like this? She was fond of George. He made her smile. He was obviously – for some unfathomable reason – besotted with her, so why the reluctance? With a shock she realised that in thinking about George she hadn't once thought about love. Was that it?

Or was it the nagging premonition of disaster that had begun to dog her waking hours? Or maybe she had developed some obscure mental condition that precluded happiness and fulfilment, something that was keeping her pinned down like a foot on the back of her neck.

'Are you with us, Withers?' George was waving his hand in front of her face.

'What? Oh, sorry.' She flashed George a consolatory smile. 'I think I'm just tired. I'll have an early night. I haven't been sleeping that well.'

George frowned. 'You haven't mentioned that before.'

The lift arrived with a *ping* and Tess drew her hand across her brow, stepping inside as the doors opened. 'Haven't I? Well, it's been a bit busy today, George—'

'It's not just today, though, is it?' George placed his foot in the path of the closing lift door. The doors slid open again obediently.

'Look, George, I just want to go home, OK? I don't have to justify my tiredness, or what I may or may not have communicated.' Straight away, she regretted her exasperated tone. George withdrew his foot.

'OK, sure. Hope you feel better tomorrow.' He forced a tight smile and walked away.

The lift doors closed again and Tess stabbed the ground floor button. Her bottom lip began to wobble. Thank God there was no one to witness her tears.

DC Schlesinger had his jacket on and was fumbling in his pocket for his car keys when George McConnell walked by and grunted a greeting. He didn't look happy. Schlesinger's desk phone rang. Damn! He had a meet with his girlfriend at half past six, and needed to squeeze in a shower and light supper before then.

'Are you going to answer that or what?'

McConnell had paused at his own workstation and was glaring at him across the open plan. Schlesinger moistened his lips. 'Well, to tell the truth I was just leaving. I'm meeting Sara – my girlfriend.'

'Are you indeed? Well, let me *tell the truth*'. McConnell took two steps towards him, an action that Schlesinger perceived as vaguely threatening. 'The truth is, laddie,' McConnell continued in a low, slightly menacing tone, 'that we're assigned to a murder case, and that means you prioritise the case over your private life until it's sorted.'

'Well, DC Martin has already gone home, so I thought—'

McConnell waved his finger threateningly. 'You thought *nothing*. For your information, DC Martin is planning to continue working from home. She's not swanning off for a pint and a pie with her paramour.'

'Oh, right. OK.'

The phone continued its insistent purring.

'Well, go on then.'

Schlesinger hesitated. Like himself, McConnell was a DC – senior, of course, but essentially the same rank. Unlike Collingworth, who had frequently made him jump since he'd joined the team a week ago, technically McConnell had no authority over him. The big boss, Moran, seemed hardly to notice him – and he was effectively retired, anyhow. Schlesinger had declined the invitation to Moran's leaving party in favour of a night out with Sara. It wasn't as if he knew

Moran, and vice versa, so…

'Answer that bloody phone!'

McConnell's face had turned puce, and he looked as though he might want to enforce the suggestion. Schlesinger had heard about McConnell's tendency to moodiness. Oh well, discretion being the better part and so on…

He grabbed the handset. 'DC Schlesinger. Can I help you?'

From the corner of his eye he saw McConnell give a brief nod and sit down. The caller had already launched into a quick-fire series of statements and questions.

'Wait. Hold on, hold on. Can I have your name again, please? Cambridge? *Levi* Cambridge? OK, what can I do for you, Mr Cambridge?'

Chapter Ten

The forensics lab waiting room was an austere and almost featureless space. Two plastic chairs, a Formica-topped coffee table on top of which lay a scattered pile of dog-eared BMA journals, a smaller corner table supporting a severely lime-scaled kettle, two plain white mugs and a jar of instant coffee – all bearing silent testimony to the low priority assigned to any brave colleagues or external visitors daring to interrupt Pauline Harris' closely managed work schedule.

Moran took a seat and prepared for a long wait. He'd passed the ceramic fragment to a masked lab assistant, who had disappeared into the lab with scarcely a word. Now he had entered what he usually referred to as idle time. But idle time was a misnomer; time spent in neutral was not necessarily idle, so long as the environment allowed for concentrated thinking. Such an environment need not be quiet, so long as it was uninterrupted. Through the semi-translucent wall, indistinct lab-coated shapes moved hither and thither as they went about their analytical tasks. Apart from the soft squeak of rubber-coated soles on antiseptically clean flooring and the occasional clink of spatula on beaker, all was still.

The fragment had been found in Marika's hair, and yet there'd been no signs of a struggle. Nothing had seemed out of place. No distressed furniture, overturned plants, broken picture frames; nothing except a small fragment of ceramic, or similar. Sure, it could have been some old bedroom breakage, an ornamental splinter inadvertently picked up from her pillow as she rose. An historical fumble, a moment's carelessness at bedtime, perhaps. But something told him this was not the case – and if Harris came up with matching pieces from the lounge carpet…

'Sorry to have kept you, Chief Inspector.' Harris appeared in the waiting room like an eagle swooping on its prey; one moment he was alone, the next he was the object of Harris' undivided attention. She stood over him so that he was unable to rise – not that she'd have allowed him time to collect his thoughts anyhow, since she'd already launched into a summary of her findings.

'We have a match, you'll be pleased to hear. We have a small collection of fragments, all from the same object, and they do indeed match the fragment you handed in for comparison. Hard to say what the original object was, but I'd suggest an ornament of some description – a statue, perhaps, or maybe a table lamp.' She shook her head, preempting his next question. 'No blood, nope. It wasn't smashed over anyone's head. I'd say it was probably dropped, or, judging by the size of the fragments, thrown down with some force.'

'Any chance of DNA extraction?'

'Sadly not. We tried, obviously, but the fragments are too small. I'd suggest that the bulk of the broken item was cleared up and disposed of by whoever broke it in the first place.'

'No chance of a reconstruction?'

Harris grimaced. ''Fraid not. Again, the bits are just too small to make any coherent sense of. Even so, though…'

'Yes?'

'Even if we did have a larger fragment, and if the object did indeed turn out to be an ornament, and if we did manage to extract DNA, it would be quite likely that it would match one of the sisters, wouldn't you say? Which wouldn't be of much help in identifying the perpetrator.'

'On the other hand, though, if it didn't, if there was no recognisable match to either sister, *that* might tell us something. It would tell us that someone else had handled the object, perhaps even broken it in anger. And for a reason.' He shook his head wearily. 'Best not to speculate, I've found. But thanks for your efforts.' Moran presented a thin smile.

Harris shrugged. 'Get me another sample and we'll keep trying.'

'I'll be in touch.'

As he negotiated the Oxford Road traffic, Moran briefly contemplated dropping in on Alice. It was just on half past seven; by now, Peter would have finished his tea and would be ensconced in the lounge in front of the TV, which would no doubt be showing some historic event from the Olympics. Alice would be clearing up in the kitchen. There'd be the possibility of a chat, a chance to reconcile. No, no need for that; it hadn't been a row as such, just a small disagreement, triggered by Alice's surprise at the news of his hasty reinstatement.

But somehow he couldn't face it. Not tonight. It had been a

long day, preceded by an unexpectedly early start. He didn't have the stamina for a heavy discussion, and certainly not for another falling out – or some worse outcome. Best to leave things to settle this evening. Tomorrow was another day, as the old saying went. Sleeping on things would give Alice time to come to terms with his situation, a chance to cool down. He was disappointed by her remark about Dawson, though, about the Scotch. It hadn't been more than half a finger, and anyway Dawson had already been well-oiled by that stage. He wasn't to blame for Dawson's accident. The suggestion had been well below the belt, and very unlike Alice.

Moran moved into second and pulled through the traffic lights at Purley.

Relax, Brendan. She was upset. She just lashed out… It was understandable under the circumstances – wasn't it?

By the time he arrived home Moran had settled his mind. Tonight would be all about a little peace and quiet, time to recharge and think everything through. All would be well with Alice. And as for the case – well, there were only a limited number of possibilities in terms of who might have wished Marika Szarka harm. He was confident they'd soon get to the bottom of the whole sad situation, make an arrest, tidy up the paperwork, present the case to the CPS, and then off he'd go to present his final resignation to the powers-that-be – this time for good, whatever else Higginson might decide to throw at him.

Would he even have to resign again? He wasn't an employee any more – not a permanent one, anyway, as Collingworth had helpfully pointed out.

Nothing to hold you there, Brendan … just the auld sense of duty and loyalty, as per usual…

Tomorrow was indeed another day – Saturday, he remembered, but he'd asked the team to present themselves promptly at seven sharp nevertheless. There was much to be done before the trail cooled.

Bernice sat at the dresser to remove her modestly applied makeup. It wasn't late, but she had an early night in mind. She felt a tingle of excitement in her spine, the promise of a new adventure. Briefing at seven, and then she'd pop down to Sussex to collect her phone. Bola was on board to cover for her. Her buoyant mood was briefly tempered by a mild pang of guilt, but it wasn't as though she was doing anything wrong, strictly speaking, and besides, she had a covering excuse for her visit, one she hadn't shared with Bola. Had she done so he'd only have gone on at her even more.

It was something she'd remembered Alastair mentioning, not about himself, but about Johnny. It had rung a distant bell, so distant that she'd been obliged to make a few discreet enquiries of her own. But her memory had not been playing tricks; she'd been right to make the association. Alastair had confided that Johnny had been educated in Berkshire, at a boarding school which had shut its doors a few years back purportedly due to financial mismanagement, but primarily because of a gruesome series of events during which DCI Brendan Moran had come close to losing his life.

The school was Charnford Abbey, and the story was that a decades-old murder had been uncovered there, and a young policeman had been savagely assaulted. Moreover, the injuries the unfortunate victim had sustained had affected his mind, caused him to go off the rails in spectacular fashion. Details were sketchy, but the old hands Bernice had spoken to were clear about one thing, and that was the perpetrator's method of assault. No knife, gun or traditional weapon had been employed – nothing so prosaic, not at all. While still conscious, the unfortunate detective constable had been nailed to a makeshift cross.

Coincidence, that Marika Szarka had suffered a semi-crucifixion? That roofing nails had been driven through her hands? A fanciful connection, perhaps, but a strange one under the circumstances. Whatever; Bernice was comfortable that she could justify her short absence by reference to this historical link, however nebulous it might seem. She wasn't worried about talking to Johnny; he was a nice lad, a little quiet, perhaps, but studious, and always busy with his music when he wasn't attending to various jobs around the estate. And her visit *would* be brief, this time – just enough for a quick lunch, a chat, a diary date for a future visit, if time and circumstance permitted.

Bernice finished her toilette and went into the kitchen to make herself a cup of hot chocolate. A framed photograph of her late mother smiled lovingly at her from the sideboard. As the milk warmed on the hob, she picked up the photo frame and hugged it to her chest.

I miss you so much, Mum. You wanted me to find someone special, I know. Well, maybe the time has finally come…

Chapter Eleven

Moran awoke well before his alarm to the sound of rain beating against his bedroom window. Late April still delivering on its damp reputation. Five forty-six, and a bleary glance outside rewarded him with a pale lightening of the sky in the east, almost hidden by looming dark clouds heading his way. A gust of wind blew more rain at the glass, impacting like wet machine-gun fire. He let the curtain fall back, made his way to the kitchen for a reviving brew.

As the kettle hissed into life Moran encouraged his brain to do similar by reference to his mental checklist. At the top of the list was a personal return to the murder scene. He liked to be alone with his thoughts at a crime scene, free from the distraction of forensic activity. He always noticed something he'd missed the first time around.

The kettle completed its task, and he dropped a tea bag into a mug, filled it to the brim. No milk this morning, just one sugar to sweeten his mood. He dunked the tea bag into the mug's depths with a teaspoon, gave it a stir for good measure, then left it to do its thing while he used the bathroom.

Two slices of brown toast completed his breakfast, and a ten minute shower rounded off his morning routine. He arrived at Atlantic House at the same time as Bola, who greeted him with his usual cheery smile.

'Morning, boss. Welcome to another wet weekend.'

'Appalling, isn't it?' Moran winced and hunched his neck further into his collar as they crossed the car park. 'Irish weather.'

Bola laughed. 'Our green and pleasant lands, eh?' Bola waved a greeting to the duty sergeant. 'Any more thoughts on the Szarkas?'

'Plenty,' Moran admitted. 'I'm going to have a wee snoop around the scene after the briefing.'

'Solo?'

'Yes. I like to feel a place. For that, I need to be alone.' Moran raised a hand in greeting to Higginson as they exited the lift; the Chief Superintendent was holding forth behind the glass of one of the small conference rooms to an audience of bored-looking junior officers. A new intake, the usual pep talk, the meeting invitation no doubt unpopularly early. How many would make the grade? Not everyone was cut out for detective work.

Moran headed straight for the whiteboard in the incident room. Most of the seats in the room had already been taken and the low murmur of conversation died out as he turned to face the assembly. Collingworth, sitting in the front row next to Bernice, looked up enquiringly and gave a nonchalant shrug as Moran shook his head. Day two, Saturday, the start of the weekend, and Moran wanted everyone to be in no doubt as to what was required of them.

'Morning all.'

The response was gratifyingly enthusiastic. They wanted this sewn up as much as he did.

'Right, let's get to it. We have one further student to speak to, and a gardener and a piano tuner, not necessarily in that order. And the neighbours – who's on that today? DC Martin and DC Schlesinger? Good.'

Schlesinger had his hand up.

'DC Schlesinger?'

'I had a call last night, sir, from a Mr Cambridge. He might have some information—'

'Yes, I know about Mr Cambridge. You can cover him at the same time. And it's guv, not sir.'

Schlesinger reddened. 'Sir. I mean, guv.'

'See that lot in the conference room, DC Schlesinger?' Moran jerked his head towards Higginson's captive audience. 'They're even newer than you. By the time they've finished induction you'll be able to show them a thing or two, won't you?'

'Yes, guv.' Schlesinger looked relieved. 'Absolutely.'

Moran nodded. 'That's the stuff. Anyone got anything else I need to know?'

Moran saw Bola glance at DC Swinhoe, who looked down at her shoes. Sensitive officer, Bernice. Thorough, and ambitious, but … there was something else, something Moran couldn't quite put his finger on. She seemed to carry a weight, the burden of some past loss or disappointment. Moran knew all about that; perhaps people could sense the same in him. He didn't like to pry. Private lives were just that. Still, she'd bonded well with the team, and particularly with Bola. They were a good partnership.

'DC Odunsi? You'll be tracking down the London student?' He went to the whiteboard, turned again to face them. 'Name?'

'Peter Kenyon,' Bernice spoke up. 'Aged twenty-nine. Plays with the London Symphony Orchestra.'

'Does he, indeed? Impressive.'

'Lives on his own in a bedsit in Earl's Court.'

Moran was scribbling. 'Good. Contact number?'

'Yes, guv. He's coming down this morning.'

Moran paused. 'To Atlantic House?'

'Yes, guv,' Bola confirmed. 'Seemed happy enough to hop on a train.'

Bernice looked as though she might have wanted to add something, but had decided to hold her peace.

'Right. And this Brooks fella. Worth a second look?'

'I'd say so, guv.' Bola scratched his head. 'His missus wasn't exactly the murdering type.'

'No? And what exactly is the "murdering type", DC Odunsi? Care to share your template with us?'

A ripple of laughter lightened the atmosphere. Bola shook his head self-deprecatingly. 'No, you're all right, guv. Point taken.'

Moran nodded. 'Everyone is capable of it, given the right circumstances, given enough provocation. Remember that, all of you. We work with evidence, not instinct. Well, perhaps a *little* instinct,' he acknowledged wryly. 'Used sparingly.' He wagged a warning finger. 'OK, onwards. Who's going to tackle the piano-tuner?'

A few hands went up. 'DC Martin? You're musical, yes?'

'Sometimes, guv. It has been known.' Tess smiled nervously.

She looked pale, drawn. Moran clocked George's look of concern; he'd be keeping an eye on her, which was comforting, but Moran worried about her fitness, her mental health. She'd been through a lot and her return to duty, although welcome, was still in its unofficial probationary period. Moran put on an encouraging smile. 'That's what I heard, DC Martin. Good. Have a look at him and see what drops out. The rest of you, acting DS Collingworth here will co-ordinate your activities – there'll be plenty to chase up, believe me. Oh, and if you can fit in the gardener, acting sergeant? That would be most helpful.'

Without waiting for Collingworth's reaction, Moran returned to the whiteboard and added names to tasks. When he'd finished he turned around and feigned surprise.

'Still here? On you go, on you go.' He shooed them out. 'Before the day gets ahead of you. Back here, five o'clock sharp.'

The clouds looked ominous as Moran pulled up outside the Szarkas' terraced property. The waterproofed but understandably glum-looking duty PC moved the chequered tape aside to let him through.

Moran stood in the hallway and sniffed the air.

After a minute or so, he began to move methodically through the house, examining each room from floor to ceiling. Nothing stood out; even the lounge carpet failed to give up additional fragments of the broken artefact. And yet someone had taken the trouble to remove it, whatever it was. Why? What was the significance?

Moran took up a central position in the room and closed his

eyes. An argument? A harsh exchange of words between a visitor and Ms Szarka? Had she been sitting at the piano, or had she been dragged there, positioned *in situ*? Unlikely; there was nothing to suggest a struggle, apart from the tell-tale holes in the piano casing. And the fragment of pottery.

Where would one dispose of a broken item? The household bins had been searched, giving up only a few items of standard packaging waste; the red recycling bin likewise. Moran frowned, went to the front door and hailed the PC.

'Sir?' The officer looked relieved at having something to occupy his mind.

'When's bin collection day for this street?'

'That'd be Tuesday, sir.'

'OK. Thanks.' Moran stepped outside and walked a few feet along the pavement. Next door to the right, the bin was empty.

'Unoccupied, sir,' the duty PC called over. 'Since Christmas, apparently.'

'OK.'

Outside the house on the left, the bin was half-full. Moran moved a few cardboard items to one side for a better look. No sign of broken pottery.

He paused, pondering. He could see a parade of shops four houses further along with two parking spaces adjoining where he was sure he'd noticed a row of larger bins. Sure enough, as he approached he could see that there were three. The first contained non-recyclables; again, no go. The second, recycling. Nothing.

The third seemed to be a mixture of the two. Unusual – or maybe the shops weren't too fussy about what got recycled and what didn't. The council would be hard-pressed to extract a confession from the businesses along the parade – they'd all deny knowledge of fly-tipping to avoid a fine.

Moran tilted the bin for a better look. Something was rolling around at the bottom beneath a loose scatter of rubbish. He laid the bin down on its side and, with some difficulty, got down on his haunches. He rolled his sleeve up and gingerly reached into the depths.

His hand closed around a smooth surface with jagged edges. He wormed the object out, held it up for inspection. It was a broken ornament, a bust. Although half the face had disappeared, reduced to shards, it wasn't difficult to recognise the subject. After all, the image had been reproduced by artists the world over, in sculptures, paintings and all manner of media. The scowl was familiar, as were the thick brows. The single remaining eye regarded him angrily, as though challenging him to find the culprit who had dared to inflict such a grievous wound.

Moran returned the baleful stare. 'Sorry, Ludwig; I'm a Mozart man myself.'

'Not dropped. Smashed.' Pauline Harris handed the ruined bust to Moran with an air of certainty. 'A blow from something heavy, blunt.'

'A hammer.' Moran made it a statement.

'That would fit the bill, Chief Inspector, yes, but anything moderately heavy would do it. The porcelain isn't as thick as it looks from the outside. It's cheap. Not an original, in case you were concerned.'

'I wasn't planning on taking it to the Antiques Roadshow, if that's what you mean.'

Before or *after* the murder – that was the question that was troubling Moran. A fit of rage after the deed, or the prelude to violence? 'Can you tell me anything more about it? Prints, stains, any traces of any sort? DNA would be nice.'

'I'll have a go, if you'd like me to. Once we've confirmed it's the same material as the other fragments.'

'Of course. I'm pretty sure it will be.'

'I like a man who's sure of himself.' Harris took the damaged bust from him, turned on her heel and disappeared into the lab, leaving an eddy of some musky perfume in her wake.

'Thanks,' Moran said to the closing door. 'I appreciate it.'

Chapter Twelve

Bernice murmured a prayer of thanks for the sparse Saturday traffic. She'd made good time, even on the unpredictable M3. According to the satnav she'd arrive at Simplicity in twenty minutes. Alastair's reply to her over-wordy text had been a single affirmative followed by a smiley face. She'd suggested lunch and a stroll around the grounds, half-expecting him to say he was too busy, or that he was sorry but no – for whatever reason. She was both relieved and excited that he'd accepted her invitation.

The satnav beeped as it recalculated her route; her lapse of concentration had made her miss a turning.

Calm down, B ... you're a grown-up, remember?

She took the fourth exit at the next roundabout and got herself back on the correct route. Somewhere in the recesses of her mind a twinge of guilt was fluttering its wings, like a butterfly reluctant to move on from a favourite flower. It was OK, she reassured herself; the guv hadn't picked up on the fact that Bola was interviewing Peter Kenyon, the London student, on his own, so ... well, technically, she hadn't lied. And besides, she needed her phone; the last few days had been a nightmare without it. No one wanted to be so dependent on a smartphone, but that was just how the world was today. Managing the day without it was akin to missing an arm or a leg.

And then there was the Charnford connection – which was probably nothing, but still worth a brief conversation with either Alastair or Johnny himself. Alastair knew all about Johnny's past, so maybe she should start there. Charnford *did* sound like a creepy sort of place; she couldn't imagine what it had been like to attend a boarding school with monks as teachers. Plain weird; no wonder things had gone awry.

And that poor police constable. Bernice shuddered. The school had closed down shortly afterwards, and good job too, but apparently the monastery was still there, albeit under different leadership. Perhaps she'd pay the abbey a visit sometime, just to satisfy her curiosity. Johnny could fill her in on the gories; even if he hadn't been around at the time of the murder, he'd be bound to know something about it.

Bernice pulled up at a busy T junction where, engine idling, she found herself wondering about the abbey and its ethos. Monks were fascinating. There was something intriguing about an individual's motivation to make such a hard choice, to eschew normality for a life of a prayerful reflection. It was not just intriguing, but appealing in a way that made her senses tingle.

What, so you're going to join a convent now, B?

Definitely not. She smiled to herself. And yet, she had to admit that something seemed to draw her to Simplicity's community ideal. Everyone self-sufficient, minding their own business, coming together every so often for communal celebration or some practical necessity – and all overseen by the benevolent Alastair. It seemed a kind of idyll; she found it powerfully enticing, so different from the path she had chosen. And, of course, there was Alastair himself...

She checked her appearance in the mirror as she waited for the traffic to clear. Subtle lipstick, a hint of foundation, minimum eyeliner, hair recently shortened from her standard and rather uninspiring shoulder-length to an edgy pixie crop which, if she said so herself, emphasised her cheekbones in a surprisingly flattering manner, just as the stylist had predicted.

You'll do, B...

The car behind honked for her attention, and she waved an apology before pulling out. She switched on the radio and hummed along to the retro tunes, idly wondering how Bola was getting on with his interview. She'd soon find out – she'd promised to be back by mid-afternoon. Any later and Collingworth would be asking questions, even if the guv hadn't twigged her absence. She shook her head ruefully. *Playing truant at your age, B...*

Her sense of excited anticipation grew as she passed through Simplicity's gated entrance and drove towards the gravelled parking area in front of the main house. She parked next to Alastair's battered old Mercedes, left the car unlocked because she knew that nobody would interfere with it – a liberating action in itself – smoothed her skirt, and took a deep draught of refreshing Sussex air. It was quiet, so quiet. At the far end of the lawn, a group of ancient oak trees towered above a scatter of huddled cabins, smoke rising lazily from their chimneys. Apart from the muffled tapping of an overall-clad workman precariously balanced on the top rung of a ladder as he attended to some minor repair, there was no sound to disturb the tranquillity.

Gravel crunched beneath her feet as she made her way to the front entrance and took the stone steps two at a time. The brass knocker felt heavy in her impatient hand.

She waited, tapping her foot and trying to resist the temptation to take out her compact and double-check her lipstick. She compromised by rooting around in her handbag for a packet of Polos she'd bought a few days ago, and popping one in her mouth.

Thirty seconds passed. No response. She knocked again. Johnny was probably immersed in his music and Alastair similarly busy with some project or other. But he knew she was coming, so…

Another half-minute passed. She frowned and tried the doorknob. It turned and she pushed. The massive door swung open easily on well-oiled hinges.

'Hello?'

Her voice echoed in the empty hallway.

'Anyone in?'

She took a tentative step forward, feeling like an intruder. *Don't be stupid, B. You've been invited…*

The hall smelled strongly of wood polish, with an underlying tang of some disinfectant or cleaning liquid. Did Alastair have a housekeeper? He'd never mentioned one. She'd assumed that Johnny took care of most of the day-to-day tasks in return for his board and lodgings.

She padded slowly past the imposing mahogany dresser and statuesque grandfather clock, her footsteps silent on the neo-classical black and white tiles – all original, Alastair had confided proudly as he'd shown her around the property. She knocked on the library door and, getting no response, quickly checked inside. Empty.

She stood in the hall wondering what to do next. Maybe they'd both had to go out on some urgent errand?

Wait.

Was that her imagination, or had she heard raised voices? Somewhere downstairs, from the gym or swimming pool? Or —?

There it was again. Definitely voices – male, and they sounded angry. Frowning, Bernice made her way across to the stairwell, peering down.

'Hello?'

No doubt about it, there was a full-scale row going on. Bernice slipped down the stairs to the pool entrance. She recognised the two voices as belonging to Alastair and Johnny. Strange; she'd never heard Alastair raise his voice before. What could be wrong?

The direct door to the pool was closed, but she got up on tiptoe to peer through the glass light in the top panel.

The two men were standing at the pool's edge. Johnny was shaking his fist and Alastair his head. Both were fully dressed, Johnny in a tracksuit and Alastair in his customary T-shirt and jeans. There was a bucket on the floor next to Johnny and a mop propped against the wall, evidence of an ongoing cleaning session.

Bernice hesitated. Should she interrupt what was going on, or retreat, leave them to it, and wait for Alastair to come back upstairs? The spat was showing no sign of ending, the shouting growing louder with each second. Bernice hated confrontation.

It always made her feel sick to her stomach.

Now she felt like a real intruder, almost like a peeping Tom – although that was more of a sexual thing, she supposed. Her ankles were complaining so she let herself down and paced the floor in a flurry of indecision. She couldn't just march in and pretend she'd heard nothing – could she?

Almost at the exact moment she'd decided to retreat to her car and telephone Alastair later, there came a tremendous crash from the poolside followed by a volley of invective, delivered in Alastair's voice.

Then all was silent.

Bernice chewed her lip. That had sounded final. She was filled with a heavy sense of dread.

Up on tiptoe again, she squinted through the thick glass and her hand flew to her mouth.

Alastair was standing over Johnny, arms at his side, breathing heavily. Johnny was on his back on the tiled floor, arms spread-eagled, as still as marble. Like a river wending its way to the sea, a widening stream of blood was spreading from his scalp towards the pool's draining gutter in a long, scarlet ribbon. Bernice felt her own blood drain from her face.

At that moment, Alastair turned and looked directly at her.

Chapter Thirteen

Bernice was frozen to the spot as Alastair walked rapidly around the pool and thrust the door open. 'B. I didn't realise you'd arrived.'

'What just happened, Alastair?' Bernice found her voice, unable to stop herself staring at Alastair's hands, his fingers stained with blood. She stepped forward and he retreated to the poolside. The door swung shut behind her.

'I didn't mean it. It was an accident. I need your help.' Alastair spoke tersely, matter-of-factly. 'We have to move him. Hide the body.' He moistened his lips, read her enquiring expression, made a gesture of helplessness. 'He's dead, yes. There's no doubt about it.' He reached out and grabbed her by the wrist. 'Please…'

Panic rushed through her like an electric shock. 'Let go!' She pulled away, but his grip was firm.

His eyes were blazing, intense. 'You saw what happened. You're part of this.'

'Wha… what do you *mean*? Let me go!'

Ignoring her pleas, he dragged her towards the pool. The door swung shut behind her with a bang. She made another attempt to free herself, twisting her wrist and yanking with all her might. Her fingers squeezed through his grasp and she staggered back, unbalanced by the force of their separation. She backed slowly away as he advanced, both hands raised in an effort to placate her.

'Look, B, calm down. It's all right. I just need you to help me, then we can talk.'

'Talk? What do you mean, *talk*? You have to call this *in*!'

'No, no. I can't do that. You know I can't.'

Hands behind her back, Bernice felt for the door handle. Perhaps she could slip through, bolt it from the outside. Did it have a bolt or a lock? She couldn't remember. 'Alastair, I'm a serving police officer.'

He was still coming towards her, forcing his expression into some facsimile of reassurance. 'Listen, be reasonable. We can work this out together.'

'We? There is no *we*, Alastair. I … I can imagine that what happened was an accident, sure, but I'm not going to be your accomplice.'

'Well that might just be a problem we have to work through, B.' He attempted a smile, but succeeded only in forming a grimace. When she didn't answer, he babbled on. 'I can't be held accountable for this. It was *his* fault. I mean, look at this place. You've felt it yourself, I know; it's perfect, an oasis of perfection in a world gone to hell. That's what I wanted it to be, and that's what I've succeeded in creating. I can't just throw it away, you must see that.'

Bernice's heart was thumping, but something in Alastair's devastated expression made her hesitate. He was right. Simplicity *was* a haven, a tiny corner of perfection in a fallen world. Moreover, it was a haven, a lifestyle, that she felt she could be a part of – truth be told, she'd thought of little else since her last visit.

Policing, or Simplicity. It was a stark choice, but if the opportunity was still there, which she believed it might well be, then … well, then it was a no- brainer.

But now? A crime like *this* – Alastair would go to prison, of course. Unless… unless… no, it was mad, she couldn't…

'You know what I'm saying is right, B. I can read it in your face. Please. This was a mistake, an accident, simple as that. Don't make me pay for it with everything I've worked for. You can be a part of our life here, you know you can. It's what you were made for.'

His words went on like a flurry of loosed arrows, puncturing her resolve until she was forced to raise both hands in front of her like a shield.

'Alastair, stop! Just tell me what happened. What were you arguing about?'

'Yes, yes, of course. It was stupid, really.' Alastair shook his head. 'Johnny wanted to practice, but there was cleaning to be done. I give him so much, you know … make so many allowances. He's not easy. Wasn't … easy. He was demanding, obsessed with his music. But there are practicalities that need to be addressed. I can't run this place solo – it's too much. I just asked him to clean the poolside, that's all, but when I came down he was nowhere to be seen. I went to look for him, dragged him down here, told him to get to work. He became abusive. I reminded him that I've always given him so much, everything he needed, but he just … went off on one. He wouldn't see reason. I got angry. And … well, you saw the end result.'

As she listened and saw the remorse etched on Alastair's face, compassion shooed away the last of her fear. It had been an accident, plain and simple. It could not be undone, but perhaps it could be mitigated.

She nodded. 'All right. I believe you.'

'You'll help me?'

'Let me see him.'

'Why?'

'I want to check. Make sure.'

Alastair hesitated but relented under her insistent gaze. 'All right. Go and look, if you must.'

Bernice walked around the pool to where Johnny lay sprawled on the tiles. She bent, felt for a pulse. Nothing. She got down on her knees beside him, put an ear to his chest. Again, nothing. She took his hand, whispered. 'I'm so sorry, Johnny. You didn't deserve this. Alastair made a mistake. He didn't mean to hurt you.'

As she spoke something caught the light, a brief movement behind the pool door's reinforced glass window. She glanced up, startled, and squinted at the door, but whatever it was had gone.

Alastair was sitting on a plastic chair by the shallow end of the pool, head lowered, hands clasped together. There was no going back from this, she knew. Everything would change from this moment; if she committed herself to helping Alastair she'd be an accomplice, pure and simple. She gently let Johnny's hand drop back to the cold floor and walked slowly over to where Alastair was sitting. 'What about his family?'

Alastair shook his head. 'None. An orphan. Brought up in

God knows how many foster homes.'

'Friends?'

'None to speak of. The residents are used to seeing him around, but he kept himself to himself.'

Bernice nodded. 'OK. So you need a story.'

'Yes, but that's for later. He can't stay here. The pool opens at four. People will come in.' Alastair's voice had steadied; he was almost back to his usual calm and unruffled self. 'I'm going to fetch a groundsheet. Don't let anyone near the poolside.' A further thought occurred to him. 'Perhaps you can guard the stairwell. It's the only way down. I'll close the pool and shutter the window, just to be sure.'

'Alastair.'

'What?'

'I didn't see this. *Any* of it.'

'Understood.' He hurried off, and as she waited for his return she tried to ignore the insistent noise of her conscience. When it became clear to her that it would not easily be silenced, she banished its noise to a secure place at the back of her mind and mentally locked the door.

No going back, B. No going back…

Chapter Fourteen

Five minutes into the interview Bola knew he was wasting his time. This skinny, serious, bespectacled young man was no killer. No way. Still, he had to go through the procedure, take the statement, make sure he didn't miss anything.

'Long way to come, London to Reading. For a music lesson.' Bola took a sip of water from the plastic cafeteria cup he'd had his coffee in earlier. Waste not, et cetera.

'You think?' Peter Kenyon pushed his glasses up the bridge of his nose, a necessity more than a habit, Bola assumed, as Kenyon had the smallest nose he'd seen on a bloke since Elton John's heyday.

'Yeah, I think.' Bola shrugged. 'Plenty of piano teachers up the Smoke, right?'

Kenyon shook his head. 'Not like Ms Szarka. She's – she *was* – special.'

Bola consulted his notes. 'And you've been having lessons since——?'

'2017. None during lockdown, of course, but then we started again. We were just getting back into the swing of things. Until … until this,' he finished, unsure as to how to describe the current circumstances. He frowned. 'It's mad. Crazy. She was an old woman. Well, elderly, I mean. Gentle, such a talented musician.' He shook his head. 'I don't get it.'

'Neither do we,' Bola agreed. 'But we're working on it.' He checked the time on the wall clock; B should be back in a couple of hours. Collingworth had already asked where she was, and Bola wasn't convinced the acting sergeant had bought the excuse he'd offered up – some unspecified medical appointment. He'd have to remember to tell B on her return, in case Collingworth followed it up.

'I can't tell you much else,' Kenyon said. 'I mean, I travel down once a week, have my lesson, go home.'

'And you haven't noticed anything out of the ordinary in recent weeks? Ms Szarka seemed normal?'

'Yes. Absolutely.' He paused, thinking. 'Her mother had died recently, that's the only thing. But she told me it was a release, really. She was in her late nineties.'

'OK. That's it? What about the sister?'

A shrug. 'Never saw much of her. Sometimes I'd hear her teaching in the dining room – oboe, not my thing.'

'And there was never any suggestion of discord between them?'

'Discord? Arguments and the like?' Kenyon shook his head again. 'Nah. They're not that kind of people.' He gave a wry smile. 'I can't imagine either of them getting mad at all.'

'And you can vouch for your whereabouts on the night in question?'

'I can. I was at home, practising. My girlfriend will confirm that. Want her mobile number?'

'Please.'

Kenyon dipped into his inside pocket and withdrew a small notebook, extracted a biro from its binder, scribbled a series of numbers, tore the page off and slid it across the table to Bola. 'Here you go.'

'Thanks.' Bola folded the note and clipped it to his paperwork. 'Use social media much?'

Kenyon made an inverted U with his mouth. 'No more than anyone else. Facebook mainly. Given up on Twitter – sorry, *X*.'

'Username?'

'My own.'

Bola nodded. There was nothing more to add, nothing to be gained from further questioning. 'I think we can call it a day there, Mr Kenyon. Thanks for your time.'

'I can go?'

'You can go.'

'OK, well, I hope you find out who did this.' Kenyon got to his feet and buttoned his jacket.

'Oh, we will, Mr Kenyon, don't you worry. We will.'

The sky darkened and a violent downpour pummelled the concrete slabs, turning the uneven pavement into a minefield of miniature lakes. Tess Martin pulled the hood of her coat as far forward as it would go, retreating into its folds like a tortoise into its shell as she waited for DC Schlesinger to emerge from the end terrace property. She was doing her best to be supportive, reassuring, encouraging, and whatever else she felt DC Schlesinger might need to compensate for his all-too-obvious rookiness. Was that even a word? Whatever, it fitted. Schlesinger's anxious persona screamed *newbie* with every word he uttered and every awkward step he took. Sure, he was a nice bloke, but there were limits to her patience, and quite frankly the last role she needed right now was babysitter. Unfortunately for her, that was exactly what Schlesinger required.

The door of the end terrace opened and Schlesinger emerged, thanked the occupant profusely and joined Tess on the pavement. 'That's pretty much all of them, right?' Schlesinger carefully ticked a box in his ever-present notebook. 'All except for Mr Cambridge, that is.'

'Saved the best till last.'

'You think?'

'I don't know, Nigel.' Tess winced at the sound of her voice – flat, monotone. *Come on, Tess...* 'Maybe he'll actually remember something significant, eh? Make the afternoon worthwhile.' She finished with a smile, but it took a disproportionate effort.

'Yeah, I hope so. I really do.' Schlesinger seemed comforted by her forced optimism.

Tess checked the time. 'OK, I have the piano tuner to see in twenty minutes. You OK with Mr Cambridge?'

'You mean talk to him *myself*? Well, I'm not entirely—'

'Yes, *interview* him, Nigel. You'll be fine. He sounded harmless enough, yes? Just don't let him run away with the conversation. Don't be afraid to cut to the chase.'

'Um – maybe we could both do the tuner, and then I could come back with you for Cambridge?'

Tess stepped over a particularly large puddle and stopped. They were two doors away from the Szarkas' property, where a duty PC was stamping his feet and trying to look as though he was enjoying his shift while the wind ruffled the tape cordon like a kite and the rain drummed relentlessly on his helmeted head.

'Look, Nigel, there are times when we have to divide and conquer. I'm not going to get to piano man in time if we stay together – especially if Cambridge likes a chat, which seems to be the case. Just listen to what he has to say, make a note of the relevant points and I'll see you back at the ranch at say—' she glanced at her watch a second time, 'four-thirty? Sound OK?'

Schlesinger shuffled his feet. 'Well, I suppose—'

'Good. Then can I suggest you get yourself in there asap, before we both catch double pneumonia?'

Defeated, Schlesinger offered a sheepish grin. 'OK then. Sure. Four thirty it is.'

Tess brushed a raindrop from the tip of her nose. 'You'll be fine, Nigel. Really, you will. Here.' She gave him the car keys. 'I can walk from here. The tuner is only a couple of streets away. I'll make my own way back.'

Schlesinger took the keys. 'Are you sure? Well ... thanks. Appreciate it.'

'Catch you later.'

Tess walked smartly to the end of the street and turned left, the rain tailing off to a steady drizzle. Her hood was annoying her and she was soaking wet anyway so she flicked it back and allowed the droplets to fall on her head unimpeded.

Matthew Potter was a rotund little man in horn-rimmed spectacles and checked jacket whose dark, angular eyebrows lent him an appearance of permanent surprise. His first action on opening the front door to his home was to blow his nose into a tan-coloured handkerchief, pausing to briefly inspect its contents before examining Tess's warrant card and ushering her into the hall.

'Shocking weather, eh? Do come in, my dear. I've heard the terrible news so your visit isn't entirely unexpected.' He led her into a tiny front room and waved vaguely in the direction of a tatty sofa. 'Take a pew.'

An upright piano was crammed into the space immediately in front of the bay window and there was also a threadbare armchair in the corner, but the room was otherwise devoid of knick-knacks and the usual ornamentation. The mantelpiece above the unused fireplace was covered in a centimetre of dust. A bachelor pad if ever there was one. Tess sat gingerly on the edge of the sofa.

'Tea? Coffee? Something stronger?'

Tess shook her head. 'No, thanks. I won't keep you long.'

Potter nodded and settled himself into the armchair. 'Two lovely old dears,' he offered without prompting. 'I'm very sad to hear what happened. Reyka will be bereft.'

'How often did you tune their piano, Mr Potter?'

'As and when.' He puffed out his cheeks. 'The instrument was in constant use – Marika was something of an obsessive, you know. Lovely tone.' He sighed. 'I wonder who'll play it now? Reyka does play a little but quite frankly—' he leaned forward confidentially, 'she's a pretty dreadful pianist. Her forte is the oboe. Quite exceptional. They'd play duets for me, you know, when they were short of cash. I took it as payment in kind. Well, one has to support the struggling artist, doesn't one. Excuse me.'

The handkerchief came out again, this time accompanied by a small silver box. Potter spread the handkerchief on the arm of the chair and clicked the box open with a practised twist of his stubby fingers. The fingers then dipped into the box and went to each nostril in turn. Potter inhaled the snuff with a hearty sniff on each side and then clicked the box lid shut.

'Ah, that's better. Now, where were we?'

Before Tess could reply, Potter made a grab for the handkerchief and bellowed a gigantic sneeze into its folds. The room was filled with a sickly sweet fragrance. Tess tried to shut off her olfactory senses by breathing through her mouth but even then she could still taste the stuff on her tongue.

'You don't mind, do you?' Potter looked concerned. 'So much better than filling the room with smoke, I've always thought.'

'No, no, it's fine,' Tess lied. 'You carry on.'

'Never understood why it fell out of fashion.' Potter shook his head. 'I mean, this vaping business – full of chemicals, you know.'

'I expect you're right,' Tess smiled sweetly. 'But let's get back to the Szarkas, shall we?'

'Yes, of course, apologies. I do get on my high horse a bit – don't be afraid to shoot me down.' He chortled as he added, 'Not that you chaps and lasses carry firearms.'

'No, quite. So, once a month, three times a year?' Tess prompted again.

Potter looked baffled.

'Your visits to the Szarkas.'

'Ah yes, sorry. Well, perhaps once a quarter. That would be about right. You'd be surprised how quickly a piano goes out of tune, especially with regular use.'

'And do you play yourself?'

'Me? Well, a little. I can find my way around the keys, you know?' He grinned self-deprecatingly. 'I had lessons until I was, oh, maybe twelve or thirteen. At that point I discovered jazz, and that was the end of my classical aspirations – or rather, my parents' aspirations for me.'

'They were ambitious for you?'

'I suppose they were, yes,' Potter admitted reflectively. 'I was a bit of a disappointment, I fear – I do feel guilty about it, you know? Even now, I occasionally dream that I'm about to perform a piano concerto at some prestigious venue. It all goes wrong, of course, as dreams do. I forget all the notes, or the piano collapses.' He chortled. 'Silly, really.'

'No, not at all, I understand,' Tess said. 'Parental ambitions for their offspring often do more harm than good. They can cause a lot of guilt and angst.'

'Quite so,' Potter said. 'How perceptive of you. I imagine you're speaking from experience?'

'Perhaps,' Tess said with a rueful smile. 'My parents weren't exactly mad keen about my career choices, but they came round in the end. Anyway, let's get back to the Szarkas. Are you acquainted with any of the sisters' friends or neighbours?'

Potter paused, stroked his chin. 'Well now, I wouldn't say I was in their social circle, exactly. They didn't socialise much at all, as far as I'm aware. Too busy with their composing and teaching. That was their main thing. Their raison d'être, so to speak.'

'Yes, that's the picture we're getting.'

'But it's an extraordinary thing, isn't it? Was it a burglar, do you imagine? Must have been some kind of intruder, surely? I

'We're keeping our options open at present, Mr Potter. How long would you spend tuning their piano as a rule? An hour? More?'

'Oh, I really can't say. I don't charge by the hour, you see. Takes as long as it takes.'

'But generally.'

'Well if you put me in front of a firing squad and demanded an answer … I'd say an hour and a half, on average. Max.'

'And the sisters were in at the time?'

'In the house, you mean? Well, yes, naturally.' Potter scratched his scalp and tapped lightly on the lid of the snuff box with his free hand. 'There was one time, though…'

'Go on.'

'When they had to go out to a recital or some such. Left me to it. But they told me there was a key under the hedgehog if I needed to pop out and come back again for any reason. Very trusting, you see. Maybe a little naive.'

'The hedgehog?'

'Yes, one of those stone scraper things on the doorstep. Quite common in animal form.'

'So, in theory, anyone who knew about that could have borrowed the key and made a copy.'

Potter looked surprised. 'Well, I really can't say. The old dears were hardly going to be the focus of a major robbery. They lived on a shoestring budget. Why go to so much trouble to rob a poor household?'

He had a point, Tess conceded. 'Robbery may not have been the motive, Mr Potter.'

'Is it true? What the local press are saying?' Potter opened the snuff box again and took another pinch. It went up his nostril with a sucking noise like a vacuum cleaner; Tess felt her stomach turn. Schlesinger had drawn the longer straw this afternoon, no doubt about it.

'I can't comment, I'm afraid. All I'll say is that it was a terrible act to commit on a defenceless elderly woman.'

'Quite so, quite so.' The handkerchief was at the ready, and Tess steeled herself for the impending explosion.

After it had passed she posed her final question. 'And where were you at the time of the attack, Mr Potter?'

Potter nodded as though he'd been expecting it, which he probably had. 'I was here. At home, tucked up in bed. I'm not a night owl. In fact, I don't think I even ventured out that day at all.' He fluttered his handkerchief like a flag and Tess tried not to cower. 'No one to vouch for me, though, I'm afraid. You'll have to take my word for it, DC Martin.'

Tess nodded, rose to her feet. 'Thank you, Mr Potter. That's all for now.'

'For now?'

Tess was already at the lounge door. She needed fresh air, wet or otherwise. Potter followed her through into the hallway.

She turned on the threshold. 'Thanks again. We'll be in touch.' Hand on the latch, she caught sight of something she hadn't noticed on her way in – an open toolbox by the understairs cupboard. On the top tray was a hefty hammer and an open bag of nails.

Potter followed her gaze. 'Sorry about the clutter. Not much of a handyman but you can't avoid those essential jobs, can you?'

Tess found a smile from somewhere and left him with it. She

pulled her hood up and made her way through the maze of back streets towards the Caversham Road. The rain had petered out and resolved into what a Scotsman would call a cauld, dreich afternoon. No matter, a brisk walk would clear her head. A bus pulled up at the bus stop a few metres ahead but she wasn't tempted; walking time was thinking time.

Potter was an oddball, no doubt about that. Hammer and nails, though… Common enough, she supposed; most homeowners kept a tool kit. Nothing unusual there. Besides, what possible motive might drive Potter to murder – and a particularly brutal murder, at that? The self-employed were usually keen to nurture their clients, rather than bumping them off, and besides, as far as she knew, piano tuning was hardly a lucrative profession.

Then again, if not an obvious motive, Potter did have means of entry – he'd known about the key. And with a little thought and patience, even the most obscure motives could be brought to light.

As Tess waited at the pelican crossing by the ironmonger's store, she came to a conclusion.

No, Mr Potter, you aren't off the hook yet.

Chapter Fifteen

Moran had just parked at Atlantic House and was toying with the idea of calling Alice when there was a tap on his car window. A woman in her early forties, smartly dressed, with flawless make up and a rolled umbrella under her arm, was glaring in at him with a stern expression. She looked as though she had something important to tell him. He stabbed the button to lower the window.

'Can I help you?'

'Are you Moran?'

'I'm sorry, I don't think we've been introduced.'

The woman's expression darkened. 'I'm Sheila Dawson. My husband died yesterday after attending a party at which you were seen to be plying him with alcohol. You are Moran, aren't you? You fit the sergeant's description.'

'Now hold on a minute—'

'I'll hold *nothing*.'

Moran could see that Mrs Dawson was barely keeping herself in check. As he got out of the car he kept his voice nice and even, his tone moderate, but firm. 'Mrs Dawson, I understand that you're upset, but I think there's been a misunderstanding.'

'Oh, you do, do you? Well, according to my source you were seen giving my husband a measure of Scotch when he'd *clearly* had quite enough. He *promised* me he wouldn't touch the hard stuff. He promised—'

Moran raised his hand. 'Mrs Dawson, I'm very sorry for your loss, but I'm not responsible for Frank's tragic accident. Yes, he'd obviously had a few – that's why I poured him barely half a finger, just a courtesy—'

'It was irresponsible. Disgraceful.'

'Look, I even offered him a lift home. He refused.'

'Did you?' For the first time, Mrs Dawson looked unsure.

'Yes. And I can offer a witness who will corroborate that.'

Her expression hardened again. 'No matter. How can a senior officer be irresponsible enough to supply an inebriated man with more alcohol?'

'Look, I—'

'I'll be taking this further, Moran. You'll be hearing from me in due course.'

And with that she turned on her expensive heels, walked smartly towards a silver Lexus ES saloon, opened the door, slipped elegantly inside and, without a backward glance, smoothly reversed out of the parking space and cruised towards the exit.

Moran watched her go and let out a deep sigh. This was crazy. First Alice, now this.

Wait.

You fit the sergeant's description…

Duty sergeant, or … detective sergeant? *Acting* detective sergeant…?

Moran locked his car and strode purposefully towards the lifts.

'He's just gone out, guv.' Bola responded to Moran's terse question with a frown. 'Problem?'

Moran puffed his cheeks. 'It's OK, Bola – it's between myself and acting DS Collingworth. Where's he gone? Any idea?'

'You asked him to track down the gardener, guv.' Bola consulted his pad. 'A Mr Harold Barlow – jack of all trades. He's local, so shouldn't take too long. Couple of hours?'

'All right. Thanks.'

Maybe, Moran reflected on his way to his office, that wasn't a bad thing. Time to cool down, get things in perspective. This situation with Dawson was getting way out of hand – *ridiculous*, for sure. Could she even threaten legal action? Surely not. The whole thing was preposterous.

Moran stormed into his office and stopped in his tracks. He had a visitor.

'Hello, guv.'

'Charlie! What on earth? I thought you'd gone back up north.'

'Sorry – bad timing?'

'No.' Moran allowed himself a rueful grin. 'It's all right. Just a bit of nonsense that got to me for a moment, that's all.'

'It wouldn't be anything to do with our friend the acting detective sergeant, would it?'

Moran went to hang his coat up, and then remembered that, apart from the single desk and two chairs, one of which had been borrowed from the open plan, the room had been stripped of furniture. He hung his coat on the chair back and sat down. 'Can't offer you anything, I'm afraid.' He surveyed the office. 'All been taken away.'

Charlie smiled. 'I've just had a cuppa in the canteen, so no probs. But still, they should have given you a kettle at least.'

'I'm a temporary resource, Charlie.' Moran shrugged. 'What can I say?'

'I reckon you could turn that to your advantage.' Charlie grinned mischievously.

'You do, eh? I'm all ears.'

Charlie laughed. 'I'll text you a few suggestions.' She folded her arms. 'Look, guv, I know you're flat out right now, so I'll make this quick.'

'Now you're worrying me.' Moran interlaced his fingers and propped his elbows on the bare surface.

'No, no. It's all good. Well, the first part is.'

'Ah, the good news, bad news routine.'

'I suppose, yes.'

Moran feigned trepidation.

'Ian and I are getting married.'

Moran smiled broadly. 'Gosh. I'm delighted, Charlie. Fantastic news. He's a good man.'

'He is indeed. Too good for me, probably.'

'I think not. When?'

'That's the thing. It's soon. We didn't want a complicated logistical nightmare – you know how these things can go. So we just thought, you know, simple. And soon.'

'How soon?'

'Next week.'

Moran's surprise was genuine. 'Next *week*? Saints preserve

us. On the Saturday?'

'Yep. Half past two, Ness Bank Church.'

'Ness Bank, as in…'

'Yep, Inverness. I know you might still be tied up with work, but hopefully…'

'Oh, don't you worry about that, I'll move heaven and earth if I have to.' He was still grinning, but then a thought occurred to him. 'Myself … and Alice?'

'Of course. You're both invited.'

'OK. Great.'

'Sure? You look like there might be a problem.'

'No, no. It's just that … well, Alice and me, we've had a bit of a misunderstanding – a difference of opinion.'

'Nothing serious, I hope?'

'Not a bit of it. It'll all be cleared up by then.'

'I really hope you can make it.'

'Wouldn't miss it for the world, Charlie. I mean that.' Moran grew serious. 'And the other thing was?'

Charlie sat back in her chair. 'Mm… well…'

'This is going to be good. I can feel it in my bones.'

'Not good,' Charlie's mouth hardened into a compressed line. 'Not good at all, guv. It's Isabel Akkerman. She's back in the UK.'

Moran sat quietly for a few seconds to let this news sink in. Isabel Akkerman. MI6 agent and double murderer. The one that got away. But he was puzzled. Charlie pre-empted his first question.

'I heard the news via one of Ian's contacts who'd been working with MI6 on an arms smuggling racket. He mentioned it in passing, but I'm not going to forget that name in a hurry.'

'She was headed for North Korea, right?'

'According to our two less-than-friendly-spooks, yes.'

'Unlikely to return, they said.' Moran sighed. 'Either they underestimated her, or the mission was aborted?'

'My thoughts exactly. But what should we do?'

Moran scratched his head. 'I'll have to run it past Higginson in the first instance. Akkerman thinks she's untouchable, but we might be able to find a chink in her armour – if we tread carefully.'

'If she's completed her mission, presumably she'll be on the bench till the next one.'

Moran shrugged. 'Maybe.' He could read the expression in Charlie's eyes. 'I know this is personal for you, Charlie – as it is for me. What happened that night in Chepstow is a story without an ending.'

'You don't mind me mentioning it?'

'Don't be daft. Leave it with me.'

'You'll keep me posted?'

'For sure.'

'Thanks. Look, guv, I'd better be off.' Charlie got up and went to the door. 'Places to be, you know.'

Moran was curious. 'Higginson mentioned a new assignment? Something special?'

'All a bit hush-hush right now, guv. I'll let you know as soon as.' She winked.

Moran touched the side of his nose. 'Got it. Take care, Charlie.'

After she had closed the door behind her Moran sat quietly, thinking. Many years ago Isabel Akkerman had ruthlessly murdered a young aircraftswoman, Laura Witney, and he had promised himself – Laura, too – that, should circumstances permit, he would bring Akkerman to account for her crimes. It wouldn't be easy. She was protected by the Official Secrets Act and all manner of MI6 obfuscation. But, given time, there was always a way, and Moran had a good idea where he might begin.

Chapter Sixteen

As Tess strode into the open plan and peeled off her sodden overcoat the first thing that drew her attention was George, who had sprung to his feet as soon as he noticed her arrival and was making a beeline towards her. The second was the fact that DC Schlesinger was conspicuous by his absence. The new officer should have been back a while ago. He had the car, and he'd started back before her – or at least he should have done. Tess hoped he hadn't bottled out, panicked and then decided he didn't want to face her or anyone else, and slunk off home – or, more likely, to his girlfriend's, with whom, by all accounts, he was completely besotted.

'All good?' George touched her shoulder.

'Yep. Potter's a weirdo, but worth keeping in the frame – he knew where the key was.' She shrugged. 'If he'd a mind to, he could have let himself in, done the deed and put the key back where he'd found it.'

'OK, I'll add him to the board. You sure you're OK? You look pale. Maybe you—'

Tess shot him a look that silenced him but then, as always, regretted her sharpness. *Don't be a cow, Tess…*

'Guv'nor back yet?' She softened her tone, reached out and gave his hand a squeeze.

George visibly lightened at this small intimacy. 'Which one?'

Tess allowed herself a small eye-roll. 'There's only one in my book, and it's not our acting detective sergeant.'

George snorted. 'Aye, I don't think anyone would disagree. The guv's been closeted with Charlie Pepper in his office. She left five minutes ago, so he's probably free if you want a word.'

'Oh? What'd Charlie want, d'you think?'

George spread his hands. 'Who knows.'

'I heard wedding rumours. Maybe related? Charlie and the guv are close.'

'Oho! I assume that my fellow countryman is the lucky guy?'

'Yep. Nice bloke, too.'

George considered this for a moment. 'Ah well, good for Charlie. About time we had something to celebrate around here.'

'Yep. Look, George, I'd better get on, get this written up.' She managed a smile and headed off towards her workstation before he could steer the conversation in a more intimate direction.

She felt his eyes on her as she logged in, made herself concentrate on the screen as it launched her Teams account. She stiffened as she sensed him approaching. 'Look, Tess. We do need to talk. I—'

'Not now, George, OK? I have to do this while its fresh in my memory. Oh, and let me know if you bump into Schlesinger. He should have been back by now.'

'All right. Sure.'

George's footsteps retreated slowly, reluctantly, a tacit mirror to her own emotional withdrawal.

DC Schlesinger was still absent when the five o'clock briefing rolled around. What could be taking him so long? He hadn't been in touch, and he wasn't responding to her calls. Tess wasn't worried, just mildly annoyed.

As Collingworth's voice, at times abrasive, occasionally pompous, rambled on, her mind began to drift. It was hard to concentrate. The room was warm and rain was beating on the windows in a hypnotic rhythm that made her eyelids feel as though small weights had been attached to them. Her chin dropped onto her chest with a bump and she jerked awake, drawing an enquiring glance from a colleague sitting beside her. She became aware that Collingworth was looking at her expectantly.

'Sorry. Can you repeat the question?'

'Are you all right, DC Martin?' Collingworth didn't look as though the question was prompted by genuine concern, but rather by the practical necessity of updating the board with new intelligence from the day's interviews.

'I'm fine. It's just a little warm in here.'

'Your update, then – if it's not too much trouble?'

From the corner of her eye Tess saw Moran wince. The guv was standing against the wall on her left, hands thrust into his pockets, his forehead creased in irritation. Tess cleared her throat, gave Collingworth what he'd asked for.

'OK, thank you, DC Martin.' Collingworth turned to update the whiteboard.

Was it her imagination, or had he emphasised the 'DC'?

'And who was speaking to this Levi Cambridge character?

DC Martin again?' Collingworth tapped the board with his pointer.

Tess flushed. 'That'll be DC Schlesinger.' She knew what was coming and stiffened for the assault.

'I don't see said DC in the room. Update?' Collingworth strode forward to the first row and tapped the pointer on an empty chair.

'Still out, DS Collingworth.' The words tasted bitter in her mouth.

'Still out?' Collingworth repeated while consulting his watch. 'Five forty-three, I make it. What could be keeping him?'

'Cambridge talks a lot, acting sergeant.' Moran spoke from the sidelines. 'I expect we'll hear from DC Schlesinger shortly.'

'I see.' Collingworth moved back to the board. 'Thank you, sir.' He sniffed self-importantly. 'Might it not have been a better plan to accompany said errant constable, DC Martin?'

'Usually I would have done,' Tess admitted. 'But time was short. I thought it would be more efficient to split up and conduct separate interviews.'

'Did you, did you.' Collingworth looked like he was enjoying himself. 'You may be interested to hear that I did a little research myself on our Mr Cambridge.' Collingworth paused.

Tess felt nauseous. Something was coming, and it wasn't good.

Collingworth withdrew a notebook from his jacket. 'Let's see. Mr Levi Cambridge, date of birth December twelfth 1976. According to PNC, we have two counts of domestic disturbance – cautioned – one count of false imprisonment – some disagreement with the postman, apparently – arrested but not convicted, primarily because he was formally declared to be mildly schizophrenic. Something of a fantasist, too, I'm led to believe. Still, he had a good lawyer. Otherwise…' Collingworth shrugged and looked up. 'Probably not an ideal or reliable interviewee.' He caught Moran's eye. 'Wouldn't you agree, sir?'

'Whether I agree or not, acting sergeant, we need to get backup over there pronto. Tess? With me, please.'

Tess stood in a daze. Why hadn't she checked?

Moran was holding the door open for her as Collingworth looked on, a sardonic smile playing about his lips. The room was quiet, the atmosphere uncomfortable. Someone coughed.

Tess flew through the open door before she lost her composure. Moran shot a parting comment over his shoulder at Collingworth.

'We'll discuss this later, acting sergeant. Carry on, please.'

This did little to reassure her. If anything had happened to Schlesinger, it was down to her, plain and simple.

'I'm sorry, guv. I should have—'

'We'll talk about it later, Tess,' Moran said, not unkindly. 'Let's see how the land lies with Cambridge first.' He stopped at the lift, and as they waited he granted her a reassuring smile. 'I'm sure it'll all be fine.'

As the lift descended to the car park, however, her nausea returned. She leaned on the lift wall for support.

'Are you OK?' Moran took her arm. The lift door opened and cold air funnelled in from the underground parking lot.

She took a deep breath. 'I'll be all right, guv. It's nothing.'

But her stomach was still churning as Moran guided the car onto the main road. A terrible sense of dread overcame her and she began to tremble.

'You can stay in the car,' Moran told her. 'I'm taking you straight home as soon as this is sorted, all right? No argument.'

She didn't have the energy to object.

Chapter Seventeen

'Finally.' Bola interrupted his journey to the coffee machine as Bernice emerged from the lift. 'What kept you?'

'Did I miss the briefing?' Bernice sidestepped the question.

'You did. But the main man didn't notice – fortunately for you. He was more interested in hauling Tess over the coals.'

'Oh – what happened?'

Bola made a non-committal face. 'Tess let Schlesinger go solo. Apparently his interviewee has what we might call a chequered history, and guess what? Our nervy new DC's gone AWOL. The guv and Tess have just left to check it out. Are you all right? You look pale.'

And she did. Her cheeks were the colour of chalk, her lips even paler. Bola frowned. 'How'd it go? Find your phone OK?'

'My what? Oh, yes. Thanks. No problem.'

Her smile rang false. Bola knew Bernice well enough to know that something was up. He postponed his quest for caffeine and walked alongside as Bernice headed for her desk. 'And how's your friend? He roll out the red carpet for you?'

'Something like that.' Bernice shrugged her coat off. 'Bloody weather. Terrible.'

'This *is* the UK, last time I looked.' Bola grinned. 'So come on. How was it? Are you an item?'

Bernice crashed into her chair and opened her laptop. 'Just leave it, Bola, OK?'

Uh oh – a push too far, Bola…

'No offence, B, honest. Look, I'll leave you to it. Let me know if you want an update before rubberdick comes snooping around asking awkward questions.'

'Sure. Will do.'

'Want a coffee?'

'Yes.' She smiled, a thin, tense smile. 'That would be nice. Sorry, I didn't mean to snap. Traffic was bad. It's been a long afternoon.'

'Hey, no worries. Black, no sugar, right? Coming up.'

Bernice watched Bola lope away across the office floor on his mission. He moved gracefully for a big man, his gait assured and confident. He had a quick mind, too, and a great sense of humour. Even though he could be a shade impulsive at times, she'd trust him with her life.

Simply put, he was the best partner she'd ever had. And now she had to deceive him, and that wouldn't be easy to keep up. He could tell she wasn't right. She'd have to be careful, so careful…

Bernice rubbed her eyes with the heels of her hands. How quickly things could change. This morning she had been full of optimism, looking forward to new possibilities, maybe a radical change, a new direction in her life. But now, after what had happened … after what she'd agreed…

It wasn't too late. She could still do the right thing and call it in.

The right thing.

The right thing would destroy her dream, and Alastair's, too. If he'd come clean right away he might have got off with a suspended sentence, but that was now unlikely because he'd have to confess to illegal concealment of a body as well as manslaughter.

And she was complicit. If she called it in there would be a reprimand – at the very least. Maybe a hearing, maybe a sacking. And then she'd be left with nothing.

All she could see in her mind's eye was Alastair's stricken expression as she'd driven away. She hadn't wanted to know where he'd hidden the body, nor where he was planning to bury it. Bad enough that she was turning a blind eye – not to theft, or a burglary, or corruption, but to a *killing...*

'Get this down your neck, B. Looks like you need it.'

Bola was balancing a steaming cup in one hand and a jam doughnut on a paper plate in the other. 'For your blood sugar.' He grinned. 'Best thing on the canteen's poor excuse for a menu if you ask me.'

His friendly grin almost tipped her over the edge; she was close to breaking down, confessing all. She took the cup and wrapped her fingers around it, wincing as the hot contents stung her fingertips.

'Careful,' Bola advised. 'I don't know why they have to boil it up so much.'

Bernice set the cup down by her keyboard. 'Better than stone cold.' The pain had distracted her, steered her away from the brink. 'Did Mr ... what was his name? The London student? Did he show?'

Bola nodded. 'Kenyon? Yep. We can cross him off. His girlfriend confirmed that he was at home on the evening in question. And the following morning, for that matter. Nothing dodgy on his social media accounts. He's just a musician, that's what he does – no way can I see him in the highest harm offender category.'

'OK, well, the narrower the search the better.'

'Yeah. Definitely.' Bola held her gaze until she blinked, pressed the coffee cup to her cheek, presented an apologetic smile. 'Look, I'd better get on.'

'Get on?' Bola consulted his watch. 'I'd get out while the going's good. You look all in, B, seriously.'

She sighed, chewed her lip. 'Yes. Perhaps I should.'

'Tomorrow's another day, right?'

'Yes.'

Bola looked on like an anxious father as she collected her things, folded her damp coat over her arm. 'Thanks for the coffee. See you tomorrow.'

'Yeah. Take care, B.'

She felt a lump in her throat as she descended to the car park. She hated lying, dissembling in any form, especially to her buddy.

She made it to the car before the tears came. It was a full ten minutes before she felt steady enough to drive.

It was raining hard as she pulled out onto the main road. Her wipers swished back and forth in a steady rhythm, mechanically mimicking the leaden beating of her heart.

Chapter Eighteen

A Sellotaped note by the bell read *not working*, so Moran rapped on the rusted door knocker. Rain blew onto his exposed neck and he turned his collar up as he waited for a response. Thirty seconds passed. He knocked again. Was it his imagination, or had there been an answering knock from inside? Yes, there, again – not a knock as such, but a faint but discernible pounding, as though someone had locked themselves in an attic and was trying to attract attention. Collingworth's summary replayed in Moran's mind: *one count of false imprisonment…*

The door opened abruptly. 'Yes?'

'Mr Cambridge?' Moran smiled a greeting. 'We spoke on the telephone. DCI Moran.'

Cambridge was a stocky, balding man in his mid forties. His eyes lit up. 'Ah, the big chief. Come in, come in, DCI Moran. Just in time. I expect you're wondering where your young man has got to.'

As if in response the pounding recommenced, this time louder and more insistent. The noise seemed to be coming from upstairs, and now he was closer to the source Moran was able to discern that the disturbance was accompanied by a faint and rather hoarse voice.

'The young man in question goes by the name of DC Schlesinger, Mr Cambridge. Is it possible, d'you think, that he might be having some difficulty exiting the bathroom?'

'I'll say, cheeky little so-and-so,' Cambridge said. 'Please, DCI Moran, come through to my humble drawing room.' Cambridge beckoned grandly as though he were showing him into some palatial suite.

Moran declined the invitation with a shake of his head. 'Perhaps you might explain the nature of your difficulty, Mr Cambridge? You see, DC Schlesinger is required for further duty,' he went on in a reasonable tone. 'I'm afraid I can't condone his being closeted in your bathroom for the entire evening.'

'Of course not,' Cambridge beamed. 'Just teaching him a lesson, that's all. If I might appeal to your sense of decency, DCI Moran – and I know that you're a decent man – I have to tell you that the nature of your young subaltern's questions rather got my back up.'

'I see. Might it be better to include DC Schlesinger in this conversation? I'm sure he'll be able to clear up any misunderstanding. He's a good lad.'

They were interrupted by a fresh fusillade of pounding. Once it had subsided, Cambridge lowered his voice and leaned forward in a confiding manner. 'Good lad, he might be, DCI Moran, but asking me if I'd spent time inside is going some way down Wrong Direction Alley, if you get my meaning. Oh, I've had my moments, I'll grant you that, 'course I have – hell, we *all* have, right?' Cambridge grinned. 'But I've *never* been inside. Never intend to be, neither. I mean, inside you've got all sorts, know what I mean? Can't trust no one, can't take a shower in peace, got to keep your back to the wall.' He paused, contemplating the imagined privations and trials of prison life. 'Anyway, I said to myself a long time ago, you aren't for the inside, Levi. You keep yourself out of mischief, keep your ears to the ground, help our boys in blue keep the peace, walk the straight and narrow.' He shrugged. 'And all things like that.'

'I'm sorry if DC Schlesinger upset you, Mr Cambridge. 'But as he's completed his penance, I propose we set him free and be on our way without causing you any further trouble. How does that sound?'

'Anything to oblige, DCI Moran. You're a decent fellow, I respect that.'

'Just a word of friendly advice, though.' Moran rested his hand on Cambridge's shoulder. 'I'd go easy on the penances in future, especially in the case of investigating officers of the law. I'd hate for you to get yourself in any kind of trouble as a result. We don't want anything to tarnish our good relations, especially as you've been so helpful.' He winked.

Cambridge cocked his head, returned the wink. 'Say no more.'

'And the bathroom is?'

'First on your right as you reach the landing. Shall I put the kettle on?'

'Have to decline, I'm afraid. Places to be, crimes to solve. You know how it is.'

Cambridge looked pleased at his implied inclusion in Thames Valley law enforcement. 'Oh yes, Detective Inspector, indeed I do.'

There was a lock on the bathroom door. On the outside. Moran slid it open and went in. Schlesinger was sitting on the edge of the bath, looking disconsolate. When he saw Moran his eyes widened and he sprang to attention. 'Sir? I'm so sorry. Erm, what I mean is—'

'Next time, if there's a lock on the outside, best to question it before entry. Agreed?'

'Yes sir. I'll make a note. But have you arrested Cambridge? He was obstructive, abusive, and then—'

'And then, in all the excitement, nature called.'

Schlesinger looked crestfallen. 'Yes, sir, but—'

'Guv.'

'Yes, guv. Look, I wasn't expecting—'

'Lesson two: expect the unexpected. He held the door open. 'Shall we? I expect you've had enough of the scenery in here.'

Moran crossed the landing and went downstairs, Schlesinger trailing behind him like a chastised puppy. They met Cambridge in the hallway. 'Thanks again for your time, Mr Cambridge. We'll let ourselves out.'

'But, *guv*—?' Schlesinger's mouth hardened.

'Say goodbye, DC Schlesinger. I think we've outstayed our welcome.'

'Glad to help,' Cambridge said as he saw them out. 'Anytime, you know where to find me.'

Moran nodded. 'Indeed we do, Mr Cambridge.'

Tess opened the car window as she saw the two men approach. The tension went out of her as she saw Schlesinger, unharmed and gangly as ever. 'Are you all right, DC Schlesinger?'

'Yes. But I'm not happy about leaving without—'

'Get in,' Tess said.

'First,' Moran said, as he buckled his seatbelt, 'it's always best to defuse rather than inflame. I take it Mr Cambridge provided *some* information before he went off the deep end?'

The timbre of Schlesinger's voice from the back seat was tentative. 'Well, yes…'

'Good. So it wasn't a complete waste of time.'

'I suppose not, but—'

Tess turned round and silenced him with a hard stare, 'Listen and learn, OK?'

'I don't understand,' Schlesinger protested as Moran eased the car out of the space and cruised towards the T junction. 'I mean, he locked me *up*. Shouldn't we—'

'Sure, I could have gone in with all guns blazing,' Moran interrupted, 'but then we might have lost the goodwill of a key witness. We're going to analyse what he told you and sift the wheat from the chaff. If we need to revisit with follow-up questions, we still have a willing witness, albeit a slightly crazy one. Got it?'

There was a pause as Schlesinger digested this. 'Yes, I see now.' Schlesinger shifted uncomfortably in the back. 'But when this is over, I want to give that man a piece of my mind.'

'You can issue a warning – when we're finished. Then and only then.'

'I'll go over it with him, guv,' Tess offered. 'I'll have a report on your desk first thi—'

'Not tonight, you won't. It's home for you. Report by tomorrow lunchtime, OK?'

'OK, guv.'

They drove on in silence. After they'd dropped Tess home, Schlesinger accepted Moran's offer of a lift into town. It was his girlfriend's birthday and he wanted to buy flowers before the shops closed. Moran told him to buy two bunches and return one to the car. Schlesinger obeyed unquestioningly and, before setting off for his partner's flat on foot he delivered a short, apologetic speech he'd obviously rehearsed while making his purchases. Moran told him to put the afternoon's events down to experience, and as the young DC scuttled off on his romantic errand he turned his mind to the problem of how to resolve his own relational impasse. Flowers always helped, but they wouldn't fix his and Alice's disagreement. For that he needed a strategy – the right words, a promise of the proverbial light at the end of the tunnel.

Because right now, from where he was sitting, the tunnel was full of darkness, not even a distant pinprick piercing the gloom. He looked at the flowers lying on the passenger seat and sighed. He had to face Alice, even with no news. He checked his appearance in the mirror and wished he hadn't. The bags beneath his eyes seemed more pronounced, the lines on his forehead more furrowed. Perhaps it was just the street lighting.

Or not.

Come on, Brendan, just get on with it. You'll think of something to say; you always do …

Right?

Chapter Nineteen

'Hello, Alice.'

For a moment Moran thought that the door was going to be shut in his face. But Alice quickly gathered herself, shook her head slowly and gave a deep sigh.

'Well, better late than never, I suppose. Come in, Brendan.'

The house was warm with the scent of fresh polish mixed with Alice's perfume. It was a female, domesticated, ordered smell. As always, Moran felt clumsy and untidy just being there. Unusually the TV was off, the lounge silent. He frowned.

'No Peter?'

'In bed with a heavy cold. He just sleeps when he's ill. He's a good patient.'

Moran frowned. 'Not Covid?'

'Can't get test kits. No one seems bothered anymore.' Alice shrugged. 'I expect he'll be as right as rain in a couple of days. So, tea? Or maybe something stronger, by the look of you?'

Moran was encouraged by her manner as he followed her into the kitchen. The prospect of reconciliation was evident in Alice's swift movements and lightness of tone. 'A small Scotch wouldn't go amiss.' He checked himself. 'Actually, no. Make that a glass of wine. Just a wee one.'

'Sangiovese?' She produced a bottle from the cabinet.

'Naturally.' He smiled.

She poured two glasses, handed him one. 'Cheers. So, how's things at the ranch? Caught your man yet?'

'Cheers.' He took a sip and the wine slipped down his throat in a warm rush. He resisted the temptation to knock the remainder back in one. 'Early stages. We've ruled out a few suspects.'

'Well, you have to start somewhere.'

'Indeed. Every investigation starts slowly. The pace picks up as we go along.'

'And how's Dawson? Still in ICU?'

Moran shook his head. 'Didn't make it, I'm afraid.'

'Oh, no. That's terrible. I'm sorry.'

Alice looked genuinely shocked. Moran was about to unburden himself by relating his encounter with Mrs Dawson, but then thought better of it. He was here to talk about himself and Alice, not himself and his problems.

Alice gestured with her glass. 'Let's go into the lounge, shall we? Take advantage of the peace and quiet.'

Moran followed her through and they sat together on the sofa, a little way apart. He was unaccustomed to the silence; Alice's autistic brother would habitually spend hours in front of the TV watching endless reruns of famous sporting events, so if they wanted to chat they were inevitably confined to the kitchen. 'Must be the first time I've been in here without the background Olympic commentary.'

Alice laughed. 'Normal service will soon be resumed, I'm

sure.'

Moran studied Alice's expression. She seemed almost her usual self, but there was something not quite right, as though she were preparing to make an announcement the nature of which he might find unpalatable. He had an inkling that the casual small talk was merely a necessary prelude to some weightier subject matter, like an orchestra tuning up before the main performance.

Better start talking, Brendan... get your move in first...

'Alice, I know this has been difficult—'

She stilled him with a look and an almost imperceptible movement of her hand. 'Brendan, don't.' She paused, looked down at her glass, swirled the wine as she took a moment to choose her words. 'I'm very fond of you, you know that. But there's something between us, something I don't think will ever change.'

'Alice, I have to retire sometime,' Moran protested, 'and it'll be soon, after this is over, I promise. I mean, I *am* officially retired—'

Alice set her glass down on the side table with a bang. 'And what about the next time? *Oh, it's just a bit of consultancy, that's all.* I can hear you saying it, Brendan. *They just want me for a few weeks, you know. They need my experience, is all.* And then you'll be sucked in again. You'll *never* be able to let go, Brendan. If you're honest with yourself, you know that.'

'I can change.'

She looked him in the eye. 'Can you? Can you honestly say you'll be here for me, and for Peter, when I need you?'

'I want to be, of course I do.'

She shook her head and shot him a bitter smile. 'You see?

You can't even give me a direct answer.'

He was lost for words. How could he turn this around? 'I won't take on any more work, I give you my word.'

'But Brendan, don't you see? You'll be embittered towards me. It's not right for me to restrict you, to make demands of you that you'll struggle to keep.'

He shook his head. There was nowhere else to go, no other avenue of compromise he could suggest. 'We can't let this spoil what we've got, Alice. It's crazy. It makes no sense.'

'No, perhaps it doesn't, to you.'

He finished his wine. 'So where does that leave us?' He set his empty glass next to hers with exaggerated deliberation.

'It leaves us as friends. But…'

'But what?' He was frightened to hear any more. Was their future friendship also to be conditional?

She looked at him, not without tenderness. 'Brendan, I need some space, a little time to myself. After that … well, we'll see.'

He stood up. 'Thanks for your frankness. At least I know where I stand.'

Her expression clouded. 'You're angry. Please don't be.'

He wasn't angry – he was confused, upset, as though the world had closed in on him unexpectedly, all hope draining away like water from a breached dam. 'I'll see myself out,' he managed. He couldn't look at her.

'Brendan—'

But he was at the front door, fumbling with the catch, found himself stumbling in a daze along the familiar path.

He drove home on auto-pilot.

The house was cold but he barely noticed. In the kitchen he found a half- bottle of scotch, poured himself a large measure, and sat down next to the casement window that overlooked his untended garden. The phone rang, but he ignored it. It rang again and still he didn't move. He remained by the window, staring out into the darkness until his glass was empty and rain began to patter softly against the leaded glass.

Chris Collingworth had had a bad day. Bad enough that his promotion had been watered down by Moran's reappointment, worse that he found himself yet again at the senior man's beck and call, and worse still that the afternoon's work had proved to be a colossal waste of time. Harold Barlow, jobbing gardener, unmarried, hard-working, average to low IQ, singularly lacking in imagination, eager to please, pleasant and cooperative to the point of irritation, had arrived on the dot for his scheduled interview, bored Collingworth silly with an unnecessarily detailed account of his work at the Szarkas' residence, and had concluded his discourse with an airtight alibi.

The only pertinent information he'd been able to provide was that the Szarka spinsters had seemed to him to be living a contented life, with Marika, the murder victim, being the more talkative and her sister Reyka the more practical. It had been Reyka who'd explained what they wanted done, Reyka who'd conducted the financial negotiations, Marika who had made him tea and kept him supplied with biscuits and sandwiches while he undertook the work. They'd paid up on time, thanked him for his diligence, and promised to contact him again if they required any further practical assistance.

So, no progress. But maybe that was good. Progress now meant that Moran got all the glory, as per usual. The only ray of sunshine that had lightened Collingworth's drab afternoon was the unexpected appearance of Sheila Dawson, an encounter Collingworth had taken full advantage of. She was looking for answers, looking to point the finger, and Collingworth had been only too happy to oblige. Dawson had had one too many on the night of Moran's do, that had been obvious to anyone with half a brain, and Collingworth had clocked Moran handing the guy another Scotch, clear as day. He'd thought nothing much of it at the time, but Collingworth prided himself on his ability to file away bits of information for future reference, because you never knew when something apparently trivial might prove useful. And boy, did this one look like it might pay off – big time. Dawson's widow was out for blood, and Moran's irresponsible gesture had lit her proverbial fuse. All he had to do to maintain his innocence was insist that he'd only described what he'd seen and heard at the party at Mrs D's prompting, and that she had demanded a fair and honest account, which is precisely what he'd given. It was hardly his fault that the guy had been plied with whisky.

Collingworth smiled to himself as he shut down his laptop and made his way out of the building. He'd had a message to say that Moran wanted a word, but they'd missed each other. Too bad. The Irishman would just have to stew till tomorrow.

Collingworth whistled a popular tune as he revved his MX-5 and shot out onto the main road. Perhaps the day hadn't gone so badly, after all.

Chapter Twenty

Bernice Swinhoe was, according to her own judgement, a self-sufficient individual. She lived alone, and felt no need for company. Boyfriends had come and gone; she enjoyed male company, but not to the extent that she required a man around all the time. Her flat was her own territory and she liked it that way. She was tidy; not compulsively so, but her living area was well-ordered, tastefully decorated, not overly fussy. She enjoyed normal activities like reading, films, country walks, lunchtime drinks in the pub, but was also fascinated by the abstract, the possibility of the existence of something other than the physical – alternative dimensions, perhaps – where mysteries hitherto undisclosed might be revealed. She was open to the possibility of the existence of a deity, and of other unseen realities hinted at in half-remembered childhood stories, folklore and mythology. She did not accept that death was an end, thinking of it rather as the gateway to something more profound, where some essence of herself might be refined and moulded into something more enduring. She thought of her late mother in this way – alive but in some new guise, fully sentient, and, although absent from the material world, nevertheless experiencing great contentment in whatever reality she now inhabited.

But she was by no means a dreamer. She had inherited a strong practical streak from her mother, and also a talent for incisive, logical thought, an attribute she had put to good use in her police career so far. She had always considered herself a well-balanced individual, confident, curious, and reliable. She was adept at dealing with problems, both in her own life and in the lives of friends and acquaintances, by whom she was regarded as a steady and sensible advisor.

Nothing, however had prepared her for her current situation. In the space of two months she had become completely infatuated with a man – a new and not altogether comfortable experience – and now, extraordinarily, bizarrely, she found herself compromised by the same individual as a silent witness to manslaughter.

Bernice rolled over and threw the duvet aside. The bedside clock read three forty-four, its luminous pointers reminding her, like ghostly, accusing fingers, of the enormity of what she had agreed to the previous afternoon. She sat on the edge of the bed and leaned forward with her head in her hands. Her eyes were gritty from lack of sleep, her stomach heavy and unsettled, as though the tension she felt in her head had somehow solidified into some internal physical weight that shifted and slipped inside her like loose cargo in a ship's hold.

She groaned as she dragged herself wearily to her feet, pulling on a dressing gown and a pair of fluffy slippers. She slid the curtains open a fraction, hugged herself and shivered. Outside the darkness was an opaque, leaden slab that squatted like some beast of prey beneath a leaden sky, pregnant with its burden of moisture.

She made tea in her small kitchen, switched on the radio – more as a distraction than from any desire to hear news or music – sat at the kitchen table and tried to calm herself. It would be all right. Alastair was a good man. Accidents could happen to anyone, after all. It hadn't been his fault. He'd been provoked. He'd been so good to that boy. If only Johnny had showed gratitude instead of attitude, then maybe things wouldn't have got out of hand. But it was done now, nothing could change that. Bernice sipped the scalding liquid and winced, blew gently over the surface of her mug.

Somehow she had to adjust to this new reality, because if she didn't, the knowledge of what she had seen would eat away at her until there was nothing left, until everything she had dreamed and hoped for was lost and ruined for ever.

Moran had emerged from his house into the rainy morning when his mobile rang. He'd slept badly and was already regretting the quantity of Scotch he'd consumed the night before. He shut the door behind him, waved a greeting to his neighbour and unlocked his car with a flourish. 'Moran.'

'Good morning, DCI Moran. Pauline Harris.'

As if the voice needed an introduction…

He ducked into his car and slid the keys into the ignition with his free hand. 'Morning. You have news?'

'The bust. It's a match with the hair fragment.'

'OK, that's good.'

'We also found chemical traces. At first I thought it might be polish – you know, Pledge or similar. Something used for dusting. That's what I'd have expected. But it's not.'

'Oh? Then what—'

'Grease. Automotive grease. A minute amount. Easy to miss.'

Moran turned on the ignition, adjusted the heater. Rain was still beating down from the endless cloud base, and the morning seemed colder than usual. 'Go on.'

'We've not found a match, yet. The team are working with the most common UK brands. All I can say at present is that it's lithium-based. But the products we've tested don't have the same chemical balance. So far.'

'Interesting. Look, I have to get to a briefing, but keep me posted, would you?'

'Of course.' The line went dead.

Automotive grease. Moran mulled it over on his way to Atlantic House. A mechanic? But the sisters didn't own a car. The gardener? But he was an outside fella, not a car mechanic. Persons unknown, then. An opportunist? But nothing had been stolen, and if any murder had been premeditated it was this one. Perhaps yesterday's interviews might have yielded something more concrete.

Well, he'd soon find out. But there was something he needed to do first – if he could find the man.

As it happened, Collingworth was strolling past the lift as Moran came out. 'Ah, acting detective sergeant.'

'Morning.' Collingworth looked as though he'd thought twice about stopping, but, reluctantly it seemed, he did.

'A word?'

Moran headed for his office leaving Collingworth to follow. He went straight to his desk and sat down behind it. Collingworth seemed unfazed as he came in, coffee cup in one hand, mobile phone in the other. He had an earpiece jammed into his right ear, an affectation that irritated Moran. It implied a strong likelihood of urgent calls, conferring a false air of importance on the wearer.

'Sit down.' Moran indicated the visitor's chair.

'Problem?'

'Problem, *sir*. You will address me appropriately while I'm SIO, acting detective sergeant. Understood?'

Collingworth sniffed. 'Perfectly. Sir.'

'Sheila Dawson. You spoke.'

'We did.' Collingworth took a sip of coffee.

'And apparently, you led her to understand that I was responsible for her husband's state of inebriation.'

'Hardly that, sir. I gave an honest report, at her request, of what had occurred at the party. I merely told her what I had observed.'

'Sounds to me as if you laid it on thick. She's holding me responsible for what happened.'

'That's ridiculous, sir, of course.' Collingworth smiled obsequiously. 'Hardly your fault that some driver wasn't looking where he was going.'

'If she takes this to court I'll be taking you with me, and you'll damn well retract your exaggerated statements and set the record straight. For your information, I was well aware that the late DCI Dawson had already had several over the odds, and the measure I poured him wouldn't have caused a mouse to stumble. Is that clear?'

'She won't take it that far, sir, surely?'

'Is that *clear*?'

'Yes, sir. Absolutely. I apologise for any offence caused.'

'I'll take the briefing this morning,' Moran said brusquely. 'I'll hand over to you to finish up when I'm done.'

Collingworth stood up.

'I haven't finished.'

Collingworth sat down again.

'DC Schlesinger made a rookie mistake yesterday. I've spoken to him. No need to haul him over the coals. Same goes for DC Martin; she's been through quite enough as it is. Do we understand each other?'

'Of course. Perfectly.'

Collingworth's attempt to mask his disappointment didn't fool Moran. The man's arrogance was staggering.

Moran checked the time. 'I'll see you in the briefing. Any updates for me?'

'Should be in your email inbox, sir.'

'Right. If I had a desktop PC, that would be helpful.' Moran swept his hand across the empty expanse of desk.

'I'll print it out for you straight away, sir. Will that be all?'

'For now, yes.'

Moran watched him go, shoulders rolling. By the time Collingworth was halfway to his desk he was on his phone, probably delegating the printing task to some hapless minion.

Chapter Twenty-One

Tess headed for the door the moment briefing was over. She didn't quite make it before Collingworth called her back.

'This Potter bloke. He had a tool box open, you say?'

'Yes.'

'And access to the property?'

'Well, in theory everyone had access – they always left a key under an ornament in the porch.'

'Yes, but he *knew* about that.'

'I suppose. But I don't think—'

'He's the frontrunner in my book,' Collingworth interrupted. 'No one else we've spoken to had access. No one else had a tool box open – and a hammer and nails in evidence, too.'

'Yes, but it's a bit of a long shot,' Tess argued. 'Where's the motive?'

'That's what we're going to find out,' Collingworth declared emphatically. 'Get your coat. We're off to visit Ms Szarka.'

'But I—'

'Car park. Five minutes. I'll drive.'

Defeated, Tess returned to her workstation. DC Schlesinger,

sitting at the opposite desk, was already busy with his newly assigned task; research into the Szarka family history.

'I'm out for a bit,' Tess told him. 'You OK?'

Schlesinger looked up and grinned; Tess thought he looked relieved to be office-bound. 'All good. Love this sort of stuff. I already researched my own family ancestry. Amazing what you can find.'

'Good, well, I'll see you later.'

Collingworth was already waiting by his jazzy little sports number. She climbed in and buckled up. Collingworth seemed in a testy mood. She'd noticed he'd been in with the guv for ten minutes before the briefing, and by all accounts Moran had read him the riot act. Some issue regarding DCI Dawson's unfortunate demise, apparently.

As they queued in the worsening traffic on the Inner Distribution Road, Tess decided that silence was the best option, unless Collingworth asked a direct question. Temporary lights had paralysed Caversham Road and both bridges over the Thames. Tess gazed out of the car window at scurrying commuters, cyclists bent over soaking handlebars, crocodile lines of uniformed kids being shepherded by harassed-looking teachers, and wondered why she was still a part of it all. Why she hadn't taken herself off to some remote island somewhere – Shetland, or Orkney, or maybe somewhere warmer… What had driven her to return to duty? George and his attentive encouragement? No, she didn't think so. Maybe the clue was in that word, 'duty'. A sense of duty had impelled her, that was all. It certainly wasn't the fulfilment of parental expectations; her mother and father, although proud of her career, had never hidden their concerns over her safety, particularly after what had happened to her in the good old line of duty.

Collingworth revved the engine in frustration as the lights at the roadworks, after less than ten seconds on green, turned red and the car immediately in front came to a sudden stop.

'That's not going to help,' Tess said. 'You'll only wind the guy up.'

'Sodding council's fault,' Collingworth seethed. 'Why can't they switch the damn lights off during rush hour? I mean, can you see any work being done?'

She couldn't; the roadworks were glaringly lacking in active personnel. All that was evident was a double line of cones, an empty mechanical digger by the side of the road, and the traffic lights themselves.

'Situation normal,' she said. 'Don't let it get to you. Incidentally, does Ms Szarka know we're paying her a visit?'

'No.'

'Want me to call in advance? I have the Goosens woman's landline.'

'No, leave it.'

Tess bit her lip. 'Don't you think that a little courtesy might help? After what that poor woman's been through?'

'I've a job to do,' Collingworth replied, steering the MX-5 through the lights like a bullet down a barrel. 'Results are what I'm after. Courtesy's for the drawing room.'

They crossed the bridge, squeezed between a bus and a parked motorcycle onto the slip road and headed out into Caversham.

'Posh out here,' Collingworth observed. 'I can smell the greenbacks with the windows shut.'

'Posh people don't use cash,' Tess corrected him. 'Even normal people don't these days. Can't remember the last time I went to a cash machine.'

'Cash talks,' Collingworth defended his assertion. 'I always keep a few large ones in my wallet.'

Tess bit her lip a second time to hold back the obvious response. It was pointless winding Collingworth up; he was irritable enough as it was.

When they arrived at the house in Christchurch Road, Fedelma Goosens answered the door and her face darkened. 'Again?'

Tess spoke quickly before the woman had time to say anything further. 'Ms Goosens – apologies for disturbing you so early, but there are some important questions we need to ask Ms Szarka.'

'And why, might I enquire, didn't you ask them yesterday?'

'New information,' Collingworth broke in. 'Won't take long. If you please?'

Reyka Szarka emerged from the kitchen, tea towel in hand. She frowned as she saw the detectives.

Collingworth marched uninvited into the lounge. Tess saw Goosens and Szarka exchange weary glances, so she conjured a reassuring smile. 'This won't take long. We appreciate your being so cooperative.'

Goosens didn't quite harrumph, but the noise she made came pretty close.

'Mr Potter.' Collingworth cut straight to the chase. 'Piano tuner. Tell me more.'

Reyka Szarka sat down on the nearest armchair. She was wearing a tasteful Laura Ashley dress and a carefully matched cardigan. 'Mr Potter is something of an eccentric,' she said. 'But he has a fine car. He hasn't been to see us since the beginning of March, so I don't quite see—'

'He knew where to find a spare key.' Collingworth had plonked himself uninvited on the sofa and was busy picking his teeth with a thumbnail.

'Well, yes, I suppose he did.' She glanced at Goosens. 'He *is* an odd little man—'

'Any arguments, disagreements of late?'

'None. Ever.'

'Not with you, or your sister?'

'No.' Her lip trembled. 'Marika was a gentle soul. I don't remember her ever falling out with anybody. Everybody loved her.'

'Are you *any* closer to finding out who did this?' Goosens interrupted. 'Why are you wasting time asking facile questions about people who are quite clearly innocent?'

Tess shook her head. 'It's not quite that straightforward, Mrs Goosens. Everyone is capable of violence, given the right provocation.'

Goosens stiffened. 'Well, I dispute that. Mr Potter might be a little strange, but it's hard to imagine —'

'You know him too, Ms Goosens?'

'We all know each other,' Goosens said airily. 'We local musicians. Mr Potter has tuned my piano on occasion, although not since last year. He has some rather unappealing habits, but in my opinion he is nevertheless a trustworthy colleague.'

Tess nodded. 'I see.'

'Did he converse?' Collingworth wanted to know. 'Did he

have much conversation?'

'Naturally we would chat about music,' Reyka replied. 'He is an enthusiast, a kindred spirit.'

'Does he have a favourite composer?'

Reyka seemed taken aback at Collingworth's line of inquiry. 'Well, I—'

'Handel? Mozart? Someone more contemporary? Glass, perhaps?'

Tess was as surprised as Reyka and Goosens that Collingworth had even heard of Philip Glass.

'Glass? Hardly.' Reyka tutted. 'Puccini, Verdi, Rossini.'

'Ah, Rossini. The Barber of Seville?' Collingworth nodded. 'My mother's favourite.'

Tess raised an eyebrow. Collingworth obviously had hidden depths – v*ery* well hidden.

'How about Beethoven?' Collingworth asked.

Tess felt her neck muscles tense. Collingworth might be an irritating pain in the posterior, but he knew what he was doing. Moran's announcement at the morning briefing of his discovery of the broken bust had caused quite a stir. It could well prove to be the connection that caught the killer.

Reyka lifted her chin a fraction. 'Now you mention it, he did tell me once that he couldn't bear the man,' she said. 'Or his music. Called it pompous. Well, I had to agree, of course.'

'Not a favourite of yours either, then?'

'No. Marika … she was the Beethoven worshipper.' Her bottom lip wobbled again.

'Is that so? The bust in your lounge – that would have been hers?'

'Yes. Ugly thing. I never cared for it.'

Collingworth folded his arms and leaned back in the sofa. 'You won't miss it, then.'

'I'm sorry?'

'You may not have noticed,' Tess said, 'but the bust has been smashed – and disposed of.'

'Was it? Well, good riddance.'

'Possibly by the killer,' Collingworth added.

'All this conjecture.' Goosens spoke up. 'Just get on and catch the man who did this. Why waste more of your time – *and* ours – on these pointless interrogations? What does it matter what's been broken and what's been stolen? A woman's life was taken. *That* should be your focus.'

'It's all right, Fedelma.' Reyka raised a conciliatory hand. 'They have to ask questions. It's just how they work.'

'Your spare key.' Tess moistened her lips which felt dry and cracked in the heat of the lounge. 'It was in its usual place at the time?'

'It's always there,' Reyka confirmed. 'We … that is to say, it was our habit … to bolt the locks from the inside at night. Whoever did this couldn't have entered by the front door after ten.'

'But earlier?'

'Possibly,' she conceded.

'Do you ever have visitors calling in the evening? Friends?'

'After we'd finished teaching for the day we would continue to work. No time for friends and social tittle tattle, I'm afraid. Far too busy.'

'Do you play in an orchestra?' Collingworth wanted to know.

'Don't be ridiculous,' Reyka snorted. 'Marika played in a quartet, sometimes a quintet. I myself always favoured an oboe and strings ensemble.'

'And may we have the names of your musical colleagues?' Tess took out a notebook.

'For heaven's sake,' Goosens interrupted. 'Pointless, pointless, pointless. The ladies in question are all above reproach.'

'That's for us to determine, Ms Goosens.' Collingworth stood up. 'If you'd like to provide my constable with the appropriate information, I'd be most obliged.'

Tess smarted at Collingworth's use of the possessive article. Bloody cheek. She kept her mouth tightly shut as Reyka and Goosens reeled off the names of their respective musical accomplices.

Tess closed her notebook and Collingworth treated the two women to an oily smile. 'That's all for now, ladies. I'd appreciate it if you'd stay in the vicinity, Ms Szarka. I take it you'll be at this address if we need to speak with you again?'

'Where else can I go?' Reyka dropped her gaze to the carpet. 'Not home, not anymore.'

As gently as she was able, Tess said, 'We'll see ourselves out.'

Chapter Twenty-Two

Alastair Catton sat behind his mahogany desk in what could only be described as a state of despair. Just days ago his world had been revolving at an optimum angle, its orbit predictable and assured. Everything was in its place, and the future looked bright and sustainable. Nothing had intervened to upset the holistic rhythm of Simplicity's bucolic way of life. No news had been good news, and Catton had begun to dare to believe that he was now free of the cords that had bound him.

She had been clear from the start that it was a dangerous mission. She had told him that her superiors had not expected her safe return, a prediction that had not seemed to faze her in any way. She had accepted the risk, confident, as always, in her own unique abilities.

And he had missed her. He had even, God help him, pleaded with her not to go. He hated her, and he loved her. How was that possible? He had asked himself this question many, many times. He needed her, desired her, and yet … her cruelty and domineering personality created conflict within him to the extent that he had thought he might lose his mind. He needed her – and he wished she were dead.

That's how it was.

Now, at his desk, a newspaper was open in front of him. A column on the second page was headed:

> *North Korean scientists die in laboratory explosion*

Three, to be precise. Top-tier brains, apparently, allocated to North Korea's defence programme and, according to something the newspaper referred to as informed speculation, key to the delivery of the closed-door country's bioweapons capability.

The newspaper, the Sunday Telegraph, was two months old. He had seen it and had at once known – it was *her* doing.

Mission accomplished. Targets down.

And then the waiting had begun. A week had passed, and then another. There was no news, and his hope had cautiously blossomed. She had succeeded but, as her handlers predicted, had paid the ultimate price. Another week, and he had convinced himself that it really was over. He was free of her, she would never return. Part of him – the carnal, possessive part – had despaired, but the rest of him rejoiced. He made himself look to the future, when the passage of time would slowly excise her from his mind, like a surgeon removing a tumour piece by piece during a lengthy operation.

Another week had passed, and still nothing.

He had relaxed. Bernice came for weekends. He enjoyed her company; she was normal, easy to be with, easy to talk to. Had no agenda. He looked forward to her visits. Maybe she would even live at Simplicity in the future; when she spoke about the possibility he could see the excitement in her eyes, as though she'd found something she'd been seeking for a long, long time.

He was free. He could make rational choices. Even Johnny was more relaxed, almost cheerful. He had never seen eye-to-eye with *her*.

The balance of life had been reestablished.

And then one day, as he carried an armful of netting to the pond with the intention of protecting his fish from the persistently murderous attentions of a heron, he had seen her. He'd been so surprised that he'd dropped the netting and frozen. She *couldn't* be here. She was dead.

But she was real. And very much alive.

'You look surprised,' she'd said as she walked slowly towards him. 'Like you weren't expecting me.'

'I thought you were—'

She'd pressed a finger to his lips. 'Don't say it. Don't think it. It's not going to happen.' She removed her finger. 'Now kiss me. I've missed you, Alastair.'

He grabbed the newspaper, tore out the offending page, screwed it into a ball and flung it towards the bin. It missed, bouncing on the rim and rolling to a halt on the office carpet.

He stood up and stretched. He was tired and stiff; he hadn't slept well since … since it happened, since Johnny… He went to the middle of the office and centred himself. Tai Chi would help. It was the only way to relax himself. He took a deep breath. *Zhan, zhuang* …

The door opened, and without preamble a female voice, dusky, exotic, said, 'Well? Have you asked her yet, my Alastair?'

He opened his eyes. Isabel was dressed in tight-fitting black leggings and a soft, grey top. Her face was devoid of makeup as usual, and her glossy black hair fell in waves over her toned shoulders. Her eyes sparkled with something like amusement.

'I'll call her today.'

'*Now* would be good, sweetie.' She went to his desk, sat on the leather swivel chair and began to spin gently around, propelling it with small movements of her unshod feet.

Catton sighed. 'Can I at least finish what I was doing?'

'If I'm to make my home with you here in Arcadia, Alastair, I need this done.'

'Very well.'

Isabel handed him his smartphone and watched as he typed. He finished and pocketed the device. 'It's done.'

'I'll wait for the reply.' Isabel got up in a languid, easy motion and came to him. She wrapped her arms around him and he stiffened.

'Oooh, so tense.' Isabel smiled. 'Want to join me for a little relaxation?'

'I have things to do, Isabel.' His voice sounded toneless to him, empty of feeling, and yet deep inside he felt the familiar stirring.

His smartphone gave a beep.

'There she is. Keen as mustard.' Isabel laughed and released him.

He glanced at the message, took a deep breath and let it out again in a long sigh. 'Tomorrow. Midday. She's in the middle of a murder investigation, so she can only stay for an hour.'

'That's more than enough, dear man.' Isabel patted his cheek. 'I could do it in half the time.'

'I don't like this. It's wrong. It's not ... fair.'

'Life's not fair, though, is it? And besides, you do want to keep me safe and sound, don't you?'

He said nothing. All he could think of was Bernice, how she would react. He felt sick. He wanted to warn her, but it was too late for any remedial action. Much too late.

'I'm going for a sauna. Want to join me?' Isabel winked.

With an effort he shook his head. 'No. Not at the moment.' He wanted to, of course he wanted to. He imagined the curves of her athletic body, the swell of her small breasts. He tore his gaze away.

'Suit yourself.' She shrugged. 'You know where I'll be.'

The door closed softly, leaving him both bereft and relieved. He went to the window and looked out at the familiar view, at the pastoral perfection of the landscape he had conceived, created and nurtured.

He covered his eyes and sobbed.

Chapter Twenty-Three

'How's it hanging, B?' Bola made sure his tone was airy and upbeat. Bernice was sitting at her workstation, toying with her smartphone. She glanced up and rewarded him with a wan smile.

'Didn't sleep so well, to be honest, Bola. Feel like death warmed up.'

Bola made a play of examining her from top to toe – well, as much of her as he could see, anyway. 'Looking A1 to me, B. Wish I looked as peng as that on one of my *good* days.'

'*Peng?* Oh God, Bola. Not you as well.'

'What?' He spread his hands in mock-innocence.

'All that *down-wiv-the-kidz-speak* in normal conversation. I despair.' She reprised the wan smile, slightly warmer this time.

'Gotta keep up, y'know.' He winked.

'Well, I don't have a clue what most youths under twenty are talking about these days, so you're way ahead of me.'

Bola was pleased he'd made her smile, but there was now no doubt in his mind. Something was up with B, and it wasn't good. Her next words confirmed his fears.

'Look, Bola, I have to pop out for an hour or two tomorrow,

late morning. I'll be as quick as I can, OK? I feel bad asking, but can you—'

'Cover for you?' He nodded. 'Sure. No worries. Anything I can help with?'

'Just keep Mr Dickhead off my scent, that's all.'

Bola grinned. 'My pleasure.' He sat at his workstation. 'How are you doing with the Szarkas' contacts?'

'Not as well as Schlesinger.' She jerked her head towards the young DC, who was typing at a speed that would put an executive secretary to shame. 'He's established the family tree back four generations. He's traced their parents' movements during and after the war. He's identified their first house in England – in Southampton, if you wanted to know – and why they eventually moved to Berkshire – the father got a new position as floor manager at Huntley & Palmers.'

'The biscuit people?'

'Yep. Reading's oldest claim to fame.'

'Oh? I thought that would be Reading Abbey, Henry VIII and all that?'

'Biscuits proved more popular.' This time, Bernice's smile was full and sincere.

'I guess.' Bola nodded sagely.

'Aha!' Schlesinger exclaimed, and they both looked over at him.

'What you got, fella?' Bola pushed his chair back.

Schlesinger sprang to his feet. He was clearly excited. 'Come and take a look.'

They went to Schlesinger's workstation. A grainy black and white photograph was displayed on his screen. It was from a local newspaper, the Reading Chronicle, and the photo was captioned: *Szarka piano quartet* and beneath it, in the usual left-to-right format, were the names of the quartet members. In small print was another name: *Leila Szarka. MD.*

Bola and Bernice exchanged glances.

'So that's Reyka.' Schlesinger jabbed the screen. 'Unusual to have an oboist in a piano quartet, but this was pretty innovative stuff apparently. And look, there's Marika – the pianist.'

'And Leila?' Bola leaned forward. 'No photo.'

Schlesinger sat back and ran his hand through his hair. 'Hang on.' He sat back down at the workstation and his fingers danced on the keyboard. Another photograph appeared. 'Here's another – at a live concert. Reading Town Hall, November 1983.'

The photograph was of the same quartet receiving post-performance applause. Standing beside the group was a stern-looking woman with her hands clasped beneath an ample bosom. The caption read: *Szarka piano quartet and musical director, Leila Szarka.*

'Ah – the mother.' Bola nodded. 'Died recently.'

'We can still get a third-party perspective on the Szarka's social habits via these two ladies.' He pointed out two serious-looking women cradling their instruments as though they were fragile infants.

'If they're still alive,' Bola said. 'It's an old photo.'

Schlesinger shrugged. 'Worth a shot. I mean, Reyka's still alive.'

'True,' Bola conceded. He turned to solicit Bernice's opinion, but she had drifted back to her workstation. She wasn't fully engaged, that was for sure. 'All right,' he told

Schlesinger, 'see if you can come up with an address or two. If you can, it's definitely worth paying a visit. Good job.' He made a fist and gave Schlesinger an encouraging bump. The young detective looked delighted. 'Let me know if you manage to track 'em down.'

'Sure. I will.' Schlesinger turned his attention back to his computer and his fingers recommenced their urgent patter. Bola left him to it.

Bernice was now absent from her workstation. Gone to the loo, or maybe having a break in the canteen? He wondered if he should mention his concerns to the guv. Not to Collingworth, no way. Bola sat down and pondered. Maybe he could offer to buy her a drink after work? No, she might misinterpret his intentions. He did, after all, have something of a reputation for the ladies.

After a while he decided that the best course of action – for the time being, anyway – would be to keep *schtum* and observe. But, then again, he wanted to know what was up. It might be something serious, something he could help resolve.

On impulse he went around to Bernice' workstation. She'd left her laptop unlocked. His eyes ran quickly over her desktop. He couldn't bring himself to open her email app – that would be an unforgivable invasion of privacy – but there were various other apps and documents grouped in typically neat rows on the desktop. Repressing a stab of guilt he guided the mouse across to a document entitled: *Notes re Szarkas.txt*. He glanced up, but there was no sign of Bernice. Schlesinger was absorbed in his research, and Tess and George were out somewhere. 'Sorry, B,' he muttered, and double-clicked the text file. With growing concern, he read:

Reyka Szarka – hands – nails

Guv – <u>Charnford</u> Abbey, 2010. Sergeant injured - crucifixion?

Simplicity – Johnny – old boy, <u>Charnford</u>. Link? Worth checking out.

The remainder of the short document contained summaries of the case briefings and task allocations. Bola closed the file and went back to his workstation. He drummed his fingers on the desk.

Johnny … Simplicity. Bola remembered the reticent young man from his only visit to Simplicity, when they had been searching for Isabel Akkerman, the MI6 agent – and murderer.

Plus a possible connection to Charnford Abbey.

And B hadn't mentioned it. *Any* of it.

Up to now he'd been concerned, but now he was worried.

Very worried.

'I want to bring the piano tuner in,' Collingworth said from the door of Moran's office.

Moran had been about to call the team together for a catch-up. 'Come in, acting sergeant.' He folded his arms. 'On what grounds?'

'Ability to access the property. An open toolbox at his place.'

'Motive?'

'I'll find one.'

Moran moistened his lips. He still felt mildly hungover, although he suspected the headache was more likely to be related to the fitful night's sleep he'd endured rather than the alcohol itself. He had tried to push Alice as far from his mind as possible, but snatches of their last conversation still intruded into his thoughts like clusters of steel barbs. For this reason, even Collingworth was a welcome distraction.

'DC Martin isn't quite as convinced, I believe?'

Collingworth sidestepped the matter of his subordinate's opinion. He placed his hands on the backrest of Moran's visitor's chair. 'What else have we got? None of the interviewees has motive, as far as we can establish. No motives *and* concrete alibis.'

'Does he drive?'

'What?'

'Does Potter drive?'

'I think so. Why?'

Moran related his conversation with Pauline Harris.

'Automotive grease?'

'Yes. And the Szarkas don't drive.'

'Right, right.' Collingworth pursed his lips and ran a finger across his cheek where his designer stubble was trimmed with great care and precision. 'I'll check it out.'

'I'm expecting an update regarding the composition and brand sometime today – or tomorrow, perhaps, depending on how the lab get on. They tell me it's an unusual compound, which may prove useful.'

'Yeah, it might.'

Moran ignored the note of doubt in Collingworth's response. 'So. Can you assemble the troops? Is everyone in?'

'Except McConnell.'

'Oh? When do you expect him back?'

'An hour ago. He's not on interviews – he's at lunch.'

Moran glanced at the time. Three thirty-six. Not lunch time. He kept his expression neutral in spite of the frisson of alarm that Collingworth's comment had triggered 'Right. Let's say four o'clock.'

'Four it is.' Collingworth departed with a brisk swagger.

Full of unease, Moran took another sip of water and tapped the empty plastic cup on the surface of the desk.

I hope you're not where I think you might be, George…

Chapter Twenty-Four

Moran's gut instinct about George's likely whereabouts would not let him rest. On his way out of Atlantic House he found Collingworth and told him to shift the catch-up to five o'clock. He didn't wait for a response.

The afternoon was cloudy and overcast, but for once the rain had held off. Moran pulled out onto the A33 and headed in the direction of the football stadium. The Atrium bar, part of an hotel complex next to the stadium, was the closest pub to Atlantic House, and only three minutes away by car. Moran knew that George had taken Tess there for a meal as a reward for enduring a football match when his team had come up against Reading FC at the start of the season. He'd also been known to take his lunch there during the working week. As he found a parking space, Moran hoped that food was the only thing on the Scot's menu today.

The bar was almost empty and for a moment Moran thought he'd got it wrong. Then he caught sight of a familiar figure tucked into a corner seat. He took a deep breath and approached the table. George looked up in surprise. 'Guv?'

'Hello, George.'

George had two glasses in front of him on the table. No food. The first glass was obviously water. The second was a chunky tumbler, half-filled with an amber liquid the composition of which required little imagination.

'May I?'

'Be my guest.' George indicated the empty seat.

'Is everything all right, George?' Moran sat down and summoned a waiter with a brief gesture.

'Not really,' George admitted. He looked at Moran. 'I haven't touched it.' He tapped the tumbler with his finger. 'I just need to know it's there.'

'George, you've done so well. Don't chuck it all away. Please.'

George sighed. 'I sometimes think, what's the point, you know? In abstinence, I mean. It doesn't make you any happier. It doesn't stop crap things happening.'

'No,' Moran agreed. 'But the other side of the coin isn't a better option. You *know* it isn't. It puts everything at risk. Job, health, relationships.'

'Relationships?' George laughed bitterly, shook his head.

'Right now, I'm struggling with mine,' Moran admitted. 'Or rather, with the end of mine – one that I thought might, finally, be an enduring one.'

'You and Alice?' George's mouth fell open. 'What's happened?'

Moran blew out his cheeks and sighed. 'I wish I knew. Well, I do know, I suppose; it's work – the new assignment. A bridge too far. Just when she thought she might get to see a little more of me. Bad timing, but what could I do?' He grimaced. 'I had no choice.'

'I'm sorry to hear that, guv.' George managed something akin to an encouraging smile. 'But I'm sure she'll come around. In time.'

'I wish I could share your optimism, George. But listen, I'm not here to talk about me.' He cocked an eyebrow.

'Och, I don't know what's happened with Tess.' George tapped his glass of water with a fingernail. 'She's not right, is all. She was better at your leaving do, seemed to come out of herself a wee bit that evening, but since then … well, she doesn't seem to want to engage. She was doing great – *we* were doing great – and then…' He trailed off.

George trailed off.

Moran said, 'She seems engaged with work all right. Almost to the point of overload.'

'Aye, that's what worries me. It's all she can think about.'

'What can I get you?' A waiter appeared at Moran's side.

'Just a still mineral water, please,' Moran told him. As the man retreated he said to George, 'Maybe the lesson for both of us is to stop fretting and give the ladies the space they need. Be there when they want us.'

'And what if they don't?'

'If they don't, they don't. These aren't things that can be forced.'

George sighed. 'Well that's cold comfort, guv, if you ask me.'

'Cold comfort's better than none at all, eh?' Moran winked but then became serious. 'Tess has been to Hell and back, George. I'm not surprised she's finding normal life a little overwhelming.'

George took a pull of water and grimaced. 'Bloody awful. Hate water. Tasteless.' He stroked his short beard. 'I suppose I just thought, you know, being together is being together. But every time I try to get under her skin, she cuts me off.' His hand strayed back to the whisky tumbler, flicked the glass with a forefinger.

'How about I take that back to the barman, George?' Moran looked at his watch. 'We've time for a coffee before the catch-up, if you fancy one?'

George hesitated, then withdrew his hand. 'Two sugars please, guv.' He watched impassively as Moran picked up the tumbler and got to his feet. 'And thank you,' he added, 'for coming to find me.'

Moran gave a brief nod and set off towards the bar.

When he came back, George had a question for him. 'I heard a rumour that wedding bells are ringing for DI Pepper?'

'Yes. I expect you'll get an invitation soon. It's all a bit of a rush – the wedding's next Saturday.'

'Next *Saturday*? Are you kidding?'

'Nope. Ness Bank Church, near Luscombe's home town.'

'I know it,' George said. 'But Saturday?' He narrowed his eyes. 'You don't suppose she's—'

Moran shook his head. 'I don't think that's the reason for the rush. I think it was just a spur of the moment decision. They don't want a long drawn-out period of preparation, they just want to get it done.'

'I'm happy for them,' George said. 'But at the same time…'

'I know,' Moran said. 'It's hard to see it all working out for another couple, while—'

'While we make a donkey's arse of the whole thing,' George finished for him.

Moran burst out laughing. 'Yes. Couldn't have put it better

myself – ah, here's the coffee.'

They sat in contemplative silence for a while. Moran stirred his Americano and George toyed with his teaspoon.

'George, there's something else I wanted to run past you,' Moran said eventually.

'Fire away.'

'Remember Isabel Akkerman?'

'The spook?'

Moran smiled grimly. 'Yep. The untouchable. She's back in the UK, so I've heard. Charlie had a tip-off.'

George blinked. 'What are you going to do?'

Moran sipped his coffee. 'They weren't expecting her to survive her last trip but it seems as though she beat the odds. To answer your question, though, I have no idea what I'm going to do. I have no power to extradite her from her MI6 immunity, but I'll be damned if I'm not going to give it my best shot.' He put his cup down. 'Would you have a think, George? Two heads, and all that?'

'Sure. Like you say, there must be something we can pin on her. Hate to think she'll get away with murder – literally.'

'I owe it to the memory of that poor girl she killed. To her family.'

George looked pensive. 'Laura, wasn't it?'

'Yes. Laura Witney.'

George shook his head slowly from side to side. 'It's the young ones that get to me. Lives cut off before they have a chance to get started.'

'Yes.' Moran nodded. 'Me too.'

George took a sharp breath. 'Well, I can't promise to come up with much, but I'll give it some serious thought.'

'Thanks, George. I appreciate it. Look, we'd better get back. Want a lift?'

'Aye.' George drained his coffee. 'That'd be grand, guv.'

Chapter Twenty-Five

Tess found a parking space and killed the engine. She checked the notes Schlesinger had compiled. *Mrs Verna Bazeley, 23 Salcombe Drive, Earley.* She squinted through the side window. Yep, number twenty-three, a tidy semi-detached property in this well-to-do suburb of Reading. Tess had volunteered to squeeze in a visit on her way home, and had confirmed a suitable time in a brief telephone conversation with Mrs Bazeley, who was keen to be interviewed and to provide whatever information might be useful to the investigation. *Profoundly shocked* were the words she had chosen regarding her friend and colleague's death.

Tess was shown into a comfortable sitting room with an ornate open fireplace and tastefully restrained decor. A music stand stood in the corner of the room by the bay window, and a low table beside it was piled high with printed manuscripts. A violin and bow were resting on a foldable stand beside the table. The violin looked old, but expensive. Noticing Tess's admiring gaze, Mrs Bazeley smiled. 'It's nice, isn't it? French. Nineteen-thirties, they tell me.'

Mrs Bazeley was a handsome woman in her late sixties with

long silver-grey hair held away from her face by a complicated arrangement of tortoiseshell clasps. She was wearing a long, floaty dress and a cream blouse. A necklace of mixed stones lay elegantly against her throat in the open V of her blouse. Tess found herself admiring Mrs Bazeley's stylish approach to sexagenarian fashion and made a mental note to attempt likewise if and when she attained the same age as her interviewee.

'It's good of you to see me at such short notice, Mrs Bazeley,' Tess began.

'My pleasure. Such an awful thing to happen. I can hardly believe it. Marika was a dear lady.'

'Tell me, how long have you known the Szarka sisters?'

'Oh, let me see.' Mrs Bazeley turned her eyes upward to the ceiling. 'I'd say … fifteen years or so, perhaps? We moved to Earley in 2006 and it took me a while to settle, to find my musical niche, as it were. Yes, it would have been sometime around 2008. I found Reyka and Marika through an online group – or rather my late husband did. I sent them a message and before I knew it we were a quartet!'

'There was another lady involved, I believe? In the quartet?' Tess consulted the notes she had made at Fedelma Goosens' house. 'A Mrs Moira Seymour?'

'Ah, Moira.' Mrs Bazeley looked down at the carpet and gave a little sigh. When she looked up again Tess detected a glaze of moisture in her eyes. 'Such a lovely woman. We became good friends. But … cancer, I'm sad to say. It was over in weeks. Liver.' She gave a little shudder. 'But when you get to our age – well, these things are to be expected.'

'I'm sorry to hear that,' Tess said. 'So, you didn't continue to play together after Mrs Seymour's passing?'

'Not in the same way, no. But I did maintain contact with Reyka and Marika. They are very keen on composition, and I was able to help them with that, but only on the odd occasion.'

Tess took out the prints of the photographs Schlesinger had found. 'I think this might be a little before your time, but I wondered if you knew any of these ladies? Marika and Reyka are there – and their mother, too, in this one.' She handed the photograph to Mrs Bazeley who donned a pair of half-moon spectacles and peered carefully at the image.

'Don't they look young? My goodness. And that's their mother? She looks rather ferocious, doesn't she!' She tapped the photograph. 'Now this lady here, Jean Harrington, Marika did talk to me about her. She was a little older than the sisters, and I believe she retired from playing – arthritis or some such ailment. But I remember Marika speaking highly of her.'

'Do you know where I might find her?'

'I'm sorry, I have no idea if she's alive or dead. She must be in her eighties now, at the very least. You might try the local nursing homes. But why would you need to visit her?'

'We're just trying to build up a picture of the sisters' social and musical activities, Mrs Bazeley. Did anything strike you about the sisters, personality-wise? Did they get on well? Would they have made any enemies, for any reason you can think of?'

'Enemies? Goodness, I doubt it. Reyka could be quite fiery, but Marika was just the sweetest thing. There were minor quarrels, disagreements about the music from time to time, of course. That's only to be expected. But that's all.' She paused. 'That's why this is so hard to understand. I mean, who would *do* something like this?' She worried her long fingers and furrowed her brow. 'Did … did Marika suffer at all? Was it a terrible end for her?'

Moran had been specific about keeping the full extent of the crime under wraps, and especially from the press; sensational headlines would be bound to bring forth the usual plethora of crazies and red herring calls. Here, however, Tess felt that she could be truthful without mentioning Marika's injuries since her death was caused not by the wounds on her hands, but by cardiac arrest. She shook her head. 'Ms Szarka wouldn't have known much about it,' she said. 'Please don't distress yourself.'

'Well that's some comfort, I suppose.'

Tess had debated whether or not to pose her next question but in the end decided it was probably best to ask, just so she had it covered. 'What about … male admirers?'

'Boyfriends?' Mrs Bazeley smiled and shook her head. 'Dear me, I don't think so. The sisters were immersed in their music. I don't remember much talk of male company at all.'

'OK, that's fine – I just thought I'd better ask.' Tess closed her notebook. 'Mrs Bazeley, you've been very helpful. I'll leave you in peace.' Tess stood up and extended her hand.

Mrs Bazeley rose elegantly to her feet and clasped it warmly. 'Goodness, it's nice to have a young person to talk to these days.' She smiled. 'Think nothing of it. It was my pleasure. I hope you find out who did this terrible thing.'

'We will, Mrs Bazeley. I promise you, we will.'

Tess drove slowly home, turning over in her mind everything Verna Bazeley had said. It seemed clear to her that the sisters' contemporary acquaintances could offer little to help unearth any skeletons in the Szarka closet, and Tess felt strongly that they needed to go further back in time to unravel the mystery.

She was still mulling it over as she let herself into her apartment. The Szarkas' mother was dead, but the woman Mrs Bazeley had mentioned, the older musician, Jean Harrington, might well still be alive. And if so, she was definitely the next on Tess's list.

After the catch-up briefing, Moran found that he didn't want to go home. He lingered in the office, his thoughts flitting between the Szarka murder, the intractable problem of Isabel Akkerman, and last, but by no means least, Alice and their recent conversation. They fluttered about in his head like a pigeon trapped in a chimney. He went to the window and looked out at the rush hour traffic, tried to nudge his weary brain back into its usual mode of logical, ordered deliberation. First, the Szarkas. Collingworth was convinced that the piano man, Potter, was a potential candidate. Bola wanted to re-interview one of the student's husbands – primarily, Moran reckoned, on the grounds that the guy had a bad attitude and not much else. Apart from the automotive grease lab report, they hadn't much else to go on. Higginson wanted a quick resolution and so did Moran, but it wasn't going to happen.

And Akkerman. She was like St Paul's thorn in the flesh – always in the back of his mind, always nagging. She was unfinished business, but he couldn't see how he could make any inroads into bringing her to justice. The fact that she was a free agent, here in the UK, made him angry – no, it made him *furious*. He didn't care how many others she'd killed for King and country; the fact was she'd also taken two innocent lives, and those were the ones he knew about.

There was one more irritant at the very back of his mind, and that was Sheila Dawson's threat. Moran wiped condensation from the window with his fingers and shivered. She was upset, understandably, and not thinking straight. Once she'd had the time and space to consider things more rationally, surely she'd realise that her accusation was groundless? How could he be blamed for her husband's accident? Nevertheless, her threat rankled. With everything else that was going on, it was something he could well do without.

He returned to his desk. Tomorrow he'd pay Pauline Harris a visit; he'd half-expected a call during the afternoon, but the boffins were obviously still working on potential matches. He was encouraged by Harris' revelation that the grease was an unusual mixture of chemicals, but at the same time worried that it might prove a fruitless discovery; the grease had yet to be matched to a potential perpetrator.

He took his coat from the chair back and switched off the light. George was still at his desk, as was the new lad, Schlesinger. Tess was out on a call. Collingworth was probably in the process of towing Potter's car away for forensic analysis. There was no sign of DC Swinhoe or Bola. He called a brief goodnight on his way to the lift but the late workers were too absorbed in their tasks to respond.

Chapter Twenty-Six

Tess was awake early, her mind spinning like a gyroscope. She swung out of bed and drew back the curtains to be greeted by a sky of solid blue. Not a cloud in the sky. It was an omen, surely?

Encouraged, she grabbed her laptop and went through to the tiny kitchen to make herself a mint tea. Since her illness she'd avoided tea and coffee – they seemed to give her headaches, or if she already had a headache at the time, which was fairly often, they made it worse. She'd grown accustomed to herbal teas and had settled on mint as a favourite. It freshened her mouth in the morning and eased her into the day just as effectively as coffee had done in the past. She was pleased not to be addicted to any substance; it felt liberating, clean and wholesome.

Sipping the hot liquid, she began her search. *Jean Harrington, musician, violin, UK*. Google duly served up several pages of irrelevant information. All the Jean Harringtons were partial matches, all irrelevant. Tess tutted, retried with *Jean Harrington string quartet Szarka*. She scrolled down the page.

There.

Reading Chronicle – violinist retires from acclaimed local string quartet
Tess clicked.

She read the short article, jotted down the details. Harrington had retired, as Mrs Bazeley had suggested, due to rheumatoid arthritis in her fingers. She read on: '*Harrington, of Glebe Road, Reading, expressed her regret at having to stand down…*'

Glebe Road. She knew it; it was a relatively short road near Northumberland Avenue. She gulped her mint tea, went through to the bedroom and threw on a navy blue skirt, a fresh work blouse and her tan leather jacket. She tied her hair back and, pausing only to give her teeth a quick brush and floss, grabbed her car keys and went out.

It took over half an hour to fight her way through the traffic, and another five minutes to find somewhere to park. She checked the time. Just after eight. Not the best time to call unannounced, but Tess was feeling optimistic. Maybe her buoyant mood was just a product of the clear skies above, but whatever the reason she intended to capitalise on it.

She stood at one end of the street and calculated how long it would take her to call on each property. Too long, probably, but then again, she might get lucky and choose the right house straight away. She began with the nearest. There was no response to her knock. Undaunted, she proceeded to the next. A flustered woman told her she'd never heard of Jean Harrington, and that she was running late for work. Tess apologised and moved on. She drew a blank at the next house, and the one after that.

Twenty minutes later she'd called at every house on one side of the street with no luck at all. Frustrated, she tapped her foot on the pavement and checked her phone. No missed calls. She looked down the row of houses on the other side. Was this a wild goose chase? Jean Harrington had probably not lived here for years. She might even have passed away.

Two houses later her luck changed. The elderly man on the threshold of number 17 nodded in affirmation in answer to Tess's question.

'Mrs Harrington? Yes, yes. We bought the house from her in … oh, it must be, let's see…'

'2004, Alec.' A female voice filled the hallway, and a stout woman in an apron appeared at the man's side. 'How can we help?' she beamed. Her cheeks were red from some domestic exertion, and she wiped her hands on the apron as she waited for Tess to reply.

Tess explained, and the woman nodded. 'She was a nice lady. Had trouble with her hands, Alec, that's right, isn't it? I believe she was planning to stay at a relative's house and then eventually move into residential care.'

'Do you recall if she left a forwarding address?' Tess almost held her breath as the couple conferred.

'Let me check the drawer,' the woman said after an inconclusive conversation with her husband. 'I'm sure we must have had to begin with. I remember receiving a few letters for her after we'd moved in. I must have sent them on.'

She disappeared into the house and Tess chatted with the husband. He was an amiable, gentle man with the air of someone accustomed to carving a quiet niche for himself on the fringes of his wife's bustling activity. After a few minutes the wife returned with a telephone pad and a look of triumph. 'Here we are. I always say to Alec, "We might need this one day, so best keep it safe."' She glanced affectionately at her husband who made a quiet murmur of acquiescence. 'Harrington, Jean (prev. owner),' she read. 'Here you are.' She passed the book to Tess with a triumphant flourish.

'Thanks, that's great.' Tess made a note of the address and telephone number. 'I really appreciate your help.'

'Our pleasure, isn't it, Alec?'

'Indeed,' Alec said.

'I hope you find your culprit, whatever he's done.' Alec's wife folded her arms.

'And I hope Mrs Harrington hasn't got herself into trouble,' Alec added, a look of mild concern creasing his forehead.

'Don't be silly, Alec. What could Mrs Harrington have done? She's an old lady.'

'It's not Mrs Harrington we're after, don't worry.' Tess smiled. 'But knowing where she might be could help us find the person we're looking for.'

'Well, that's a relief,' Alec said.

'Sorry to have disturbed you.' Tess slipped her notebook into her jacket pocket.

'Not at all,' Alec said. 'Mind how you go now, young lady.'

Tess returned to the car, touched by the elderly man's concern. Decent people still existed, if you were patient enough to seek them out.

She set off for Atlantic House with a light heart, pleased with her morning's work.

'Later,' Collingworth said. 'After you've checked out ANPR for Potter's vehicle's movements – forty-eight hours before and after, got it? If he was anywhere near, I want to know about it.'

Tess held herself in check. 'Have they found any trace of

anything suspicious in the car so far?'

'Not as yet, but that doesn't mean they won't. And you were late this morning, by the way. Good job briefing's been put back till eleven.'

'I was working.' Tess was seething now. 'And I think I have a useful contact.'

'Think away. ANPR first.' Collingworth walked off.

Tess stayed where she was, motionless, trying to calm herself. Collingworth was an idiot. An oaf. He was like a horse wearing blinkers; he just didn't have the breadth of vision to cover all the shifts and changes of an investigation. Should she go over his head, talk to the guv? No, that'd just add fuel to the fire. But her contact needed checking out. What if it turned up something useful, or critical, even?

As she deliberated, Bola came into view carrying a cup of coffee and a paper bag. 'Aha. Morning. How are you feeling today?'

'Annoyed, frankly,' Tess said.

'Don't tell me – our great captain and commander wound you up again?'

'You guessed it.'

'Want to talk about it?'

Tess exhaled slowly. 'Sure, why not?'

'Come on, then. Canteen's quiet for a change.'

Bola led the way back to the canteen and chose a spot some distance from the only other occupied table. He placed his breakfast items carefully on the table top. 'What can I get you?'

'A mint tea, please. Thanks, Bola.'

'That won't hold body and soul together for long. Sandwich? Sausage roll?'

'I'm good, really.'

'OK.' Bola looked doubtful. 'Mint tea it is.'

She watched Bola's familiar lope to the counter. He was a good guy. She trusted his instincts, and his advice was usually solid. Sure, he'd had his past indiscretions, but who hadn't? The guv trusted him too, and that was an endorsement in itself.

She took a breath and tried to settle herself. Collingworth was hard work. Insensitive. How had he passed his sergeant's exam and interviews? Tess grudgingly conceded that Collingworth presented well – when it suited him. Anyway, it was no use fretting about her colleague's temporary elevation. They were stuck with him for now, and they'd all just have to get on with it.

'Here you go. Smells awful, but whatever.' Bola set down a mug with a mint teabag colouring the boiling water a greenish hue.

'It's good for you. You should try it.'

'Nah. Caffeine man through and through, me.' He flashed her a wide smile. From the paper bag he extracted a cheese roll and a buttered bun, smoothed the bag with the palm of his hand, and placed the items carefully on top. 'So,' he said, 'what's the problem?'

Tess dunked the teabag with her teaspoon. 'Apart from a severe personality clash?'

'Yeah, well, we all have that.'

She smiled ruefully. 'I suppose.' She fished out the teabag and dropped it onto a side plate that hadn't yet been cleared from the table. 'I was in a really good mood until I got here. I called in on one of the quartet contacts Schlesinger dug up yesterday, and from there I got an address and phone number for one of the older ladies involved in the Szarka musical setup from years ago. I think she could help us get a clearer picture of the sisters, but Sergeant Bonehead wants me to waste time checking ANPR for Potter, the piano tuner.'

Bola nodded sympathetically. 'I get your point. I can do a little ANPR research, if you want to follow your musical lead. I'm planning to revisit our friend the evasive husband sometime today, but I can leave that till this afternoon.'

'Would you, Bola? I really appreciate that.'

'I'll mail you anything I find, in case you-know-who asks any questions – you can update him.'

'You're an angel.'

'Funny shape for an angel, but OK, if you say so.' He grinned.

'I do.' Tess sipped the mint tea, winced and blew over the top of the mug.

'Mind if I ask you a personal question?' Bola took a bite from his buttered bun.

'Sure.'

'How are you and George doing?'

'Ah.' Tess dropped her gaze to the table top.

'You don't have to tell me if you don't want to.' Bola munched his bun. 'That's fine. I just wanted to make sure you were OK, that's all.'

'That's kind, Bola. Truth of the matter is that I don't really know. Recently I just feel … I don't know, like I need some space. Maybe it's to process what happened, try to come to terms with those lost months. George is sweet but…'

'He's too in your face.'

'Yeah. In a way, maybe. I mean, I'm fond of him. I don't want to hurt him. We get on really well, but…'

'Have you thought about taking a sabbatical? You know, just six months on your own, just you and the wild blue yonder, that kind of thing? It might give you the headspace you need to think it all through.'

'Oh, Bola. I can't tell you how many times I've wished I could just take off somewhere and … I don't know, just be me. Do nothing. Walk, swim, visit places, you know? But I feel so guilty. I've only just come back.'

'Maybe it wasn't quite the right time to come back?' Bola finished his bun with an appreciative smack of his lips and moved onto the cheese roll.

'Yeah. Maybe it wasn't.'

Bola raised his free hand. 'Hey, I'm not saying you can't do the job – don't get me wrong.'

'I know. I know you're not.'

'So. Talk to the guv. Sabbaticals are commonplace these days – and no one could argue that you're not a prime candidate for taking one.'

Tess reached across the table and patted Bola's hand. 'You're a good friend, Bola. Maybe I'll do that. When this case is over, maybe I will.'

'George'll get it,' he reassured her. 'He'll understand.'

As Bola made short work of the remainder of the cheese roll, she sipped her tea and thought about George's anxious and regular enquiries as to her wellbeing. A sabbatical. Would he get it?

Somehow, she doubted it.

Chapter Twenty-Seven

Bernice tried to calm herself as she motored along the main road towards Horsham. Alastair's text had been terse, short to the point of rudeness. She put it down to his mental state – if he was struggling mentally, well, that was hardly surprising. He'd killed someone. Someone he cared about. And he'd have to live with that for the rest of his life.

And if she continued to play along with his deception, so would she.

Over the past twenty-four hours she'd come so close to reporting the murder. She'd seen herself knocking on Moran's door, sitting down to face the guv and confessing all. It had been a comfort to imagine Moran's kindly response, his empathetic reaction, and to fantasise about the relief of being able, finally, to unburden herself, whatever the consequences.

But she hadn't. The lure of Simplicity and her affection for Alastair had proved the stronger impulse. She was well aware that the longer it went on, the longer she remained silent, the more she would distance herself from any possibility of redemption.

So today was make or break day. Whatever had prompted

Alastair to summon her would clarify her intentions. Whatever he had to say would form the basis of her decision. Bernice felt for the water bottle beside her, unclipped the lid and took a long pull. Her satnav told her she was ten minutes away. Ten minutes until a life-changing decision had to be made.

No pressure, then.

She passed through the familiar gateposts and parked in her usual spot. She locked the car and breathed deeply. The air tasted the same. The vista was the same, smoke rising lazily from one or two chimneys, a few folk out and about or working their gardens. And the big house, majestic, heavy stones piled upon heavy stones. The imposing steps to the front door. Everything was the same.

And yet everything had changed.

The front door opened as she approached, and Alastair was there. He raised his hand in greeting but there was something about his demeanour that set alarm bells ringing. This was not the man who had intrigued her with his assured, yogic grace and confident, articulate conversation. This was a shadow of the man who had shown them around the site and led her and Bola to Isabel Akkerman's cabin all those months ago.

'B. Good to see you.'

His voice was flat, devoid of emotion. A frisson of panic rose in her gut. Something was wrong – badly wrong.

'Hello. I was worried,' she began. 'You sounded strange … your text…'

'I'm sorry, Bernice.'

His body language reignited her anxiety. It didn't sound as though he was apologising for the terseness of his text, but for something more weighty –perhaps even for something that was about to happen.

'Come in.' He stood aside.

She entered the house and heard the door shut behind her. There was an atmosphere of tension, of something lying in wait.

'Come upstairs.' Alastair beckoned and set off up the main staircase.

She followed him, her heart thumping in time with her footsteps. 'What's wrong, Alastair? What is it?' She addressed the back of his T-shirt, beneath which his toned muscles moved like miniature tectonic plates as he climbed.

'I'll explain in a moment.'

They walked along the gallery towards his office. She half-expected Johnny to appear with a tray of refreshments as he had done on her early visits, but of course she knew that that was impossible. Johnny was gone.

Alastair opened his office door and, once again, stood aside and ushered her inside.

She went in and stopped dead.

A woman was seated at Alastair's desk. She rose to her feet with a wide smile and brought her hands together in the universal sign of reverence and respect. 'Bernice.' The voice was deep and mellow. 'How nice to finally meet you.'

Bernice hesitated and glanced at Alastair in the hope that he would make some kind of introduction. The woman looked Chinese, or Malay perhaps, but her accent was pure English middle class. It took a few seconds for Bernice to put two and two together and the realisation was accompanied by a jolt of fear.

This was Isabel Akkerman, the woman with multiple

passports, the woman whose cabin she had searched with Bola.

'You're Isabel.'

'Among other things, I suppose I am, yes.' Isabel walked around the desk and came right up to her. 'Hm. You're quite pretty. I understand that you and Alastair have been getting on like – what was it you said, Alastair? A house on fire?'

Bernice was rooted to the spot. She had no idea what was going on, or what Akkerman's presence might imply. She glanced at Alastair, but his expression revealed nothing. It seemed he had assumed the role of a passive onlooker, with Akkerman clearly in charge of the situation.

'What's this about?' Bernice stood her ground. Her heart was pounding, but she wasn't going to be intimidated.

'I'll tell you, dear girl.' Isabel returned to the desk and opened a drawer. 'But I'm not sure you're going to like it very much. Take a look at these.'

Bernice went to the desk and looked at the photographic prints Isabel had placed on its leather surface.

'Go on. Take a peep.' Isabel sat back down in Alastair's chair, crossing one shapely leg over the other.

Bernice picked up the first print. It was an image of Johnny's body lying by the poolside. Bernice was crouched beside it, looking towards the camera. She remembered catching a glimpse of someone at the window; just a flash, just a moment…

She hadn't imagined it. Isabel had witnessed and recorded the whole episode.

Bernice swallowed hard and picked up the remaining photos. They were all of her, and the last was particularly damning, showing her standing over the body, fists bunched at her sides, her expression hard, angry-looking.

'Good, aren't they?' Isabel steepled her hands. 'Glad I was around to capture the moment.'

Bernice looked at Alastair but found no comfort in his dejected expression.

'You're going to be a good girl and provide me with a little assistance, Bernice. And I'll be very much obliged.'

'What kind of assistance?' Bernice's mouth was dry. 'And I'm DC Swinhoe to you.' There was little consolation in reminding this woman that she was addressing a police officer; Bernice knew she was caught in Akkerman's trap, whatever that might involve.

'A police officer.' Isabel let the words hang in the air. 'Now then, I'm not sure a serving police officer would aid and abet a murder. What do you think?'

Before Bernice could formulate a reply, Isabel went on. 'Or maybe even *commit* a murder? I mean, after all, that's what these photographs appear to show. And what happened to the body, mm? I bet the coroner doesn't know anything about it.'

Now Bernice understood how completely she'd been caught. She dropped the photos on the desk.

'One makes very few friends in my line of work, *DC Swinhoe.*' Isabel leaned back in the chair and examined her nails. 'But one does find that one has made a good few enemies. And the old adage always applies – you know the one? *Keep your friends close, but your enemies closer.*'

'I'm not sure I understand. What is it you want from me?'

'Your boss, the Irish fellow. You see, DC Swinhoe, I know when I've made an enemy – I could see it in his eyes.'

'DCI Moran? He's retired.'

'Oh? I heard on the grapevine he'd been recalled.'

Bernice said nothing.

'Well, he has, hasn't he? And you're working under him on the new homicide – sorry, *murder*. I forget I'm not in the US, sometimes.'

'I still don't understand what you're getting at.'

'DCI Moran is one of those tiresome individuals who thinks they'll be able to … what's the term? Oh, yes, *bring me to justice.*'

'I'm sorry, but I have no idea what DCI Moran's intentions might be.'

'No? Well, that's going to change because *you*, DC Swinhoe, are going to find out exactly what your boss's intentions are, vis-à-vis yours truly.'

'You want me to be your undercover informer.'

A look towards Alastair. 'She *is* a bright girl, isn't she?'

Alastair spoke up at last. 'Look, Bernice – B – I'm so sorry. I had no idea this—'

Isabel chortled. '*B*? How charming. Pet names already?'

'I'm sorry, B. I really am.'

Bernice turned on Alastair, anger welling up inside her, an eruption of bottled-up emotion. She heard herself shouting, screaming, at him. 'Sorry? *Sorry*? First you make me promise to keep quiet about Johnny, which makes me an accomplice. Then *this*? You're going to let her do *this* to me? You *bastard*!'

'Now, now. Let's calm down, shall we?' Isabel gave a languid wave. 'It's not as bad as it sounds, DC Swinhoe. Just keep me abreast of your guv'nor's thought processes concerning myself, and all will be well. If nothing happens then…' She made a dismissive gesture. 'All of this might just go away.' She smiled. 'Storm in a teacup. Who knows?'

'And if I don't do what you want?'

Isabel made a chagrined face. 'I'd be very disappointed, DC Swinhoe. And the photographs, well … they'll take some explaining, won't they?'

Bernice took a gulp of air. Her throat was parched. 'Alastair, you'll tell the truth, won't you? You won't let me take the rap?' She fought to keep the desperation from her voice.

Alastair couldn't meet her eye.

'You can go now,' Isabel said. 'And remember. The slightest hint that your guv'nor is formulating some move against me, or even if you hear something from anyone else that you consider to be pertinent, I want to know. And if you fail to comply, if I find that plans have been laid which you were party to or even aware of, then I, or Alastair, will make these public.' She tapped the photos with her fingernail.

'Alastair? You wouldn't accuse me of murder, would you? Please tell me you wouldn't…'

Alastair looked down at his shoes. His silence roared through her like a hurricane.

'Cheerio, then. Drive safely.' Isabel shooed her away with a dismissive gesture.

Stunned and shaking, Bernice left the room and returned to her car. She sat motionless for a full ten minutes before she found the wherewithal to turn the key in the ignition and drive away.

Chapter Twenty-Eight

Bola kept a close eye on Collingworth as the morning progressed. Fortunately the acting sergeant was more preoccupied with stripping Potter's car than checking up on his staff, and consequently Bola hadn't yet been obliged to provide excuses or resort to dissembling in order to cover for his colleagues' unsanctioned activities. Tess had the bit jammed firmly between her teeth and her contact, if traceable, quite clearly had potential. As for Bernice, though … he didn't know the reason for her latest absence, and she was the one giving him cause for worry. There was a fine line between a listening ear and a desire to pry and, although his curiosity had threatened to get the better of him on more than one occasion, it was a line he didn't want to cross. He could only hope that she would do whatever she needed to do and return to the fold asap.

But in the end Bola found he couldn't concentrate on his work. He couldn't keep his concerns under wraps any longer; Bernice might be in danger – or they might even miss something significant because of her clandestine behaviour.

You know what you've got to do, Bola…

He locked his laptop and went to find the guv.

As he left the guv's office, Bola felt a strong sense of relief. Moran had listened to what he had to say and assured him that he'd done the right thing by sharing his concerns. Bola had taken Moran's parting words on board – 'Leave it with me, DC Odunsi. I'll have a think about how to tackle this.' He could trust the guv to do the right thing, and Bernice would understand –maybe not at first, but eventually – why he felt he'd had no choice.

It was coming up to lunchtime and he was scheduled to have another chat with Mr Brooks, Miss Manning's unsupportive husband. There was something about the guy that didn't add up. Bola prided himself on sniffing out when someone was withholding or hiding information, and if Brooks wasn't sitting on something illegal he'd be very surprised. Even if it was unrelated to the Szarka case, there was something lurking beneath the surface of the Brooks household just waiting to be uncovered. Miss Manning herself seemed almost too sugary, too twee to be real. She was unquestionably under Brooks' thumb; the spectre of domestic abuse was a distinct possibility, but as far as Bola had been able to determine, Manning had been unmarked.

Of course, abuse could take multiple forms, and physical abuse was just one of many possibilities. Psychological scars were harder to spot, and even when they were brought to light the sufferer often refused to press charges or take sides against the perpetrator. Mistreatment was always a tricky proposition, but this morning Bola was in the right mood to tough it out, and in this positive frame of mind he threw his coat on and made his way down to the car park.

The nursing home was tucked away in a side street about a half-mile from the town centre. Tess pressed the buzzer and waited impatiently for someone to open the door. She was on a roll. The address given to her by Alec and his wife in Glebe Road had still been occupied by the family who had taken Jean in for three years before her eventual departure to Abbey Court Nursing Home. Moreover, they had been in contact with Jean just a few months earlier and despite her advanced age they had found her in good health. As she waited Tess muttered a silent prayer that that would still be the case.

'Hello. Can I help?' A uniformed care worker opened the door and looked her up and down. Tess showed her warrant card.

'Mrs Harrington? Goodness, what's Jean been up to?'

'Nothing at all,' Tess reassured her. 'I just have a few questions for her about a family she used to know.'

'I see. Well, come in – if I can ask you to sign the visitor's book, just there. That's it. Now then, Jean's in the day room. She's been a bit sleepy this morning, but I'm sure she'll perk up when she realises she has a visitor. I'll bring tea – or would you prefer coffee?'

'A fruit tea, if you have one. Thank you.'

'Jean's mad on Earl Grey,' the care worker said over her shoulder as Tess followed her past the reception desk and along a wide, wheelchair-friendly corridor. Handrails had been installed along the corridor's length to assist the more physically challenged residents. Tess found herself shallow-breathing to alleviate the strong scent of micturition that always seemed to be a permanent feature of residential care. The accompanying combined scents of boiled vegetables and some cloyingly sweet air freshener made the overheated atmosphere even more challenging and Tess prayed that Mrs Harrington's location in the day room might be situated near a window that opened.

They overtook an old lady making laborious progress with the aid of a Zimmer frame. 'That's it, Barbara.' The care worker raised her voice. 'You're doing great. That's my girl.'

Tess smiled at the old lady as they passed but received no response. The woman's head was bent down, all her energy focused on taking the next painful step forward.

This could be you one day, Tess …

The day room was wide and bright. Several residents were sitting in armchairs, mostly women apart from a solitary man in a green cardigan and beige trousers sitting on his own reading a newspaper. A television on a tall stand was broadcasting some daytime chat show on low volume, although no one seemed to be paying any attention to it. The care worker took her over to a group of three ladies seated by a window which, Tess noticed with dismay, was locked firmly shut.

'This is Mrs Harrington,' the care worker said to Tess. And then, again in a slightly raised voice, 'Jean, you have a visitor. A nice young lady detective.'

Jean Harrington looked up. She had obviously been dozing and looked a little disoriented. 'Oh. How lovely.'

'I'll make your tea,' the care worker smiled. 'I hope you have a nice chat.'

'Hello, Mrs Harrington. I'm sorry to visit unannounced,'

Tess began. 'I do hope you'll forgive me. My name is DC Tess Martin from Thames Valley Police. I wanted to ask you about some musical colleagues of yours, the Szarka sisters – and their mother, if you remember her.'

'Marika and Reyka? And Leila?' Jean Harrington's eyes widened.

Tess could see that in her youth Mrs Harrington would have been an attractive, if not beautiful, woman. Her eyes were grey and clear and her face was remarkably unlined for a woman in her nineties. 'You remember them?' Tess felt a shiver of anticipation.

'Oh *yes*. We had some wonderful times together.' She gave a small cough. 'Excuse me. But what have they done to attract the attention of the police?'

'Nothing at all.' Tess laid her hand on Mrs Harrington's arm. 'So you mustn't worry. I'm just trying to find out a little more about them. About their friends and colleagues.' Tess hesitated. Should she come clean and mention Marika's murder? She didn't want to cause any distress.

'Something's happened, hasn't it? Something bad.'

'Turn the damn thing off!' The man in the green cardigan was on his feet. He had discarded his newspaper and was shaking his fist at the television screen, appealing to the other residents. 'Why do we have to watch this drivel? No one's remotely interested. I know I'm not. Bloody distraction, that's all it is.'

With that he sat down again, retrieved his newspaper and continued to read.

'Never mind Bill,' Mrs Harrington said. 'He always gets cross about the TV.'

The care worker returned with a tray. 'One chamomile tea, one Earl Grey. I assumed no sugar.'

'That's right.' Tess took the mug. 'Thank you.'

The care worker found the TV remote and switched it off on her way out. 'There we are, Bill,' she said in a tone that implied a regular repetition of the scenario. 'All off now.'

Tess passed Mrs Harrington her tea. 'Shall I stir it for you?'

'No need. Kathy will have brewed it nicely for me,' she replied. 'She always does. She's a sweetie.' Mrs Harrington took the cup and saucer and balanced her beverage in her lap. Her hand was quite steady. 'Now then. Are you going to tell me what you're here for? Please don't treat me as though I need to be cosseted. I'm quite robust, you know. We oldies lived through a world war, after all.'

Tess smiled. 'Of course.'

'I'm all ears.' Jean Harrington leaned forward. 'We don't get much excitement in here.'

'There's no easy way to say this, Mrs Harrington. I'm afraid it's Marika, I'm sorry to say that she was murdered.'

Mrs Harrington leaned back in surprise. 'Murdered? Well, I wasn't expecting that, I must say. Poor Marika.' She stirred her tea with a steady hand.

'I wondered if you might remember anything about the sisters, their mother. Anything that might help us. Did they all get on? I mean in your musical circle, at the time?'

Mrs Harrington didn't reply straight away, but closed her eyes and rested her head on the antimacassar. She was silent for so long that Tess thought she might have drifted off into another doze, but as Tess was considering how best to awaken her without causing alarm, her eyes opened and she began to speak.

'The mother, Leila, she was the driving force. She worked her daughters hard – right from the beginning. I first met them when they were much older, of course, but Marika used to confide in me about their practice regime – how hard they were made to work. There was a tutor, I forget the name now, an old school musician who was a stickler for accuracy. Marika was always nervous before her lessons, but, dear me, she needn't have worried.'

'Oh? Why was that?' Tess asked, pleased that Mrs Harrington could recall conversations from such a long time ago. She was all there mentally, that was for sure.

'Why shouldn't she have worried? Well, it's quite simple; Marika was one of the most talented pianists I ever had the pleasure of playing with. She rarely made an error – in fact I can't remember even one, in rehearsal or performance.' Mrs Harrington paused and closed her eyes a second time. Tess waited patiently for her to gather her memories. One of the seated ladies began to sing in a low, tuneless voice that sounded like a lament, and Tess wondered if she ought to go and comfort her or ask if she wanted anything to drink, even just distract her from whatever it was that was causing her such mental anguish. Just as she was about to get up, however, Mrs Harrington opened her eyes and went on.

'Reyka wasn't as blessed with natural talent, you see. She tried and tried but it was no use. I think her mother despaired of her ever becoming a competent pianist. I don't know why she was made to continue for so long before she was allowed to change instruments; things were so much better after that.'

Tess was forming a new question when her mobile rang. Her

heart sank. It was Collingworth. 'Excuse me, I need to answer this.'

'Of course,' Mrs Harrington said. 'I'll still be here, don't worry.'

Tess went out to the corridor. 'DC Martin.'

'Where are you?'

'I'm interviewing a Mrs Harrington. She remembers the Szarkas well from back in the day.'

'That's not what I asked you to do.'

'No, but…'

'Exactly, no buts. Get your arse back here. Now.'

Tess ended the call and returned to the day room. *What happened, Bola? You were supposed to cover for me…*'

'I'm sorry, Mrs Harrington, but I'm needed elsewhere. Thank you for talking to me. Can I come back soon, so we can chat a little more?'

'I'd be delighted.' Mrs Harrington smiled. 'I'll be able to have a good think about Reyka and Marika in the meantime. So sad…' She shook her head. 'A delightful lady.'

Tess briefly rested her hand on Mrs Harrington's shoulder. 'You've been very helpful. I'll see you soon – I hope.'

Chapter Twenty-Nine

Moran's day had begun with the unexpected, and looked to be continuing in the same vein. He'd scarcely taken his coat off when there'd been a knock on his door. Bola's expression had been all anxiety, and what he'd had to say had transferred much of the same to Moran.

The ghost of the Charnford Abbey murders had apparently risen in the shape of an ex-pupil known to DC Swinhoe via her contact at the Simplicity commune in Sussex. Bola had discovered – he had not specified exactly how – that Bernice had pencilled a possible connection between this same pupil and the Szarka murder. He'd gone on to confirm that there was no *known* link – so far as he was aware – between the Szarkas and this ex-pupil, save for the perpetrator's MO, i.e. that the murder had featured the penetration of the hands with nails.

It was a long shot. The pupil may or may not have been aware of the events surrounding the death of the Abbot and the injuries sustained at the time by the late ex-Detective Sergeant Gregory Neads, and Bola was unaware of any likely motive that might have driven this ex-pupil to murder an elderly musician in Reading. However he surmised that Bernice may – or may not be – in possession of further information which, for reasons unknown, she was reluctant to share.

Bola's concern was that Bernice had failed to mention her theory. A secondary concern was that, also for reasons unknown, Bernice had taken three hours off this morning, and Bola suspected that her absence might be related. He didn't like to pry, but he was worried about DC Swinhoe. There was something playing on her mind, and he thought she might be in some kind of trouble – that's the only reason he'd felt it necessary to let Moran know. He didn't want to be thought of as a snitch.

Moran had reassured him that he'd done the right thing and, thus unburdened, Bola had departed to keep an appointment with his POI.

Charnford. Not a place or a time Moran wanted to be reminded of. He'd almost died at Charnford. He'd almost died in the months leading *up* to Charnford, in an RTC nightmare not of his own making. And the nightmares had continued long after the disturbing events at the abbey; indeed they still continued, although less often and more sporadically. Surely history would not repeat itself in this roundabout way?

He sat back in his chair and closed his eyes. Bernice's contact was an ex-pupil, but the school had closed years ago. If the pupil in question had been in attendance at the time, it would hardly be surprising if he had been traumatised by what had happened. So – not just an ex-pupil, but maybe a *disturbed* ex-pupil? Leading to a copycat murder?

Moran drummed his fingers and pondered. It wasn't

inconceivable, but it was hugely unlikely – unless some strong motive was unearthed. Still, he'd have to talk to Bernice. Whatever was bugging her had to be brought into the light; after all, this was a murder investigation, and secret assignments were very much off Moran's agenda, even for promising young members of the team.

But that was for later, for when DC Swinhoe returned from her outing. What Moran needed right now was concrete information from Pauline Harris regarding the grease analysis. He picked up his mobile to call her, but as he did so a text message came through.

Alice.

Should he ignore it?

His inclination was to do just that. What was the point? She'd made her position clear. Why torture himself by dragging it out?

Emotion vs. logic.

Logic should win. Every time. Emotional reaction was a sure-fire way to misery.

He tapped his phone on the desk, as though trying to fire the bits and bytes that made up Alice's message back into the ether where they could no longer unsettle him.

Emotion vs. Logic.

Only one possible response.

He opened the message.

Hello Brendan. Thought you should know that Peter was admitted to hospital in the early hours. Doctors say bad chest infection. I want to say that I'm not worried, but that wouldn't be honest. He is very poorly. I've told Emma. She's on her way. Nothing you can do. Just wanted you to know. A.

Moran put the phone down. Guiltily, he recalled Alice telling him that Peter had been unwell and bedridden during his last visit, but he hadn't given it a further thought. Still, infections could be controlled, and mental eccentricities notwithstanding, Peter was physically robust enough to put up a fight. He'd be fine, right enough. But visiting him in hospital would be good, when he was on the mend. Should he reply to Alice's message? He was reluctant to reopen the conversation, but…

His thoughts were interrupted a second time by Collingworth, a wiry bundle of nervous energy. The acting sergeant barrelled into the room, pulled up a chair, crossed one leg over another and fixed Moran with a baleful look. 'Any news re the grease? Motor's been stripped. Got some samples from fixtures and fittings, engine casing and so on. Been serviced regularly at the Car Bar, so Potter says.'

'Come in, acting detective sergeant, why don't you?'

Collingworth looked around the office pointedly. 'Not interrupting anything, am I?'

'Only my thinking time.' Moran returned Collingworth's steady eye-to-eye.

'Oh, well then.' He shrugged. 'So? Any news?'

'I'm about to give them a call. I'll let you know.'

Collingworth was already on his feet.

'Let me know when DC Swinhoe reappears, would you?' Moran said. 'I'd like a word.'

'Sure,' Collingworth called over his shoulder as he left the room. 'If I remember.'

Moran's eyes narrowed.
Let it go, Brendan. Save him for later…

Clive Brooks looked even more irritated than before, and that was really going some. He didn't bother looking at Bola's warrant card, just said, 'Now what?'

'A few more questions, I'm afraid, sir. Won't take a minute.'

'Fi's out.'

'That's not a problem, sir. May I come in?'

Brooks grudgingly held the door open. '*I'm* going out in five.'

Once in the lounge Bola was not invited to sit, so he folded his arms and dived in. 'Can I ask about Fiona's temperament? She seems a little edgy.'

'Her temperament?' Brooks frowned. 'She's a bit highly strung. Not very practical, head in the clouds most of the time. Leaves the running of everything to me.'

'Any instances of a loss of temper? Arguments? Can she be reactive?'

'What are you getting at?'

Bola spread his hands. 'I'm just asking if there's another side to her character, that's all. It happens. Sometimes the meekest people have hidden depths that only show up on rare occasions. Like, during times of stress.'

'She's a good girl,' Brooks said, shuffling his feet. 'Never gives me any trouble.'

'That's not quite what I asked, sir.'

Brooks coloured. 'Look, where is this going? I've told you, Fi's all right.'

'Any objection if we take a look at her car?'

'Her car? Why?'

'Mr Brooks. Miss Manning was probably the last person to see Marika Szarka alive. It's important that we cover everything – every possibility – very carefully.'

Brooks was shaking his head. 'You think Fi had something to do with this? With a murder?' It sounded as though the possibility had only just occurred to him.

'As I explained, we're just following all possible lines of enquiry. We're not accusing anyone of anything right now.'

'Fi, a killer?' Brooks looked horror-struck. 'I mean, she gets cross sometimes, yeah, but—'

Bola was keeping a careful eye on Brooks' body language. 'If I can ask you to cast your mind back to when Miss Manning returned from the lesson in question, sir. Did she seem upset in any way? Agitated?'

Brooks' chin was stuck out, his fists bunching at his sides. 'I already told you; she's highly strung. Sure, she can get agitated about stuff – anything, really, even something trivial.'

Bola heard a key scrape in the front door lock, a waft of cool air as someone entered the hallway.

Good timing, Miss Manning…

'Clive?'

'In here.'

Fiona Manning came in wearing a long quilted coat and a quizzical expression. 'Oh. The police again?'

'I told you your bloody piano gets in the way of everything, didn't I? Now we've got this to deal with.' Bola could see that Brooks was more frightened now than angry; his fists had relaxed, the fingers visible once again.

'Just routine, Miss Manning.' Bola smiled reassuringly. 'I realise this might be a little inconvenient, but I wonder if you might allow our forensics team to have a look at your car? It won't take long – a morning should do it.'

'My car? But why?'

'They think you might be the killer,' Brooks said, 'is why.'

Manning's forehead creased in a mixture of puzzlement, irritation and concern. 'No they don't, Clive. They're just dotting the Is and crossing the Ts. It's detail. There's nothing to find.'

'Well, you're not using my car. I need it every day this week.'

Manning let that go and instead said to Bola, 'Of course it's all right. Just let me know when. Will you do it here, or shall I drive it to the police station?'

'We'll collect it,' Bola said. 'We don't want to inconvenience you more than we have to.'

'Not much.' Brooks glared.

Bola sidestepped the acerbic response he'd have liked to give and turned to go. 'Thanks again for your time. I'll leave you in peace.' He paused at the lounge door. 'Oh, sorry, almost forgot, you didn't answer my last question, sir, about Miss Manning's state of mind on her return from said lesson.' He beamed at the couple who were now standing together, at least physically.

They looked at each other.

'I was a bit upset, I suppose,' Manning confessed. 'It was a difficult lesson.'

'Oh? In what sense?' Bola cocked his head.

'It was a difficult piece to manage, technically,' Manning said. 'The one we were studying, I mean.'

Brooks rolled his eyes.

'May I ask which piece?' Bola asked.

'The *Diabelli Variations*,' Miss Manning's brow furrowed again at the memory. 'The sixth. It's full of arpeggios and trills. So hard to play at speed.'

'The composer?' Bola's eyebrows rose a fraction.

'It's by Beethoven. You know it?'

Chapter Thirty

'Schles? Where's Bola?'

Tess threw her coat across the chair back and plonked herself down, rubbed her eyes with the heels of her hands. Mrs Harrington had turned out to be a greater mine of information than she could have hoped for, but now she had to waste time tracing registration numbers. Bloody Collingworth. She needed to vent. '*Schles*! I asked where Bola was.'

'Mm?' Schlesinger looked up. He appeared distracted, lost in thought. 'Sorry. No idea. Oh, maybe an interview. Yeah, that's it, the Brooks/Manning place.'

'Did he say when he'll be back?'

Schlesinger shook his head. 'Nope – ah, here's Bernice, she might know.'

As Bernice headed towards them Tess stage-whispered, 'Don't call her that within earshot. It's B to us, OK?'

Schlesinger made a face. 'OK. Whatever.'

Bernice gave them a desultory wave and disappeared behind her workstation.

'Back in a mo.' Tess went over to Bernice's workstation and stopped short. Bernice's head was in her hands, and when she looked up, Tess saw that huge, fat tears were rolling down her cheeks.

'Babe? What's the matter?'

'*Babe*? Bloody hell, Tess, that's worse than Bernice.' Bernice took out a handkerchief and blew her nose.

'Yeah, I suppose. Sorry… but what's up? Can I help?' Tess rested her hand on Bernice's heaving shoulder. She waited a few seconds for the stifled sobs to subside, and then tightened her fingers. 'Right, young lady. Come on – we're going for a cuppa.'

Bernice allowed Tess to lead her by the arm in the direction of the canteen. 'It'll take more than a cup of tea to fix this, Tess.' She blew her nose again. 'Hell, what a state. Sorry.'

'No need to apologise – you can tell me all. And don't worry, we'll find a way, OK?'

'OK.'

Bernice sounded doubtful. The canteen was sparsely populated. Tess sat her down and went to get the drinks.

When she returned, Bernice had calmed herself. She managed a weak smile as Tess passed her a cup of breakfast tea. 'Thanks.'

Tess waited to see if Bernice would volunteer anything. Silence was OK in the meantime. They were comfortable with each other.

Eventually Bernice said, 'I'm sorry. I don't often lose it like that. It's just been a tough day.'

'Sure. I get it. Did you manage to sort out what you needed to sort?'

A pause. 'No, not really.'

'Want to tell me about it?'

'I can't.'

Tess waited again to see if Bernice would offer any word of explanation. When she didn't, she tried another approach. 'Old rubberdick is causing me all kinds of grief today.'

'Yes?'

'Yep, he sure is.' Tess went on to explain Collingworth's tunnel-visioned mandates regarding Potter's car, but after only a short while she could see that Bernice wasn't really listening. She was making the right noises, but her eyes were distant, focused on something else entirely. Tess tapped her spoon on the Formica. '*Hello, Beeeee* … are you there?'

'Mm? Oh, yes, sorry,' Bernice said, shaking her head. 'I just have … stuff on my mind, you know? It's OK. I'm fine.'

Tess gave her a hard look. 'It's *not* OK and you're obviously *not* fine. You need to spill, B, seriously.'

Bernice's face crumpled again. 'Oh, Tess. I don't know where to start. Really, I don't.'

Tess took her hand and squeezed it. 'At the beginning. That's always the best place.'

Tess was silent when Bernice finished her story, processing the information, sifting it through. Bernice was right. It wasn't a promising scenario.

Bernice's hands were cupped around her empty mug, her lips pressed together. She was very pale.

'I told you it was worse than bad.'

Tess nodded. 'You did.'

'You think I'm an idiot, right?'

Tess took her hand. 'Don't be daft, B. You've been set up, big time. How were you to know? You were just there at the wrong time.'

'I could go down for this.' Bernice's eyes filled again.

'You won't go down for anything. We'll fix this, I promise.'

'But how?'

Tess leaned forward, squeezed Bernice's limp hand. 'This Isabel. She's escaped custody by virtue of her MI6 connections, right?'

'Right, but…'

'So, somehow, we need to cut the tether, cut her loose.'

'Can't be done.' Bernice shook her head. 'She's a highly prized asset. That's what I've heard, anyway.'

'Supposedly.' Tess thought some more. 'But she's also a murderer. If we can figure out a way to discredit her, maybe, to remove her protected status, somehow…'

'Two coppers on our own? We'll never be able to do that.'

'Not just you and me, no. We need help, B. I think you should tell the guv. He knows about this woman. He's still mad that she's walking free.'

'No way.' Bernice shook her head emphatically. 'I can't. Once he knows, that's it. Game over. I'll be locked up.'

'No, you won't. The guv's a wise man. He'll know how to handle this. Trust me.'

Bernice's face fell. 'I don't know, Tess.' She looked at her friend beseechingly. 'I don't know *what* to do.'

Tess folded her arms. 'I'll tell you what you're going to do. You're going to sleep on it tonight, and then we'll talk some more in the morning. In the meantime, you can help me with the ANPR searches, OK? Take your mind off it for a while. It'll help.'

Bernice offered the suggestion a weak smile. 'All right. If you say so.'

'I do. Come on, let's get to it.'

They bumped into Bola on their way back to the open plan. 'Great news,' he told them with a wide grin. 'Captain Knobhead's getting another car to pull to bits.'

'Anything that'll keep him out of the way for a while,' Tess said, 'is OK by me. Whose car?'

'Fi Manning's. She gets tetchy if her lessons don't go well, so my mate Clive Brooks tells me. She didn't deny it. She wasn't in a good place after her last lesson with Marika Szarka.'

'Like I said, Bola, I can't see her nailing a woman's hands to a piano.' Bernice said. 'If anyone's guilty, my money's still on Brooks.'

Bola clucked his tongue. 'We'll see. It's the quiet ones you've got to watch.'

'True.'

Tess was encouraged by Bernice's comment, suggesting that she'd been distracted enough to refocus on the case. Distraction was the best therapy until they could figure out a way to extract her from the mess she'd got herself into. She was sure that Moran was key, and that Bernice would have to bite the bullet in the morning. She'd support her all the way, but everything hinged on Moran's reaction, whether he would side with them or against.

She hoped, for B's sake, that her gamble would pay off.

Chapter Thirty-One

Moran was on his way to the Royal Berkshire Hospital. He'd come to the conclusion, after his conscience had nagged him for the remainder of the afternoon, that it would be best to visit Peter straight away. Alice may or may not be there, but he was mentally prepared either way. He couldn't allow their difficulties to influence his relationship with Alice's gentle, autistic brother. They'd always got on well, and he was sure that his visit would have a positive effect – if not on Peter's condition, then certainly on his mood. Moran smiled to himself as he thought of Peter's innocent face lighting up as he recognised his Irish friend *Brennan*, as he always called him despite Moran's patient attempts at correction. But would they allow him into the ward? If he was still in ICU, it was doubtful. Usually they allowed family members and no one else. Well, if push came to shove, he had his warrant card. He didn't like using it in that way, but there were times when it was excusable.

He allowed his mind to shift back to the Szarka case. Two cars now under suspicion, belonging to a student with a temper and an eccentric piano tuner. Another waiting game as forensics went through both vehicles – and still no word from Pauline Harris.

His mobile rang. Moran stabbed the *accept call* button on the screen. 'Moran.'

'Pauline Harris. I have some news.'

'Ah. I was just thinking about you.'

Harris stepped smoothly over Moran's ambiguity. 'Can you come over? I think you'll want to know what we've found.'

'When?'

'Now would be good.'

Moran sighed. Here it was again, the conflict between work and a normal life. This is what had driven the wedge between himself and Alice.

Harris sensed his hesitation. 'It's a significant find. I think it will help.'

'I'm on my way.'

Harris rang off.

Sorry, Peter. See you later, son…

Harris met him in the waiting room. 'Have a seat, Detective Chief Inspector.'

She pulled up a chair on the other side of the bare table. 'It's taken a bit longer than usual, but we have some interesting results.'

'You mentioned lithium?'

'Yes, the grease is lithium-based. But the interesting thing is the additives.'

Moran frowned. 'Additives?'

'All automotive grease contains additives. Thickening agents for starters,' Harris explained patiently. 'The solubility of the grease is directly related to the solubility of the thickener used to manufacture it. Lithium hydroxide and the thickeners typically used in its manufacture have very low water solubility. This means that lithium grease has excellent resistance to water washing and water absorption.'

'OK.' Moran's forehead was still creased.

'And there are other additives to aid lubricity, thermal insulation, and oxidisation resistance. This is where it gets interesting.'

'I was wondering,' Moran said.

'Graphite is a common additive. The most effective additive range for graphite is between three and five percent. But graphite isn't cheap, at least not through the most common European outlets. That's why the additive percentage tends to be around three percent for most of the lubricants available in the UK.' Harris hooked a loose strand of hair over her ear. 'You're wondering where I'm going with this.'

'You read my mind,' Moran said with a half-smile. 'But I think you're getting there.'

To his surprise she smiled back, a wide, transformative expression that softened her face and made the light dance in her eyes. 'I am. You're a patient man, I can see that.'

Moran cocked his head self-deprecatingly. 'It's been said before. Who am I to deny?'

The smile came again, unforced, natural.

A small voice whispered, *You're making progress here, Brendan…*

With an effort, he nudged himself back into professional mode. Harris was showing him a printout. She slid it across the table with an easy gesture. Her fingers were long and slim, the nails unpainted but neatly trimmed.

'You can see here that in this case the graphite percentage is much higher – just under five per cent. That's quite a difference, and as I said, unusual for the UK and European markets. All popular and widely used brands of automotive grease come in at around three percent, without exception.'

'Meaning?'

'Meaning that this particular sample comes from a batch manufacturing process that took place somewhere Graphite is more readily available, and therefore cheaper.' Her eyes lit up again. 'I did a little research for you. Only one manufacturer uses such a high ratio of graphite in the manufacture of automotive grease – an Indian company, based in Mumbai. India has huge reserves of graphite. It's big business.'

'So this grease must have been bought in as a special order, by a particular company?'

'I'd say so, yes. And before you ask, it's not Reading Transport. We checked their suppliers. Good old Castrol, three percent.'

'OK.' Moran leaned forward in his enthusiasm. 'So we're not looking at an individual driver here, we're looking at a company, an auto company.'

'Yep. A garage, perhaps, with contacts in India.'

'Or,' Moran said, 'a local taxi or minicab service.'

Harris nodded. 'Over to you, Chief Inspector.'

DC Nigel Schlesinger was on a mission. It was a mission he knew he had to undertake – and undertake alone – in order to prove his competency, not merely to the team, but also to himself.

He hadn't been able to shake off the shame, the sheer

mortification, of having to be rescued from Levi Cambridge's bathroom by the DCI. It had stung. He'd cried himself to sleep that night, for the first time since childhood. The humiliation had somehow only been made worse by DCI Moran's kind and sympathetic assistance. The way the DCI had handled the situation had been a revelation to Schlesinger. The calmness, the way in which Moran had disarmed Levi Cambridge and brought him back onside, had been poetry in motion to witness. Schlesinger knew he had a lot to learn.

He'd tried to cut himself some slack. *You're new to all this. It was a simple mistake.* But he couldn't shake off the feeling that the incident would follow him around like a stray dog, that it would resurface in meetings, or in the pub, or at work-based social functions, to the delight of his colleagues and his own resentful shame. He'd tried at first to see the funny side, but quickly gave that up. There was nothing remotely amusing about what had happened, not to him. He had been taken for a complete fool.

Schlesinger felt his face redden at the memory. He swore under his breath and indicated right to join the Inner Distribution Road, slipping in between a taxi and a Sainsbury's van. 'This time,' he said aloud, 'this time, Nige, you're going to handle it better. You're going to come away with something useful, something that matters. You're going to make a meaningful contribution to the team, justify your placement and DCI Moran's faith in your abilities. You can do this.'

He turned off the Caversham Road and into the familiar street. There was one space, a bit of a squeeze, but he skilfully manoeuvred his vehicle into the gap and switched off the engine. He could see the on-duty constable stamping his feet outside the Szarka residence. It had been a cloudless afternoon but an evening chill had crept in at sundown. Having to hang around semi-motionless for hours on end wasn't a lot of fun; Schlesinger knew all about that; he'd done it himself. The PC was pacing up and down on the pavement now, poor sod. Schlesinger sympathised, but no way was he ever going back to that. No, sir.

Schlesinger gave the lad a wave as he knocked on Levi Cambridge's front door, but the PC was miles away, most likely fantasising about warm firesides, or pints of lager, or weekend football, or anything other than what he was actually doing at that moment.

He waited, worried that Cambridge might be out, but suddenly the curtain to his right was moved aside and Cambridge peered out, only to instantly disappear. Schlesinger wondered briefly if he would refuse to come to the door, but a few moments later it opened and Cambridge greeted him with arched eyebrows.

'And what do you want *now*?' he enquired, the emphasis not lost on Schlesinger.

'Just a word, Mr Cambridge. It won't take long.'

'Hope you're going to be polite this time,' Cambridge said as he held the door aside. 'And behave yourself.'

Schlesinger followed him inside. 'This is a murder investigation, Mr Cambridge. We're all on our best behaviour. We want to find out who committed this terrible crime just as much as you do.'

'Is that so? Have a seat.' Cambridge pointed to the tatty armchair. The place felt damp and Schlesinger noticed a snail trail at the edge of the carpet. Blown damp proof course, most likely.

'Tell me about that evening, Mr Cambridge – the evening of the murder. The last time we spoke you mentioned that you went out for a brief period that evening, that you returned home at around ten, and—' Schlesinger consulted his notebook, '—that you watched TV till midnight or thereabouts and then went to bed.'

'Yes, very good. That's spot on, young man.'

'Tell me about your brief period out. Where did you go?'

'Nowhere, really. See, I like to get out for a stroll, breathe a bit of fresh air. Sometimes I stop for a quick one at the rub-a-dub, other times I just walk. Not much to tell, to be honest. I'm a simple man. Simple pleasures, y'know?'

'I understand.' Schlesinger was making an effort to maintain a professional air, to sound as if he carried authority. So far, it appeared to be working. 'So, along the road? To the local shops? Or maybe the recreation ground?'

'Let's see now.' Cambridge stroked the grey stubble on his chin. 'Along the main road, past the Co-Op, didn't go into the park. Didn't stop for a pint, I don't think. Just me and my thoughts, and all things like that.'

'Do you recall anyone else being around? This would be, what, around ten o'clock ish?'

'That's correct. I remember getting back at ten-thirty. I watched Silent Witness. Recorded it earlier, see?'

'So, the streets were deserted?' Schlesinger pressed on.

'Good series, Silent Witness. Forensics and all things like that. It's the Fox girl, you know? Day of the Jackal's daughter.'

Schlesinger nodded. 'Yes, I know the one. But your walk, sir. Is there anything you can recall that might be of interest? Did you see anyone else out and about?'

'There are always folk out and about, aren't there?' Cambridge drummed his fingers on the arm of the chair. Schlesinger sensed irritation creeping into his replies. 'Youngsters coming out of the pubs, people at the bus stop. People getting dropped off. But—' he paused briefly, blinking as the memory came back to him, 'yeah, now you mention it, there was someone I thought I didn't recognise – and I know most people around here. Been here twenty-five years, now.' He chuckled. '*Tempus fugit*, young man. Enjoy life while you're young, that's my advice.'

Schlesinger wanted him back on track. He smiled. 'I'll remember that,' he said. 'Thanks for the advice.'

Cambridge brightened at Schlesinger's reply. 'My pleasure, young fella.'

'So, this person you didn't recognise?'

'Yeah. I remember 'cause he was in a suit, climbin' out of a minicab. Businessman late from the office, I thought. Then I thought, hang on Levi, it's Saturday. Maybe … maybe he's visiting the house of ill repute, that's what he's up to. That's why the cab.'

'Ill repute?'

'Knocking shop. See 'em come and go all the time. Embarrassing, it is. You lot should shut it down. Surprised your boss hasn't told you about it.'

'OK.' Schlesinger felt his face reddening as he scribbled in his notebook. 'You think that's where he went?'

'I dunno, do I?' Cambridge looked irritated again. 'I'm not the morality police, am I? I walked behind the bloke for a bit until I turned off at the end of my road and went around the block.'

'Wait, so he *could* have been heading here – into your road, I mean?'

A shrug. 'Maybe. Can't say. I walked on and that was that.'

'Can you describe this person?'

Cambridge closed his eyes. 'Tallish. Short, grey hair. Specs. Like I said, a suit. Grey, or some such. Walked a bit stiff, like 'e 'ad an apple up his bum. Had a brolly, or a walking stick. Maybe. I wasn't paying that much attention.'

'Right, thanks. And do you, by any chance, remember the minicab type?'

'Blimey. Don't want much, do you? No idea. It was white, or light coloured, leastways I think it was.'

'Registration?'

Cambridge guffawed. 'You're kidding, right? What d'you think I am? Some kind of anorak taxi-spotter? I've no bloody idea what the registration was. I just noticed it 'cause of the bloke, that's all.'

'You've been very helpful, Mr Cambridge.' Schlesinger wanted to quit while he was ahead, but there was one more obvious question that, as far as he knew, no one had yet asked. He steeled himself and went for it. 'Oh, by the way, do you play the piano?'

'Me? Ha ha!' Cambridge put on a sly expression. 'I know where you're coming from, lad. Sure, I had a few lessons when I was a nipper, but the teacher told me I had cloth ears. My old ma was sad about it, but what can you do, eh? You've either got it or you ain't. Abrupt end of said piano lessons, my musical career, and all things like that.'

'No lessons with the Szarkas, then.'

'Watch my lips, son. *Never.*' Cambridge mimed the word in a slow growl.

Aware that he'd slid back onto thin ice, Schlesinger stood up. 'Right. Got it.' He beamed a positive smile. 'Well, thanks again, Mr Cambridge.'

'Don't want to visit the bathroom tonight?' Cambridge offered with a sly wink. 'It's a free service.'

'I think I'll pass, thanks all the same.' Schlesinger returned a complicit smile.

As the front door closed behind him, Schlesinger felt a small spark of elation ignite in his stomach.

There we go. Piece of cake, Nige, wasn't it? Nothing to it, nothing at all...

Chapter Thirty-Two

Moran was woken by a bleep from his mobile. He fumbled for the device in the gloom of his bedroom and groaned at the time. It was twenty-five past six. He squinted at the glare from the small screen. A text message.

Morning, guv. Sorry to message early but I need to speak to you urgently before the briefing this morning. Can we meet in Costa at seven thirty? Tess wants a word, too. Hope that's OK. Sorry for short notice. Thanks & regards, Bernice S.

Moran sighed and clonked the mobile onto his bedside table. His head was still clogged with fragmented images from the last stages of REM sleep. Peter in hospital, Alice dressed in a nurses' uniform. The hospital was a pet shop, the cages filled with musical instruments. His eyes flickered and closed. A piano suddenly appeared, and the pianist, DCI Dawson, took his place in a slow motion dance. His bicycle was propped against the piano, a tangled wreck of metalwork. Dawson had no hands. How would he play? Pauline Harris came in and screwed a pair of prosthetic hands onto Dawson's outstretched arms. The music began, a Beethoven sonata. Or was it Mozart?

Moran jerked awake and swung his legs out from beneath the duvet before he could drift off again. His feet touched the floor.

Grounded…

As the kettle boiled he gazed out into the wilderness of greenery that was his garden. The rain had returned and his unkempt shrubbery had grown at least another six inches over the last week of downpours. He'd have to think seriously about hiring someone to come in and cut it all back. The neighbours routinely teased him about his lack of green-fingered expertise, but he could hear the implied criticism. The Bakers' garden was immaculate, every blade of grass trimmed to precision, the small pond neatly delimited by tasteful stonework and, as spring turned to summer, their herbaceous borders thrived and bloomed like an artist's palette.

Guiltily, Moran turned away and busied himself with the coffee machine, averting his eyes from the bottle of Scotch which, unlike his garden, seemed to have shrunk since the previous evening by some considerable volume.

Not good enough, Brendan…

As the coffee percolated he wondered how his alcohol intake would be affected by his retirement. At least while he was working there was a cutoff point beyond which he knew he could not go – if he wanted to be able to perform his duties adequately, that was. After the job had gone, his self-imposed moderation might also disappear. It was a worrying thought.

He drank his coffee and took a quick shower. When he left the house the rain had settled into a familiar, steady rhythm, a damp declaration of intent to continue in the same vein for the remainder of the day.

Traffic was, for once, relatively thin for rush hour, and Bernice and Tess were waiting for him as he arrived at the Costa outlet. There was a small queue at the counter but Tess waved him over.

'Morning, guv. I got you a medium cappuccino – that's right, isn't it?'

'Spot on,' Moran said, sliding into the bench seat opposite the two detective constables.

'Sorry about the cloak and dagger approach, guv,' Bernice said. 'I'll come straight to the point, because I know time is short. I'm in a fix and I need to tell you about it.'

'I see. Well, fire away. I'm listening.'

As Bernice began, watched anxiously, Moran noticed, by Tess, he saw that her hands were trembling. As her story unfolded, he understood why. He sipped his coffee, and every so often, stopped her for a point of clarification. But mostly he just let her talk.

When she'd finished, he nodded. 'Thank you, DC Swinhoe, for your honesty. That must have been difficult.' He paused, both detectives hanging on his next word. 'There are a number of issues here,' he continued after a moment. 'So we'll deal with them one by one.' Now he smiled and the tension eased. 'This is not the end of the world, DC Swinhoe. It might seem like it is, but it isn't. Between us we'll concoct an action plan to bring this to a speedy conclusion. However—'

The women glanced at each other.

'Some of it will necessarily be off grid.' Moran took a pull of his coffee. 'I'm already aware of Isabel Akkerman's repatriation; DI Pepper informed me a few days ago. But first things first – I want you to put this aside during the working day in the knowledge that, a, the situation has been shared with a senior officer, and b, that, somehow or other we're going to bring this woman in.' Moran looked at each of them in turn. 'Let's not kid ourselves, though. The photographs you mentioned could cause you considerable inconvenience if published, there's no doubt about that. I imagine that Isabel and this Catton character intend to testify against you if push comes to shove?'

Bernice nodded miserably. 'Yes.'

Moran opened his hands. 'All right. Let's not be naive. If that happens, the court may find against you, DC Swinhoe. At worst, manslaughter, at best a suspended sentence based on your excellent record and the testimony of colleagues.'

'I'll not plead guilty,' Bernice said quietly. 'No way.'

'Let's not worry about that now.' Moran went for an encouraging smile. 'Our priority is to formulate a plan to expose Akkerman. And,' he added with a wag of his finger, 'I've an idea how that might be achieved, but I need to do a little research first.' Moran paused. 'Before we finish, I think we should also address your concerns regarding a possible connection to Charnford Abbey?'

Bernice sighed. 'I don't think it's relevant, guv. If I'm being honest, it was just an excuse to visit Alastair – a nebulous connection. And Johnny's dead, so…'

'So we'll never know how much he knew?'

Bernice shrugged. 'Alastair told me Johnny had never been back to Charnford – he left before sixth form, so he'd have been young, fifteen or sixteen around the time of the murder –

and he also told me that Johnny hadn't left Simplicity at all over the past few weeks, not even to go into town.'

'I can't pretend I'm not relieved to hear that, DC Swinhoe,' Moran said. 'Charnford is one stone I'd rather leave unturned.' He looked at his watch. 'OK. Time to go. Let's meet up again this evening at, say, eight? If you're amenable, I'd like to get Bola involved – and possibly George. I trust their integrity, and we need to put our heads together.'

There was a brief silence as the detectives digested Moran's proposal.

'All right,' Bernice said eventually. 'I'm so sorry to drag you into this, guv. I mean, with the Szarka case, it's not what you need right now.'

'I've weathered storms before, DC Swinhoe, and this is just more of the same. Speaking of which,' he glanced outside at the teeming rain, 'I hope one of you had the good sense to bring an umbrella.'

Chapter Thirty-Three

'She's a sweetie,' Tess told Bernice as they sheltered beneath the nursing home's front porch. 'Totally with it. Her memory's better than mine.'

Bernice laughed. She felt lighter in spirit after their meeting with Moran, a lightness that even Collingworth's boorishness during the morning briefing had failed to dispel. He'd wanted to veto Tess's suggestion to revisit Mrs Harrington, but Moran had overruled him, and Bernice had wanted to cheer – as had everyone else if the expressions on their faces had been anything to go by.

The atmosphere in the Incident Room had lightened even further as, for the first time, the team sensed a narrowing of the search criteria. First up had been Moran with the forensic results from the grease, which suggested an automobile company as the substance's origin. Second came DC Schlesinger with an unexpected update regarding Levi Cambridge's testimony, which pointed, potentially at least, to a new POI and a link with a minicab company. Predictably, Collingworth had tried to dismiss both as unlikely candidates for further investigation, but only, Bernice knew, because they cast doubt on the validity of his own fixation with the Potter and Manning vehicles. After a heated discussion, Collingworth had announced that he intended to continue his line of enquiry until both vehicles had been declared forensically clean, and abruptly left the briefing. As the door closed behind him, the assembled officers heaved a sigh of relief. In closing the meeting, Moran tasked George and Bola with contacting local cab companies while Tess and herself had been given the green light to reinterview Mrs Harrington.

'Hello. Can I help?' A smartly-uniformed lady appeared on the threshold. Her name badge read: *Mary Elvey – Manager.*

They showed Mrs Elvey their warrant cards, and Tess confirmed that she had met Mrs Harrington on a previous visit.

'That's fine. If I can just get you to sign in? Mrs Harrington's in the lounge. I'll let you find your own way – we're rather busy this morning with two new residents, it takes a while to get them settled.'

Mrs Harrington was seated in the same chair as before. There was no sign of the grumpy TV resident anywhere, but there were several elderly ladies Tess hadn't seen on her last visit gathered in a corner of the room, some dozing over Sudoku puzzles, some conversing in low voices, the remainder just content to sit and observe. Tess led Bernice through the maze of chairs, tables and parked walking frames until they arrived at Mrs Harrington's side.

'Morning, Mrs Harrington. It's me again.' Tess rested her hand on Mrs Harrington's shoulder.

'Oh! Hello, dear.' Mrs Harrington stirred from her reverie. 'And you have a friend with you today, I see.'

'This is DC Bernice Swinhoe,' Tess said. 'We're working on the case together.'

Mrs Harrington's wrinkled face broke into a smile. 'Nice to meet you, young lady. It's wonderful to see you bright young things showing the men how it's done.'

'We do our best.' Bernice returned the smile.

'I'm quite sure.' Mrs Harrington beamed. 'But, please do have a seat – there, that's right. Now, what else can I help you with?'

'You were telling me about Reyka Szarka, how she struggled with the piano. And how Marika was so proficient.'

'Yes, yes. It was a shame for Reyka. And Marika, of course, would always get a great deal of male attention. That didn't help, either.'

'She was prettier?' Bernice asked. 'Than her sister?'

Mrs Harrington paused. 'Marika was pretty, yes, but I think it was more a case of temperament. She was so sweet-natured. The boys loved her.'

'But she never married,' Tess said.

'Oh, wait! I remember now, Reyka *did* have an admirer for a while, but it didn't last. She broke it off and went to stay with a friend in Scotland – or was it the Lake District?'

They waited patiently as Mrs Harrington sifted through her memory's dimming corridors.

'Anyway,' she continued at last, 'wherever it was, she seemed to get over it. I'm sure it was all about the music for both girls, you see.'

'And Marika's paramours?'

'She never married. As I said, both sisters were married to their music and, of course, there was the mother to deal with.'

'She looks rather strict in the photographs we've seen,' Bernice said.

'You have photographs? Oh, I would love to see those.'

'The mother – Leila?' Tess prompted. 'You told me that she worked both girls hard.'

'Oh yes, she did indeed, especially poor Reyka. But you see, Reyka's problem was simple, but it was something she couldn't fix.'

'Oh? And what was that, Mrs Harrington?' Bernice asked.

'She was a girl. You see, Leila had wanted a boy – after the miscarriage.'

'Miscarriage?' Bernice prompted.

'Yes. The first child was stillborn. A boy – it's always so sad, isn't it? I don't believe mothers ever get over something like that, do you?'

'I suppose not,' Bernice agreed. 'But then Reyka came along?'

'Yes. She came next, but by all accounts Leila never warmed to her.'

'That must have been hard for Reyka.'

'Yes. I believe it was. She could never please her mother enough.'

A clattering in the corridor announced the imminent arrival of the tea trolley. The chatter in the corner of the lounge tailed off in anticipation of its arrival.

Tess said, 'You also mentioned a tutor?'

Mrs Harrington's expression darkened. 'Miss Keane.' She fell silent and closed her eyes. When she reopened them, they were clouded by a thin film of moisture. 'She was an ex-nun. We heard that she was dismissed from her order because she couldn't live peacefully within the sisterhood. There was a rumour of abuse, a hint of scandal. But she seemed to rise above it, turned to teaching privately – perhaps because no schools would take her. Beatrice Keane.' Mrs Harrington's gaze was focused on the grey skies outside the window. 'She was Reyka's nemesis. And I saw the evidence with my own eyes.'

'What evidence was that, Mrs Harrington?' Tess caught the look in Bernice's eye. There was something here worth uncovering.

'Oh, look, call me Jean, please. I can't abide formality, can you?'

'All right,' Tess agreed. 'But here's the tea trolley. Can I get you something?'

'I'll have a milky coffee, please dear. It'll keep me alert.' The eyes twinkled again.

'I'll get it,' Bernice offered. 'Tess?'

'I'm OK, thanks. You go ahead.'

When Mrs Harrington had been given her coffee and a chocolate digestive, she continued. 'All the students who went to her were frightened. Thank the Lord I wasn't one of them.' She munched her biscuit and crumbs fell unheeded onto her tweed skirt. Tess and Bernice waited patiently for her to finish as she sipped her coffee and then set the cup down on the arm of the chair. 'Beatrice Keane was an unpleasant woman. I remember catching a glimpse of Reyka's wrist after a lesson. She'd been crying, I could see.'

Tess felt a wave of revulsion. 'What was wrong?'

'It was red and sore. Miss Keane used a steel ruler. I imagine Reyka still bears the scars to this day.'

'That's terrible.' Bernice looked horrified.

'It was.' Mrs Harrington lifted her teacup and took a sip. 'But do you know, years later I discovered something very interesting about Miss Keane. I hadn't been in contact with the sisters for a decade or more but then I saw an obituary in the paper. Keane had made a name for herself in the classical music world, you see, and someone felt that she merited a few lines in a national. No one had ever come forward to complain about her – I imagine they were all too frightened to say anything. Anyway, there was a photograph. I recognised it; it was her all right, but the obituary told a different story to the one we'd been familiar with.'

Tess and Bernice had unconsciously moved closer so they could hear Mrs Harrington above the clink of teaspoons and the encouraging chatter of the care worker as she distributed her wares. 'Go on,' Tess said.

'Whoever wrote the obituary had obviously done their homework. It turned out that Keane wasn't her real name at all. She was from an Irish background and had a rather chequered past. She had a daughter out of wedlock at a very young age and had to leave her hometown in disgrace, taking the baby with her. It was either that or incarceration in a Magdalen laundry, and give the baby up to the church's ministrations. So she came here, and, well, of course she couldn't manage, in a strange country with a child to support. So eventually she gave the baby up for adoption on the understanding that the child retained her surname. Shortly after that she joined the convent. It must have affected her mind, the way she'd been treated by her family, the stress of it all. When I read the obituary I finally had a sense at last of what might have caused her bitterness, why she'd had to take out her anger and frustration on her students.'

'Do you recall her real surname, the one from the obituary?' Tess asked.

'I do. It was an unusual name…' Jean Harrington knitted her brow. 'Oh, dear, can you believe it? It's gone. I had it there on the tip of my tongue.'

Bernice looked at Tess with a *what can you do?* expression.

'Have some more coffee and think about something else,' Tess advised her. 'That's what I do.'

But ten minutes later there was still no progress. Mrs Harrington's mind had gone blank.

'We'll pop in another time,' Tess told her with a sympathetic smile. 'It's no bother. It's probably not important, but you never know.'

'I'm so sorry, my dear. I hope I've been of some use.'

'You most certainly have, Mrs Harrington.' Bernice took her hand and shook it gently. It was cold and dry. 'We'll see you soon.'

Chapter Thirty-Four

Moran's brain was a fizzing kaleidoscope of activity, his thoughts flitting from one conundrum to the next so rapidly that he was in serious danger of losing his ability to focus altogether. The double-sided coin of Bernice Swinhoe's confession had both unnerved and excited him. It was a serious situation for the young DC, but she'd done the right thing in coming forward. Any judge in his right mind would cut her some slack, given the circumstances – *if* it came to trial. And the other side of the coin was engraved with an invitation to once again lock horns with Isabel Akkerman – but maximising that opportunity would require careful thought, and for this he needed support.

Rain spattered against the office's external window in a violent gust that made him step back a pace. Atlantic House living up to its name. Flood warnings were beginning to filter into the news, with many low-lying towns under threat. The Thames had burst its banks in his own village and many other waterways would follow suit if the weather continued in the same vein.

Moran returned to his desk, closed his eyes, and tried to

prioritise his main concerns. The Szarka case was moving forward, albeit slowly. Schlesinger's possible lead was encouraging, both for the newbie detective and for the team as a whole. The lad had done well. He'd faced up to his mistake, used his initiative and come up with a possible new POI, an unknown male disembarking from a taxi and walking to an unknown destination. Maybe the Szarka residence, maybe not, but Pauline Harris's forensic analysis made the presence of a taxi more than plausible. Definitely worth following up.

Collingworth, on the other hand, seemed intent on flogging the dead horse of his two impounded vehicles. No convincing evidence had been found so far in either of them, and neither had any realistic motive been uncovered that would suggest either Potter or Fiona Manning as a possible suspect.

Moran was also conscious that he had not yet made it to the hospital to visit Peter. This nagged at the back of his mind, just ahead of Mrs Dawson's threat to hold him responsible for her husband's accident. And then there was Alice, but he still felt too emotionally vulnerable to ponder how the sudden severing of their relationship might be repaired.

He needed relief, some grounded conversation. He went to check on the team's progress. Bola was on a call, but George looked up as Moran approached.

'Any joy?'

'Getting there, guv.' George tapped his screen. 'I'm compiling a list of garages used by local taxi companies for servicing. Bola's made a start with the phone calls – he's working his way through them as I add more. First question is the drop-off on the night in question. If we score on that, we'll follow up with the service centres. So far, no drop-offs that fit the bill.'

'All right. Keep at it. Tess back yet?'

'Not yet.'

'Checked ANPR re taxi drop offs?'

'I have, guv. Problem is the nearest camera to the supposed drop-off site – the recreation ground – is by the station bridge. And I don't need to tell you how much traffic flows along the IDR during an average evening.'

'Sure. Just a thought.'

They looked up as the lift doors opened and Bernice and Tess stepped out.

'News?' Moran prompted hopefully.

'Lots of background about the Szarka sisters, guv. Mrs Harrington remembers them well – they were teens together in the early seventies.'

'But anything pertinent?'

Tess puffed her cheeks. 'Not really. Marika was the favourite, Reyka not so much. They had an evil piano tutor with a dodgy history. Once Reyka had changed instruments all was well, but the poor woman had a hard time of it. Used to get her hands rulered on a regular basis.'

'I can relate to that,' Moran said.

'Watch out – talking of rulers, here comes the lord of misrule.' Bola had ended his phone call and was nodding towards the lifts.

'Acting DS Collingworth, anything to report?' Moran addressed the acting sergeant while he was still making his way across the open plan towards them.

'Actually, yes.' Collingworth looked smug. He found a nearby vacant chair and sat down on it in reverse, his arms draped over the back of the chair like a commando hugging his parachute.

'Don't keep us in suspense,' George said. 'I might pass out with anxiety.'

Collingworth ignored George's quip. 'As it happens, we found something in Manning's car.'

'Go on.' Moran wondered what was coming.

'A piece of porcelain. And I'll bet it matches your broken bust.' He glared triumphantly at Moran. 'Right colour, for a start. It's with forensics now.'

Fiona Manning was pale and tearful. She'd appeared shocked, but was fully compliant as Bola and George read her her rights and escorted her from her house. Brooks had watched the drama unfold in uncharacteristic silence, shaking his head in disbelief. His only words had been quietly articulated, and directed solely at his girlfriend. 'I can't *believe* you would do something like this, Fi.'

'You are entitled to a solicitor,' George told her as he booked her in. 'But we can make a start straight away, if you wish.'

'No. I want a solicitor present.'

'Fair play.' George pointed to the desk phone. 'It's all yours.'

The solicitor arrived twenty minutes later, a middle-aged man with a goatee beard and longish hair which he wore combed back behind his ears. He was carrying a small scuffed briefcase and seemed surprised to find himself in a police station so late in the afternoon. 'You'll have to forgive me,' he told George. 'I'm due at the airport later this evening. Hope this won't take long?'

'I'm sure you have your client's best interests at heart,'

George replied coldly. 'This way, please.'

Collingworth was waiting impatiently outside the interview room. 'Let's get on, shall we?'

Once the tape was running, Collingworth cut straight to the chase. For once, George approved.

'What time did you leave the Szarka household on the day of your last lesson?'

'I.e the day of the murder of Marika Szarka,' George clarified.

'I had nothing to do with Marika's death,' Manning insisted. 'I went for my usual lesson, that's all. I went. It was hard, yes. We finished, and I left.'

'Answer the question,' Collingworth barked.

'I got there a little late, as I told you before,' Manning said. Her hair was disarrayed, ruffled by her subconscious habit of pushing it away from her face at regular intervals. 'The lesson was an hour, so I must have left the premises at around four forty-five.'

'Can you be specific?'

'No.' She shook her head. 'I didn't look at the clock, but I went straight home. I was home by five. You could work out the time I left by subtracting my journey time home.'

'Do you recall a bust?' George asked. 'Of Beethoven?'

Manning frowned. 'Yes. It was on the mantelpiece, as usual. Marika loved Beethoven.'

'Intact?' Collingworth chewed his pen.

'The bust? Yes – but I don't understand. What do you mean?'

'My colleague means, did you smash it in a fit of temper?' Collingworth rapped his pen on the table.

'Smash it? No! I mean, why would I do such a thing?'

'Because you get frustrated,' George reminded her. 'You were working on a Beethoven piece – a hard one. You told us it had been a tricky lesson, right?'

'Yes, but I didn't break the place up because of that. I was cross, of course, but I loved Marika. I wouldn't break any of her possessions just because I felt bad about my performance.'

'Are you sure about that?' George pressed the point.

The solicitor coughed. 'My client has answered your question. Please continue with another line of enquiry, if you have one.'

'Did you dislike Marika Szarka? Because she highlighted your deficiencies as a pianist?' Collingworth's eyes sparkled. George glanced at his colleague with unease. He was enjoying this, the thrill of the chase.

'Dislike her? No! I've already told you, I *loved* Marika. And she would never point the finger like that. I mean, I know I'm only an average musician. I don't need anyone else to tell me that; Clive has that one covered.'

George noted the bitter tone; Brooks sounded a right bastard. It made him even more determined to treat Tess well, to encourage her in every possible way.

Collingworth settled back in his chair and folded his arms. 'You know what I think, Fiona? I think you lost it. I think your frustrations finally got the better of you. You can't take it out on your live-in lover boy, so you lashed out at poor Marika. That's what happened, isn't it?'

'No. You're wrong! I wouldn't, I *couldn't*.' Manning began to sob.

The solicitor stood up. 'I think that's quite enough. May I

suggest a more empathetic approach? Perhaps one of your female officers?'

Collingworth looked at first as though he might refuse to entertain the request, but after a short hesitation and to George's surprise, he reached across the desk and hovered his finger over the recorder button. 'Request noted. Interview suspended at five forty-three.'

Click.

Collingworth stood up and George followed suit. 'I'll see who's available. George? Can you sort out tea and coffee for our guests?'

They left Fiona Manning, still sobbing, in the interview room, her brief looking on impotently and trying to pretend he was somewhere else.

George was bristling. *Tea and coffee? Cheeky sod.*

Chapter Thirty-Five

'This is DC Bernice Swinhoe,' Tess said. 'And I'm DC Tess Martin. Are you happy to continue?'

The solicitor nodded. 'I'm not sure that *happy* is the appropriate sentiment, but yes, my client is content to proceed.'

'Miss Manning,' Tess began, 'you are aware by now that our forensics team has confirmed that evidence in your vehicle suggests you were present at Marika Szarka's home at – or after – the time the Beethoven bust was broken. But you maintain that when you were at the Szarka residence that day, the bust was intact and in its usual place?'

Manning was pale, but had regained her composure. 'Yes. I have no idea how or when it was broken, and I can't imagine how a piece of it came to be in my car.'

'It is hard to imagine, isn't it?' Bernice chipped in. 'You can understand why we are suggesting the most obvious possibility – that it was transferred to your vehicle after you left your lesson, perhaps under your shoe, or maybe caught in your clothing.'

'I understand. But there is no way that it could have

happened the way you are suggesting. The bust was whole when I left. The fragment you have must be from another ornament.'

Tess shook her head. 'I'm afraid not. Our forensics team are very clear about that.'

'Then someone must have deliberately put it there.' Manning chewed her bottom lip. 'But that sounds completely mad, doesn't it?'

'Who might want to make you out to be a potential murderer, Miss Manning?' Bernice said. 'Do you have any enemies?'

Manning dipped her eyes. 'I hardly have friends, let alone enemies.'

'Tell me about Clive Brooks, Fiona,' Tess said gently. 'He doesn't seem very supportive.'

'Clive? He's all right. It's just his way. He doesn't mean to put me down.'

Tess could sense Bernice's reaction to this statement, a slight tensing of her muscles, and she shared her colleague's irritation at Manning's docile acceptance of Brooks' psychological abuse. But how had their relationship begun? She asked the question directly.

'How long have you been together?'

'Eighteen months and two days.' Manning smiled for the first time.

'That's very precise,' Bernice said.

Manning flushed. 'I don't have much history with … ah, with men. Relationships, you know?'

'OK.' Tess smiled. 'That's all right. Men are optional extras, right, DC Swinhoe?'

'Absolutely.' Bernice caught on. They needed Manning onside, all girls together. Maybe Collingworth wasn't so dumb after all.

Manning flushed. 'Well, they weren't even on my radar until I met Clive.'

Tess poured herself a glass of water from the jug. She could feel another headache coming on. 'OK, so where exactly did you meet?' She sipped the water – luke warm, but at least it would hydrate her.

'At the Szarkas house.'

Manning's reply froze, like a paused videotape, in the space between them.

Bernice was first to recover. 'You met Clive Brooks at the *Szarkas*? That's quite significant, Fiona.'

'I'm sorry, but no one asked about Clive before.'

'What was he doing at the Szarkas', Fiona?' Tess relaxed her grip on the glass tumbler.

'He does handyman work – it's a secondary income source for us. He's always done it. He's very good with his hands. Good at mending things, you know? He's in the local directory – you can check. He has a limited company for it. It's all above board.'

'I'm sure it is. And that's when you first met him? You were attending a lesson, and you got talking?' Bernice wanted the whole story. 'And one thing led to another.'

Manning nodded. 'He always seemed to be around. We'd chat in the hall, or outside. One day he asked me to dinner. I was taken aback. No one had ever asked me that before.'

'And how did Clive know the Szarkas? How did they find him? The local directory? Or a friend?'

'I've no idea. I've never asked him. If you're a good handyman, word gets around.'

The solicitor looked at his watch and then enquiringly at Tess. She ignored him. 'Fiona, you said that Mr Brooks' handyman work was a secondary employment. What's his other job?'

'He's a minicab driver.'

Bernice gave an exclamation of surprise.

Tess said, 'Right. I'm going to pause the interview here, Fiona. We'll continue a little later. I'm afraid you'll have to remain in custody for the time being.' She stopped the recording.

Manning looked distraught. 'But can't I go home? I won't go anywhere, I promise.'

'I'm sorry, Fiona,' Bernice said. 'We have to follow procedure.'

Outside, Tess leaned against the wall, her head throbbing. Collingworth was advancing along the corridor, his body language forming a giant question mark. 'Well?' The voice cut through her.

She closed her eyes.

'What's the matter with you?'

She opened her eyes. 'Just a headache, that's all.'

Bernice emerged from the interview room, followed by a dejected-looking Manning and her impatient brief.

'I need to speak to the guv,' Tess told Collingworth. 'Is he still here?'

'Right,' Moran said. 'I'll get acting sergeant Collingworth onto Brooks. He'll enjoy having another car to play with.'

Tess repressed a smile.

'Think Manning's telling the truth?'

'I think she is, guv. I never thought she looked like a killer—certainly not one capable of that kind of brutality. I think she's a victim of abuse, frankly – verbal abuse, certainly, psychological abuse, possibly. Brooks seems like a controlling sort of individual.'

'He does indeed. I think we'll let Manning stew overnight, nevertheless.' Moran studied Tess's face. 'Good work, Tess,' he said. 'But you look all in.'

'A headache, guv, that's all. And just for the record, DC Swinhoe was interviewing with me. She was amazing, considering ... what we discussed earlier.'

'And on that note,' Moran fished his coat from the back of his chair. 'I'd like to convene a quick meeting – offsite, naturally.'

'I might have to sit that one out, guv. Sorry.'

'Sure. I'll have a chat with Bola and George – and DC Swinhoe, of course. Leave it with us for now.'

'Are we bringing Brooks in yet?'

Moran considered. 'He has a link with the Szarka household. He's a handyman, and a minicab driver. All ticks in our boxes, but I don't want to spook him. Not yet. I want to be sure. He doesn't know what Manning's told us so far – and let's keep it that way, no phone calls home for her this evening.'

'She doesn't use a mobile, guv. Apparently Brooks doesn't allow it.'

'Sounds like a charming fella. So, we'll start with his car, give him the routine angle. He won't like it, but that's tough. And in the meantime we can keep a close eye on him. Perhaps you'd like to take that up first thing?'

'Will do, boss.'

Moran made his way through to the open plan. George and Bola were still hard at it, and Bernice was also at her workstation. Good.

'You three.' Moran beckoned. 'I need you for half an hour.'

George looked at Bola and Bola looked at George. Bola shrugged. 'Sure thing, boss. Your office?'

'Just follow me, please, DC Odunsi, if you would.'

In reception they were approached by Manning's solicitor. He looked flustered. 'Look, I have a flight to catch. Are you intending to continue interviewing my client this evening?'

'You're free to go,' Moran told him. 'I take it you'll be sending another representative of your firm in the morning, since you'll be unavailable?'

'Yes. It's all arranged.'

'Good.'

The solicitor hurried away to catch his flight, and the three detectives exited the building.

From his vantage point at the top of the staircase, Collingworth watched them leave. Something was up, something he'd been excluded from. But DC Martin was still around somewhere, nursing a headache, probably getting her things together to go home.

Not before he'd had a word, though. Collingworth walked quickly back towards the open plan. He was good at winkling out information, especially if the informant was feeling under the weather.

That made it almost too easy.

Chapter Thirty-Six

Moran chose a quiet corner of the atrium. The bar was quiet, early evening – precisely what he wanted. They ordered coffees and teas from the waiter, and when they were settled Moran began.

'I wouldn't normally do this in the middle of a murder investigation, especially after this evening's revelations, but these are extraordinary circumstances, and I need your help. Whatever we decide here, we need to set it in motion sooner rather than later.'

That got their attention. George paused, his cup half-way to his mouth. Bola looked as though he had an inkling of what might be coming, but Bernice sat quietly, avoiding eye contact, pale, tense and apprehensive.

When Moran had finished explaining the problem, with occasional clarification from Bernice, Bola and George were silent for a while, digesting the information.

'This isn't good,' George said finally. 'Where the hell did Catton bury this guy?'

Bernice spread her hands. 'I have no idea. I didn't *want* to know. I thought – at the time – that I could still salvage something from what I hoped might happen.'

'You and Catton?' George's mouth twisted into a half-smile, half-sneer. 'From what Bola's told me, he's an eco-weirdo.'

'You don't understand, George. He's so much more than that. He—'

'He's killed a man, B.'

'All right, all right,' Moran broke in. 'This isn't helping. Our focus is Isabel Akkerman. We'll worry about what happens to Catton once she's accounted for.'

'This is *way* risky, guv.' George didn't look happy. 'Best to just let the Sussex lot investigate, don't you think? They can bring Catton in.'

'You're not taking DC Swinhoe's situation into account, George,' Moran said patiently. 'Akkerman releases those photographs and our colleague is in hot water, no question.'

'But she didn't do it – it's a stitch-up.'

'I know, I know, but an investigation'll take time – a suspension from duty, a possible series of court appearances, and so on and so on – before we get a resolution. And even then, there's no guarantee DC Swinhoe will emerge unscathed.'

'The guv's right, George,' Bola said. 'Akkerman needs to be brought to heel. After that, things'll get easier.'

'And how do you propose to achieve said bringing to heel, eh?' George's face was reddening. 'Walk in there, bump her off and dump her body as well?'

'Enough!' Moran rapped the table top. 'I have some thoughts, if you'll be good enough to focus. We don't have long – there's a murder case to be solved, and thanks to some useful interviewing on the part of DC Swinhoe and DC Martin this evening, not to mention DC Schlesinger's latest contribution, we've just had a breakthrough. I want to pin the Szarka case down as soon as, and we're *this* close.' He held up his thumb and forefinger with the minutest gap between them. 'Clear?'

They quietly chorused their agreement. More people were starting to arrive for post-work drinks or early pre-dinner snacks. There was a growing background buzz of conversation, which suited Moran fine.

'Good. Now listen up. This is what I think needs to happen. Firstly, you may or may not be aware that Isabel Akkerman was sent on a mission to North Korea. Her remit – and this is confidential – was to eliminate the top brains working on that country's bioweapons programme. According to her MI6 minders, whom I had the pleasure of meeting a while back, they weren't expecting her to return.'

'But she did.' Bernice murmured.

'She did, and she accomplished her mission. The news was in the papers a while back. An explosion, top scientists killed outright. Now, how do you think the North Koreans feel about that?'

'They ain't gonna be happy, that's for sure,' Bola said, toying with his mug.

'Exactly. But still, she evaded capture and managed to flee the country.'

'If the North Korean secret service couldn't nail her, what hope do we have?' George was still ploughing his field of negativity.

'Probably still out for her blood,' Bola said.

'Precisely.' Moran leaned forward. 'But they don't know who she is. She's a ghost. They thought they knew her, but they didn't.'

'A woman of many identities,' Bernice said thoughtfully. 'Hard to pin down.'

Moran said, 'So we do have one advantage.'

'Right. We know exactly where she is,' George said, in dawning understanding. 'I think I see where this is going.'

'Any more drinks for you?' The waiter had appeared at their table and begun to clear their empties. George licked his lips and glanced wistfully towards the bar.

'We'll have a jug of iced water, if that's possible,' Moran said. To the others he said, 'Helps the concentration, I find.'

The waiter departed and Moran continued. 'Yes, George, We know where she is. We don't know how long she's going to stick around at Catton's holiday park, so we need to act quickly.' Moran spotted Bernice's pained expression at his description of Catton's commune. 'Sorry, DC Swinhoe, no offence.'

'None taken,' Bernice replied with a weak smile. 'But I do prefer sustainable communal permaculture project.'

'Rolls off the tongue,' George said.

'All right, concentrate.' Moran scowled. 'As DC Swinhoe has pointed out, Akkerman has many identities. She'll have passports, documents, perhaps even sensitive mission information, all held somewhere secure. But she also needs to have these to hand, so my bet is that they'll be stored on some secure drive that only she can access.'

'Or at MI6 HQ,' Bola said.

'Undoubtedly,' Moran agreed. 'But she's a field agent. She needs what she needs in the moment, not when MI6 gets around to furnishing her with the necessaries.'

'Oh, right,' George said. 'So all we have to do is locate her sensitive information and steal it. That'll be hard enough. But then what?'

Moran lowered his voice. 'Once it's in our possession, we hold the trump cards. She'll know that we can expose the information to whomsoever we choose. Her covers will be blown, MI6 will be less than impressed and my guess is that she'll be cut loose – at least for a period.'

Bola whistled softly. 'She'll be out there on her own.'

'Yes. And that's when we take the kid gloves off,' Moran said. 'That's when we make the information available to interested parties.'

George's eyes widened. 'I see what you mean. The North Koreans would pay a lot to get hold of her.'

Moran sat back. 'Indeed. And when she realises she's a marked woman – and more importantly, an accessible one – she might come round to my alternative proposal as not such a bad option.'

Bola smiled. 'You arrest her for the murder of Laura Witney.'

'Spot on. And she gets to stay in a nice, safe English gaol out of reach of those nasty North Koreans.'

'It might just work,' George said. 'But first we have to steal the data.'

'That's the tricky part,' Moran conceded. 'So let's put our thinking caps on and come up with a plan.' He looked at Bernice. 'We do have one advantage, and that's you, DC Swinhoe. You have access to Catton's estate, and you have a reason to visit. Akkerman wanted updates, yes? Well, like a good blackmail victim you can feed her updates. And while you're about it – and with support, of course – you can have a sniff around the place to figure out where her crown jewels are kept. You've already visited her lodgings once, so you have a head start, yes?'

A tentative nod.

'A *very* dangerous game, guv,' George said.

The waiter arrived with the iced water.

'Help yourselves,' Moran said.

'There's another issue, guv.' Bola was first to pour a glass. 'Why do they put *lemon* in it?' He fished the offending chunk of fruit out of his glass with an unused teaspoon.

'That's not such a serious issue,' George said.

Bola looked exasperated. 'Not the lemon. The *data*. Even if we can get hold of the tablet, laptop or whatever it might be, we've still got to crack the passwords, encryption etc etc. And you can bet it'll be encrypted to the nth degree.'

'It will be,' Moran agreed.

'Well, who's going to take that on? I'm no cyber hacker.' Bola wiggled his fingers in imitation of rapid key strokes.

'I know someone,' George said. 'Correction – I don't *exactly* know them, but you do, guv. A certain someone who'd relish the opportunity to have a crack at Akkerman.'

'Is that so, George?' Moran considered and his eyes widened. 'Ah! I think I know who you mean. But no, that'd never work.'

Bola looked lost. 'Care to elaborate?'

George picked up the lemon segment and sucked it noisily.

'That's disgusting, George.' Bernice wrinkled her nose.

'Sharpens the brain.' George dropped the segment in his glass.

'Come on, George, who?' Bola repeated his question.

Moran sipped his water and dried his lips on a paper napkin. 'Problem is, she's in prison.'

'No way.' Bola gave a low whistle. 'You can't mean Connie Chan. Surely not?'

'She's an adroit hacker. We know that,' Moran replied. 'My guess is she'd do anything to get back at Akkerman, after what she put her through. But it'd be too difficult to set in motion. Too much red tape, and far too visible, considering we have to do this quietly.'

Bernice reached across the table and grabbed George's wrist as he was about to retrieve the lemon. 'Behave, George.' She looked at Moran. 'I might know someone, guv. George, you remember the guy – the Indian lad who got married last month? Shared all that amazing food with us? What was his name? Began with a V…?'

'Vishal,' George said. 'Vishal Shrivastava. The new team lead on cyber security. Newish, anyhow. Been in post around six months.'

'Right. Vishal. He did an amazing job on that bank account, remember? No one else could crack it, but he did.'

'Yeah, but would he do it under the proverbial radar?'

'He's one of the guys,' Bernice said. 'I can have a word.'

Moran was listening. 'OK, but he'll have to work offsite. I don't want to wreck the guy's career before he gets started. We're happy that he's conversant with the language of IT hackery?'

'Absolutely. He's super-skilled. The old lags were shaking their heads in admiration. But … well, it's risky, guv.' Bernice's lips hardened to a compressed line. 'What if it all goes wrong?

I don't want to be responsible for—'

'I'll worry about that, DC Swinhoe.' Moran tapped his forehead. 'Your job – and DC Odunsi's – is to figure out where Akkerman stores her data. Once we have that, provided your young whizz kid is in place, we're good to go.'

George put his hand up. 'If I may volunteer—'

'You may not, George. I need you on the Szarka resolution. Still plenty to do there.'

George sat back, resigned. 'Whatever you say, boss.'

'Thank you, George.' Moran finished his water and set the glass down with a decisive thump. 'DCs Swinhoe and Odunsi, I'll cover for you as much as I can, but it goes without saying that your task will be best performed in the strictest secrecy, and inevitably out of working hours.' He looked at the three officers in turn. 'I trust we're all on the same page?'

No one disagreed.

Chapter Thirty-Seven

'Still here, Brendan?' DCS Higginson filled the doorframe of Moran's office.

'Apparently so, sir.'

'Mind if I interrupt?'

Moran gave a mental sigh. 'Not at all.'

Higginson pulled up the visitor's chair and sat down. His uniform, as always, was perfectly presented – not a single mote of dust, no blemish to spoil its perfection.

'I hear things are moving? You have a suspect in custody?'

'We do, yes,' Moran said, guardedly.

'And a possible lead from our new young talent, DC Schlesinger?'

'That's correct, sir.'

Higginson waved his hand in the air. 'Never mind the *sirs*, Brendan.'

'We're hoping for an early resolution, that's for sure.' Moran folded his arms, waiting for the real reason for the chief's visit. Something else was on Higginson's mind, that much was obvious.

'Indeed, as am I, Brendan. But I knew you were the man for

this. Tragedy about Dawson, but, well, between you and me and the bricks—' Higginson glanced theatrically around the office. 'I was never a hundred percent convinced he was the right man to fill your shoes.'

'It's kind of you to say so, sir. But I suspect that Dawson's ghost will be dogging my footsteps for a while yet – at least in the shape of his widow.'

Higginson looked puzzled, so Moran explained.

'That's absurd. Man couldn't hold his drink. I'll vouch for you, Brendan, no need to worry. She'll never take it to court. It's a knee-jerk reaction; understandable, of course, given the circumstances, but unfortunate for you.' Higginson pondered the threat. 'It's illegal, of course, for a licensed premises to sell alcohol to someone already intoxicated, but I don't believe there's any law that prohibits procuring a drink for an inebriated person at a private party.'

'I don't believe there is, sir, but it's nevertheless a little embarrassing, given that the party was thrown for myself, held on police premises, and there is definitely the slight possibility that although I only gave him a small whisky, it might have contributed to his accident. Who can say?'

'Yes, yes; I see what you mean.' Higginson stroked his chin. Moran suspected the DCS would be more concerned about reputational damage than the likelihood of Moran's being prosecuted, but he felt slightly better for having shared the problem.

'Still,' Higginson adopted a blustering tone, 'I'm sure it'll all come to naught. No point worrying about things that haven't happened yet, eh?'

'I suppose not, sir.'

'Which leads me to another subject, Brendan, if you'll allow me a few minutes more of your time.' The DCS looked a little uncomfortable. He cleared his throat. 'I've heard a rumour on the grapevine that this Akkerman MI6 woman is back in the UK. Diplomatic immunity, wasn't it? MI6 closed ranks, and so on? Now, please don't take this the wrong way, Brendan, but I'm aware that Akkerman – how can I put this – got under your skin a little.'

'We have corroborated witness statements concerning her various murderous activities, sir, so yes, it does trouble me that I was unable to present her case to the CPS because of said diplomatic immunity.'

'Quite. I understand. But let me be clear, it would cause me a … well, a considerable amount of anxiety if I thought you might be considering the prospect of … ah, hatching some kind of maverick plot to reverse her fortunes. To bring her in, as it were. Make her accountable.'

Moran maintained as neutral an expression as possible, but he knew where this had come from. Collingworth. Had to be.

'I'm not sure where that suggestion might have originated, sir, although yes, DI Pepper did mention Akkerman's repatriation to me a few days ago. Of course, she'll still be shielded by SIS, so I don't see that there's much more I could achieve, even if I wanted to.'

'I see. Well, good, good. That's reassuring, Brendan. We mustn't let personal vendettas rear their ugly heads, mm?'

'Indeed not, sir.'

'Well, then, that's all for now. I'll leave you to it. You'll let me know if we manage to nail down the Szarka culprit? Ahh…' Higginson coloured. 'That was very clumsily put, and not intended. Forgive me.'

'No problem, sir. I'll call you as soon as we have something tangible to report.'

'Day or night, Brendan. Don't hesitate.'

'Sir.'

'Well, goodnight, then. And good luck.' Higginson stood up and marched out with a ramrod-straight back and a slight self-deprecating, shake of his head.

Moran exhaled slowly. *Nail down the culprit. Nice one, sir.*

His expression hardened as he thought of Collingworth. How had the man known? Had he somehow eavesdropped? No, they'd been offsite. Except for Tess … who'd been suffering from a headache and heading home. That was Collingworth's way. That was how he operated: find a weakness, exploit it.

But Moran trusted Tess. She wouldn't have let much slip. Bare minimum, hopefully, but he'd need to check. If Bola and Bernice were to succeed, their mission had to be watertight, sealed, no leaks.

He checked the time on his phone. Just after seven. Could he risk a quick trip to the RBH? No texts, so hopefully no news was good news. Moran cracked his knuckles, reluctantly elected to stay put; things were moving. He should check on George and young Schlesinger, see how they were getting on, provide some encouragement.

Collingworth intercepted him en route. 'Still here?'

'If I were given a twenty-pound note every time I'm asked that question I'd be a richer fella than I am now,' Moran said.

'Sorry, seem to have left my wallet in my coat pocket,'

Collingworth said. 'I've got Brooks in number four. Unhappy bunny.'

'You've got *what?*' Moran felt his blood rising. 'I didn't want Brooks brought in yet.'

'Must have missed that one.'

Moran fought to keep himself under control. He had two choices – he could bawl Collingworth out or let him run with it. The damage was done; Brooks would be on his guard now anyway, so the interview might as well go ahead. As calmly as he could, he said, 'And are you inviting me to participate?'

'I think I can handle it. Blooding the new boy. We'll see what he's made of.'

'You're taking DC Schlesinger in with you?'

'Sure am.'

'What's your angle with Brooks?'

'Find out when he worked at the Szarkas. What he did there. If he holds a grudge. For starters.'

'And Manning?'

'Leaving her to stew till the morning. We'll see what Brooks comes up with, see if their stories dovetail.'

'Brooks has a brief?'

'Yep. A tad more committed than Manning's, too. She's here for the duration, so she says.'

'OK. You know where to find me.'

'You'll be kept in the loop – guv.' Collingworth walked away.

Moran took a moment and two deep breaths before moving on. The ceiling lights flickered to life as he approached George's workstation. 'Any news, George?'

'None worth shouting about, guv.' George leaned back, stretched. 'Not yet, anyhow.'

'Our acting sergeant has Brooks in custody, did you know?'

'Aye, I know – he's taken Schles in with him. I thought we were going to cut Brooks some slack, keep an eye on him?'

'That was my intention, George. I obviously hadn't made that sufficiently clear.'

George nodded diplomatically. 'Aye, well. Let's hope they get something out of him.'

Moran grunted. He was more angry with himself for the miscommunication than with Collingworth. 'Yes, let's. For sure, Brooks knows something. Manning too.' Moran grabbed an empty chair and sat down. 'They're connected to this, somehow – and it's not just that she's a Szarka student.'

'I agree,' George said. 'So, 'd'you reckon Manning put Brooks up to it, for whatever motive?'

'Or vice versa,' Moran said. 'Can't rule that out.'

George grunted. 'The fact that Brooks worked at the Szarkas has to be significant.'

'For sure.'

'But Manning – a killer? None of us think so.'

'I'm inclined to agree, George. But then, what does a killer look like?'

'Aye, I know.'

'And if the motive's not money, or sex – I think we can rule that one out in this case – what are we left with?'

'Burying a secret? Or the old chestnut – revenge?'

'OK, let's work with that. What possible motive could anyone have for murdering an elderly spinster?'

George knitted his brow. 'We have to get into their mindset – a genteel, musical mindset. A life of constant practising, public performances, composition. In all other areas, austerity. No sex, no high living, no holidays. Just music.'

'An element of competitiveness, you think?'

'No one has their hands nailed to a piano for suggesting a C major instead of an A minor.'

'Fair point. But these classical types … they take their music *very* seriously.'

'I don't know, guv. A musical disagreement? Too extreme a reaction, seems like.'

Moran was silent for a moment. 'What else has Collingworth got you on?'

'Brooks' accounts.' George indicated a large box file on the floor by his desk. 'Wants me to check for anything anomalous. Dates, times and so on. Running checks on his bank account, too – and Manning's. We'll see.'

'Anything interesting on social media?'

'Nope. Manning doesn't use it; she has a Facebook account but her last public update was two years ago, some comment on a local concert. Brooks has nothing, just email. All innocuous chatter. I wouldn't say he was the most IT literate guy; spelling's bloody awful. He's a manual sort of bloke. Drives, mends things.'

'No correspondence with the Szarka sisters?'

George shook his head. 'They don't use email, so no. There may be a paper trail somewhere, but Brooks doesn't seem a correspondence type of bloke, either.'

'No, quite.'

'Might be something in his cab, guv. It's a local firm he works for; he uses the same vehicle on a regular basis, and he was working that night. I'll get onto them in the morning. We might get your grease match.'

'I hope so, George. I hope so.' Moran felt a bone-deep weariness creep over him, as though the spirits of all his past investigations had gathered to point invisible fingers at his shortcomings and failures. He made a quick decision. 'I'm heading off. We'll work through everything we've got so far at the nine o'clock briefing. Don't burn too much midnight oil, George, and if you need to call, don't hesitate.'

George looked as though he wanted to say something else. 'What's on your mind, George? Spit it out.'

'I just wondered how Tess seemed when you spoke earlier. She hasn't been herself lately.'

'She's all right, George. She had a migraine. She'll be fine tomorrow, don't worry.'

George didn't look convinced.

'She's done amazingly well. Let's not forget where she's been. Just give her a little space; that's what she needs.'

'Aye. That'd be right, guv. Thanks.' George smiled, but Moran could tell it was forced.

As he headed for the car park, Moran briefly considered checking in on Tess. But then again, she might be asleep, and he didn't want to disturb her.

We all have our problems, Brendan. Some big, some small.

A half-remembered Bible verse from childhood came, unbidden, into his mind: *Who of you by worrying can add a single hour to your life?*

It was good advice, no doubt about it, but then good advice was never easy to follow.

Chapter Thirty-Eight

'CCTV?' Bola asked as Bernice brought the car to a halt before Simplicity's gates.

'Nope,' Bernice said. 'Alastair doesn't agree with it. This place is off the grid. That's the point.'

'OK.' Bola wasn't convinced. 'Must be *some* kind of security, even if Catton hasn't mentioned it.'

'No, there really isn't. And that,' Bernice said patiently, 'is why Akkerman feels so damn safe here.'

'I guess. So we leave the car here? Walk in?'

'Not me. Too suspicious. I'm supposed to be the bearer of news, remember? No reason for me not to rock up and park in the usual place. So this is where we part company.'

'Uh huh. Ready when you are.'

Bernice hesitated. 'Bola, I want you to know that I appreciate this. I know you don't have to do it.'

'Come on, B. We're partners, right?'

'Sure. But thanks, anyway. I mean it.'

'Don't mention it.' Bola opened the car door. 'So. Akkerman's cabin. Far as we know, it's the same one?'

'Yes.'

'Near the pond.'

'Yes. Wait for my signal. I don't want you to wind up getting shot.'

'Mm. Not too keen on that option myself.'

He waited until Bernice's tail lights had disappeared before slipping through the gates, hugging the shadows as he made for cover. The pond was off to the left, and he wanted to find a good vantage point so he could check out the area while he waited for Bernice's all-clear.

As his night vision improved he began to pick out familiar landmarks. The giant redwood holding court near the first group of cabins. The thick laurel bushes that camouflaged the pond and one isolated cabin – Akkerman's.

The silhouetted manor house loomed proprietorially against the night sky, the windows dark and vacant. Bola fretted about Bernice, what might happen if Akkerman turned on her.

Concentrate, Bola ...

The smell of woodsmoke hung in the still air like sweet tobacco, evoking memories of Scouts, midnight barbecues, campsites...

Night games ... here we go again...

He found a clump of alder and settled down behind it to wait. No one was about, but now and then the sound of a cabin door closing, or a distant hailed greeting, floated across the estate. The cabins themselves were spread far and wide, each with its own vegetable garden or animal pen. The homes had been thoughtfully placed, Bola remembered, so as not to intrude upon each other and to allow each homestead a good measure of privacy.

He looked at his watch and made sure his phone was on

silent. B had assured him there was no onsite security, but he found it hard to believe that Catton would risk leaving his precious self-sufficiency project exposed to the possibility of malicious intrusion.

Ten minutes passed. No signal.

Another five.

He had to move. He was getting cold, and he could feel his leg cramping.

He ran forward in a half-crouch towards the laurels and hunkered down, listening intently. He peered through a gap in the foliage. The pond was a darker oval beyond, and the cabin itself was unlit, no sign of life.

Should he move in? Or wait?

His mobile vibrated. Text message. One word: *Clear…*

That's it, my boy … Let's go.

He was at the cabin door in seconds. Locked. Of course it was.

Moving along the side, his back to the rough wood of the cabin exterior, he came to a window. Shut and bolted. Naturally.

He froze at a sudden, sharp *crack* – a foot on an uneven surface, a branch, a loose stone…

Something.

He waited. His chest was heaving, not with exertion but with the effort of keeping completely still. And another thing…

Fear.

He knew about Akkerman. What she could do. Charlie had told him. *She took the gun off me as though it were a toy … like I was a child…*

He wiped a trickle of sweat from his brow.

You're a big guy, Bola. You can take care of yourself. Right?

All was still. Maybe it had been an animal – a squirrel or a fox.

He peered around the corner. There might be another window at the rear – a bathroom, perhaps. Maybe left open for ventilation.

He edged around the corner, rough wood brushing his fingertips.

Nothing there. Bola breathed again.

Something caught his attention at the limit of his peripheral vision.

Coming fast…

A heavy blow caught him on the side of his head, just above his eyebrow and threw him against the cabin wall. Stunned, he tried to raise his fists to square up to his attacker, but a powerful beam shone directly into his eyes, blinding him. He ducked, shimmied to the right, but a second blow drove into his stomach. He doubled over, gasping for breath.

'Nah, mate. You're going nowhere.'

Bola didn't have enough air in his lungs to speak, but he gave it a go. 'I'm a … I'm a…' He reached into his jacket.

'Don't care what you are, mate. I said *nope*.'

Another blow, this time on his bicep – not as hard as the first, but enough to deter him from further movement. Bola let his arm drop to his side.

'That's the way. You're getting the hang of it. Now, when you've got your breath back, maybe you'd like to tell me what the hell you're up to.'

The accent was unmistakably Aussie, the tone not entirely unfriendly, but firm. It wasn't Isabel. That, at least, was a bonus.

'I'm a … police … officer,' Bola managed eventually.

'Ah shit, no way.'

'If you'll allow me?' Bola went for his jacket pocket again.

'Easy, mate. Nice and slow.'

Bola carefully withdrew his warrant card and held it up for inspection.

The torch beam tracked downwards. 'Well, well. So you are.'

The beam vanished. Bola blinked, his night vision wrecked.

'OK, sorry for the heavy intro. Can't be too careful these days, right? So, maybe you'd care to explain?'

'I don't have long.' Bola gingerly touched his forehead. It was sticky with blood.

'Just a scratch, mate. You'll clean up all right. The name's Ben Runnalls.' He offered his hand. 'I'm the senior camper here. Old mate of Al's.'

Bola shook his hand. 'DC Bola Odunsi. This is Isabel Akkerman's cabin, right?'

'Yep, sure is.'

'I need access.'

'I'm guessing you'd rather she didn't know?'

'You guess right.'

'Odd fish, that one,' Runnalls said. 'Got some kind of hold over Al. Things haven't been the same since she's been around.'

'There's a good reason for that.'

'Yeah? I'll bet. But listen, mate, I'm not up for any heavy scenes these days. I just live my life; me and my woman and the kids. That's why we're here. No stress, no worries, you follow?'

'Sure. I get it.'

'You do? Good to hear.'

Bola's night vision was slowly returning. Now he could see Runnalls instead of just a silhouette. The Australian was around six feet tall with a plaited beard and shoulder length hair. His eyes were piercing, full of restless intelligence. He was holding a stout length of birch in one hand and a fat Maglite torch in the other.

'Look, I'm kind of in a hurry,' Bola said.

'Yeah? And here's me jabberin' on like a Kookaburra. So, you want in?' Runnalls produced a set of keys from his jeans pocket and dangled them in front of him. 'Allow me.'

'You have a key?'

'I built the cabins, mate. All of 'em. I keep a master, just in case.'

Bola followed Runnalls to the front of the cabin. The door was open in seconds.

'Do what you've got to do, mate. Catch you later. Sorry I gave you a smack. No hard feelings, eh?'

'None.'

And with that, Runnalls was gone.

Bola hesitated on the threshold. He'd used around twenty minutes of their agreed thirty. Which left … not enough time. He checked from left to right, scanned the area by the pond and then as far as he could see through gaps in the laurel. No sign of movement, no noise.

He went in.

The cabin was orderly, simply furnished, as he recalled from their previous visit. Bola took out his own torch, a pencil-thin version of Runnalls', and played the beam around the interior. There was the desk where they'd found the passports. He checked there first. No laptop, no external drives, no memory sticks. He progressed to the bedroom. Both bedside cabinets were empty.

He stood in the centre of the room. Where would he hide valuables? A safe? He quickly scanned the walls, moved two framed prints aside. Nothing. The floor was uncarpeted, the boards partially covered by a rectangular Chinese rug. He bent, rolled up an edge, probed the area with his foot. Nothing loose.

Where, then?

The kitchen.

He went through each cupboard. Crockery, pans, and in the last, an iPad. He knew there'd be nothing on it. He left it where it was.

One room left.

He checked outside. No movement.

The bathroom was small, but luxuriously fitted. He examined the laundry basket, the wall-mounted cabinet.

He checked his watch.

Out of time, Bola, my lad…

What was left? The bath…

The cistern.

He eased the porcelain lid from its base and looked inside. Water, the float, the flush mechanism.

He was about to replace it when something beneath the lip caught his eye. He laid the lid upside down on the floor and experimentally probed the interior. His fingers brushed something plastic, like a sealed inner envelope. He checked around the edges of the lid, found a clip, and another. The envelope dropped into his hand.

He slid his fingers inside, withdrew a slim external memory drive.

Bingo…

He slipped the drive into his pocket, replaced the cistern lid, crept back into the main living room and moved cautiously to the front door. He had one hand on the door handle when he caught sight of a torch beam playing along the grass by the laurels. Runnalls?

Maybe, maybe not.

And then, from the opposite direction, another light. Bola slipped outside, closed the door softly behind him and looked for cover. He was two metres away from the alder, the nearest option, but if the first torch owner turned the corner he'd be seen immediately.

'Ah, Miss Akkerman.' A voice floated towards him through the night air. 'Nice to see you out and about on this fine evening.' The accent was unmistakeable, as was the intent.

Runnalls, giving him a chance to get away.

'And what are you up to, sneaking around in the dark?' A deep female voice replied, half-playfully.

'Just security checking, you know me. Never leave anything to chance.'

'Is that so, Mr Runnalls?' The voice took on a flirtatious tone.

'Al OK? Haven't seen much of him lately, since you pitched up again.'

'I like to keep my men busy,' Akkerman said.

Bola made his move, covered the gap between the cabin and

the alder, squatted behind it. The cabin would be unlocked. Was that a problem? Maybe Akkerman left it like that from time to time. Or maybe she'd know instantly that someone had broken in…

He watched from his vantage point as both torch beams converged and approached the cabin frontage.

'Mind if I test a new key? Just had it cut – you know how they can stick when they're new?'

'Ah, the master key. How masterful,' Akkerman purred. 'Be my guest.'

Bola relaxed; Runnalls had him covered.

'All good,' he heard Runnalls say. 'Lock turns like a dream.'

'Thank you, Mr Runnalls. I know who to ask should I be careless enough to lose my own.'

'No worries. Have a nice evening. Say hi to Al for me – tell him he still owes me a return match.'

'The battle of the grand masters continues? Of course – I'll be sure to.'

Runnalls' beam retreated, and the cabin door opened and closed.

Bola turned to scan the drive, a dark ribbon scored through the landscaped gardens between the main house and the gates. Two headlights pierced the gloom next to the house, began a slow crawl along the drive.

'That's my girl,' Bola muttered, and began a brisk trot towards the gates.

The car cruised by, went through the gates, turned left. Bola followed it. If Akkerman went straight for her hard drive she'd be down on them like a ton of bricks. And Runnalls might be in the firing line as a result. But he couldn't help that. Panting, he made the gates and headed quickly towards B's car.

'All good? What happened to your head?' Bernice's face was a mask of concern.

'Made a new friend from down under. But yeah,' he patted his pocket. 'I have what we wanted. What story did you spin Akkerman?'

'Gave her a load of hot air about how she was a low priority, given the severity of current caseloads. Plus a few other inconsequential bits and pieces of trivia.'

'And Catton?'

'Keeping out of my way, by the look of it.'

'Wise man. Let's get the hell out of here.'

Bernice floored the accelerator.

Bola shut his eyes.

Chapter Thirty-Nine

Moran looked out at a sea of weary faces, a dozen pairs of eyes following him as he approached the whiteboard.

'Morning everyone. All right, let's try to pull it all together. I want to concentrate on Clive Brooks, the possibility that he might have set Manning up. Acting sergeant Collingworth and DC Schlesinger interviewed said gentleman last evening. Over to you, acting sergeant.'

Collingworth's customary swagger was strangely absent as he came to the front of the room. After his brief and inconclusive summary, Moran understood why; Brooks' interview had yielded nothing new. It would have been so much better to monitor Brooks' movements from afar than try to pin him down at interview, but that option had gone.

'Thank you, acting sergeant.' Moran took his place by the whiteboard. 'Let's have a quick round the room. I'll transfer anything relevant to the board, and we'll see where we are. We'll start with you, George. Any joy with Brooks' minicab employers this morning?'

George flipped his notepad open. 'Yep, I made contact, but sadly no joy. Yes, he works for them. Yes, he was on duty that evening, but they have his fares all written up and printed out. No drop-offs in the area of interest, and the cab company has its own maintenance operation. The gaffer there confirms that their fleet sticks to a single supplier for automotive maintenance peripherals – a UK-based operation by the name of Malvern and Whitcomb, and they buy in Castrol products exclusively.' George closed his notebook with a snap. 'Sorry, guv.'

Moran did his best to mask his disappointment. 'Thank you, George. I suggest we cast the net wider. Let's include minicab companies from further afield – to cover Slough, Maidenhead, Newbury. Can you run with that?'

'Will do, guv.'

'Did you get a chance to check through Brooks' accounts and invoices?'

'Ongoing, guv.'

'Good. How about you, Tess?'

Moran followed George's anxious glance, and was relieved to see that Tess looked better, for sure. Her cheeks had regained some colour. 'What's your take on the Szarka situation? You've interviewed an old friend, a Mrs Harrington?'

'Yes, guv. She remembers the sisters well. They were all into music as young adults, and they frequently met up to play together. She mentioned a tutor, a sadistic woman.' Tess consulted her notes. 'A Beatrice Keane. She gave Reyka Szarka a hard time.'

'Oh yes?'

'Marika was a naturally talented pianist, but Reyka had to work at it, and her mother pushed her hard.'

'Do I detect a sibling rivalry?'

'I thought about that, guv. I mean, yes, Reyka would obviously have felt it – any normal person would. But Mrs Harrington assures us that the sisters loved each other, and after Reyka switched instruments things seem to have got much better.'

Moran nodded. 'And Reyka has an alibi. Do we trust it?'

'No reason not to,' Tess said. 'Ms Goosens seems reliable, and she has no reason to lie. She's very concerned about Reyka's wellbeing.'

'Seriously? Can you *honestly* see the old dear nailing her sister's hands to a piano?' Collingworth broke in, casting about him for support. There were a few guffaws, some murmurs of agreement. 'I mean, come on, *please*. It's either Brooks or persons as yet unknown, and for your info I'm still on Potter's case. He's not off my hook yet. Let's get real here.'

'Thank you, acting sergeant.' Moran turned to write on the board.

'One more thing, guv.' Tess put her hand up.

Moran turned around in mid-sentence.

'Yes, DC Martin?'

'Not sure if it's relevant, but the sisters' mother died a few months ago. She was living with them; they were all together, the three of them. It must have been upsetting for Marika and Reyka when Leila passed away.'

'Thank you, DC Martin. Until we're further forward, *everything* is relevant, right acting sergeant?'

Collingworth simmered.

'Er, may I suggest something?' DC Schlesinger tentatively raised his hand.

'Go ahead, DC Schlesinger.'

'Have we considered the possibility that Reyka and Ms Goosens are, er … you know? How can I put this?'

'Out with it, DC Schlesinger.'

'Well, I thought maybe a motive could be … well, let's see.' Schlesinger began to tick events off on his fingers. 'The mother dies. The dynamic changes. Maybe Reyka doesn't want to live with Marika any more. Maybe she cooks up a plot with Ms Goosens to get rid of Marika, so they can live together as … well, you know…'

Collingworth had his head in his hands.

Moran was taken aback. The lad had a point. Why had he not considered it?

'Thank you, DC Schlesinger. That's an interesting theory. Goosens' alibi for Reyka could be false, is what you're saying?'

'Yes sir – sorry, guv. Goosens could be covering for her. Reyka sneaks off, does the deed, comes back, plays the bereaved sister card. Goosens supports the whole story.'

'What about the ceramic shard in Manning's car?' Collingworth reminded them. 'Forensics have confirmed it's part of the same ornament – the Beethoven bust. How'd that get in there? How does that fit your theory, Sherlock? It's Brooks or Potter, or like I said before, persons as yet unknown. Got to be.'

'Maybe Manning did the deed on Reyka's behalf?' Schlesinger spread his hands. 'They conspired.'

'OK, but for why?' Collingworth wanted to know. 'She's got nothing in her bank account, right George?'

George read from his notes. 'A hundred and twenty-three pounds and twenty-two pence.'

'Hardly an assassin's fee, is it?' Collingworth smirked. 'And look at the woman. She couldn't kill a goldfish, let alone an old biddy.'

'But there is the shard, as you've reminded us, acting sergeant.' Moran said.

'So, maybe it was planted,' Schlesinger said. 'A frame-up.'

'Again, maybe so.' Moran stroked his chin as he considered the best course of action. 'Right, this is what we're going to do,' he said. 'George, carry on with the garage checks and Brooks' accounts. DC Schlesinger – you're with me. We're going to pay Reyka another visit. Tess, you carry on with Szarka research. Is there any dirt? Anything off kilter? Your Mrs Harrington? She might remember a great deal more with prompting. Try and fit her in if you can. Acting sergeant? Keep at Brooks, if you would, please, and then back to Manning. All of you, report back every hour today, please. I want regular updates. Ladies and gents, we're getting closer. Keep it up, and thanks for your hard work.'

'And DCs Odunsi and Swinhoe?' Collingworth raised his voice over the scraping of chairs and hubbub of rekindled conversation. 'Any idea where they might be this morning?'

'They're doing a job for me, acting sergeant,' Moran said. 'Not your concern. Oh, DC Martin?' he caught Tess's eye. 'A quick word?'

'Yes, guv?'

Moran waited for the team to disperse. 'Not a problem – no need to look so worried. I just wondered if our acting sergeant approached you regarding the Akkerman development?'

'He did, guv, yes. But I didn't give him much – honestly. I just said we'd been informed that she was back in the UK and you'd made a mental note.'

Moran nodded. 'OK, that's fine. We need to keep this well under wraps for DC Swinhoe's sake – Higginson's caught a scent.'

'My lips are sealed, guv. I won't breath a word.'

'I'm sure. Thanks, Tess.'

Chapter Forty

'I never knew there were so many minicab companies in the county,' George said. 'I mean, how many do you need?'

Tess grinned across the space between the workstations. 'Keep going. You'll get there.'

'By Christmas, maybe.' George moved to the next on his list. 'Here we go again.'

But it was another blank. No drop-offs in the area that evening – or even that week. Hardly surprising; it was a Hungerford minicab company.

'I've had enough for a bit,' George said, exasperated. 'Back to the accounts.'

'Break it up, that's the way,' Tess said. She lowered her voice. 'George, there's no sign of the two Bs this morning. I'm worried.'

'Hm. I was wondering, too. I'm sure they're OK.'

Tess's voice was a hoarse whisper. 'I wish I shared your optimism. I mean, *anything* could have happened.'

'Give them till lunchtime. They'll show.'

She sighed. 'All right. If you say so.'

She shot him a quick smile, which pleased him. She seemed

altogether brighter, despite her concern about their absent colleagues. He'd been thinking about suggesting a coffee break, but decided in the end he couldn't face rejection. Besides, it sounded as though she was well stuck into her Szarka research, and he was reluctant to interrupt her flow. He was reaching for Brook's box file when Tess gave a small cry of surprise.

'What is it?'

'Marika's performances back in the day. She was very popular. Even played the Albert Hall. On the … let's see … twenty-first of April, 1980.

'Rings a bell.' George frowned. 'Hang on, that's the date of the murder.'

'So it is,' Tess confirmed. 'And here's another clipping from the Evening Post. Reyka, this time.' Tess fell silent. 'Oh dear.'

'What?'

'Bad review. And take a look at this.'

George joined her at her workstation, pleased that she'd called him over. 'What am I looking at?'

'This woman in the photo. See the caption? It's the tutor, on the left there – Miss Keane. Look at that face – like thunder.'

'And that's Reyka?' George tapped the screen.

'Yep. But read the review.'

George scanned the few lines that some classical reporter had penned. It wasn't exactly positive. Words like *disappointing*, and the recurring phrase, *poorly interpreted* peppered the narrative. The final paragraph made him exclaim aloud. He read it again, but there was no mistake. *Miss Keane, musical director, was scathing in her criticism, particularly of the oboe in the second movement, blaming the errors and lacklustre performance on the performer rather than her arrangement of the popular piece.*

'That would have hurt,' he said.

'And then some,' Tess said. 'Poor Reyka. It's hardly a review, more a public humiliation.'

'Are we looking at motive here?'

'We're certainly looking at disappointment, and not a little bitterness and frustration.'

'But Keane must be long dead,' George said. 'She looks ancient in the photo.'

'She is, but I'll bet Reyka wasn't first in line to pay her respects. What an awful woman Keane must have been. Mrs Harrington certainly painted a picture. Imagine being put down like that in a newspaper. I mean, it's only a local rag, but still.'

'Worth a mention,' George said. 'Keep going. I'd better crack on with the accounts.'

An hour later it was George's turn. He stretched and rubbed his eyes. 'Well, that *is* weird.'

'Hm?' Tess's response was semi-automatic.

'Brooks' accounts. He's actually pretty fastidious. I can link all dates and invoices, except for one thing.'

'Oh? What's that?'

'There are no invoices for the Szarka jobs. None at all.'

'Maybe he keeps them somewhere else?'

'But why would he?'

'He definitely did work for them in the financial year you're looking at?'

'Yep. Three jobs, according to Captain Motormouth. Brooks confirmed that during his interview last night.'

'So he didn't charge them?'

'Apparently not.'

'OK, so what possible reason could he have had? He's not a charity.'

George looked at Tess. 'Supposing you were an odd job person. Who would you waive your charge for?'

Tess shrugged. 'Friends?'

'Uh huh. Or?'

'Or family.'

'Right. Didn't your Mrs Harrington recall Reyka taking an extended trip to Scotland back in the day – after some kind of break-up?'

'Or the Lake District. She wasn't sure.'

George put on a knowing smile. 'There you go. Bet she was away for eight or nine months – probably with a relative, an aunt, maybe, or some family friend.'

Tess looked impressed. 'Nice one, George. I'll get Schles to do some digging.'

Moran slammed on the brakes as a van pulled out in front of him. '*Damn!*'

'Post Office, guv,' Schlesinger said. 'All their drivers are mad. Seriously. I avoid them.'

'I'm glad I avoided that particular one, DC Schlesinger.' Moran steered the car around the roundabout and headed out of Reading along the A33 towards Atlantic House. The visit, in his view, had been inconclusive. Goosens had stuck convincingly to her story about their being at home all evening on the night of Marika's demise. Reyka was clearly still emotional, and seemed genuinely discombobulated by her sister's murder. Schlesinger's LGBT theory had also taken a nosedive under Moran's careful perusal of the two women's mannerisms and body language. He'd seen lesbian partnerships before, and this one didn't fit the bill. Reyka was beautifully turned out in a long, patterned dress, comprehensive, albeit subtle, make-up applied, with feminine earrings and elegantly styled hair. Goosens too was dressed conservatively, but also in a genteel style very much favoured by ladies of her generation, with not a hint of sexual ambiguity.

In short, he felt discouraged, but was trying, for Schlesinger's sake, not to show it.

His mood lifted, however, when he caught sight of Bola's car just ahead and about to turn into the station car park. Relief washed through him. Had they succeeded? Whatever, at least they were back in one piece.

As he turned in behind them and looked for a space, Schlesinger cleared his throat. 'You recall I excused myself at Ms Goosens' house, guv?'

'I do. And I'm glad I wasn't obliged to come to your assistance this time, DC Schlesinger.'

Schlesinger looked uncomfortable. 'Yes, guv. Anyway, er, I had a little look around while I was upstairs. Hope that was OK?'

'Did you indeed?'

'I slipped into the spare bedroom. They're definitely not sharing.'

'Yes, thank you. I'd figured that out myself.' Moran watched Bola's car as it slid into a parking bay and its tail lights flicked off.

'Thing is, guv, I couldn't resist the handbag on the bedside chair. It's Reyka's, definitely. There was a diary with her name inscribed on the cover – a five-year diary.'

'Anything of interest inside?'

'Maybe.' Schlesinger nodded. 'She's circled a few dates. I took the liberty—' He showed Moran his smartphone. 'I noticed a consistent marker on the fifteenth of January, every year – look.'

Moran peered at the small screen. 'Date's circled. What's that? *T*?'

'I think so, just the letter T.'

'Someone's birthday, perhaps?'

'And there's this.'

Moran looked again. 'Twelfth of February. *Mother has passed.*' His eyes tracked to the next line, written in the same precise handwriting. He read aloud, '*And now T is here. Such bliss. I feel … liberated. Such love for T…*'

'Odd, don't you think, guv?'

Moran grunted. 'Could mean anything. Run them past Bola and Tess, would you?'

'Will do. I did find something else, too.' He held up a small plastic vial of clear liquid. 'I squeezed out a sample – not enough that it'd be noticed.'

Moran's heart lifted as he saw Bernice disembark from Bola's car, followed by the big man himself. He turned his attention back to Schlesinger. 'What is it?'

'I thought it might be holy water at first – you know, a Catholic thing. But the viscosity looks wrong. I'll get it over to the lab, shall I?'

'*Holy* water? Saints and sinners, lad – are you having me on? Here, let me see … just hold it under my nose, that's it.' He took a sniff. 'Hm. Definitely not holy water.'

'Bottle was unmarked, so probably not prescribed medication, either,' Schlesinger said.

'Indeed not. All right – to the lab with it.'

'Yes, sir.' Schlesinger got out of the car and scurried off.

As Moran clicked the key fob and made his way to the lift, his mobile bleeped. Text message. He thumbed a button and stopped in his tracks.

Brendan. I'm sorry to tell you that Peter passed away in his sleep during the night. I'm also sorry you weren't able to find the time to visit. A.

Chapter Forty-One

'Schles? What happened at Goosens'?' As she spoke, Tess clocked Moran storming into his office and slamming the door. Moran never slammed his door.

'I found something—'

'Never mind that. What's up with the guv?'

'He was fine a minute ago.' Schlesinger shrugged. 'Really. I have no idea.'

At that moment Bola and Bernice appeared from the direction of the canteen carrying mugs and an assortment of rolls and sandwiches.

'Hey.' Tess fist-bumped Bola's shoulder. 'I was beginning to worry. Busy morning?'

'Had to see a man about a dog,' Bola said, with a sly wink.

Schlesinger was looking at Bola. 'What happened to your head?'

Bola fingered a deep cut on his forehead which had been sealed with two Steri-Strips. 'Banged it on a scaffolding pipe. Careless, as usual. It'll heal.'

'Never mind his head,' Tess said to Schlesinger. 'We think Reyka Szarka may have had a child – late eighties, early nineties. Probably adopted. So, can you check aunts, cousins, family friends living in the Lake District or maybe Scotland.'

'Really? OK, will do.' Schlesinger looked pleased with his new assignment.

'Bola? You fit for some minicab calls?' George called from his desk.

'Fit for nothing, more like.' Bola booted his laptop. 'Pass the list.'

George selected the next two pages from his minicab checklist. 'Here you go.' He glanced around to see if anyone was within earshot. 'Well?'

'Sussex was OK. This morning with Mr Shrivastava less so – but I got at least every other word he was saying. Mostly.'

George grinned, punched in the next phone number with his biro. 'Should have paid more attention at school.'

'They hadn't invented IT when I was at school, buddy.'

Three rings. George held his hand up. A female voice.

'Hello, EasyCabs – time and location required, please.'

Moran sat very still in the vacuum of his office. He was conscious of the usual day-to-day noises filtering through from the open plan. He recognised some of the voices – Bola's easy laugh, George's urgent chatter, Tess Martin's cultured and reserved tones. But they came from another place, another world. In here, in his inner sanctum, there was only sadness and deep regret.

Peter was dead. How was it possible? A chest infection and then, in all probability, pneumonia. Moran was used to sudden death, but this was so totally unexpected, so tragic, so close to home – or what he had almost come to the point of considering as home.

And he had not visited. He'd intended to, of course he had. But the case, along with DC Swinhoe's dilemma, had swept away his opportunity to do the right thing, to provide Alice with some badly needed emotional support. If their relationship had been on the rocks before, it was now forever shipwrecked, that was a given. Surely there was no way back from this terrible sin of omission.

Moran leaned on his elbow and cupped his forehead with his hand. Peter, gentle, harmless, innocent Peter, was gone. It was little consolation that Alice would have her sister and brother-in-law to support her. He had been absent and even if Alice could find it in herself one day to forgive him, he knew that he would never forgive himself. How to respond to her cold, factual text? There was nothing he could say, nothing he could do.

A personal visit, then? Better late than never? Or just leave it, give her time to be with her sister?

He looked up, startled, as the office door flew open and George appeared, red-faced, animated.

'Guv – sorry to interrupt, but we've found it, the cab company I mean. Fleet, of all places. Drop-off checks out, so I called their maintenance garage, and guess what? They import parts, oil and peripherals directly from India, from Mumbai.'

'Mumbai? That's spot on, George, according to Pauline Harris' research.'

'Gets better, guv. I spoke to the cabbie and he remembers the fare, thought he was a bit of an odd bod. Description fits Schlesinger's intel from Levi Cambridge: tall, grey suit, short – no, cropped – grey hair. Specs. Carried a small briefcase.

Wanted to be collected from the same spot an hour later.'

'They get a name?'

'Tarzan.'

'Are you kidding?'

'I know. Guy said that's what it sounded like, anyhow.'

'Where was the pickup?'

George was almost apoplectic as he tried to get his words out. 'Herbert Road. Just round the corner from the shopping parade, you know, the one with the curry house, the bike shop —'

'And the hardware store? Yep, I know it.' Moran closed his eyes, tried to visualise the area. 'Wait, that's pretty close to—'

'Goosens' place, yes.' George bobbed his head like an excited terrier.

'Hm. I'd say about the same distance from Brooks' house, too.'

'But still, guv…'

'OK, can you arrange a sample of lubricant from the cab? I'll get forensics onto it. Should be quick enough to establish a match with the shard sample.'

'Aye, it should.'

'One thing…' Moran frowned. 'The description doesn't match Brooks. Too tall. Brooks is a stocky guy.'

'I was thinking the same.' George hovered by the door.

'You think Reyka and Goosens hired someone? A hit man?'

'Sounds unlikely, doesn't it? I mean, how would they know where to look?'

'True. Another thing, guv – Brooks' accounts. He didn't charge the Szarkas for any of the work he did for them. Nada. Tess and I, we thought it might indicate a relationship, some closer connection.'

'Go on.'

'So maybe they're more than acquaintances, or friends. Odd to have a young guy friendly with two old spinsters. I mean, they're not exactly moving in the same social circles, are they?'

'You're thinking family.'

'Yep.'

'A well-kept secret? A son?'

George nodded. 'Yep, maybe. DC Schlesinger is checking it out.'

'So potentially an accomplice.' Moran scratched his chin. 'Collingworth still grilling Brooks?'

'I believe so, yep.'

'Let's do this properly. Can you arrange a DNA sample from Brooks, George. Interrupt, if you need to.'

'On it, guv.' And the Scot was gone.

Moran sat quietly for a while. *Tarzan?* That was just plain crazy. The Szarkas were of Hungarian origin, though, so maybe…

He thumbed his smartphone. *Hungarian names. Male.*

He scrolled down the list of the first website to appear in the search results.

Szevér,
Tabor,
Taksony,
Tardos,

Tarján…

They were two minutes from the nursing home when Bernice began to tremble. Tess shot her an anxious look. 'You OK, B?'

'I thought I was, but—'

'Delayed shock,' Tess said. 'Hardly surprising.' She indicated and pulled over. 'Look at you. You're exhausted. You need time out.' She made a snap decision. 'I'm taking you home. You can have a shower, sleep for a couple of hours. No arguments.'

'But, I'm on du—'

'Not any more you're not. I just signed you off.'

'*Tess*—'

'No arguing.' Tess checked her mirror and pulled out. 'It's home for you. We'll be there in five minutes. I'll talk to Mrs Harrington. It's fine. She's not going to bite me.'

Bernice was holding her wrist tightly but the tremors were still noticeable. 'OK. If you say so.'

'I do say so.'

They were at Bernice's maisonette in three minutes flat. 'Right. Out you get. I'll talk to the guv, don't worry.'

'Thanks, Tess. I appreciate it.'

'Don't be daft. You'd do the same for me. See you later – and don't rush back.'

Tess waited for Bernice to let herself in. She turned at the door, waved and disappeared inside.

Tess made a U-turn and headed back the way she'd come. She'd done the right thing, absolutely. B was stressed out, big time – and no wonder; anyone would be in her situation. Thank God she'd come clean and told them what had happened. The guv would fix the Akkerman problem – Tess had no doubts about that – but she was still cross with herself for talking to Collingworth – not that he'd given her much choice. He'd caught her in a weak moment; the guy just had the knack of knowing when something was up…

Tess chewed her bottom lip. She'd given nothing away; she'd been upfront with Moran. And he'd believed her, so … Tess drummed on the steering wheel. But … it was bugging her, nevertheless. Collingworth was *so* annoying. The last thing she wanted was for Moran to think she was untrustworthy, that she might betray confidences. She shook her head angrily.

Come on, Tess … concentrate on the job in hand.

When she arrived at the nursing home it was Mrs Elvey, the manager, who answered the door. Her face immediately told Tess that bad news was coming.

'I'm afraid Jean had a bad turn just before lunch. The doctor thinks it might have been a mini-stroke, but we're hoping it was just a dizzy spell. Do come in, though. She's in her room resting. I'll see if you can pop in to say hello, but extended conversation is out of the question – I am sorry. If you'd like to wait in reception, I'll be back shortly.'

Tess waited as instructed and Mrs Elvey returned a few minutes later.

'She's fast asleep – I think it's best not to disturb her. We'll see how she is later, and perhaps you could call back? It's hard to predict how she will be at the moment. I'm sure you understand.'

'Did she, by any chance, mention anything about a name? She was trying to remember for me.'

'You're DC Martin? Jean did write you a note. She asked me to post it for her, but one of our staff members lives near your building – Atlantic House, that's right, isn't it? So I asked her to drop it in by hand. She went off shift a couple of hours ago, so I imagine it'll be waiting for you by the time you get back. Jean was very pleased she'd remembered. She hoped it would be helpful.'

'Oh, that's great – please pass on my thanks.'

'I'll be sure to. I'm sure she'll be fine – she probably just needs to rest. Call me for an update later, if you like.'

'I will. Send her my best wishes, won't you?'

'Of course.'

Her mobile rang on her way back to the car. Collingworth. Just what she needed.

The acting sergeant's voice, eschewing preamble as usual, cut through her like a knife. 'DC Martin – as you're out and about get yourself over to the Goosens' house. I want a DNA sample from Reyka Szarka. Quick as you can. We've got a sample from Brooks in the lab already.'

'Well, as you've asked so nicely…'

'Just do it.'

Tess gritted her teeth. 'All right – one thing, though.' She caught him before he ended the call.

'What?'

'Mrs Harrington's been taken ill, but a letter should have been delivered on her behalf to AH this morning, addressed to me. Can you check to see if it's arrived? Open it – it might be helpful.'

'All right.'

Collingworth rang off.

Twat.

Unlocking the car, Tess opened her glove box where she kept

a range of accessories, including DNA sample kits. She hadn't restocked recently, but fortunately she had one unopened box.

Fine. This wouldn't take long.

On her way to Goosens' property she amused herself by imagining all the things she'd like to do to acting sergeant Collingworth, all painful and none repeatable in company.

Chapter Forty-Two

Fedelma Goosens looked up from her manuscript. The solemnly ticking grandfather clock told her it was three forty-two. Goodness, how time flew when one was working; it was past tea time, and neither of them had noticed. Reyka must be still napping upstairs, otherwise she'd have had the kettle on twenty minutes ago.

Goosens worried about Reyka. She'd been so tired these last few days – all that emotional stress, though, so it was hardly surprising. And those police officers! Why couldn't they just leave her to grieve? But oh no, they had to come back, time after time, asking the same questions. What was the point? There was a madman out there and they'd be better employed going out and catching him, instead of causing more distress to an already traumatised woman.

Her ears pricked up at the sound of crockery being laid out. 'Reyka? I thought you were asleep?'

'No, I finished my nap, dear. Would you like tea?'

Goosens smiled. 'Yes, please. I'd lost track of time.'

'How are you getting on?'

'Rather well. I think you'll like it. I had a little trouble with the second movement, but then I had a brainwave. I can't wait to play it through with you.'

Goosens played the first few bars. 'What do you think? I've transposed it to D major.'

'Better. Much better.' Reyka's voice floated from the kitchen. 'And it'll be easier for me to play, too.'

Goosens felt a warm glow of contentment. However sad the situation was with Marika's passing, it was nevertheless lovely to share these moments with a like-minded friend. Every cloud, she thought happily, every cloud. Perhaps this could become a permanent arrangement. She would be only too happy to have Reyka as a full-time housemate. They were so ideally suited. Not for the first time, she found herself thinking how unpredictable life could be. One moment she had been a lonely, single woman, the next … companionship and happiness.

'Here we are.' Reyka emerged from the kitchen with a tray. 'Earl Grey, as usual. I've made a pot. Will you have it where you are, or in the lounge?'

'I should have a proper break, really,' Goosens said. 'In the lounge is perfect. Be with you in a moment.'

Goosens pursed her lips, made a small adjustment to the manuscript in front of her. Tested the change with a brief flourish of the piano keys, nodded with satisfaction. She yawned. She could do with a nap herself. All this concentration. She marked her place with the pencil and hurried through to the lounge.

Reyka was already seated by the coffee table. 'Shall I pour?'

'Thank you, lovely. You know, *I* should be doing this for *you*.'

'Nonsense,' Reyka said. 'My pleasure.'

Goosens put her hand on Reyka's shoulder. 'You're too good to me. What have I done to deserve you?'

Chapter Forty-Three

'Boss, we have something.' Bola popped his head around Moran's office door and promptly disappeared again. Moran followed him to find George concentrating hard on his screen.

'Look,' George said. 'Five days after Marika's recital, Reyka's concert took place in Reading Town Hall.'

'The hatchet-job review,' Bola said.

Bola cast a sideways glance as Collingworth sidled up to Tess Martin's workstation, picked up an envelope. What was he snooping around for?

George was still chattering about the photographs. '— featuring quotes by none other than this Beatrice Keane woman.'

Collingworth stood next to Bola. He was opening an envelope. 'Relevance?'

'Dates,' George said. 'Maybe a coincidence, but—'

'No,' Moran said. 'These are the same dates circled in Reyka's diary.'

Collingworth took a slip of paper out of the envelope, glanced at the contents.

George said, 'Reyka's disastrous concert—' he tapped the

calendar on his desk, 'was held on today's date.'

'And Marika's murder happened on the anniversary of her triumph in London,' Bola chipped in. 'Two anniversaries. One big success, one big failure.'

Collingworth dropped the letter onto George's desk. 'This has just come in.'

Moran frowned. 'What is it, acting sergeant?'

'Read it for yourself.'

Moran spread the paper out. It was a short note written in beautiful, copybook handwriting, the like of which was a real rarity in the age of text-speak. It read:

Dear DC Martin

I racked my brains last night until I became quite exhausted, but in the middle of the night, it came to me – as these things so often do. Beatrice Keane's original surname was Goosens. I do hope that you find this helpful, and that you will pop in to visit me again sometime. It was so nice to meet you.

With kind regards,

Jean Harrington

'Goosens,' Moran said. 'That can't be a coincidence.'

'The tutor,' George said, 'had a daughter out of wedlock, or so Mrs Harrington told Tess. Given up for adoption, but she kept the same surname.'

Bola said. 'That's not all Mrs Harrington told Tess. She talked about the Szarkas' mother, Leila, and how she was bitterly disappointed Reyka wasn't a boy – the first male child was stillborn. You thinking what I'm thinking?'

Moran swore under his breath. 'DC Schlesinger's screenshots of Reyka's diary – there was an entry … *now T is here. I feel … liberated. Such love for T…* or some such. The reference is to the dead child, Tarján, surely? Levi Cambridge's pedestrian – it's not a man we're looking for…'

Bola's voice was barely a whisper. 'Reyka's assumed her dead brother's identity.'

George said, 'Reyka's still camping out at Goosens' place.'

'…with a handy bottle of GHB in her handbag,' DC Schlesinger's voice piped up from behind them. All heads turned to the new arrival, and Schlesinger gave them a thumbs up. 'Lab just confirmed it.'

There was a stunned silence.

'*That's* why Goosens was so sure of her alibi.' Moran was first to recover. 'A small dose and she'd never have noticed Reyka slip out.'

'You should probably know,' Collingworth said quietly, 'I've just asked Tess to pop over to Goosens' place to get a DNA sample.'

George stood up. 'You sent her there on her *own*?'

Collingworth shrugged. 'DNA samples, pronto. That's what was required for both Brooks and the Szarka woman.'

George's face was puce, his hands bunched into fists. Moran caught him by the arm. 'Leave it, George.' He addressed them all. 'Blue light time. George, you're with me. Acting sergeant, Bola, I want Brooks hauled over the coals. I suspect his intention was to fit up Fiona Manning to take the rap, hence the bust shard in her car, and if Reyka *is* his mother I'm betting they cooked this up between them.

Schlesinger cleared his throat. 'Er, she is indeed, guv. Furness General Hospital just confirmed a birth: February 1989. Clive Spencer Szarka, mother Reyka Szarka. A DNA test will confirm, and I haven't got the adoptive details yet, but —,'

Bola whistled. 'You don't hang about, Schles, do you?'

Schlesinger shrugged. 'I got lucky. There are only so many functional Maternity Units in the Lake District.'

Even Moran looked impressed. 'Thank you, DC Schlesinger. Acting sergeant, tell Brooks we know. Give him a phone, get him to call his mother; it might stall her, give us time to get over there before we have another killing on our hands.'

Fedelma Goosens' consciousness returned slowly, as if she was rising from the bottom of a lake to the distant surface, but with weights attached to her legs. Everything was moving at half-speed. She willed her eyes to open, but her eyelids were heavier than the rest of her body.

After a tremendous effort she finally succeeded in opening them just enough to allow her a glimpse of her surroundings, but her vision was blurred, unfocused. She thought she recognised the shape of her piano, squat in the distance, just beyond the open louvre doors which separated the instrument from the rest of the house, but it was too hard to keep her eyes open, and the darkness closed in again.

Some time later, or it may have been immediately after she closed her eyes, she experienced a dream: she was performing with the London Symphony Orchestra, and her mother was conducting. She didn't remember her mother, though, and so the conductor's face was a blank oval, devoid of features or expression. She knew her mother had been a skilled musician, that she had taught many students in her lifetime, but Fedelma had been warned by her adoptive parents that she must not try to contact her in later life, and she had respected this – although not without a deep sense of regret. Nevertheless, some instinct assured her that her mother was indeed guiding this surreal performance with swift, confident gestures of her baton, and Fedelma threw herself into the music with gusto, wild flurries of notes flying from her fingers like audible colours of the rainbow.

The dream ended abruptly as she felt a penetrating pain, as if a bee had stung her, or a sharp splinter had embedded itself in her wrist. The phantom orchestra disappeared and she opened her eyes. The room was still fuzzy around the edges, but this time she was able to discern a little detail. She was seated at the piano, looking into the lounge. Someone was standing beside her – she was aware of their presence – but could only pick out a vague, grey shape in her peripheral vision.

'Good. You're back with us. Can you feel that?'

The voice was low, familiar, although oddly distorted. Fedelma tried to moisten her lips, which were dry and sandpapery, but she couldn't move her tongue; it wouldn't obey her command to form the sounds she asked of it.

'Don't worry. It's difficult to talk, I know. I'll press a little harder – that'll do just as well.'

The pain this time was more intense, like a sudden jolt of electricity. She cried out wordlessly, and heard her voice echo and bounce across the walls of some distant chamber.

'Ah, there we are. You *can* feel it. Good.'

Fedelma heard a name issue from her parched mouth, not perfectly articulated, but close enough that the meaning could be understood. 'Reyka?'

'Reyka has gone,' the voice said. 'Now you have me.'

Fedelma felt her hands being lifted together, as if they were about to be placed on the keyboard to begin playing a piece of music. Then they were dropped into her lap. She had no control, was helpless to perform any independent movement.

'What fine piano hands you have. Like your mother, I think.'

'M–my mother?'

'Yes, dear one. She taught your friend, Reyka. For many months. So many lessons.'

Fedelma felt her heart judder, a brief but noticeable fibrillation. It resumed with deep, resonant thumps, like a battering ram against the solid wood of a stately home's front door. Her body went rigid as her rational mind whispered:

You are in the presence of a madman…

Her chest heaved as she tried to inflate her lungs. She would call for help, someone would come. It was going to be all right…

'Don't waste your energy, Fedelma,' the voice advised. 'You'll need it all later, after I'm finished.'

Fedelma gasped and the small amount of air she had managed to inhale escaped from her slack mouth in a defeated *whoosh*.

'That's better. Now, try to relax. I'm almost ready to begin.'

'W–why … are…' Fedelma gave up. The formation of a sentence was beyond her.

'Questions, always questions. Why do I always have to

answer questions?' The voice grew louder, angrier. 'I wish simply to do what I have to do. There is no point asking why this, why that. It is necessary, that's all. Some things are necessary. The things we wait for are necessary. We must finish. Do you understand?'

Fedelma heard the scraping of metal on wood, the sound of some tool being lifted from a hard surface.

'Reyka? Wh—?'

'Is absent.'

Fedelma took quick sips of air, the effort of speech making her feel faint, her skin clammy.

'Do you know what date it is?' More scraping and shuffling.

More scraping and shuffling.

'Date?' Fedelma tried to make sense of the question.

'No, of course not,' the voice said. 'I don't expect you do. After all, why would you? Shall we have some music?'

Footsteps clacked on the music room's parquet floor and then abruptly softened as her tormentor reached the lounge carpet. Fedelma was dimly aware of a low muttering, a conversation between two people, or so it seemed, and the sound of record sleeves being shuffled as one was rejected in favour of the next. Eventually, a choice was made, and a few moments later the mournful opening to Chopin's Piano Concerto No. 1 in E minor filled the room.

Fedelma started as a quiet voice whispered in her ear. 'I expect your mother could play this. Could you, I wonder?'

Terror gave her strength. 'W–who are you? What have you done with … with Reyka? Let me go, *please*…'

'Just listen to that arpeggio. Beautiful, isn't it?'

'Let me go. Please—'

'I shall be able to play at a higher level than this, dear Fedelma.' The voice softened to a barely audible whisper as it slipped into introspection. 'I'll have all the time in the world. No one to interrupt me. No one to distract me. No one to correct me. No one to *hurt* me – not that I would allow that, of course. Not *now*.'

Fedelma flinched as something slammed down beside her, and again as gloved fingers softly caressed her neck.

'Dear Fedelma. What a lovely name you were given. Your mother's choice, of course. Sad, I imagine, never to have known your mother. Of course, dear Reyka spent many hours with her. Hours and hours and hours. I wonder what you were doing when she was with your mother?'

'I … *oh*!' Fedelma groaned as a hand gripped her shoulder and squeezed hard.

'Shh! Do not interrupt.'

Fedelma whimpered. Her heart redoubled its pounding.

'It took dear Reyka *so* long to find you, but she was determined, you see. We needed to find you, to make things right.'

The doorbell rang.

Chapter Forty-Four

No answer. Tess noticed that the front room curtains were still closed. She rang again. Maybe they were out? Shopping, or…?

She peered through the letter box.

All quiet.

No, wait.

She put her ear to the door. Classical music was playing softly. She didn't recognise the piece – not her thing.

Another ring.

No response.

Tess turned around. School kicking-out time. Mums and kids walking past, laughing and chatting.

The door opened behind her. Taken by surprise, Tess spun on her heel.

'Oh! I thought you were out – so sorry to disturb you, Ms Szarka – I'm aware you've already had a visit today, but I just need to do a quick test. Is that all right?'

'Of course.' Reyka Szarka held the door open. 'Come in, my dear.'

The lounge was dimly lit by a standard lamp in the corner of the room. Tess didn't enquire as to why the curtains were drawn. Perhaps Ms Szarka had been having a nap. 'Ms Goosens is out?'

'She is busy, yes,' Reyka said. 'Would you like a drink? Cold, or tea perhaps?'

Tess was parched. 'A mint tea would be nice, thank you.'

'Of course. I won't be a moment.'

Reyka left the room, and Tess settled herself on the sofa. It was actually nice to stop for a moment, let her thoughts drift. The music was soothing. Maybe she should check out some classical music sometime. She might get to like it.

Her ears pricked up as another sound reached her ears, a little higher-pitched than the violins, woodwind and piano notes coming from the two floor-standing stereo speakers on either side of the bay window. A cat, maybe?

'Here we are.' Reyka returned with a silver tray, two cups and saucers, a cosy-covered tea pot, granulated sugar in a small bowl adorned with flowery motifs, a matching jug of milk, and a smaller pot Tess guessed contained her mint tea.

'Thank you. You shouldn't have gone to so much trouble.'

'One ought to serve tea in the proper manner.' Reyka smiled. 'Fedelma – well, I've tried to educate her, but she insists that a tea bag in a mug does just as well.' She rolled her eyes.

'This certainly looks prettier.' Tess laughed. 'Thank you.'

Reyka settled herself in an armchair. She was wearing a pair of grey, pinstripe trousers and a white blouse. Her shoulder-length silver hair was neatly brushed, tortoiseshell combs keeping stray strands away from her forehead. 'So, this test you mention. Is it absolutely necessary?' She lifted the lid of the larger teapot and stirred the contents with a silver spoon, poured a little into her cup and sniffed. Satisfied with the result she poured a full cup for herself and then, from the smaller pot, a cup of green mint tea for Tess.

'Here we are.'

Tess took the dainty cup and saucer, scared that she might drop it, or that her finger might be too fat to fit through the thin bone china handle. She politely sipped the hot, fragrant liquid and replaced the cup in its matching saucer, carefully setting it down on the side table next to her. 'I'm afraid so. It's just a formality – for our records.'

Which wasn't quite true, but she didn't want to elaborate, not until they had a better grasp of the facts.

'I see. Well, let's enjoy our tea first, shall we?'

Tess smiled. Five minutes. What harm?

Bernice had always been blessed with what her mother would have described as a sixth sense, although she herself interpreted the gift as more of an attribute of the soul, or spirit. Whatever word one used, it had proved invaluable many times in her past, particularly on one occasion when she had felt a strong sense that she should not take her usual train to Oxford for a regular Saturday meet with two close friends. The train had derailed just before Didcot Parkway and nine people had been injured.

In the moment she waved to Tess, closed the door and breathed in the atmosphere of her home, she knew.

She was not alone.

She hung her coat on the stand she had recently bought from IKEA, retrieved a beech walking stick – her late father's – from the downstairs loo, took a breath and went into the living room.

Isabel Akkerman was seated at the breakfast table. The larger of Bernice's cooking knives and a businesslike silenced hand gun were laid next to each other on the table top, both within easy reach.

'Good afternoon, DC Swinhoe.'

'You're in my house.' Bernice stood her ground, tightened her grip on the walking stick.

'As you were in mine, I believe? Or rather, I suspect, as was your accomplice – I do hope you're not intending to do anything foolish with that stick?'

'What do you want?'

'Silly question.' Isabel picked up the hand gun, slid its magazine out, inspected it, clipped it back into place. 'I'll spell it out, shall I?' She pointed the gun directly at Bernice. 'I've come for what you stole from me.'

'If you shoot me, you'll never get it back.'

Isabel laughed, a rich, throaty chuckle. 'Oh, I have plenty of other options, don't fret.' She tapped the automatic's muzzle on the tabletop. 'Let me explain what you're going to do, DC Swinhoe. You're going to retrieve the hard drive from wherever you've secured it, return it – solo, you understand; no lurking backup, if you please. I'll then leave you in peace. Provided you continue to toe the line, of course.'

'It's too late,' Bernice said. 'The drive is with our cyber team. Once it's decrypted, we'll have access to all your sordid little secrets.'

'You won't break it.' Isabel's tone was firm.

'I think we will. We have a very talented team.'

'You start down that road, young lady, and you'll be all over the internet before you have time to draw breath. You'll be arrested. It'll go to court. Two reliable witnesses will testify what they saw. There'll be photographic evidence to back it all up. A no-brainer for the jury, career over for you. Probably a prison sentence – and you an ex-copper. Not exactly the best place to hang out.'

Bernice's resolve began to waver. What if Isabel was right? What if Vishal couldn't break the encryption? By then Isabel would have made good on her threat, and like some slo-mo vintage horror movie the whole nightmare scenario would have begun to roll. She could easily return to Atlantic House, retrieve the disk drive from Vishal… Her grip on the walking stick loosened.

'You know I'm right.' Isabel ran her finger up and down the automatic's black casing. 'I'm a patient person. I understand that you felt the need to try to extricate yourself from the tangle you're in, but no one crosses me and gets away with it. So, off you trot – here, take my car.' She dangled a set of keys. 'I'll be waiting – oh, and remember, no conferring.'

Chapter Forty-Five

Tess felt herself drifting as a voice faded in and out of a gentle ocean of music. The swelling harmonies wrapped themselves around her; it felt like being cosseted in the softest cotton. She was pleasantly sleepy, but the voice, slipping between the melodious notes, kept her from completely going under. It was hard to understand exactly what was being said; the words seemed jumbled and, like blind letters rushing around an empty room, their meaning was impossible to decipher.

'I don't care for tests, I'm afraid.' The voice had dropped in pitch to a gravelly monotone. 'My mother wouldn't approve in any case. She's very protective of me, you see. I'm her special one.'

Tess's eyes closed. She was no longer present in Fedelma Goosens' lounge; instead she was floating in a world of soaring scales, stirring crescendos and whispered diminuendos. Each note had its own colour, although she couldn't be sure which was which, or how each was assigned a particular shade. She was on a journey, and was content to go where the music led her.

When Reyka Szarka stood over her, she knew nothing about

it. Neither was she aware of the louvre doors sliding open, nor of Fedelma Goosens' panicked, wide-eyed stare as Reyka slipped on a matching grey jacket, fastened a thin striped tie around her neck and adjusted her collar, retrieved a pair of gold-rimmed glasses, hooked them around her ears, and finally removed her fastidiously groomed wig, placing it carefully on a scarlet-covered occasional chair in the corner of the piano room. Her cropped grey hair was combed back at the sides with styling gel, a finishing touch that had pleased her when she had inspected herself post-application in the bedroom mirror.

'I'm so sorry to have kept you waiting, my dear. But let's have a little silence.' The music was turned off.

The spell was broken. With a huge effort, Tess lifted the twin weights of her eyelids. A tall, slim, figure was preparing something on top of the piano casing. Fedelma Goosens was seated at the instrument, head lolling, arms spread in front of her and resting on the woodwork.

Tess tried to speak but nothing would come. She rolled off the settee and sprawled on the carpet. The stereo system was a metre away.

She started to crawl.

As Tess inched towards the sideboard, the individual words of the monologue began to make sense, like a hand of cards being rearranged in order of suits.

'How shall we proceed, I wonder? Shall we use the ruler first? Or shall we be kind and get it over and done with? Oh, Fedelma, if only you knew how patient I have been; tracking you down, biding my time, tempting you to move nearer to your musical sisters.'

A pause.

'I've waited *so* long, you know, dear Fedelma, so long. But the day has finally arrived. You'll forgive me if I savour the moment – just a little? Of course you will.'

Tess had reached the sideboard with its modest rack of CDs. She pawed at the row of plastic, her movements uncoordinated, clumsy. Four or five CDs fell from the rack onto the carpet. She tried to focus her eyes on the covers. She knew what she was looking for, but it was hard, *so* hard to stay awake. She could just rest her head, lie here, let sleep claim her.

No. You'll die…

She spread the CDs on the carpet. Chopin, Handel, Debussy…

There.

Beethoven.

With fumbling fingers she prised the CD from its casing.

The player was right in front of her. Dead ahead.

She stabbed the eject button, tossed the emerging CD away, slid the new one into place, nudged the drawer closed and collapsed onto her back.

The opening of Beethoven's Fifth Symphony flooded the room with its familiar dramatic minor key motif.

The effect was immediate.

'Who told you to play this … *aberration?*'

Tess felt hands on her lapels, and she was pulled into a sitting position.

'This is not music. It is the devil's gratings. It is the sound of *pain*. Do you understand?'

The palm of a hand struck her cheek. 'Yes, yes. I do.' Tess's response was slow and slurred, but a small beacon of hope had begun to blink in the depths of her anaesthesia; above the thunderous swell of the Fifth Symphony, her ears had detected the sound of a car engine. With her remaining strength she reached out and wrapped her arms around the trousered legs, held on tight.

'Let me go, girl.'

'Enough.' Tess held on, mouthed the words against the rough material. '*Enough.*'

Strong, wiry hands plucked at her arms, something hard, metallic banged against her ribs. She tightened her grip, shoved her shoulder against her assailant's hips like a rugby player in a loose ruck. Something heavy struck her between the shoulder blades and, although the pain was dulled by whatever drug she'd ingested, it was still enough of a shock for her to cry out. To her relieved amazement, a response came from the direction of the hallway.

'Tess? Are you in there?'

George.

The letterbox flapped, a metallic butterfly in her mind.

She opened her mouth to reply but another blow fell, this time catching her on the collarbone. She felt it snap with a brittle, sharp stab of pain. She let go of the legs, hugged her arm to her torso.

'I *warned* you.'

From the twin speakers the horn section sounded a plaintive call to arms.

The telephone rang.

For a moment, the scene froze. Tess shuffled backwards until her spine was pressed against the sideboard. Her shoulder was a fiery agony. The music rose to a crescendo, the violins chasing over one other until they reached an abrupt stop, briefly relinquishing their dominance to flutes and sundry woodwind before reasserting themselves in a fortissimo sixteenth note spiral that mirrored, with metronomic precision, the rapid beating of Tess's heart.

Loud banging on the front door. *Tess! Can you hear me?*

An arm reached over her shoulder. The music died, cut off.

'Hello? Who's calling, please? Ah, it's you. Yes, yes, I'm listening…'

Tess drew a breath, filled her lungs. No good. It was too painful, too much effort.

'I see. Well, I have to finish this, Clive. As you know. It's what we decided. I can't possibly stop now. You do understand, don't you? Good.'

The conversation seemed surreal to Tess. Mad. She had reached the end of her reserves of energy. Her head fell back until it banged on the sideboard, causing her to jerk awake again.

'Police! Open this door! Now!'

A tinkling of glass, then an almighty bang.

Her head tipped forward onto her chest and the room slipped away.

Chapter Forty-Six

Bernice's mind was in overdrive. The encrypted disk was all they had, the only card available to play. Returning it to Akkerman would mean total defeat. That wasn't going to happen.

Think out of the box, B, come on...

She hurled the car into a vacant space and took the emergency stairs instead of the lift. This was her problem, her mess. Bola had already stuck his neck out, and almost had it chopped for his trouble. The guv had been amazing, but this was her battle.

There was no one from the team around. She hoped that was good news. She glimpsed DCS Higginson in the corridor, and avoided him by ducking into the loo. She still felt nauseous, but her sense of outrage at Isabel Akkerman's intrusion was overriding it, giving her a second wind.

She headed for her workstation and booted up the laptop. The germ of an idea was forming, if she could work out how to execute it without suspicion on Isabel's part.

She typed rapidly into the search bar on the homepage.

North Korean Embassy, London.

Google duly delivered several pages of material. She clicked on the Wiki link and her heart gave a little flutter. It looked perfect, too good to be true. But was Isabel aware? She was a foreign operative, familiar with the Far East, and North Korea in particular, but had she ever had cause to visit the London embassy?

Bernice read on, her heart pumping now with excitement. *Located in a detached house in Ealing, notable for being one of the few embassies in London located in a suburban area, away from the central diplomatic areas of the city…*

The photograph showed a regular detached suburban house with double bay windows on the ground and first floors.

It was a gamble, a huge gamble. Did she dare?

There were two preparatory actions she had to take. She found the handbook she was looking for in Bola's desk, flicked through the pages.

There.

She scrawled down the telephone number.

Next, she zipped through the internal directory and found the high-tech unit.

Tapped the extension number.

Please be there…

'Vishal Shrivastava. How can I help?'

Bernice tightened her fist. 'Hi Vishal – DC Swinhoe here. How's it going with the disk?' She listened, nodded. 'OK, we knew it would be tough. Look, I have an idea – can I run it past you?'

She met Vishal at reception twenty minutes later, thanked him for his promptness, and quickly returned to her desk. She glanced around the room. No one was paying any attention, no one was within earshot. She puffed out her cheeks, took a deep breath and picked up the phone.

Dialled the number.

It was answered immediately, a pleasantly accented female voice.

This is the North Korean Embassy. To whom may I direct your call?

Bernice raced home to find Isabel reclining on her sofa. It was now or never. Would she take the bait?

Isabel listened and nodded. 'OK. That's sounds doable. West London? That's, what, forty minutes?'

Bernice nodded. 'Yes, roughly. Our technician usually works from home. He has all his equipment there, in situ.'

'Come along then, young lady.' Isabel stood up. 'I'd like this little problem resolved as soon as.'

'You want me to come with you?'

Please, please…

A shrug. 'Of course. I like to have an insurance policy with me at all times.'

'All right.'

'Good girl – after you.'

Chapter Forty-Seven

A voice, a familiar voice, calling from a long way off. Tess groaned. Her eyes slid reluctantly open. Her head was throbbing and the pain in her upper arm and shoulder was making her feel sick.

'Take it steady. Don't try to move.'

She became aware of people moving about the room, terse commands and snatches of brief, instructional conversation.

'George.' It was all she could manage.

'The very same. You're all right. Thank God.'

Slowly her vision cleared. Fedelma Goosens was seated on the armchair that Reyka Szarka had previously occupied, being attended to by a female uniformed officer.

'Is she hurt?'

'No, just scared out of her wits,' George said. 'You stopped it happening, Tess – and I have no idea how.'

'Beethoven helped.'

'Pardon me?'

'Tell you later. So, Reyka and Goosens?' Clarity was returning rapidly now.

'Goosens is Reyka's old tutor's daughter.'

'Revenge across the generations?'

George gently slid his arm around her. She was OK with it – more than OK with it. He said, 'Seems that way. And Brooks – her son – he helped her set it up.'

Tess gingerly moved her arm and winced. 'Her son? Right. These demure ladies and their amorous trysts…'

'Aye, I know.' George gave a dry laugh. 'Nothing's ever quite as it seems, eh?' He squinted at her shoulder. 'Looks like the collarbone – might be fractured.'

'Tell me about it. And no thanks, I've had enough medication for now, cheers all the same.' She smiled weakly. 'For a lifetime, actually.'

'Best leave that decision to the paramedics, OK?'

'George – don't fuss.'

'Let me help you up, then. Here you go.'

Tess found her feet, gasped as her collarbone grated. 'Maybe I do need a little something.'

Reyka Szarka appeared from the direction of the kitchen, flanked by two uniforms. As she was led past she bared her teeth and hissed, 'Interferer.'

George stepped in between them. 'That'll do, Ms Szarka.'

'Tarján. My mother named me *Tarján*.'

'Whatever.' He stayed put until Reyka was safely outside.

Tess blinked and exhaled slowly. Reyka Szarka's face had left an imprint on her retinas that would take time to fade; she knew from experience that the same image would return to haunt her when she was low, when her defences were down.

DCI Moran came into view. 'DC Martin. All in one piece, more or less? Good. Get yourself out to the para boys. They'll check you over.'

'Yes, guv.'

'And Tess?'

'Guv?'

'I'm recommending you for a gallantry award. That was exceptional work. Very well done.'

'Thank you, sir.'

She allowed George to lead her outside to the waiting ambulance, whose flickering blue lights had attracted a small crowd of concerned neighbours. She smiled at the well-wishing comments, the anxious enquiries.

'You all right, darlin'?'

'God bless our coppers – they're the best.'

'Can I make you a nice cup of tea, love?'

And to the paramedics: 'You look after her, mind.'

George shooed them off, but in a kindly way, and they dispersed, chattering and speculating in ones and twos.

Tess lifted her face to the grainy April sky, climbed the steps into the ambulance and sat down. She followed the paramedics' instructions automatically as the echoes of Beethoven's Fifth filled her head with the eccentric sounds of genius.

Chapter Forty-Eight

Bernice drove with her heart firmly in her mouth. This was crazy. Her plan was wild, bound to fail. What if Akkerman knew? What if she recognised the house? It was an all or nothing gamble, for sure.

The M4 junctions sped by: 10, 8/9, 7, 4a...

'You're very quiet, DC Swinhoe. I wonder what you're thinking. Nothing detrimental to our agreement, I hope?'

'I'm not thinking anything.'

Bernice swallowed and concentrated on the road. Her handbag was on the back seat, and for a moment prior to their departure she'd thought Akkerman might ask her to open it, but no such request had been made and Bernice had breathed again. But surely her face would give her away?

The Embassy had initially been suspicious, but after waiting on hold for five minutes a second official had come to the phone and posed searching questions about her intentions. How long would she be? Would she be alone with Akkerman, or would there be others present? Was Akkerman likely to be armed? Did Bernice have the encrypted drive in her possession? What did she want in return? In the end they had agreed to allow her to carry her plan through.

Junction 2.

Bernice followed the satnav, hit the elevated section and prepared to turn off towards the A406. She recalled a hard left turn ahead which led through a width-restricted shortcut she'd used many years ago when travelling to the training school in Hendon. Yes, here it was. Up to the top, turn right and then left. They were five minutes away.

'Made progress, your friend, has he? Like I said, I'd be awfully surprised.'

Bernice indicated right, pulled out onto Popes Lane. 'I think you're going to be very surprised.'

'Well,' Akkerman purred, 'we'll see, hm?'

Bernice was conscious of Akkerman's automatic, still cradled in her hand. She would not hesitate to use it, that was a given. Bernice knew, by reputation, what Akkerman was capable of.

Bernice turned left into Baronsmede. The Embassy was at the end of this road on the left. Bernice prayed that the North Korean official had made sure that, as agreed, the frontage would appear totally anonymous. They'd had over an hour to sort it out; if they'd neglected to do so, the game was up – for them and for her.

'Here we are.' She murmured a prayer of thanks as she saw no tell-tale signage. She had fretted that a high-end Lexus or ostentatious Mercedes sports might be parked outside, some classy vehicle out of kilter with the earning power of even a highly competent IT nerd. She needn't have feared; there was only one other car in the drive, an innocuous-looking, mid-range saloon. Bernice breathed again.

'Charming property. Your colleague must be doing well for himself.'

'He's a very skilled guy.' Bernice parked and switched off the engine. 'Much in demand.'

The windows of the house were covered by net curtains, obscuring the interior.

'Let's make this quick.' Akkerman gestured with the automatic. 'Out you get.'

Bernice's pulse quickened as she imagined for a split second that Akkerman intended to stay in the car, but the MI6 agent joined her on the driveway and inclined her head towards the front door. 'Well?'

Bernice approached the imposing frontage with more confidence than she felt. Cold beads of sweat prickled her hairline as she rang the bell. She could sense Akkerman behind her, alert, but not yet suspicious. So far, there was no movement behind the twin oval, translucent glass panes set into the front door. Traffic skimmed by on the A406, London's historic orbital road, and the metallic tang of exhaust fumes stung her throat. She was scarcely aware that her tongue was stuck to the roof of her mouth and that she badly needed a drink of water. A pedestrian passed the side of the house, their head and shoulders just visible above the neatly trimmed privet hedge.

'Nobody in? You did tell them to expect us within the hour?' Isabel was at her shoulder, close enough that Bernice could smell her pungent, musky perfume.

'Yes. He'll answer in a moment. He's always busy.'

Bernice sensed that Isabel was taking stock of her surroundings. She felt the other woman stiffen and heard her make a soft cluck of concern. 'Your friend has a flagpole?' She began to back away, turning her head to the right and left, the automatic swivelling in a wary semicircle. Bernice followed her gaze and her heart missed a beat. To their immediate left a white flagpole was resting horizontally alongside the herbaceous border, parallel with the opposite hedge. It was hinged, she saw, at its base, allowing it to be swung upright into position or laid down for a flag to be attached or detached as necessary, or perhaps for maintenance work to be carried out.

Bernice forced a laugh. 'He's a little eccentric. Scottish – very patriotic. He flies the Scottish flag to let everyone know. Not always, usually on special saints' days and the like.'

Isabel hesitated, assessing the explanation for plausibility.

A slight movement behind one of the ground floor windows caught Bernice's eye. A second later, the front door swung open.

A dapper looking man, unmistakably Korean, stood on the threshold. He was wearing a dark suit, a pristine white shirt, and a tie in the red and blue colours of the North Korean flag.

'*Bitch.*' Akkerman hissed in her ear.

To their left and to their right a phalanx of similarly-attired men, one or two wearing dark sunglasses, had soundlessly slipped into position while four dark-suited figures were blocking the exit, all cradling neat but businesslike silenced semi-automatics.

The dapper man stepped forward and gave a small bow.

'Miss Akkerman. Or perhaps I should say, Ms Ahn Kwan? Or is it Yoon- suh Mook? Well, whichever, I'm so pleased you have come to visit. I have spoken to our great leader, Kim Jong Un. He is *very* much looking forward to meeting you.'

Akkerman's reaction was immediate. She ducked, snapped off two quick shots right and left, dropped the automatic, and launched herself at the space vacated by one of the agents she had clipped. Bernice guessed her intentions; vault the hedge, look for cover behind whatever cars were parked nearby…

But it was hopeless; Akkerman was both outnumbered and outgunned. She made it as far as the hedge, and had scrambled halfway over it before the nearest Embassy guard took leisurely aim and placed a bullet with easy precision into the soft flesh of her thigh. Akkerman yelled and collapsed onto the hardstanding, arms flailing at the privet as she tried to haul herself upright. The shooter caught her by the arm and began to drag her towards the front door. His colleagues followed, supporting their wounded comrade. The dapper man stepped aside to let them pass. No more than forty seconds had passed since the front door had opened.

Traffic continued to roar past on the A406, oblivious to the unfolding drama being enacted just metres away.

'And now, I believe you have something else for me?' The dapper man still wore his welcoming smile.

Bernice dipped into her handbag and withdrew the external drive. 'I was never here,' she said.

'I quite understand,' the man said. He took the hard drive from her and bowed. 'On behalf of my country, may I express my grateful thanks.'

Fat drops of rain blurred the windscreen as Bernice waited for the tremors in her hands to subside. She had just delivered Akkerman to certain death, and guilt was an ugly, pressing weight in her stomach. But what choice had she had?

The background drone of traffic seemed to merge with the throbbing of her head as the enormity of the risk she had taken hit home.

Reaction, B. Hardly surprising…

She couldn't wait here any longer. Maybe the North Koreans would change their minds. Maybe they would come for her, too.

Bernice slammed the car into gear and butted herself into the traffic queue on the North Circular, provoking a raucous chorus of indignant horns.

She made it as far as the A33, just ten minutes from Atlantic House, before her stomach gave up the struggle. She pulled into an industrial park near the football stadium, threw the door open and let nature take its course.

Chapter Forty-Nine

'You did *what*?' Moran was dumbfounded. 'The *Embassy*? Are you kidding me?'

'I'll explain everything, guv. I just need a moment.'

'Take all the time you need, DC Swinhoe.'

Moran watched Bernice walk purposefully across the office towards the ladies'. The pallor of her cheeks, the barely discernible quiver of her bottom lip, the way her left hand firmly grasped the fingers of the other, all bore testimony to the strain she had been under.

He shook his head in wonder. *By God, I underestimated you, DC Swinhoe, by a long way…*

Moran went to his office. He needed a moment, too. He sat at the familiar desk, with its familiar view of the half-blinded window looking out onto the open plan, and tried to imagine not being here every day, not being involved with whatever new case his talented team might be tasked with. His final case was closed, the reasons for Marika Szarka's sad end had been explained, and a further crime averted. Reyka Szarka would serve time, or be referred for psychiatric assessment, or maybe – most likely – both.

He took out his mobile and placed it on the desk. No calls. No texts. What to do? How should he approach Alice? That was a priority, for sure, now the case had been resolved.

Chris Collingworth's strident tones made him look up. He took a breath, and then raised his voice to pre-empt the uninvited intrusion. 'Come in, Chris.'

Why not? Why maintain a hostile stance? No point. In all likelihood he'd never see Collingworth again, not after today.

Collingworth appeared distracted – probably, Moran speculated, in view of George's reaction to the order he'd given to Tess. He'd be advised to avoid contact with the volatile Scot for a while, but that was his problem. Moran put up his best effort at cordiality.

'Hello, Chris. Have a seat. All's well, I hope?'

Collingworth slumped into the visitor's chair. 'Yeah. Brooks admitted planting the shard in Manning's car. Reyka gave it to him – oh, the DNA matches, by the way. Brooks *is* her son. They both set Manning up to take the rap. Unbelievable. Relationship was a total fake from Brooks' perspective; Manning was just glad to have a bloke. She's not so happy now, I can tell you.'

'I can imagine,' Moran said.

'So Brooks was dirty, like I said.'

'Sure.' Moran was hardly surprised at Collingworth's attempts at self-justification. It was a measure of the man. Maybe he'd change, maybe he'd become a little less self-serving with the passing years. Moran hoped so, but somehow doubted it. He said, 'DC Martin has been sent home from A&E. You might pop over to see her? Her collar bone is broken, but aside from that, no serious injuries.'

'Good to hear,' Collingworth said, but Moran could tell that his mind was elsewhere.

'In view of her past history, it might be an idea to keep a close eye,' Moran added. 'She's an asset to the team. You wouldn't want to lose her.'

'No. She did good,' Collingworth conceded.

Moran sensed that Collingworth was hesitating on the brink of making some kind of request. It looked as though he was having trouble getting himself over the line.

'Anything else on your mind, Chris?'

Collingworth sniffed. 'Well, there was one thing. I wondered if … you might put in a good word with the DCS for me? I mean, all in all, like you said, it's worked out well.'

With you spending most of your time chasing your tail… That was Moran's first thought. But instead he said, 'Of course. I imagine you'll be on your way soon, in any case.'

Collingworth brightened. 'Thanks. No hard feelings, eh?'

'None at all.'

'Right, well, see you later.'

Collingworth left the office with his ego intact and a little more spring in his step.

Moran shook his head with exaggerated deliberation. In some ways he was surprised at himself, in some ways not. *You let him off, Brendan, you auld softie…*

'I need hardly remind you that this goes no further.' Moran looked at each of them in turn. The atrium bar was filling rapidly, and he didn't want to linger. 'Anything you want to add, DC Swinhoe?'

Bernice shook her head. 'That's how it was. I rolled the dice and it worked out. The only thing on my mind now is Alastair.'

'I wouldn't waste any sympathy on that bastard,' George growled. 'He dropped you right in it – to save his own skin. The only consideration I'd have is which part of him I'd choose to punch out first.'

'Thanks, George,' Moran said. 'I think we get where you're at.' He sighed. 'I'll have a word with the Sussex fellows; no doubt they'll be wanting to pay Mr Catton a visit. I'm happy to play middle man, DC Swinhoe.'

Bernice shook her head, 'Thanks, guv, but I need to be there.'

'If you're sure,' Moran said. 'I'll be glad to have you along.' He paused. 'I'd like to thank you, too, DC Odunsi, for your part in bringing this to a conclusion.'

Bola shrugged. 'No problem, boss.'

'Head healing all right?'

Bola gave a wry smile. 'My own fault, guv. I'm on the mend. No problem. I don't blame the guy – he thought I was an intruder.'

'You *were* an intruder,' George said, sipping his orange juice.

'Pedant,' Bola said. 'You know what I mean.'

'Ben's a good guy,' Bernice said. 'I've met him on a few occasions. He's been there the longest. I think he'd be up for managing the estate in Alastair's absence, if it comes to that.'

'Oh, it'll come to that,' George said. 'Don't you worry.'

Moran had fallen silent. There was one matter left to clear up, and he didn't know how to broach the subject. The implications were potentially far-reaching, and he was still in the dark as to whether Bernice had thought it through.

Well, it had to be addressed. Might as well get on with it. He coughed. 'One last thing. I'm sorry, DC Swinhoe, but I need to bring it to your attention.'

'Oh, yes?'

'The encrypted disc,' Moran said. 'We have no idea what data it might contain. It's possible that it contains names, locations, alter egos, whatever, of any and every active MI6 asset. For all we know.'

Bola and George looked at each other.

Bernice nodded. 'Yep, I thought of that.'

Bola said, 'Official Secrets. If the North Koreans decide to share what's fallen into their possession, it'll be curtains for us.'

'It's all right, Bola,' Bernice said softly.

'All right? Doesn't sound all right to me. Sounds like life imprisonment.'

George said, 'At least they don't hang people for passing on official secrets these days.'

Bola wrinkled his nose. 'That's great, George. Good to know.'

'Well, not in the UK, anyway,' George added. 'Torture, maybe. These MI6 characters – you know, I've heard that—'

'It really is OK,' Bernice interrupted. 'They don't have the disk.'

There was complete silence.

'I swapped it,' she explained. 'Vishal found a similar disk. If and when the North Koreans crack the encryption Vishal created for me, they'll find that it's completely blank. Null. Empty.'

Chapter Fifty

As Moran walked up the short path to Alice Roper's front door he was acutely aware that he had never been so frightened in all his life. In the course of his career he'd faced bombs, assassins, crazed drug dealers, a mortar attack, a skilled and deadly hunter, double-agents, bent coppers and much, much more. He'd endured physical pain and lived with the scars of emotional trauma for more years than he cared to remember, but this … *this* was real fear.

What if she shut the door in his face? What if she raged at him for his failures and emotional inertia? It would be well-deserved. No doubt about it. He stopped before he reached the narrow porch, hovering on the threshold, almost paralysed by the enormity of the occasion. This wasn't a mere physical threshold; it was the threshold of the rest of his life. He stopped before he reached the narrow porch.

The situation was too momentous, too weighty for him to manage. He half-turned, one hand stuffed in his raincoat pocket, car keys digging into his fingers.

Away, Brendan, away and be done with it.

'Hello, Brendan.'

There she was in the doorway, elegant in a black long-sleeved midi dress, composed and calm, an exact counterpoint to the wildly spinning thoughts in his own head.

'Won't you come in?'

'Sure. Of course.'

He followed her into the familiar hallway with its faint trace of her scent, on this occasion mingled with the sweet fragrance of flowers. There were fresh blooms in the hall, the lounge, and in the near distance more bouquets and floral packages on the kitchen table in mid-preparation for display. 'People have been so kind,' she said. 'We've had so many visitors.'

'Emma and Adam are still here?'

'No, they left earlier today. The funeral's not till next week, and Adam has to work.'

'Of course.'

They were in the kitchen, where they'd spent many a convivial evening while Peter had sat in the lounge riveted to his beloved sports reruns. Today, the television was silent. Moran didn't know where to begin. He hovered awkwardly by the draining board.

'It's all right, Brendan.' Alice sat at the table and resumed her interrupted task of freeing another flower delivery from its cardboard packaging. 'I'm not going to start screaming at you.'

'I … Alice, I'm so sorry. I can't believe it. It happened so suddenly.'

'Yes.' She snipped at the package binding with a pair of scissors. 'It went to his lungs, and he didn't respond to antibiotics. I don't think he suffered, though.' Her voice caught a little and she cleared her throat. 'They were all lovely in the ward. They did their best for him.'

'Alice, I wanted to visit. You *know* I did, but…'

'Yes. I know.' She put the scissors down and unpacked the contents of the box. 'Look at these! Gorgeous. You'd think they'd wilt and die all trussed up like that, but no.'

'I feel terrible.' Disarmed by Alice's self-possession, he nevertheless felt compelled to carry on – not in any attempt at self-justification, but simply to share his feelings. 'I was very fond of Peter. He was a lovely, innocent soul.'

'He loved you, too, Brendan. He told me so.'

Moran managed a thin smile. 'And Emma? How is she coping?'

'Upset, of course. Like all of us.'

'I would have come before, Alice. I—'

She paused her activity momentarily and raised her chin, a quick glance at him. 'You're here now.'

'Yes.'

Her hands resumed their busyness. 'Then I presume it's over? You found the killer?'

He nodded. 'Yes. The team did a great job. The suspect is in custody – two suspects, actually.'

'So you're free?'

'Almost. Just one loose end to tie up in Sussex, then that's it.'

'Am I really to believe that?' Alice slid a cut glass vase towards her and began to arrange the flowers inside it.

'I'd like you to.'

'And then?' Alice paused again and looked him in the eye.

'And then I was hoping you'd like to … you might want to … in spite of what was said a few days back…'

'Oh please, Brendan. Just spit it out, would you?' She stood up and came to him, her arms encircling his waist.

He was so taken aback that the words stuck in his throat. His arms went around her and he pulled her to him.

She whispered in his ear. 'I feel guilty.'

He drew his head back. 'Guilty? Why?'

She looked at the floor. 'I feel guilty because – I couldn't see how it *could* work out between us … with Peter. I mean, he loved you, like I said, but I suppose I thought that … well, he was *my* responsibility, you know? Not yours. And to have him here, in the middle, between us, well, I just couldn't see how it would work out.'

'I understand. And so?'

'That's why I feel guilty. He's gone. And I'll always miss him – terribly – but now here we are, and it's just you and me, and…'

'It's all right,' Moran said, and hugged her close. 'Everything is all right, now. Everything is just fine.'

Chapter Fifty-One

Moran was feeling lightheaded and a little dehydrated – reason being, he surmised, the combination of the shuttle flight's dry air and the surreal delight of being accompanied by the extraordinary woman sitting next to him in the taxi. He still couldn't quite believe, considering the events of the past week, that they were here together.

'It's a fine morning, isnae it?' the taxi driver said. 'No a cloud in the sky – and they say we never get the decent weather. Well, here you are, Scotland's own riviera.'

'It is lovely,' Alice said. 'My first time this far north.'

'Aye? It's a wedding you're here for?'

'That's right,' Moran said.

'Couldnae've have picked a better day.'

The driver chattered on for the remainder of the twenty-minute journey until they turned into Great Glen Way adjacent to the river, and pulled in.

'Here we are – seems tae me you're in the right place.' The driver turned in his seat and grinned.

To the left of the Gothic-style church was a small, low-fenced garden, beside which a small crowd of wedding guests had gathered.

'All the best to ye. Have a grand day.'

'We will,' Alice said.

'Haste ye back, mind.' The driver tipped his cap and drove away.

They walked to the railing and drank in the scene. The River Ness sparkled in the late morning sunshine, the trees on its far side standing serenely to attention, green-plumed and rustling gently in the mild breeze.

'I was going to bring a raincoat and a brolly,' Moran said. 'Life is full of surprises.'

'Isn't it just.' Alice smiled. 'We'd better join the other guests – it'll be time to go in soon.'

Alice took his hand and they strolled across to the neat little garden.

'Morning, guv.' George was animated and cheery-faced, the reason for which was clear to Moran; just behind him, talking to DCS Higginson, was Tess, her arm in a dark blue sling to match her dress and flighty-feathered fascinator. George followed Moran's appreciative gaze. 'Aye, looking good, eh? As, I must say, are you both.'

'Thank you, George.' Alice accepted the compliment with a dismissive wave. 'You're a close second. Very impressive. Is the kilt McConnell tartan?'

'Aye, it is indeed.'

The church interior was cool, the atmosphere electric with anticipation. DS Ian Luscombe was already seated at the front pew on the right next to his best man. Moran watched them enviously as they shared a joke. The best man leaned over and patted Luscombe's cheek, who grinned in return and made a pretend fist. Lucky man; Charlie Pepper was a great catch. Attractive, bright, with a great sense of humour and an incisive, analytical brain. The couple would make a great team.

They found an appropriate pew half way along the aisle on the left and settled down to wait.

Alice reached over and took his hand as the organist began the first of his introductory hymns. The minister appeared from the wings, spent a few moments chatting to Luscombe and his pal, and then made his way to the lectern to prepare himself for the bride's arrival.

When the organ fell silent, all heads turned to the rear. The opening bars of Purcell's Trumpet Tune in D struck up, and there she was. Charlie paused to exchange a nervous glance with her father, a grey-haired, slightly stooped gentleman in a dark morning suit, white shirt and tartan tie. He was grinning all over his face.

But all eyes were fixed on Charlie.

'Oh!' Alice let out her breath. 'Wow!'

Charlie advanced slowly up the aisle to audible gasps of admiration. Her dress was stunning: silk taffeta with a puff ball hemline, tartan sash and train. Her bridal bouquet was of purple heather, thistle and berry, and she wore a matching wedding crown, her hair caught in a knotted milkmaid braid.

'Every inch the Scottish bride,' Moran whispered.

As she reached their pew Charlie paused momentarily and shot them a radiant smile. Moran felt his eyes prickling.

You sentimental auld eejit, Brendan ... get a grip ...

But Moran's emotions remained volatile for the rest of the service, especially during the exchange of vows, prompting

Alice to stage-whisper, 'Are you quite all right, Brendan?'

By the time they emerged into the sunlight and assembled next to the garden for photographs, Moran hoped he'd got himself under control. He thought he knew what was responsible for his fragile state of mind: his final case, Bernice's dilemma, Tess's near miss with Reyka Szarka, Peter, Alice, and the happiness of this particular occasion, and … well, just *everything*. It was no use; he was overwhelmed. He excused himself and walked briskly back into the church, followed by Alice's anxious glance.

The minister was pottering by the choir stalls, collecting hymnals and blowing out candles. He looked up as Moran approached. Without knowing quite what he was going to say, Moran heard himself blurt a question.

'Is there … hope? For people like me? Is there anything I can … trust?'

'Goodness, what a question for a day like this.' The minister was a young man in his thirties. He had piercing blue eyes and an easy manner.

'Is it all hopeless? Everything, the world, people…' Moran was standing in the part of the church known as the Sanctuary.

'Not at all,' the minister replied with a sympathetic smile. He half-turned towards the Sanctuary. 'It might appear that way, but…' He pointed at the wall-mounted crucifix above the altar. 'Fifteen years ago next month I finally understood why that was necessary. I'd recommend giving it some consideration yourself.'

Moran followed his gaze and nodded. He could relate to sacrifice, physical pain, betrayal; he'd been through it all. But redemption? He shook his head. 'I've tried. In the past, I mean

—' Moran felt the words catch in his throat.

'Forgive me, but perhaps that's where you're going wrong. It's not about trying. It's about accepting. By that I mean accepting who and what we are – and more importantly, who he is.' The minister seemed to sense Moran's perplexity. 'Look, I'm always happy to chat. Feel free to call me. Anytime.' He smiled again and puffed out the last candle.

Moran found his voice. 'Perhaps I will. Thank you – I appreciate it.'

He made his way back out into the open. Alice looked relieved to see him. 'You're just in time,' she said. 'Come on – come to the front with me.'

Moran took his place next to Alice as the photographer, a young man in a white jacket and sporting a ponytail, called for silence. 'OK, I only get one shot at this, as do you lovely ladies.'

'The bouquet,' Alice said.

'Ah. Of course.'

Charlie turned her back on the assembled guests. 'Count me down, then.' She threw her head back and laughed. Moran thought it was the most wonderful sound he'd heard for a very, very long time.

'Three … two … *one*!'

As if in slow motion the bouquet sailed into the clear air, turning over and over.

Alice leaned forward on tiptoe, reached out with both hands…

Epilogue

'She'll not be back? What exactly do you mean?'

Bernice shuffled her feet. This was harder than she'd imagined. Alastair was standing next to his pedestal desk, looking thinner – gaunt even. Dark circles underscored his eyes, in which the light seemed to have vanished as though into a black hole. The man she had met in this very room all those months ago had been swallowed up as if consumed by some wasting disease of body and soul. The yogic, easy movements, the centred confidence that had so fascinated her were now just memories. This was a broken man standing before her.

'It's over, Alastair. And I think that's probably a good thing for you. In the long term.'

'What happened to her? I need to know.'

'And I'll tell you. When we've finished our business here.'

'We?'

Bernice sighed. 'My boss, DCI Brendan Moran, is outside with a team from the Sussex constabulary. They'll be asking you – and me – specific questions about the events leading up to and including Johnny's death.'

'You've betrayed me.' His fingers scrabbled at the tooled

leather desktop.

Now Bernice saw red. '*I've* betrayed *you*? Can you hear yourself? You threw me to the wolves, Alastair, you let Isabel Akkerman – a proven killer – set me up. You let her *use* me!'

'I never wanted that.' He shook his head.

Bernice heard herself ranting on. 'To save *yourself*, Alastair. Your own skin was more important than mine. And I thought we *had* something here. I had no idea that this woman, this *bitch*, had her claws into you the way she did.'

'I didn't think she was coming back,' Catton said miserably. 'I thought I'd be free, but then…'

'Well she isn't coming back now, that's for certain.'

'I'm going to lose everything.'

'And I should care? I should give a *toss*?' Rage was a bubbling cauldron inside her. She knew she should stop before she became incoherent. 'Ben can look after the place while you're gone – *if* they convict you, and they bloody well should. And he'll make a better job of it than you ever have.'

'That's just cruel. Unfair.'

'Where's the body, Alastair? They're going to find it whatever, so you might as well tell me.'

He moistened his lips, took a step towards her. 'Will you – put in a good word for me? Tell them I didn't mean it?'

Bernice backed away. 'I'll tell it as I saw it. Hire a good lawyer. That's my advice.'

'I'm so sorry, B.'

'Too late. Now, where is he?'

Catton looked down. 'At the end of the rose garden, there's a compost heap. The far end, by the hawthorn. It's deep. Bernice, please—'

Her tone was icy. 'Don't *ever* call me that. We're done here.'

She turned her back on him; he'd never see the tears she'd fought so hard to suppress.

She threw her parting words over her shoulder. 'I'll send Detective Chief Inspector Moran up. He's a good man. He'll treat you fairly.'

She shut the door behind her, leaned hard on it, took a deep breath, and went to find the guv.

Moran surveyed his desk. His empty desk. Having cleared it once before, there was little to pack away now. Would he be back? No, not this time. He was done.

He shrugged on his coat, peered out of the window to check the weather. The forecasted fine drizzle was pattering on, misting the glass and dampening the spirits of the homebound commuters in their little tin vehicles, wipers thrashing ineffectually. Ah well, situation normal. For him, it was home to Alice, a log fire, perhaps a glass or two of Sangiovese.

He looked up at the brief, yet familiar, Morse code of Higginson's knock.

'Ah, Brendan. Glad I've caught you. This came for you in the late post. I suspect I know who it's from. Recognise the handwriting.'

'Thank you, sir.' Moran took the envelope.

'Last post, eh?' Higginson chuckled.

'Last—? Ah, very good, sir.' Moran awarded Higginson a smile.

Moran pulled a letter opener out of the box on the desk and slit the envelope. He read:

Dear DCI Moran

I feel I should apologise for my rather threatening behaviour in the car park the other day. You should perhaps be aware that your Sergeant Collingworth called me yesterday to set the record straight. He felt that he'd exaggerated your involvement in my late husband's final hours and wished to retract his opinion that you were responsible for my husband's state of intoxication. Sergeant Collingworth appears to be a fine young man, and I am content to take him at his word. I understand that you will be leaving at the conclusion of your current caseload. May I take this opportunity to wish you a very happy retirement.

Yours sincerely,

Sheila Dawson

'Sheila Dawson. Am I right?' Higginson said.

'Yes. Apparently I now have no case to answer. Collingworth has vouched for me.'

'Good lad, good lad.' Higginson seemed pleased.

Moran adopted a suspicious expression. 'You wouldn't have had anything to do with that, sir, would you?'

'Me? Well, perhaps I greased the wheels a little, Brendan. Least I could do.'

Moran laughed. 'In what way, sir?'

'Told the young fella that I might be able to speed up his substantive posting if he played with a straight bat – if you get my drift.'

'I do indeed. And I appreciate the gesture.'

'Well, as I said, Brendan, it's the least I could do after you stepped in so graciously to handle the Szarka case.'

Moran allowed Higginson's selective memory of his press-gang style re-recruitment to pass without comment. 'And very well done, too,' Higginson continued. 'I understand that Reyka Szarka covered her tracks rather well?'

'Yes, sir. She disguised herself as a man, called a cab from Fleet, met the cab in an anonymous location, paid in cash, entered the house via the rear. Her mistake was the bust. She wore gloves, but one of the broken pieces nicked a hole large enough to transfer a trace of lubricant from her finger to the shard.'

'And the lubricant came from the taxi?'

'Yes, from the internal door handle. Key evidence for the CPS.'

'Remarkable. Woman had some mental issue, I believe?'

'It seems that the mother's death triggered a long-suppressed desire for revenge. Reyka Szarka lived in her stillborn brother's shadow all her life, and Leila Szarka never let her forget it.'

'Tragic. And very sad,' Higginson reflected. 'Nevertheless, excellent work, Brendan,' he added. 'Absolutely top notch.'

'Credit must go to the forensics lab, sir – Pauline Harris and her team.'

'Quite, quite. Well, I mustn't keep you, Brendan.' Higginson stuck out his hand – clearly enough detail was enough. 'May I wish you a very happy and fulfilling retirement. Keep in touch, won't you?'

'I will, sir. Thank you.'

Higginson didn't exactly click his heels as he turned and marched from the office, but the formal style of his exit had much the same effect.

Moran sighed.

At last, it was time.

He flicked the light switch, closed the office door behind him with a definitive *clunk*, and walked resolutely along the corridor towards the lift, his waiting car, and the unknowable future.

Character Outlines

DCI Brendan Moran

Moran is a loner, but not a natural one. Born and raised initially near Cork and later in Co. Kerry after his parents moved away during his teens, he was left in the care of the Hannigan family where he met and fell in love with Janice, the Hannigans' eldest daughter. They were engaged to be married, but Janice was tragically killed in a car bomb incident in the late 1970's. The bomb had been meant for Moran, but a change of work routine that day prompted Moran to suggest that Janice borrow his car. He has never forgiven himself for Janice's death, nor has he been able to settle into a relationship since.

Moving to England in the early nineteen-eighties, he joined the Thames Valley Police and rose through the ranks on merit. Moran has experienced various setbacks in his career since Janice's death: he was almost killed in a car accident in bad weather conditions near Reading, and after his recovery was also injured during the course of an investigation into a suspicious death at Charnford Abbey ('Black December').

Despite this, he has a warm sense of humour, a great sense of loyalty to his friends and colleagues and an acute knack of being able to figure people out. He has a taste for Italian wine, preferably Sangiovese, and any quality scotch whisky. He is an appalling gardener and owns a hyperactive cocker spaniel named Archie. He has lately formed an attachment to Alice Roper, the sister of one of the main characters in 'The Cold Light of Death.' He is approachable, reliable, a little old-fashioned, intuitive, optimistic, and something of a romantic at heart.

DI Charlie Pepper

Originally from the Midlands, Charlie Pepper is a career police officer. She has been on the receiving end of violent crime more than once, but has been able to overcome her fear and continue in a senior role. In a relationship with DS Ian Luscombe, whom she met while working on the mysterious care-home murders in 'When Stars Grow Dark'.

DC George McConnell

George is an irascible Scot. Short in stature but in possession of a big heart, he has struggled in the past with alcohol addiction, but is now teetotal and intends to stay that way so as not to affect his blossoming relationship with DC Tess Martin. Excellent detective, but can be distracted by personal matters.

DC Bola Odunsi

Bola is a well-built, athletic black guy with an eye for the ladies – a trait that has caused him problems in the past. His enthusiasm is offset by a tendency to rush in and ask questions later, a pattern that has often drawn unwanted attention from his seniors. Despite this impetuous streak, Bola always has his fellow officers' backs, and is a popular and sociable member of the team.

DC Chris Collingworth

A good detective, but his character tends towards the self-serving, a trait that often lands him in trouble. Following an embarrassing and dangerous error of judgement ('When Stars Grow Dark'), Chris has made some effort to reform himself, but still has a way to go. He passed his sergeant's exam with excellent marks, and is looking forward to a future role in the new grade. The rest of the team are also looking forward to his departure. Although married he has a roving eye, and female team members tend to avoid social contact with him for this reason.

DC Tess Martin

Tess is a tough, determined police officer but suffers from bouts of self-doubt and depression. She hit a low trough during the investigation into the death of the singer, Michelle LaCroix and fell foul of the assassin, Ilhir Erjon, in 'Gone Too Soon', succumbing to a potent cocktail of drugs and lapsing into a near catatonic state. It was feared that she would not recover, but thanks to a combination of excellent care and George McConnell's encouragement, she is now making good progress.

DC Bernice Swinhoe

One of the newer members of the team, Bernice is naturally shy, but has a well-ordered and disciplined mind. Her casework is both methodical and logical, and she shows great empathy for victims of crime. Her mother died when she was young and this is a matter of great sadness for her. She is a serious thinker, in touch with her inner self and her spirituality. Hates her Christian name. Prefers to be known as DC Swinhoe, or DCB, as her colleagues often call her. DI Charlie Pepper is a role model, and Bernice aspires to ascend the ranks as she gains experience in Moran's team.

DS Ian Luscombe

Scottish detective sergeant seconded to Moran's team from Police Scotland, Aviemore who were running a parallel investigation re the care home murders in 'When Stars Grow Dark'. Has formed a relationship with DI Pepper. A reserved but capable officer, he keeps himself in peak physical condition and is no stranger to the tougher side of police work.

Isabel Akkerman

Isabel Akkerman is an MI6 operative and serial killer, responsible for the murder of RAF Aircraftswoman, Laura Witney, ('Closer to the Dead') but, due to diplomatic (SIS) immunity, DCI Moran was unable to bring her to justice. She is an exceptionally dangerous and capable MI6 resource – as exemplified by the case in which she got the better of Connie Chan, another of Moran's murderously capable adversaries.

Connie Chan

Real name Zubaida Binti Ungu, native of Malaysia. Wanted by Malaysian authorities. Suspected of killing her uncle and absconding with his worldly goods. Arrived in the UK 1990 or thereabouts. Escaped from hospital following attempted murder of Duncan Brodie. Also wanted in connection with several care-home-related murders. Ruthless, driven, yet emotionally flawed.

Alice Roper

Sister of Emma Hardy, the police officer who went missing in 'The Cold Light of Death'

Peter Hardy

Alice and Emma Hardy's autistic brother. Lived originally with Emma, but now lives with Alice. A sports fanatic, his favourite pastime is watching reruns of the best Olympic moments through the history of the games.

The DCI Brendan Moran Series – have you read them all?

Black December

DCI Brendan Moran, world-weary veteran of 1970s Ireland, is recuperating from a near fatal car crash when a murder is reported at Charnford Abbey.

The abbot and his monks are strangely uncooperative, but when a visitor from the Vatican arrives and an ancient relic goes missing the truth behind Charnford's pact of silence threatens to expose not only the abbey's haunted secrets but also the spirits of Moran's own troubled past . . .

Black December is an atmospheric crime thriller that will keep you on the edge of your seat until the stunning climax. This is the first in the DCI Brendan Moran crime series, one of the new breed of top UK Detectives.

'…gripping, with a really intriguing plot.'

Creatures of Dust

An undercover detective goes missing and the body of a young man is found mutilated in a shop doorway. Is there a connection? Returning to work after a short convalescence, DCI Brendan Moran's suspicions are aroused when a senior officer insists on freezing Moran out and handling the investigation himself.

A second murder convinces Moran that a serial killer is on the loose but with only a few days to prove his point the disgruntled DCI can't afford to waste time. As temperatures hit the high twenties, tempers fray, and the investigation founders Moran finds himself coming back to the same question again and again: can he still trust his own judgement, or is he leading his team up a blind alley?

'…non-stop action and convoluted twists. Another brilliant read in the Brendan Moran series…'

Death Walks Behind You

DCI Brendan Moran's last minute break in the West Country proves anything but restful as he becomes embroiled in the mysterious disappearance of an American tourist. Does the village harbour some dark and dreadful secret? The brooding presence of the old manor house and the dysfunctional de Courcy family may hold the answer but Moran soon finds that the residents of Cernham have a rather unorthodox approach to the problem of dealing with outsiders…

'…a pleasure to read – gripped from start to finish…'

The Irish Detective - digital box set

The first omnibus edition of the popular DCI Brendan Moran crime series. Contents includes the first, second and third in series, plus an exclusive CWA shortlisted short story 'Safe As Houses'...

Silent As The Dead

A call from an old friend whose wife has vanished from their home in Co.Kerry prompts DCI Brendan Moran to return to his Irish roots. The Gardai have drawn a blank; can Moran succeed where they have failed?

Moran's investigation leads him to a loner known locally as the Islander, who reveals that the woman's disappearance is connected to a diehard paramilitary with plans to hit a high profile target in the UK. Time is running out. Can Moran enlist the Islander's help, or does he have to face his deadliest foe alone?

'Superb storyline with plenty of twists and turns…'

Gone Too Soon

Moran is called to a burial in a local cemetery. But this is no ordinary interment; the body of a young woman, Michelle LaCroix, a rising star in the music world, is still warm, the grave unmarked. A recording reveals the reason for her suicide. Or does it?

Why would a young, successful singer take her own life? To unlock the answer, Moran must steer a course through his darkest investigation yet, as the clues lead to one shocking discovery after another…

'…endlessly twisty – an explosive finish…'

The Enemy Inside

DCI Brendan Moran's morning is interrupted when a suicidal ex-soldier threatens to jump from a multi-storey car park ...

Moran soon regrets getting involved when an unexpected visitor turns up on his doorstep to confront him with what appears to be damning evidence of past misconduct. Can the Irish Detective clear his name, or must he come clean and face the consequences? One thing seems certain: by the time the night is over, his reputation may not be the only casualty…

'…a cracking, fast-paced thriller.'

When Stars Grow Dark

A fatal road traffic collision uncovers a bizarre murder when it transpires that an elderly passenger in one of the vehicles was dead before the accident. All indications point to the work of a serial killer – but with little forensic evidence, how can DCI Brendan Moran and his team run the killer to ground?

To add to Moran's problems, an unexpected discovery prompts the Irish Detective to undertake a dangerous and unscheduled journey to Rotterdam where he believes his former friend and MI5 agent, Samantha Grant, is being held.

Can Moran succeed in his rescue mission whilst juggling the heavy demands of his most perplexing murder investigation to date? *When Stars Grow Dark* is number seven in the popular DCI Brendan Moran crime series

'…another brilliant outing for the DCI. No red herrings, page fillers or unnecessary characters, just gripping story leading to an unexpected ending…'

The Cold Light of Death

July, 1976 – Thames Valley, UK. Long, scorching days of blue skies, water shortages, and record temperatures. A newly promoted Detective-Sergeant is tasked with investigating the murder of a local shop owner – an investigation that goes tragically wrong...

Fast-forward forty-five years to 2021, when a chance discovery exposes a grim secret that forces a reexamination of the circumstances surrounding the ill-fated murder inquiry.

DCI Brendan Moran is assigned this coldest of cases, and it soon becomes apparent that he is dealing with a cold and calculating criminal mind. Can Moran and his team piece together the events of that long forgotten summer and unmask the killer before history repeats itself?

'A most satisfying read, with a plot zooming back to the mid 70s. As usual, wonderfully evocative. The entire series is a must for any crime fiction fan'

Closer to the Dead

A new cold case for DCI Brendan Moran coincides with the unexpected reappearance of a dangerous adversary.

As Moran grapples with an ever-changing work culture and begins to get to grips with the forty-year old murder of a young RAF aircraftswoman, an unexpected complication arises in his personal life that threatens to sabotage a promising relationship before it even begins. Could his new friend really be involved in the shady financial dealings of a cold case murder victim?

With this uncertainty playing on his mind, Moran throws himself into the new investigation, but as he digs deeper it becomes clear that the original case was sloppily handled, the interviews poorly conducted and critical evidence overlooked. Under the watchful eye of a newly-appointed Crime Investigations Manager, the team begin the painstaking process of tracing the original persons of interest.

Progress, however, is glacial, and so, when presented with incontrovertible proof that their progress is being monitored with alarming accuracy by someone who seems to always be one step ahead of the official investigation, Moran begins to wonder if he can make an arrest before the perpetrator falls into the hands of an antagonist with a very different idea of justice…

'Great story telling from a master of the crime thriller novel. Sometime Baterista, Scott Hunter, weaves a thread of names, characters and dark deeds past and present in a complex but eminently readable tale to match the best of British crime writers.'

The Irish Detective 2 digital box set

The second omnibus edition of the popular DCI Brendan Moran crime series by CWA shortlisted author, Scott Hunter. Contents includes the fourth, fifth and sixth in series, plus an exclusive short story 'Inside Job'…

A Crime For All Seasons (short stories) - FREE via website

From the midwinter snowdrifts of an ancient Roman villa to a summer stakeout at an exclusive art gallery, join DCI Brendan Moran and his team for the first volume of criminally cunning short stories in which the world-weary yet engaging Irish detective reaffirms that there is indeed a crime for all seasons…

'…great characters, plot lines and dialogue. More please!'

For more information – www.scott-hunter.net

Printed in Great Britain
by Amazon